PRAI

THE
BEAUTIFUL

QUARTET

"An incredibly ornate, lush New Orleans; characters who imprint themselves on your memory forever; a story that is nail-biting and swoony and satisfying and tense ALL AT THE SAME TIME. And of course . . . VAMPIRES."

—Sabaa Tahir, *New York Times* bestselling author
of *An Ember in the Ashes*

"Darkly delicious." —*BuzzFeed*

"*The Beautiful*, which kicks off a new series, returns the vampire novel to popular form, evoking the style of Anne Rice and breathing fresh life into the genre." —*Entertainment Weekly*

"It's intoxicating. *The Beautiful* has that decadent, slow-moving horror that feels like a dream slipping to nightmare. It's like walking alone down a twilight street and feeling the snap of a branch behind you and that acidic heart-in-your-throat rush of knowing that you're being followed. Stalked."

—Roshani Chokshi, *New York Times* bestselling author
of *The Gilded Wolves*

"[A] romantic and adventurous story of vampires, fey, and magical worlds." —*POPSUGAR*

"It's true: Vampires are back, and they're more seductive than ever." —*Bustle*

"Ahdieh's New Orleans is lushly atmospheric, permeating this series opener with an undercurrent of violence within a seductive underworld around Mardi Gras . . . Fans will clamor for the continuation to this captivating volume."
—*Publishers Weekly*

"Darkly glamorous . . . Compelling."
—*The Bulletin of the Center for Children's Books*

"Ahdieh brings New Orleans vibrantly to life, particularly when exploring the complicated racial and gender restrictions of high society through main and supporting characters of mixed-race origin. Sure to please fans of the author and of the vampire-romance genre."
—*Kirkus Reviews*

"Vampires never stay dead for long, and bestselling Ahdieh's approach—part homage to the classics, part fresh-eyed revitalization—will intrigue all but the most committed skeptics."
—*Booklist*

"Expansive worldbuilding . . . Romantic . . . Steamy . . . Decadent escapism."
—*Kirkus Reviews*

"The first in a series, this mystery novel shines when it focuses on Celine and her struggle to fit into society while trying to be true to herself."
—*School Library Journal*

"Forbidden romance and harsh consequences set up this highly anticipated sequel that will leave you wanting so much more."
—*Seventeen*

"A worthy sequel that builds upon the world set up in book one and takes our characters to far darker places than before."
—*Culturess*

"*The Damned* continues the thematic elegance and glamour found in *The Beautiful* and manages to take it up another level . . . There is a deep and seductive ambience that weaves throughout the story and leaves you feeling like you are reading the novel while lounging in a richly appointed New Orleans drawing room . . . nothing short of fantastic."

—*The Nerd Daily*

"Forbidden love, sultry romance, and clashing immortal factions fill this sequel . . . [and] will keep readers engaged . . . For fans of vampire love stories."   —*School Library Journal*

"Pippa and Arjun's compatibility allows for a quickly building romance . . . [and] the worldbuilding further expands with deceptions and dangerous fey schemes coming to fruition just in time for the sequel. Racism, colorism, and colonialism are confronted."   —*Kirkus Reviews*

"The romance is delightful, as is the sex positivity, intersectional feminism, and discussions of colonialism . . . an easy recommendation to fans of Holly Black's *The Cruel Prince*."

—*School Library Journal*

"An enjoyable continuation to The Beautiful series that sets up for the next book rather nicely. By focusing more on minor characters from the previous books, Ahdieh makes the story fresh."   —*Book Riot*

"The best part of the book remains Ahdieh's writing. Its lyrical quality brings the world to life once again . . . [and] gave Ahdieh's story a fairy-tale feel."   —*Bookstacked*

"A big, bold, high-cost end to a lush quartet." —*Kirkus Reviews*

THE
RUINED

RENÉE AHDIEH

NANCY PAULSEN BOOKS

NANCY PAULSEN BOOKS

An imprint of Penguin Random House LLC
1745 Broadway, New York, New York 10019

First published in the United States of America by G. P. Putnam's Sons,
an imprint of Penguin Random House LLC, 2023

First paperback edition published by Nancy Paulsen Books,
an imprint of Penguin Random House LLC, 2024

Visit us online at PenguinRandomHouse.com.

The Library of Congress has cataloged the hardcover edition as follows:
Names: Ahdieh, Renée, author.
Title: The ruined / Renée Ahdieh.
Description: New York: G. P. Putnam's Sons, 2023. |
Series: The beautiful quartet; book 4 | Summary: "Bastien and Celine look for allies
and rally friends as war breaks loose"—Provided by publisher.
Identifiers: LCCN 2023034958 (print) | LCCN 2023034959 (ebook) |
ISBN 9781984812643 (hardcover) | ISBN 9781984812650 (ebook)
Subjects: CYAC: Vampires—Fiction. | Fairies—Fiction. | Supernatural—Fiction. |
New Orleans (La.)—History—19th century—Fiction. | LCGFT: Paranormal fiction. | Novels.
Classification: LCC PZ7.1.A328 Ru 2023 (print) | LCC PZ7.1.A328 (ebook) | DDC [Fic]—dc23
LC record available at https://lccn.loc.gov/2023034958
LC ebook record available at https://lccn.loc.gov/2023034959

Printed in the United States of America

ISBN 9781984812667

1st Printing
LSCC

Design by Suki Boynton
Text set in Warnock Pro Regular

To Anne Rice, who first made me
believe in the power of stories

To Mushu, for fourteen years of love

And for Cyrus, Noura, and Victor, always

Give me my Romeo; and, when he shall die,
Take him and cut him out in little stars,
And he will make the face of heaven so fine
That all the world will be in love with night
And pay no worship to the garish sun.

From Romeo and Juliet
by William Shakespeare

For I have learned that every heart will get
What it prays for
Most.

From "A Potted Plant"
by Hafez

PROLOGUE

eath meets us in the darkness. There, in that moment, all
the moments before it take shape to form the lines and
contours of a life, like a vessel on a potter's wheel.

For an instant, the measure of a life can be seen.

Was it a life of emptiness? Was it misshapen, its cup filled
from another's well? Was it cracked and leaking? Perhaps chipped
from so many lessons learned?

These were Suli's thoughts as he held on to Sunan's hand. He
wondered what would become of them, now that his brother's
magic could no longer protect what remained of the Winter
Court.

Their court of ice and darkness had once been great, its ram-
parts carved deep into the heart of a glittering mountain. The
vampires and the werewolves had ruled from this lofty perch,
their coffers overflowing with gemstones mined from this very
fortress, its caverns veined with gold and iron ore, its alcoves
spangled with rubies and diamonds.

But in the end, their greed cost them everything, and the
mountain had fallen still. Looters and profligates tried to tunnel

their way to what remained of the riches, but the caverns collapsed on them, burying them in tombs of stony silence.

The mountain faded into remembrance, its once-glittering halls empty.

Now its formidable shell provided their kind with a place to call home. In recent years, Sunan had kept the creatures of the Sylvan Wyld—and all those who needed it—safe. He was great indeed, and Suli was proud to call him brother.

A humble goblin like Suli learned long ago to accept that he was not fated for the same kind of greatness. Standing in the shadow of his brother—the most famed illusionist the world of the fey had ever known—had not bothered Suli much. He'd seen the cost of Sunan's so-called gift. Better that Suli keep to his own clumsy conjurings. They had given him solace after he'd lost his family to the mirror, and they would undoubtedly do so once again.

Now that he would be the only member of their family left.

"Out with it," Sunan whispered in a raspy voice, his brow knotted. "You . . . have s-something you wish to say."

Suli glanced at the soaked dressings pressed against the wound in Sunan's side. "Don't waste the energy to speak," he said in the language of their kind. Already his brother's injury was stinking of rot, the swelling and the charred blue flesh around Sunan's stomach preventing a healer from sewing it closed.

"Should I be s-saving it for something else?" Sunan's eyes twinkled, despite his obvious pain. "Perhaps . . . a jaunt through the f-freshly fallen snow?" He snorted. "I'm dying. The l-last joy I have is to s-speak my mind."

Suli sighed. "I suppose you're right."

A shudder wracked through Sunan's tiny blue body. He gripped Suli's hand. "Brother, you must p-protect our kind. The mirror . . . you m-must see it d-destroyed. Promise me."

"You know I cannot."

"P-please." Sunan swallowed. "Promise me."

"I swore on my children's graves that I would never again stand close to that mirror, much less make use of its power, even to destroy it." Suli took a deep breath. "I'm sorry, brother. I cannot accept this responsibility. The mirror is a curse to all who behold it."

Sunan wheezed, his features twisting in dismay. "I—I thought Arjun Desai w-would be the one, but"—he coughed, and blood dribbled down his chin—"now w-we must turn to the prince." He winced again, a single tear trailing toward his right ear. "He m-must know. He—"

"Sébastien Saint Germain is not up to the task." Suli's voice rose. "He is as selfish and calculating as his uncle ever was."

"He s-stayed to help us."

"A mere two days of him caring for our wounded does not sway me." Suli's features hardened. "A true leader does not wait for smooth waters. He faces the hurricane."

"We c-cannot expect him to change overnight."

"You wanted him to take a stand against Lady Silla that afternoon by the river. He did not, nor will he, so long as he loves her daughter. Our people will never follow him, despite the noble blood flowing through his veins."

Sunan's yellowing eyes widened. "If y-you will not lead, h-he must be the one." He tried to sit up. "He m-must protect our kind. He must s-safeguard the mirror. Or . . . s-see it destroyed. It is his birthright. His . . . d-duty. Promise me."

"I promise you that I will speak with him on the matter."

Sunan nodded, his exhaustion plain. "Th-thank you, Suli."

Suli sighed to himself as he eased his brother back to the threadbare pillow, straw poking through its seams. He wanted to argue more with Sunan. Give voice to his exasperation, as he'd done for centuries.

All at once, Suli realized that time was at an end. The comfort he'd felt in that closeness would be gone from him in a matter of moments. Loss took hold of his heart. It blossomed in Suli's chest, the ache creeping up his throat. He gripped Sunan's hand.

"I . . . shall miss our conversations," Suli said.

Sunan smiled at him, another tear etching down his blue skin. "I shall miss *you*."

"Some mortals believe in an afterlife." Suli's own eyes welled. "I hope they are right."

"If they are, I w-will tell our f-family you love them."

"Thank you."

Sunan took a trembling breath, his voice fading to a whisper. "I'm f-frightened."

"That is unlike you."

"Knew . . . this time . . . would come."

"The mirror allowed you to foresee your death, yet you are still frightened," Suli murmured. "Knowledge alone is never enough."

Sunan nodded, another bout of coughing tearing through his body. He groaned and pressed his lips together.

"You don't have to fight anymore," Suli said softly.

Sunan swallowed. A gasp flew from his lips, his eyes wide. With a final burst of effort, he gripped Suli's hand in both of his own. "She will . . . never . . . choose her."

"What?" Suli bent closer.

"Silla. Will . . . kill the child . . . first." Bloody sputum poured from Sunan's mouth.

Suli shook his head, tears coursing down his cheeks. "Don't fight anymore, Sunan. Be at peace."

"Tell . . . Bastien. Celine . . . will die. Hallowtide."

Realization struck Suli like a bolt of lightning piercing the night sky. "Lady Silla intends to kill her own daughter during mortal Hallowtide?"

Sunan wheezed. "Stop . . . them. Destroy . . . the mirror. Do . . . what I . . . failed to do."

"I will do whatever I can. Be at peace, brother. You have more than earned it."

With another shudder, Sunan exhaled. Suli watched the life leave his brother's body. Still he did not release Sunan's hand. He sat in silence, honoring the moment of his brother's passing. Many long years and many hard losses had taught Suli that this was not a time for anger or pain. That time would come later, like waves crashing upon a dark shore.

5

Now was a moment for quiet. A moment for respect. A moment for love.

Tomorrow there would be pain. Tomorrow he would allow the anger to race through his veins and the pain to rip through his chest. Tomorrow he would make sense of it all.

One day, perhaps there would be justice.

With a heavy heart, Suli let go of his brother's hand for the last time.

Sunan had charged Suli with knowledge. And knowledge alone was never enough.

Suli swore on their family's graves that he would pass the mirror's curse to Sébastien Saint Germain . . . or die trying.

THE RUINED PRINCE

The events of that afternoon along the riverbank was seared onto Bastien's memory like a brand. He returned to the scene as if it were a daguerreotype brought to life.

Chaos reigned around him, silver-tipped bullets flying through the twilit sky. The fog from Sunan's illusion began lifting, and a pack of werewolves emerged from the tree line near the bridge linking the wintry land of the Sylvan Wyld to its summery nemesis, the Sylvan Vale.

Bastien watched the wolves prowl from the frosted woods, intent on severing the last threads of truce and crossing into the Vale unchecked. His feet moved. He felt an irrepressible desire to strike out at them. To act, rather than remain neutral.

From his experience, werewolves brought nothing but disaster. Striking them down would be justified. But Bastien forced his feet to remain still. Celine was on that bridge. If he acted from a place of recklessness, the wolves' retribution would be swift. So he stood immobile, caught between action and indecision.

The next memory caused Bastien to press his eyes shut, his chest tightening like a drum.

The daguerreotype in his mind flickered to life. Philippa Montrose darted through the confusion, fighting to make her way over that same bridge to Arjun Desai, without care or consideration to anything around her. Bastien knew she saw only Arjun.

The werewolf who struck Pippa first was missing a front paw. Just like Bastien's sister, Émilie Saint Germain. The one he had banished to the frozen wastelands in a foolish attempt at mercy.

In his mind's eye, Bastien watched himself race toward the bridge. He could no longer stand idle along the shore, hoping to remain above the fray. Impossible choices enclosed him on all sides. Left him tangled in a thick web of uncertainty.

It was not Bastien's place to embroil himself in fey politics. Nor was it his job to defend the downtrodden remains of the Winter Court against the aggressions of the Summer Court.

But he would protect those he loved—his family—with everything he possessed.

Pippa Montrose had become family. She was the treasured friend of Bastien's true love, Celine Rousseau. The cherished wife of his brother Arjun Desai.

His heart in his throat, Bastien bent his head. In his mind, he watched the consequences of his failure. That cursed second of indecision.

Without flinching, he bore witness to the final moments of Pippa Montrose.

Bastien refused to turn away when the first of Pippa's screams tore through the air, her blood staining the white snow and splashing against the mossy stone along the bridge. He listened to her thrash and flail as the pack of wolves dragged her dripping body back toward the icy tree line. As their howls faded to silence, the last of her cries ringing through the darkness.

He would not look away from the sight of an inconsolable Celine being hauled from the bridge by her mother's grey-cloaked soldiers. Nor from the horror fixed on Arjun Desai's face as he fell to his knees and raged against his captors, his anguish echoing in Bastien's ears.

Now Bastien sat in the hollows of the cavern, his face covered by his crimson-stained hands. His cowardice cocooned around him like a wet cloak. Cold fury raked across his skin. He lingered deep in the heart of the mountain fortress that had once been the stronghold of his vampire ancestors. Around him lay the bodies of the fallen, along with the Sylvan Wyld's wounded and the dying. The wretched souls fated to stand along the wintry embankment, there to witness what was meant to be a peaceful exchange.

Until some worthless fool loosed an arrow on the Lady of the Vale.

Bedlam had followed the sight of Lady Silla being felled by her enemy. The Summer Court's forces had unleashed hell upon the bedraggled gathering of winter fey waiting on the opposing riverbank. Though a healer had been summoned, the injuries inflicted upon the winter fey by the summer fey's new-fangled weapons were grave, the silver-tipped bullets ripping through wings and embedding themselves beneath skin, fur, and scales to fester and rot.

Bastien grimaced when he recalled the way the arrow had

struck Celine's mother. The way it had sailed through the sky—undeniably fired from the Sylvan Wyld's icy reaches—before slamming into its mark, who had collapsed on the bridge upon impact.

His expression hardened. Try as he might, Bastien could not overlook the obvious. The last time his world had been turned upside down, his sister, Émilie, had been the orchestrator of its destruction. It could not be mere coincidence that she was there that day, waiting in the shadows beyond the river, ready to pounce on Pippa Montrose.

When it came to Émilie, he believed there was no such thing as coincidence.

The scent of freshly spilled blood drifted in Bastien's direction. Another wounded creature collapsed to the ground a stone's throw from where he sat. When the horned fey recognized Bastien, she shrank back in fear, clutching the open wound beneath her neck with both hands.

It didn't matter. The smell of her blood beckoned to Bastien, as ever.

The lone vampire among them, crouched in the darkness.

In the past, there had been many blood drinkers who called the Sylvan Wyld their home. They'd ruled the Winter Court until their insatiable appetite for control had cost them everything. By rights, Bastien should never have been allowed to return. But there was no one left to enforce the exile.

And Bastien had never been the sort to comply.

A sweet perfume rose from the fey blood glistening on the stone floor. The young female—her horns curved and her hooves cloven—rasped another breath, the long gash along her collarbone continuing to spill, warm and rich and fragrant. The blood called to Bastien with a forbidden melody. Cursedly beautiful. Deliciously damned.

He locked his jaw, even as he felt his features start to transform. His fangs cut through his bottom lip, bringing the taste of his own blood onto his tongue.

Bastien had never fed on a fey creature. The scent of their blood was enough to promise that its taste would be like water on the lips of a man lost in the desert.

He inhaled. Then exhaled.

Monstrous. Even now, after all the suffering he'd witnessed, still his thirst sang the sweetest song. Bastien forced himself to look away from the ruby-red blood just as commotion resounded from the blue darkness closest to the mouth of the cavern.

A tall fey creature struggled against the grip of their captors.

Despite the murk, Bastien's heightened senses recognized the familiar garb of a Grey Cloak warrior, one of the elite guards tasked with protecting the Lady of the Vale.

Bastien stood, his hands turning to fists at his sides.

What was a Grey Cloak doing in the Sylvan Wyld?

A massive centaur held the Grey Cloak with one arm, while a redcap goblin prodded the warrior from behind with a spear. The third dark fey, this one a lean, dark-haired amabie, grasped the end of an iron chain bound to the Grey Cloak's joined wrists. As the warrior fought their restraints, a faint sizzling sound emitted from the parts of their skin touching the dark metal.

The Grey Cloak was not alone in their injuries. Half the

centaur's face was burned from where silver bullets had grazed his cheek. A makeshift binding was wrapped around his right shoulder and forearm. The redcap was missing an eye. And though the diminutive amabie appeared unscathed, her hands and sleeves were covered in dried blood.

It was likely someone the amabie loved had died in her arms.

The Grey Cloak warrior winced and straightened to face Bastien. Even in the dim light from deep inside the mountain, Bastien could see the disdain on his handsome face. A sneer curled his lips. It was clear from the cuts and bruises along his jaw and knuckles that he'd fought his captors every step of the way.

All those around Bastien fell silent, watching intently.

The ebon-haired amabie spat beside the Grey Cloak's feet, her white fingers curling tighter around the iron chain. "We caught this one just beyond the reaches of the mountain." She looked around, her beak-like mouth shaping into a sneer. "What should we do with him?"

"Feed him to the children!" cried a creature from above.

Another screamed, "Burn the skin from his body with iron tongs."

"Tear him apart, limb from limb," yelled a mushroom-headed hob.

"No," boomed the voice of the massive centaur. His gaze locked on Bastien. "Ask the vampire. The one whose arrival portended our suffering." Accusation flashed in his eyes. "The one who—despite his bloodline—holds such affection for summer scum. Let us see if Nicodemus' heir knows how to mete out justice."

Anger flared in Bastien's body. He stood, his chin high, ready to fight. Then an injured winter fey groaned nearby. Bastien glanced around.

They had suffered enough. He would not be baited by their pain.

Instead, Bastien fixed his attention on the green-eyed stare of the grey-cloaked warrior. "I gather," he began, "that you were sent to find the Lady of the Vale's assassin."

The warrior's nostrils flared, his sight narrowing.

Bastien stepped closer. "You take umbrage with what I said?" He kept his voice even.

"I take umbrage with your very existence, filthy leech," the warrior ground out. "Nothing as paltry as a single arrow could kill Lady Silla. She alone wields the powers of air and of earth. None are her equal."

Loose-tongued lout. It was the first time any member of the Summer Court had acknowledged the extent of Lady Silla's abilities in front of Bastien. He was unsure if even Celine understood the magnitude of her mother's powers.

The Lady of the Vale commanded the air and the earth. In recent years, it had become a rarity for even the most powerful among the fey gentry to conjure more than a simple spell, much less wield elemental magic like earth, air, water, or fire. For Lady Silla to control two of the four meant she was formidable indeed.

Bastien studied the warrior for a moment. "I never said the Lady of the Vale was dead. But thank you for confirming the good news that she is not."

Despite the summer fey's pompous appearance, his hands shook. The burns on his wrists had chafed through the skin, exposing raw flesh to the wintry air. His eyes darted from one corner to the next. The Grey Cloak was agitated. Distracted by obvious pain. Perhaps he would not be as guarded as he should be.

"How many of you crossed the bridge to find the one responsible for firing the arrow?" Bastien asked him point-blank.

The Grey Cloak flinched and pressed his lips into a line.

"Definitely more than a single soldier," Bastien mused. "*You* would not be enough."

Irritation etched lines across the summer warrior's brow.

"Two?" Bastien continued.

The warrior did not react.

Bastien stepped closer, letting his voice drop to a whisper. "Three? Four?"

Something tugged at the corners of the Grey Cloak's lips.

Dark satisfaction warmed through Bastien's chest. "Four, then. It makes sense for General Riya to send at least that many soldiers to chase after Lady Silla's assassin."

"You are so certain it was a lone wolf?" the Grey Cloak said under his breath.

"I am," Bastien replied without missing a beat. "After all, your queen fell under the weight of a single arrow. Its high arc and speed suggest that it was fired from a far distance, which further supports the theory that the perpetrator worked alone. Four warriors fanned out in several possible directions would be a prudent effort to rout out the culprit." Bastien tucked his hands in the pockets of his trousers. "Though I must say, how embarrassing for your great leader—one with the power to control both air and earth!—to crumble in the face of such a paltry threat."

The Grey Cloak bared his teeth. "Soon Lady Silla will rise up and wreak summer's wrath on all you winter abominations, of that you can be—"

"Enough!" the centaur bellowed, his hooves striking against the stone floor with a booming clatter. "I grow weary of such talk, Sébastien Saint Germain," he said. *"Where is your justice?"* Fury mottled his features. "I suppose I should not be surprised. You are your uncle's blood, after all. A puppet master lurking in the shadows, afraid to sully your elegant hands."

His words struck a harsh blow in Bastien's stomach. The air left his body in a rush.

Bastien's failure to act had resulted in his uncle's execution and the destruction of his home. Just as his failure to mete out justice on his sister, Émilie, had led to the death of Pippa Montrose. No matter where Bastien looked, he was confronted by the cost of his indecision.

"Now is the time for action, Sébastien Saint Germain," the centaur continued. "Not speeches."

"This vile summer swine," the amabie said, yanking on the

chain in her hand for emphasis, "carved a path through our kind on his trek toward the mountain. It did not matter whether he encountered the elderly or the infirm." Tears welled in her eyes. "He struck down younglings. *Younglings.* The blood of our children is on his hands."

A single cry echoed through the cave, followed by a whimper.

Bastien took a careful breath. "Now is the time for justice," he agreed. "Not speeches."

"And what would be the appropriate manner of justice?" the centaur asked, his equine features appraising. "Should we kill him as he killed us? Should we burn his skin with flesh-flaying weapons, or perhaps feed him piece by piece to the ice sabers that lurk at the foot of our mountain?"

Discomfort knifed through Bastien's chest. He did not care for the way the winter fey watched him, stalking his every move. Like a predator to its prey, lying in wait for his next misstep. "The warrior's fate is not for me to decide," Bastien said.

The centaur looked to the curved ceiling of the cavern. "Then who among us should decide the fate of this summer swine? Who among us is to take responsibility?"

He was met with silence. His voice fell to a vicious whisper. "I say we place the weight of our plight on the shoulders of the one who brought this violence to our doorstep." Again, he pitched his words louder. "Who among us agrees the vampire is responsible?" The centaur's question was answered with a low hum of assent. "Look around you." He raised his hands and turned an accusing eye toward Bastien. "Before Sébastien Saint Germain and his ilk returned to our woods, we knew peace.

Perhaps we were not happy with our lot. But at least our children were not being murdered beneath the light of our mother moon."

Bastien's cheeks hollowed. "I understand why you wish to hold me accountable. But this fight between summer and winter existed long before me. It is not my responsibility to right these wrongs."

The redcap finally spoke, his voice gravelly and resonant, like the echo of a gong. "In the Wyld, we believe in reaping what you sow. It is not a coincidence that your arrival heralded the end of our treaty with the Vale." He stepped back, his hands wrapping tighter around the spear in his hands, his slub garments in tatters. "Your attachment to Lady Silla's daughter is the reason this destruction was brought upon us, and you *will* take responsibility for it."

Tears of fury coursed down the amabie's cheeks. She swiped at them with her stained forearm, leaving a smear of crimson along her jaw. "I lost my sister today. My only sister. *My twin.* I watched her drown in her own blood." Her naked pain cut Bastien to the quick. "Blood drinkers ruled our lands for millennia. Under their protection, the Sylvan Wyld prospered. We had no need to fear." She pursed her bird-beak mouth. "You will fix this. You will take responsibility. Because I will see you burn in the sun before I allow you to turn your back on us." Her body shook as she spoke, and her fury reminded Bastien of Celine.

How she, too, would never let him forget how she lost Pippa.

Guilt settled on Bastien's shoulders like a heavy yoke.

"Deal out your justice, vampire. Make a choice," the redcap

said quietly. "Do you stand with your fellow creatures of the night? Or will you allow summer to murder and maim us until we are no more?" With his spear, the redcap prodded the back of the Grey Cloak.

The Grey Cloak scoffed. "Goblin, look around you. *You are already no more.*"

The centaur knocked the summer warrior's legs out from under him, and the Grey Cloak fell to the ground with a thud, his face striking a protruding rock.

The Grey Cloak began to laugh. "You think this pathetic rabble threatens the supremacy of the Summer Court? You saw how quickly I vanquished your line. How many weak winter fey I was able to cut down before—"

With a warlike shriek, the tiny amabie kicked him in the side. Then she turned toward Bastien, her chest heaving, the chains clanking around her as she drew the Grey Cloak in like a fish on a line.

Bastien waited for the rest of the chamber to rally and howl as he would have expected. Instead they all looked to Bastien. Still lying in wait for his next misstep.

When the Grey Cloak rose to his knees, fresh blood dripped from his nose and chin.

The hunger roared to life inside Bastien. He struggled to silence it. To quench his thirst. He'd thought it was the right thing to exile Émilie. An eye for an eye left the world blind, did it not?

But Bastien's mercy had inescapable consequences.

Once again, Pippa's screams filled Bastien's ears. As did the memory of Arjun's anguish as the wolves hauled away Pippa's bleeding body.

The price of Bastien's unconditional love. For Émilie. And for Celine.

The Grey Cloak struggled to stand, putting one foot on the ground, his gold-heeled boot caked in mud. "The Ruined Prince of the Wyld . . . and his court of nothings." He glanced around at the vestiges of a lost world. The injured, the dying, the forlorn. His laughter was like cracking ice, cold sweat beading on his brow. "What happens to me is immaterial. We will overrun you in a fortnight. And do not fear for your halfblood lover, vampire. We will make short work of her, too, and then our land will be as it once was. Pure and untainted. United under a blazing sun." His eyes gleamed with feverish intensity.

Bastien had expected his rage to get the better of him, especially in the face of such brazen taunts. He waited for the wrath to take hold. Instead he felt nothing but cool defiance. His gaze met that of a nine-tailed gumiho, her fox eyes lambent in the darkness. Filled with sadness, yet flashing with something else.

A light . . . a hint . . . a suggestion of more.

In the end, it was not rage at all. Calm descended on Bastien like a thick woolen blanket. Without a second thought, Bastien yanked the warrior to his feet by the collar of his grey cloak.

The warrior flinched, and for the first time, Bastien detected a hint of fear in him.

"Good," Bastien said. "You're afraid. I appreciate the honesty."

"I'm not afraid, vampire. It is you and your kin who will know fear."

"I welcome it." Bastien smiled. "Fear and I have been bedfellows for many years."

"Do your worst," the Grey Cloak spat. "I will not beg for mercy from the likes of you."

"A pity." Bastien yanked him close and bared his fangs. "Why is it that no one knows how to beg anymore? It's been far too long since I've been asked what *I* want."

A muscle jumped in the warrior's jaw. He clenched his teeth shut. The blood from his broken nose continued to flow past his lips and drip down his chin.

It smelled like springtime. Like fresh strawberries and new wine.

"What is your name?" Bastien asked softly, his mouth going dry.

The warrior's blond hair fell into his green eyes. "Anurak."

"Anurak." Bastien nodded. Then he breathed in, letting the perfume of Anurak's blood fill his nostrils. The change began. Instead of fighting it, as he had ever since he'd first set foot in the land of the fey, Bastien allowed the magic to take hold. He watched Anurak's eyes. Saw the terror build in them as his reflection transformed from that of a man into the perfect image of a monster.

"Since you refuse to ask," Bastien growled, "I will simply tell you." He spoke in Anurak's ear, as if he were sharing a secret. "I want to go home to New Orleans. I want to be with my family. To lie beneath the stars with my love. To savor every mortal moment as I walk down the streets of my beloved city, far away from you and from this world and all its madness." Bastien let his fangs graze his lower lip, his fingers forming claws against the warrior's shredded grey cloak. "But the Winter Court offers you its thanks," he announced so that everyone around him could hear. "The beasts of the mountain—and their *ruined prince*—are now awake." He crushed Anurak to his chest and buried his fangs in the fey warrior's neck.

Anurak struggled against Bastien, a stifled scream on his lips. He tried to push Bastien away, but the amabie yanked on the iron chain, keeping him restrained. The silence in the cave thickened as Bastien drank.

He'd always wondered what the blood of a fey would taste like. Each mortal Bastien had partaken from had blood with a unique flavor. Some were savory, like cured meat paired with the finest burgundy. Some were sweet. Mille-feuilles, layered with crème pâtissèrie.

The taste of Anurak's blood surpassed them all. It was like fresh herbs harvested from a French mountainside, then mixed with newly churned butter and rubbed into the rarest cut of lamb.

Anurak's memories were chaotic. As if Bastien were witnessing the musings of a drunken man. They lacked the sharpness and clarity of a mortal's thoughts. He witnessed flashes of violence interspersed with excess. A taste for both mortal and fey fruit. For honeyed liquor and sweet-smelling opium, along with the charms of countless beautiful men and women and lieges, their limbs willowy and perfumed, their moans of shared pleasure like distant music.

Bastien knew he should stop drinking. If he let Anurak go now, the fey warrior would be debilitated for a night, but likely to survive the encounter.

Bastien had faced many crossroads in his life. This was one of them.

It was time for him to make a choice.

Anurak had warned that the whole of the Summer Court would descend on the Winter Court. Overrun them in a fortnight. He'd threatened and mocked them.

The Summer Court may very well destroy Bastien.

But he would take a few of their immortal lives first.

As Bastien committed to this action, he recalled Anurak's words regarding Celine's mother, the Lady of the Vale. His confirmation that a single arrow could not destroy a being so powerful. If that was true, then why had Lady Silla allowed two days to pass without word of her survival?

He had an answer. It was not a good one.

Bastien had tried, time and again, to protect Celine from her mother's duplicity. He'd watched the Sylvan Vale silence her. Under the protection and supposed guidance of her mother, Celine had faded to a shadow of herself.

She'd become easy to control.

This, too, could not be mere coincidence. The thought of someone controlling Celine stoked the anger building inside him. So he drank and drank and drank. Until Anurak's attempts to fend him off grew feeble. Until the last drop of his blood touched Bastien's lips.

Anurak fell to the ground, his body drying into a husk.

Bastien watched the husk shrivel. Watched it shrink into itself, folding and constricting until it resembled the silken wrappings around ears of corn, artfully arranged in a pile of bloodied clothing. Dispassionately, he considered what remained of Anurak.

Then he glanced around at the shattered Winter Court. The centaur nodded with approval. Still others stared at him unflinching. As if they gazed upon Bastien in earnest for the first time.

In their eyes, Bastien saw a hint of expectation. Perhaps even of hope. It unsettled him almost as much as the centaur's reaction. Caused an odd stirring of pride to form in his chest. As if he had looked to his uncle or his father for praise and found what he sought.

A muscle tightened in Bastien's jaw. "The bridge."

"What?" the centaur said, taking a step forward.

The amabie and the redcap—as well as the assortment of winged fey hovering in the ledges above—eased closer.

"We should destroy the bridge connecting the winter lands to the summer lands," Bastien continued. "The summer fey are using it to send Grey Cloaks to the Wyld in search of the assassin. We need to destroy the bridge to hamper any more summer fey from crossing. And to send a clear message that we will not stand idly by as they make plans to invade."

The amabie agreed. "We should recruit the riverfolk and the ice nymphs to stand guard at the crossing."

Bastien nodded. "Do we have ways of demolishing the bridge quickly?"

"Blasting the keystone and piers should be effective." The centaur glanced up toward a group of fey with multicolored wings like those of dragonflies. "Bagus, the stores of niter you still possess for burrowing into rock tunnels can be used for this, can they not?"

Bagus started to reply, but the shadow of a small figure graced the entryway below him, leading to the heart of the mountain. The shadow lengthened as Suli stepped forward, his features weary. "Sunan is gone," he said without preamble, in a simple, sad voice.

Bastien had not known the small blue goblin well, but he felt the weight of Suli's words as the cavern descended into silence once again. Several winter fey began crying softly. Bastien knew enough to realize that Sunan's powers had kept those of the Winter Court safe for many centuries.

Suli's attention settled on Bastien. "I would speak with you, Sébastien Saint Germain."

Annoyance took root in Bastien's chest. Why did the entire Winter Court seem to feel as though he alone were responsible for their misfortunes?

Suli sighed when Bastien failed to reply. "Make no mistake, vampire. You are not my first choice. Nor are you my second. Were it left to me, I would not involve a blood drinker in our affairs. But my brother's last request will be honored. You will follow me. Now."

What kind of deathbed request would Sunan the Unmaker have of Nicodemus Saint Germain's blood heir?

Without a word, Bastien fell into step behind Suli, who began leading him through the darkness, deeper into the mountain. To a place Bastien had once dreamed of finding and now dreaded with every fiber of his being.

His past. His present. And his future.

THE RUINED PRINCESS

Frenetic energy tingled in Celine's fingertips. She shook her hands in the air, then continued pacing at her mother's bedside, her mind in a whirl.

Pippa could have survived. She was still fighting the wolves when they dragged her into the woods. Pippa would never give up. Pippa is alive.

Pippa. Pippa. Pippa.

The name of her best friend echoed through her like a heartbeat. Celine covered her ears and cried out, the pain in her throat threatening to become a roar.

Again, the memory of Pippa's flailing body raked across her vision.

The blood. So much blood.

Celine fell to her knees and sobbed. She stuffed the skirt of her rose silk gown in her mouth and screamed until her voice went hoarse. Through her tears, she thought she saw her mother's hand twitch.

"Umma?" Celine knelt in haste at the Lady of the Vale's bedside. Breathing in short bursts, she swiped the tears from her chin and laced her fingers through her mother's hand.

Her mother did not reply.

Celine's eyes welled again, her frustration mounting. "Why won't you wake up?" she murmured, her grip tightening. "They all want to know what we should do. What you would do. Please come back to us." Her words fell to a whisper. "They are talking about war. *War.* Please, Umma. Please tell us what we should do. Help me."

A voice—one whose absence had grown apparent the longer Celine lingered in the Vale—stirred in the furthest reaches of her mind. A more carefree version of herself. One who grinned in the face of danger and dared darkness to look her in the eye.

Why do you care what your mother—who left you as a child—*would do?* the voice said. *Perhaps you should ask what* you *would do.*

"This is not my world." Celine bristled at the insult to Lady Silla. "How would I know what to do? I've never been anything close to a general or a warrior."

Remember what Papa used to say? Who you were has never mattered.

Celine swallowed, a bitter taste collecting on her tongue. For the tenth time in as many minutes, she wished she could speak with Bastien.

The voice inside her head grew even more annoyed. *And now you are waiting for a ridiculous boy to tell you what to do? Why are you so afraid?*

"Because I'm alone," she shouted through the silent stillness. "I'm alone, and I'm tired of being alone. I want to be with my mother. I want to be with Bastien. I want to be with"—she swallowed, refusing to allow the worst of her fears to take root—"Pippa and Odette. I want to feel as if I belong *somewhere*. As if I finally, finally know who I am and what I'm meant to do."

How come you don't know who you are?

Celine did not have an answer.

So you are merely weak. How . . . disappointing.

"Go away," Celine said. "I don't need you. I've never needed you."

Liar. I am exactly what you need. I am the only thing you need. I am you.

"Whenever I listen to you," Celine said through her teeth, "I lose everything that matters."

You are wrong. But don't worry. As long as I am with you, you will never be alone.

Celine gritted her teeth and squeezed her eyes shut. "I sound like a madwoman, talking to myself like this."

And what of it? Simply be who you are, Marceline Rousseau.

"Stuff and nonsense," Celine muttered. "I am better than I was before. I am the daughter of a fairy queen." She turned her attention toward the sleeping figure of her mother, who rested on a bed of scented pine with eiderdown pillows and a coverlet of quilted gold silk. A dazzling haze encircled the carved pine bed, a charged warmth emanating from it. Though Celine had very little understanding of magic, she recognized this strange halo of energy. Powerful wards kept Lady Silla safe while she convalesced. The expression on her face was oddly peaceful.

If Celine had not been there two days ago beside the bridge to witness the moment the arrow struck her mother, Celine could believe that Lady Silla might awaken the next instant, a graceful smile on her face, her willowy arms ready to take her daughter into an embrace.

But Celine had been there. She'd seen the way the arrow struck her mother, slamming Lady Silla's slender body to the ground with an astonishing amount of force. Everything that had followed had been a blur. She and her mother had been taken from the bridge in a whirl of motion, encircled by a bastion of Grey Cloak soldiers. When the arrowhead had finally been removed, the injury in her mother's chest had bled like a river released from a dam.

Twice before, Celine had witnessed this much blood flow from a single wound. The first occasion had been when she struck the young man who had tried to violate her on a fateful winter night at the atelier in Paris, half a world and a lifetime ago. The second time was when Celine watched Bastien bleed to death in her arms after he'd rescued her from Nigel that horrific evening in the cathedral in Jackson Square.

Both events had marked life-altering moments in Celine's life.

Neither of them had prepared her for now.

Celine was not afraid of the unknown. But the world of her mother was a different world in truth. And Celine had not been in the Sylvan Vale for long, though the days passed differently here. Months had surely gone by back home in New Orleans. It was spring in Louisiana when Celine had first learned of her mother's existence. Now it was likely fall.

Much about the Sylvan Vale remained a mystery. Its rules. Its customs. Its magic. Everything eluded Celine. But she was determined to find a place for herself here. The Vale was a world made for someone like her. A world without restrictions, where enchantment itself was entirely possible. In the realm of the fey, even her dreams could be made real.

All her life, Celine had wanted so much more. She'd craved it. A life of danger and excitement. The thrill of the unknown and the power to chase after it.

The chance to know her mother better was reason alone to remain in the Vale, at least for a time. But Celine would be lying if she claimed she wasn't also drawn to the power available to women in the Summer Court. Lady Silla's presence as its ruler was nothing like the middling kind of influence afforded to women in the mortal world.

A knock echoed through the chamber. "Lady Celine?" The attendant who entered the room had the ears and tail of a sea mink and the yellow eyes of a cat, her long lashes curving toward her temples.

Celine stood at once. "Have they found any trace of Pippa?"

The attendant shook her feline head. "I'm sorry, my lady."

Inhaling, Celine forced herself to smile and her trembling hands to still. "Don't apologize, Vanida. But please be sure General Riya and the Grey Cloaks inform me the moment they have word."

"Of course, my lady. I've brought you something to eat."

"Thank you." Celine stood. She wasn't hungry, but it had been too long since she'd eaten a proper meal.

Vanida stepped toward Celine, her lush tail swishing as she walked. In her hands she bore a wooden tray of food, the platter carved from pale ash, and the dishes molded from gold.

Celine watched Vanida set down the tray on a small table near Lady Silla's bedside. There had not been many occasions for Celine to speak to her mother's personal attendants without being overheard. "May I ask what could be considered an impertinent question?" she said as Vanida began lifting the conical lids to uncover the artfully arranged dishes of food.

"You are the only daughter of my lady," Vanida said. "You may ask anything."

"Why is it that some of the fey possess attributes of animals and others do not?" Celine glanced sidelong at Vanida while removing a small silver container of salt from the skirt pocket of her gown.

Vanida wrinkled her nose. "Are you speaking about my ears and my tail?"

Celine nodded.

Vanida said, "These I purchased from an illusionist who specializes in changing appearances."

"Then they are not real?" As she'd been instructed by her mother, Celine began sprinkling a small amount of salt on each uncovered dish, waiting to see if the clear granules changed color on contact, indicating the presence of a spell or a possible poison.

"What is real?" Vanida lifted a shoulder while she watched

Celine season the food. "The fur on my ears feels soft to the touch. My tail whips through the air as I move. And if I wish to alter their hue or see them gone at any time, I can do so in the matter of a moment, provided I am able to pay the price."

Celine considered Vanida's words. In the last few weeks, she'd asked her mother several questions about the Vale's magic, but Lady Silla had a way of replying without offering any real answers. "And why are some fey magical and others not?"

Vanida began serving small portions of lavender-scented cheese, spiced lentils in a buttery tomato gravy, tiny aubergines simmered in a mint-green sauce with palm sugar and fresh herbs, and a selection of steamed dumplings shaped into pastel-colored flowers. "That is more difficult to answer." The attendant hesitated. "Many believe our magic has diminished because we have mixed with lesser creatures."

"You mean mortals."

Vanida straightened, alarm flashing across her feline features. "I meant no disrespect, Lady Celine."

"I know you didn't." Celine removed a lace handkerchief from her other pocket and toyed with its scalloped edges.

Vanida poured tea sweetened with a fruit like crushed black-berries into a golden chalice. "It is a rarity nowadays, but there are also those among our gentry who choose to couple with fey who never possessed magical ability, like myself."

"I see," Celine said. "May I ask how you feel about the summer gentry?" Knowing how the powerless spoke of those in power was an important lesson Celine had learned from experience.

Vanida paused before replying. "I am . . . grateful to them. When I was given this job serving in the Summer Court, everyone in my family rejoiced. It is a great honor to attend the Lady of the Vale."

Celine reached for a steamed dumpling pressed into the shape of a pink rose. Vanida caught her hand before she could touch the food. "My apologies, Lady Celine," Vanida said. "But I'm afraid the salt is no longer enough. You must wait until your meal is tasted."

"Why?" Celine frowned. "My mother told me salt would detect the presence of anything harmful." On food that was spelled or tainted, the salt flakes turned odd shades of grey or blue-green, causing the meal to savor of metal on a mortal's tongue. "My food has never been tasted before," she said. Realization dawned on her the next instant.

After her mother's attempted assassination, were the fey worried that someone would try to kill Celine?

Vanida's cheeks hollowed. "Forgive me, Lady Celine, but I always tasted your mother's food. It is only natural for me to taste yours as well. If the unspeakable were to happen and Lady Silla never wakes, there are many in the gentry who would look to you for leadership."

A bubble of fear caught in Celine's throat at the idea of her mother never waking. She blinked. "I'm half mortal. Most of the gentry tolerate my presence out of respect for my mother. The idea that they would support me in any leadership role is ludicrous."

Averting her gaze, Vanida proceeded to chew on her lower lip. Hesitation clouded her features. The fey was hiding something important.

"Please, Vanida," Celine said. "Speak in earnest. I know there is much I have to learn, but how will I ever begin to understand if I continue to be kept in the darkness?"

Vanida toyed with the rose-colored dumpling between her glossy fingers. Minuscule flower petals and flakes of gold were embedded in her talon-shaped nails. They matched the pattern painted on the tightly laced corset cinching the attendant's tiny waist.

Like most of the fey who resided in the Vale, Vanida enjoyed beautiful things.

"Vanida," Celine pressed, her tone gentle. "Please."

The attendant nodded. Her voice dropped to a whisper. "There will always be members of our court who will refuse to bow to an ethereal, no matter her parentage." She paused. "But they cannot ignore the importance of the magic linked to the Horned Throne. Those who are most loyal to Lady Silla would see the power of the throne pass to her own kin. It is the only way such great magic is sure to remain intact."

"Magic?" Celine's eyes went wide. "My mother's powers are passed to her kin?"

Again Vanida nodded. "When the first Lady of the Vale knew she was near the end of her life, she used her last breath to create an unbreakable enchantment to prevent those at court from overthrowing her young heir. It is the kind of magic only the greatest among us can perform. Her blood heir alone is meant to inherit her powers. If the one who inherits the title is not the first living daughter of our lady, the magic of the Horned Throne is lost to us forever."

Stunned by this news, Celine took a step back and nearly fell, her ankle catching on the leg of a gilded chair. All at once, it made sense why her mother had been so keen to foster a connection with her. Celine sank into the plush velvet seat, her thoughts churning like the sea in a storm.

No one had done so much as hint that her mother's powers might pass to her.

Celine didn't even know what her mother's magic could do. She'd watched Lady Silla manipulate air on several occasions and coax flowers and trees to grow on others. As for displays of real power? The kind that would press an entire court of fey creatures to pledge their fealty?

Celine could not fathom what that sort of magic might mean.

Hot on the heels of this revelation followed a twist of anger. "Why did my mother never tell me this?"

Vanida continued fidgeting with the pink dumpling, which began falling to pieces between her painted nails, the sweetened filling of nuts and spices crumbling like flakes of snow. She opened her mouth to speak, then closed it the next instant before finally saying, "In the past, daughters have wished ill on their mothers in an attempt to obtain this magic."

A chill passed through Celine's bones. She understood this as well. Her mother's magic—like so much of the magic that had enthralled Celine as a young girl captivated by dark fairy tales— came with a price. In the world of the summer fey, daughters had likely tried to steal it from their mothers. Mothers had deceived and manipulated their own children to maintain it.

But the most haunting thought of all was this inescapable truth: In Celine's bloodline, magic and murder had long existed hand in hand.

Like puzzle pieces joining together, everything aligned to form a clear picture. Celine had held an attraction to power, even at an early age. The very idea of it had intoxicated her. If she was honest with herself, her attraction to power was what had brought her to the doors of La Cour des Lions . . . and into Bastien's arms. "My mother barely knows me," she murmured. "And I barely know her. But I do know that I would never kill her in order to steal her magic."

"A thousand apologies, my lady, but it is one thing to say that, and another thing entirely to mean it," Vanida said. "I would wager that Lady Silla intended to tell you eventually, in time. But it is important that you learn the truth, now that"—she glanced with unease toward the sleeping figure of Celine's mother—"she is indisposed. The magic of the Horned Throne means you would reign over the lands of the Vale and conduct the wind as it flowed through the trees and command the very roots of all living things to bend at your will. It is a power almost anyone in the Vale would kill to possess. And that is only the beginning. A skilled enchantress could learn to control the forest below and the skies above. A few blood heirs have wielded the magic differently from their predecessors. Some become even stronger. Or manage to control the air itself to conjure illusions of their own."

For an instant, Celine imagined being able to manipulate the wind in the trees and the roots at her feet. Like some kind of dark symphony. How the branches above would bow to her. How the ground below would tremble in her wake.

The thought alone was delicious. But Celine could never fathom a world where she would sacrifice people she loved for power. More than anything, Celine hated being alone. And power for its own sake would leave her with nothing else.

It was as the fairy tales always foretold.

Just as that thought occurred to Celine, the doors to her mother's chamber opened once more, and Lord Vyr—the highest-ranking member of the gentry, in Lady Silla's absence—strode across the marble threshold without so much as a knock or a request.

Celine frowned. He'd twice requested an audience with her for this afternoon, and Celine had ignored him for a myriad of reasons, least of which was the fact that she felt supreme discomfort in his presence. The fey lord with the silver hair and the enviable wardrobe had failed to ingratiate himself to her. He had the look of someone who would strangle his own brother if it suited his needs. Nonetheless, Celine understood that Vyr was a better ally than an enemy, and someone of his standing supporting her was more important now than ever.

"Lady Celine." Vyr offered her a quick bow, his curtain of straight hair falling over both silk-clad shoulders. "I apologize for my impatience, but I have a matter to discuss of grave importance." His eyes glinted as he gazed down at her, a hint of malice curling his lips.

Celine wanted to dismiss him outright. She did not owe anyone in the Vale her allegiance, and she disliked the way he looked upon her with such condescension. But she'd watched, time and again, while Bastien navigated such intricacies in New Orleans, and ignoring Lord Vyr would not do her any favors now.

Bastien. Pippa. Celine closed her eyes for a moment. If something unthinkable had happened to the ones she loved, her heart would know it. Wouldn't it? This was why she refused to accept that Pippa had succumbed to the wolf attack on the bridge. There was too much hope left in Celine to accept that possibility.

But why was there still no word on Pippa? And to where had Bastien disappeared, without a word?

Distress wove through Celine's stomach, causing her nerves to quake once more. The next second, she hardened her resolve. Bastien was a vampire from one of the most powerful lines of winter fey. He moved like lightning and healed in the blink of an eye. It was likely that he'd stayed behind in the Wyld to tend to the wounded or perhaps to care for Pippa. Perhaps they were together even now.

She swallowed, clinging to every shred of hope she could muster.

Pippa wasn't dead. She was alive. Just like Bastien. They simply had to be.

Celine opened her eyes. "Yes, Lord Vyr." She did not apologize for keeping him waiting. It was something else she'd learned, not from Bastien but rather from Odette, who often said that women apologized far too often for her taste. "Thank you for coming to see me." She lifted her chin to match his condescending stare.

Lord Vyr bowed again, this time more deeply. "I have come because it is long past due for you to address the court. We must take action for what the Sylvan Wyld perpetrated against us two days ago."

Despite the irritation flaring through her, Celine kept her features expressionless. "I—" She stopped herself before she could give voice to her protests. "May I ask what General Riya has suggested we do?"

"Our general remains along the border, coordinating efforts to find the ones responsible for trying to murder Lady Silla. We have not received word from her since yesterday." The right side of his mouth curved into a cold smile. "Which you would know, had you attended the summit of the Fey Guild earlier today." He attempted to appear sympathetic. "But I understand the injury to your mother and the death of your beloved friend must have been shocking. I suppose it is difficult for you to weigh these heavy considerations during such a trying time."

This conceited ass. Dress him down. Don't tell him who you are. Show him.

Such reckless behavior was bound to cause Celine nothing but trouble. With effort, she attempted to silence the voice in her head. "I . . . do not believe my friend is dead, Lord Vyr," she said. "And as for my mother . . . you advised Lady Silla in the past, did you not?"

Coward.

"Yes, my lady. I often gave her counsel." His expression turned haughty. "She said on more than one occasion that I possessed the same eye for strategy that the blood drinkers employed against us centuries ago."

"And what would you counsel we do in this situation?"

Lord Vyr's features turned shrewd. "I would fortify our forces. Increase the guards around the Ivy Bower. Prepare for an incursion into the Wyld." He paused. "And I would ready plans to destroy what remains of their troops, once and for all."

A shiver chased down Celine's spine. She had little doubt as to Lord Vyr's designs on the land of the winter fey. If he were left in charge, he would force the whole of the Otherworld to bow at the feet of the summer gentry.

And he would not hesitate to kill anyone who stood in his way.

Then strike him down before he has the chance.

Celine gripped her skirts, fighting to hold her tongue.

"If I may," a male voice said from beyond the open double doors of Lady Silla's chamber, "there may be a less intrusive way of seeking justice." The clear voice grew louder as its owner paused just beyond the threshold to await permission to enter, in contrast to Lord Vyr.

"Before making a decision that could be seen as hasty," Haroun al-Rashid continued, "perhaps it would be prudent to send a small party of scouts to explore the Wyld and determine what their intentions might be. And, in particular, who might be the one giving the orders."

"Ali," Celine said, still using the name he'd first given those at court. "Please come in."

Haroun entered the chamber, a hand on his curved sword and a careful look on his chiseled face.

A sense of calm descended on Celine. She had not called for "Ali" since their conversation two days ago beside the dais upon which the Horned Throne sat. His presence now made her feel less alone. She wondered why she'd chosen to keep him away. Haroun trusted Celine with his identity. Why he'd felt the need to conceal who he was from those of the Summer Court, she had yet to understand, but if he trusted her, she wanted to trust him, and he'd never given her reason to doubt his intentions.

Of course, Bastien had never liked Haroun. But then, Bastien seemed to dislike everyone he met in the Sylvan Vale. A pang of longing cut through Celine's stomach.

More of this nonsense. As if you don't have better things to do.

Fretting about Bastien, Pippa, and her mother had consumed Celine for the last two days. Her mother had yet to wake. Pippa could be in grave peril. And Bastien had failed to send a whisper to Celine of his condition or whereabouts. The distance that had been growing between them since they'd returned to the Sylvan Vale a few weeks ago was now distance in truth.

It wearied Celine, body and soul.

"I'm curious . . . if the arrow fired upon Lady Silla was fired from the icy reaches of our greatest enemy, who else do you think could be giving the orders?" Vyr fixed his icy stare on Haroun.

Haroun tilted his head. "That would be a better question for you, would it not, Lord Vyr? Seeing as how you are the one with the most experience on these matters."

Vyr's lips pursed, his eyes narrowing to slits.

Celine almost smiled. "Will you share a meal with me, Ali?" she asked Haroun. She waited while Vanida used a small pearlescent spoon to taste each item on a golden plate. After Celine sprinkled the food with more salt—just to be certain—she passed the plate to Haroun.

When he looked her way, he offered a kind grin. His irises were gilded like those of a jungle cat, and his brown skin glowed in the warmth radiating throughout the chamber. He wore the lustrous garments of cream silk and sage-colored damask as though he'd been born into the fey court. Haroun always appeared strong and capable. Attractive in that unassuming manner of a young man at ease in his own skin.

Celine's mother liked Haroun a lot. There was a time when Lady Silla had subtly nudged Celine to engage in a dalliance with him. But Haroun had never quickened her heart or stolen the breath from her body. He did not haunt her dreams, nor did he set her mind adrift in fantasy.

No. There was only one young man who had ever done that.

"If we could continue, Lady Celine." With a glare at Haroun, Lord Vyr crossed his arms and tapped his foot on the marble floor. "We've sent countless spies to the Wyld over the centuries. It is clear their growing weakness has caused them to act out of desperation. Now is the time to strike with decisive action, not excuses." Again, he glanced in Haroun's direction.

"I agree with you, Lord Vyr," Haroun said. For a moment, his acquiescence disarmed Vyr. "But any actions taken by the Summer Court must be from a place of careful consideration."

"Mortal warfare is not fey warfare," Vyr countered. "The time we waste collecting information is time that would be better spent on the offensive."

"It is true," Haroun replied, "that fey warfare differs from mortal warfare in many respects. But I would wager that I've experienced mortal warfare more recently than those of the Summer Court, who have known nothing but peace for centuries." He turned toward Celine, his brow furrowed. "Lady Celine, I would avoid an offensive until we know exactly what we are facing."

Dry laughter flew from Vyr's lips. "Have you not heard?" He grinned. "Oh, forgive me, a mere mortal such as yourself would not be privy to such information, nor were you present when the winter scum tried to murder our lady. Their forces are non-existent. That day on the riverbank, we learned that the Winter Court has relied on the conjurings of an illusionist to deceive their enemies with respect to their strength. They are bedraggled and run-down, with limited weaponry and less than a hundred warriors in their ranks."

Haroun said nothing for a time. Then he rested both hands on the hilt of his curved sword. "And would that not be yet another wonderful illusion to cast? Would it not be the strategy of a brilliant mind to lure the Summer Court into such an attack?"

Vyr took in a sharp breath. "They lack the leadership for this kind of complicated strategy."

"Forgive me, Lord Vyr, but that is simply untrue. You said it yourself. Lady Silla never forgot how shrewd the blood drinkers were. Nicodemus Saint Germain's heir stood along the banks of the Wyld that day. Or have you forgotten?"

Vyr no longer cared to conceal his fury with Haroun. "Sébastien Saint Germain never impressed me. The vampire is little more than an animal familiar, nipping at the heels of his mistress." He gestured at Celine with his chin.

"You and I disagree on that front," Haroun said. "There is more to Bastien than you or I know."

Though Haroun spoke as if he were complimenting Bastien, Celine could not help but detect a sharp note to his words.

A part of Celine wished to defend Bastien, especially against Vyr's petty incitements. But what could she say? That he would never take up arms against them? That if he were any kind of animal familiar, he was a snake, and that Vyr would not see him strike until it was far too late?

Celine knew Bastien would never hurt her.

But the rest of the summer fey?

If Bastien thought them to be a threat to anyone he loved, he would not hesitate to attack first. Haroun's suggestion was well warranted. A mind like Bastien's working in opposition to Lady Silla's court would pose a serious threat to the Sylvan Vale.

More serious than Celine wished to consider.

Would he act against the Summer Court? Against . . . her mother? Was it possible?

It is. You know it is. And you may have to choose. Your family? Or your love?

The golden spoon in Celine's hand slipped from her fingers to the floor, clattering against the marble with all the grace of a newborn foal. Celine stared at the splatter of food across the otherwise impeccable white stone. Overwhelmed, she closed her eyes and tried her best to drown out the ceaseless debate in her own mind.

She was so tired. So troubled. So alone.

More than anything, she wanted a place to rest her head. Something that tasted of home. The bread at Jacques'. A plate of something rich and warm and thick, with a sauce that clung to her ribs and spices that livened her tongue. Odette's ribald laughter. Pippa's sage advice. The smell of Bastien's skin. Bubbles of champagne frothing in a crystal glass. The hiss of the lamps on Decatur Street. The scent of the musky Mississippi wafting through the warm summer breeze. The clatter of hoofbeats and the echo of something that was once beautiful.

Damn it, she even longed for the clouds of blood-drinking insects.

She missed it all. Their city. Their home.

New Orleans.

"Lady Celine," Vanida said, her tone gentle as she placed her clawed fingers on Celine's shoulder. "Would you like for me to prepare a bath for you? Or perhaps ready your chamber so that you might sleep?"

Celine shook her head. "Lord Vyr," she began. "We will send scouts before launching any kind of offensive."

Vyr cut his eyes. "Lady Celine, I—"

"Now is not the time for haste." Celine spoke even louder, letting her voice fill the chamber. "We will lead with the head above our shoulders, not the one below it."

Vanida tittered. Haroun's eyes went wide.

"Are you"—Vyr's nostrils flared—"are you speaking of my phallus?"

Celine nodded. Something sparked in her chest, behind her heart. "Just this once, Lord Vyr, for it is not a topic I wish to discuss ever again."

A flush crept up Vyr's neck. It was the first time Celine could ever remember seeing the haughty fey look embarrassed. "I—I have no need to make decisions according to the whims of my phallus, Lady Celine," he seethed. "If you wish to insult my sexual prowess, there are countless members of court who can attest to the contrary. My mate, Liege Sujee, can speak to all the ways I please them. I would prove it to you myself, but I do not bed ethereals on a matter of principle, no matter how much they might beg me." He raised his chin, his eyebrows curving into his forehead. "And you would beg, Lady Celine." His teeth shone as he appraised her figure. "I would almost lower myself to your level, just to see you beg."

Vanida gasped at the insult, her nails forming claws. "How *dare*—"

Celine took Vanida by the hand and offered her a grateful nod. "I would *never* beg, Lord Vyr," she said to the fey lord, her voice growing softer.

"Ah, so you have never begged for pleasure before?" Vyr continued. "The vampire is as pathetic a lover as he is in all things. Take a summer fey into your bed. Then you would know why mortals lose their minds to us in the Vale."

"Rest assured, Lord Vyr, the dark fey who shares my bed would put you to shame with nothing but a glance." Before Vyr could offer a rejoinder, Celine spun on her heel, anger flashing hot through her veins. She knew her cheeks were pink, and her eyes were wild. She felt . . . alive. It wasn't just the anger. It was a feeling of purpose. A feeling of . . . power. She cleared her throat. The voice inside her head laughed, the sound throaty. Filled with delight.

Vyr muttered something under his breath. A word Celine could not make out.

A hiss flew from Vanida's lips. She stepped between Celine and Vyr, her feline whiskers trembling. "That is the second time you've dared to insult our lady's only daughter, Lord Vyr. Persist, and I will inform the court."

"Do as you will, kitten," Vyr countered. "I would be interested to see what comes of it. Where we all stand in the end." He smoothed the front of his pristine garments. "Indeed, who remains standing at all."

Though Haroun said nothing, Celine did not fail to recognize the shift of his hands on his curved sword, as if he were about to unsheathe the blade at a moment's notice.

Vyr's words were true. The coming clash between them for the Horned Throne was imminent. For an instant, Celine toyed with the idea of provoking the fey lord further.

But Celine did not think she could weather the storm that would follow. Not now. She needed to rest. To calm the tempest in her mind.

And quash this insect beneath her boot.

Celine began with a smile. "Vyr," she said softly. "It's quite possible that there are members of our court who conspired to overthrow my mother in the hopes that they might better control me, *her blood heir.*" She spoke in low tones, her words easy, though fury flashed before her eyes. "If you do not wish for my suspicions to fall on you as their ringleader, I suggest you follow my orders. Send out scouts with all haste. Wait to see what our soldiers say before taking any kind of offensive against the Sylvan Wyld." She stood on her toes, her words a mocking whisper in his ear. "And if you insult me one more time, I will feed your tongue to kittens back home in New Orleans." She smiled. "Even our Crescent City babies have a taste for blood."

Silence filled the space. It turned heavy, until Celine almost believed she could hear every swish of Vanida's tail. Something brash began to churn through her blood. A recklessness she hadn't felt in far too long. For an instant, she thought about striking Vyr, just to see how it would feel.

The echo of her own laughter reverberated through her head.

How I have missed you. Stay with me, and we will do great things.

Vyr swallowed. Celine watched his throat move, as if he were choking on something bitter. "Yes, my lady," he said in clipped tones. Then he bowed once before taking his leave without uttering another word.

"Well," Vanida said once Lord Vyr was no longer in earshot, "I enjoyed that more than I've enjoyed anything in a very long time." She purred contentedly as she leaned back against the wall with a huge grin.

"He will not suffer that in silence," Haroun warned, his palm still gripping his sword.

"I do not expect him to." Celine sank into the gilded chair, her features weary. She pressed a palm to her forehead. "But if I bought myself one day more, I will be content."

"My lady." Vanida crouched beside her. "By my count, you have not rested for more than a few hours. Please take care of yourself." She brought a goblet to Celine's lips, urging her to drink. "Lord Vyr will be the least of our concerns if you fail to maintain the appearance of strength, now of all times."

"Vanida is right," Haroun said. "You need to rest."

"No," Celine murmured. "I don't need rest. I need answers." She sat up at once. "I need to know that at least one person I love is no longer in harm's way."

Understanding settled on Haroun's features. "You cannot journey to winter's shores, Celine."

"No," Celine agreed. "But I can go home."

"To New Orleans?" Haroun's brows rose.

Celine nodded. "I can see with my own eyes whether Odette survived. And ask my family for advice."

The moment she uttered the words, Celine's heart leapt at the idea of returning home. The chance to smell the sultry air of the French Quarter. To bite into a rare steak and laugh with her Court of the Lions family, even if it was just for an hour.

But could she dare?

"No, it's a bad idea," Celine whispered, her shoulders falling. "What if something happens while I'm gone? What if . . ." Her voice trailed off, her gaze returning to her mother's silent figure.

Vanida tilted her head to one side. "It isn't a bad idea at all. If you journeyed there for a mortal day, it would be a matter of less than an hour here in the land of the fey. Provided you remain in one place, it will be easy to return using your mother's tare. The work of a moment."

Temptation gripped Celine's heart. The thought of returning home for even a breath of time—of seeing Odette's smiling face and asking for Jae's help to strategize—warmed her soul.

Again, Celine's attention drifted toward her mother. "You are certain word can reach me easily?"

Vanida nodded. "Of course. But you will have to take two Grey Cloaks with you to stand guard."

Celine's heart dropped, though she understood why. Her family in the Court of the Lions would not be pleased that summer fey warriors were in their city.

"I would like to accompany you as well," Haroun offered.

The chamber fell silent while Celine considered her options. "Forgive me," she said. "May I have some time to myself to consider the best course of action?"

Haroun placed a hand on her shoulder and nodded, the warmth in his features once again reminding Celine to keep him in close company. Vanida quietly followed Haroun from the chamber, pulling the double doors shut as she left.

Celine sat beside her mother, her bones weary, aching as

though they were carrying an unseen weight. The world of the fey had never felt more unfamiliar to her.

She needed the guidance of the family she'd chosen for herself. Even more than that, she needed to look at Odette's face and believe—in her heart—that all would be well once again.

A renewed sense of hope was what Celine needed now, more than ever.

"Umma," Celine said. She reached for her mother's hand. "I will be gone from the Vale for no more than an hour. But I need to return home to New Orleans. Once I clear my head, I will come back to the Vale, and I promise we will all be the better for it."

Celine swore Lady Silla squeezed her hand in response. Her heart stuttered in her chest, hope flooding her veins. It was as if her mother wanted to tell her she understood.

"Thank you," Celine replied. "When I return, we will right what has been wronged." Determination filled her words. "I will not fail. The Horned Throne is safe. I swear to you, I will keep it safe."

It might have been a trick of the light, but Celine thought she saw one side of Lady Silla's mouth curve into a peaceful smile. With that, she called for Vanida to lead her to the tare reserved for the Lady of the Vale's private use, her throat tight with anticipation.

In a few minutes' time, Celine would be home.

She would be in New Orleans once again.

The Ruined Son

A shot rang out in the darkness with a noise to wake the dead. The silver bullet ricocheted off the back of a metal pan before striking the packed-earth ceiling. Bits of soil crumbled to the ground like salt flakes off a fisherman's net.

Arjun Desai snorted, then coughed from the gunpowder lingering in the air. In the past, the way the peppery residue collected in the back of his throat had been pleasing. It reminded him of eating something spicy, the way it warmed his body long after he'd finished a meal. Now the dust from the powder settled on his tongue and made his mouth feel dry.

"There's a solution for that," he slurred. He took a long swig from the green bottle of mystwine in his other hand. Then he aimed his revolver at a bundle of herbs hanging off a carved wooden rack suspended from the ceiling. The silver bullet severed the herbs in two, and Arjun took another deep breath of the blue smoke surrounding him. While he coughed, he held the smoldering barrel of his weapon upright, his forehead pressed against the hot metal, scalding just enough to cause pain, despite his drunken haze.

Arjun laughed at nothing and took another draught of

mystwine. He slumped farther down the wall while he drank. Once he managed to drain the dregs of burning liquid from the bottle, he paused to stare through the emerald glass, then hurled it against the solid silver stove gleaming along the right side of one of the Ivy Bower's largest sculleries.

The bottle shattered into pieces, joining the broken shards of glazed pottery, terra-cotta jars, and glass vials that Arjun had spent the better part of the afternoon destroying. Bits of food and pools of honey and dried fruit—along with smashed beans and dustings of colorful spices—were scattered across the floor as if a trip of goats had gotten loose in the larder.

It was a mess. But it was Arjun's mess. And he wouldn't apologize for it.

He groped through the shadows, searching for something else to drink. Liquor. Mystwine. Shroom tea. Tincture of a coblynau's nipple.

"Ah," Arjun shouted. "Bollocks!"

There was no more mystwine. If he wanted to continue drowning his feelings, he would need to stand and seek out the spirits for himself. Or do what he dreaded most and speak to another living being in the Ivy Bower.

He sank lower, until most of his body was lying supine on the polished stone floor, the side of his head propped on a curved ledge. Arjun closed his eyes and breathed through his nose. The mystwine circled through his mind at a slow roll, almost as if he were in a gentle, dizzying spin.

Through this swirl of thoughts, Pippa's face came into sudden focus. But this time it was different. It wasn't the image of her smiling or laughing or fighting to keep Arjun safe, her back to his.

This time he saw her sleeping.

The ache in his chest almost consumed him.

Even in this inebriated state, Arjun's memory continued to torture him with its ability to capture such exquisite detail. The one and only time Pippa had slept in his arms, Arjun had awoken in the dim reaches of dawn and felt her soft breath against his neck. Her long eyelashes had cast ribbons of shadow across her lightly freckled skin. She was so beautiful that Arjun had looked away a moment.

When he glanced back, her blue eyes were open. She smiled, her gaze heavy-lidded. Beguiling in a completely innocent way. He'd felt himself falling, as if he were diving into an azure pond beneath a sea of puffy white clouds. And once he landed, he'd floated beneath that sky, his mind at perfect ease.

All Arjun's life, he'd lived along the fringes. He never sought to meet the gaze of anyone at court, because he dreaded the notice of any member of the fey gentry.

For the first time, Arjun thrilled at the chance to lock eyes with someone, without fear. To glance at another person with love and hope in his heart, ready to dive in headfirst, without a second thought. He knew without hesitating that, wherever he was, he would look up and find Pippa in a crowded room. That she could find him. And neither of them would need to search for something alone, ever again.

Rage clawed up his throat. Tears burned hot and fast in his eyes.

The wolves. The damned werewolves. The beasts that had attacked Pippa on the bridge. There was only one reason for them to have done that. Before marrying Arjun Desai, Philippa Montrose had been a mortal girl of little to no significance to any fey of any court, light or dark. But the day she'd become the wife of General Riya's only son?

She'd become a pawn. Something to toy with. Something to sacrifice.

Something to lose.

Arjun surrendered to the darkness, as if he could banish the memory of that afternoon from his mind. Still he heard Pippa's screams. Felt the grip of his mother's soldiers as they held Arjun tight, preventing him from racing to her aid.

The blood. Her screams. The hiss of the bullets raining down around them.

By all rights, he should be at the vanguard of the coming fight. His mother would relish finally having her only son join the ranks of their esteemed warriors. But Arjun had always refused to play their games. Refused to become embroiled in fey nonsense. He would not be drawn into their endless cycle of spite, where he was destined to suffer even more pain and loss, until nothing remained of him but skin and bones and hate.

Even if it cost him everything he had, he would not fall prey to the evil of the Vale.

Arjun yelled and fired another round from his revolver at nothing. Then another. And another. Until the chamber emptied and the clicks echoed into the dimly lit ceiling.

"Are you finished?" a soft, feminine voice asked, cutting through the darkness with the precision of a knife.

"Not nearly," Arjun muttered from his position on the floor, his ears ringing from the noise.

He listened while exacting steps moved across the room, booted feet crushing broken pieces of glass and dried herbs and shattered carafes of trickling liquids. Disoriented from the mystwine and his own unshed tears, Arjun did not recognize Yuri at first. He'd half expected his mother would be the one to yank him from his drunken stupor, as she usually was.

But General Riya was not at the Ivy Bower. She was protecting the border and seeking out the ones who had dared to fire an arrow in an attempt to kill the Lady of the Vale.

Arjun's jaw clenched. He wondered what it would be like to have a mother who cared enough to console her son in any meaningful way. To know his mother valued something beside her position as general of the Sylvan Vale's fighting forces.

"Did my mother send you to spy on my pathetic state?" Arjun said, his tone flat. "Be sure to say how disappointed you are. Stress how predictable my behavior is."

Yuri said nothing in response.

Arjun peered up at her through one eye, squinting from the light of the single lantern she held aloft in her left hand. Despite the play of shadows, it was impossible to miss the look of pity on the young Grey Cloak's face. He hated it. Her pity made him feel like he was a boy again. That small ethereal boy, fighting to feel significant and, at the same time, dreading anyone's notice.

Arjun struggled to sit upright. He wanted to ask the most important question but didn't know if he had the strength for the answer. "D-did they find her?" he whispered, his voice gruff.

"No," Yuri replied. "General Riya has not found any further trace of Philippa Montrose . . . or her body. Our runners followed the werewolves' tracks along with the trail of her blood into the rocks beside the mountain. The entrance to their cavern must be concealed or warded." It was strange to hear a note of sympathy in Yuri's voice. At least it sounded like sympathy. Arjun had not experienced many occasions in which any member of the Summer Court expressed a drop of understanding for mortal emotions.

He tapped the barrel of his revolver against his knee. He swallowed. Arjun could not decide if the news Yuri had presented was good news. If the pack of werewolves had taken Pippa with them, she might still be alive. But . . . why would they keep her alive? If they wished to make demands of the Summer Court to secure her release, where was their request?

Yuri hesitated. "If it is any comfort to you, I . . . do not think Lady Pippa is still suffering. It would be difficult for a mere mortal to survive extensive bite wounds from werewolves. If there were fey blood in her lineage somewhere, it might be possible, but there has never been any indication of that in her past. Has there?"

A knot of anguish pulled taut in Arjun's stomach. He shook his head. "No. Pippa is wonderfully, perfectly mortal." He laughed, the sound dark. Like acid dashed against stone. "I'm sure my mother would have uncovered any proof to the contrary. In any case, I'll bet General Riya was thrilled about losing track of the werewolves."

"Why would General Riya be thrilled by that?" Yuri asked. "Your mother does not enjoy seeing you in pain, Arjun Desai, despite what you may think."

He opened both his eyes to look up at her this time.

Yuri, the youngest Grey Cloak ever to take up arms. Sworn into the service of the Lady of the Vale as soon as she'd finished her early schooling. A gifted warrior, rider, archer, spear thrower, and climber. Unquestioningly faithful. Equally unyielding. She'd been raised in General Riya's care after her parents' untimely demise in a tragic lovers' quarrel. Yuri was everything Arjun's mother could want in an offspring. Though she was not of General Riya's blood, her loyalty remained unmatched, as though she were indeed a member of their family. Whatever Arjun's mother had asked of Yuri, the young fey warrior had answered, without hesitation.

But something about Yuri had troubled Arjun from the start, even when they were children. Her face was too symmetrical. It lacked a single blemish. Perhaps a scar from childhood or an imperfect, lopsided smile might have lent her features an air of authenticity. But it was as if her appearance was frozen in time, childlike, with glass skin and upturned eyes of shining jet black. Arjun could not reconcile a warrior so deadly in the tiny body of someone who appeared so harmless at first blush. As if a fluffy bunny had sprouted fangs and leapt in the air, intent on tearing him limb from limb.

"If you think my mother doesn't enjoy seeing me suffer," Arjun said, "then congratulations on being duped, you baby-faced ninny. Your life is a lie. Now join me for a drink. I'll have another bottle of mystwine, thank you."

"Don't you think you've had enough?"

Arjun recognized the disdain on Yuri's face as she stared down at him. It was the same look she'd given him since they were children.

He laughed again. "If you're not going to get me a drink, then what in hell are you doing here, Yuri? The zoo is closed. Read the signs." His gaze hardened. "Don't feed the bears."

"I am here because I want to help coax you from this pitiable state."

Arjun's laughter grew louder. "And how would you do that? With your charming wit?"

"With an appeal to reason. Or with the hope that, as your childhood peer, I could convince you to see beyond yourself."

"That doesn't seem to benefit me, though, does it?"

Her lips pursed to one side. "Your mother told me she thought this was a fool's errand."

"Unsurprising." Arjun snorted. "What else did she say?"

"She wanted me to determine if you had any idea what the vampire might do next."

Arjun quirked a brow. "Bastien?" Low laughter flew from his lips. "He had nothing to do with the attack on Lady Silla. Why would he? He's in love with her daughter. It would be illogical for him to try to kill Celine's mother. Besides that, his interest in fey politics is nonexistent."

"He is Nicodemus Saint Germain's heir," Yuri insisted. "He would be the one to sit upon the Ice Throne, had it not been shattered centuries ago by our ancestors. He has everything to gain from throwing our court into disarray by murdering the Lady of the Vale."

"Ugh," Arjun groaned. "You're making my head hurt. If my mother thinks Bastien is responsible for what happened that afternoon on the banks, then I congratulate her on being duped as well." He plunked his revolver down on the floor and threw his arm over his eyes as if he were shielding himself from the sun. "Please save me the trouble of having to continue this conversation. What do you really want from me, Yuri?"

She sniffed, annoyance causing her chin to tip upward. "I suppose I harbor the vain hope that I might convince you to finally take your place among the warriors meant to defend the Vale from its enemies." Yuri took a step forward, her booted heel crunching on glazed pottery. "Or at least I hoped to help you stand on your own two feet, son of Riya. And maybe—just maybe—I could ask you to come with me to the border. Join your mother. Help us search for the girl you love and seek justice for the wrongs that have been done to us all."

Arjun exhaled in a huff. "Justice?" he said, using his elbows to move into an upright position, shards of glass shifting around him. "In the Vale?" He snorted. "What a piss-poor joke." He slid to the floor again.

"You are the poor joke, Arjun Desai. You, who were destined for such greatness."

He sat up in a quick motion that caused his head to pound in protest. "You can fuck right off with that nonsense. No one in the Vale has ever thought an ethereal was destined for greatness."

Yuri crouched to look him in the eye. "If you are angered by what I said, there is a way to channel that anger toward something good. Something helpful."

"Helpful to whom?" Arjun narrowed his eyes. "War is never good. Though I doubt you would agree. Without war, you and my mother wouldn't have a profession."

"I suppose you think this is a valuable use of your time, then?" Yuri asked as she glanced around at the destruction that was once the larder.

Arjun's thoughts turned circumspect. Despite his wiser inclinations, he decided to be honest with Yuri for a moment. "Letting my emotions be known is indeed a valuable use of my time. I'm not bottling them up as I did before I met Pippa. That . . . would be a dishonor to what we shared together." He followed Yuri's gaze, his attention landing on a shattered bit of porcelain. Then he locked eyes with his mother's favorite, struggling to keep his voice from breaking. "The world around me matches the world inside me now. I do find that strangely comforting. At least there is some part of me that refuses to lie." Then he grinned. "But don't worry; it's only a small part of me. The rest is happy to keep lying for the rest of eternity."

Yuri's features clouded over. "I . . . am not indifferent to your pain, Arjun Desai."

Arjun's hand slipped out from under him, nearly causing him to fall back onto the shards of glass strewn across the floor.

"Will wonders never cease?" he mocked. "What is it like, for an automaton such as you to feel something besides indifference for someone else's pain?"

With great care, Yuri pushed aside broken bits of pottery and sat before him. "Do you think I never loved anyone before?"

"I think . . . I am not drunk enough for this conversation." Arjun groaned. He propped his elbows on his knees so he might rest his head in his hands. "Again, would you care to assist me on that score?"

She glared at him. The hint of hurt in her expression caught Arjun off guard. He sighed, his fingers tearing through the ruin of dark hair on his head. "I think you live for a word of praise from my mother. You wouldn't notice a loaf of fresh bread in your pocket even if you were starving." Arjun averted his gaze, his voice softening. "But I know how that feels. It's a world I inhabited for far too long."

Yuri said nothing to him for a time. "I will tell you something I've told no one else, Arjun Desai, if it will make you stop acting like such a selfish ass."

"I'm listening. But only because you said a naughty word."

She studied the shadowed scullery around them, careful to check all the corners and every eave before speaking.

"Don't worry," Arjun said. "The wisps that were here earlier scattered when I started throwing things. They haven't returned for hours."

She nodded. Then took a deep breath. "I . . . loved a dark fey once," she said softly.

"Shocking. That's forbidden." Though Arjun meant to tease

her, he did in fact feel a jolt of surprise at this admission. Yuri admitting she loved anyone—let alone a dark fey—was as if a stone had rolled up to him at sunset to confess its undying adoration for a fish.

"I know well how forbidden it is," Yuri said. "We knew it well. It is why we are not together now."

Arjun swiped a hand across his face. The pain in his forehead continued to grow, mirrored by the ache in his heart. He needed another drink. He needed Yuri to leave him alone. He needed anything but this. This would not help him forget.

"I'm listening," he repeated, despite his better judgment.

"It was before I formally joined the Grey Cloaks," Yuri continued. "When I was still in training, I was asked to patrol a section of the border close to the largest underwater city of merfolk."

He paused in thought. "Five Waters, I believe it's called."

"Yes." Yuri nodded. "For the five tributaries joined in one place. The merfolk there are interesting, as they don't necessarily adhere to our boundaries underwater, regardless of their alliances to dark or light fey. Underwater, they often trade freely in goods between the Vale and Wyld, likely because it is difficult for us to enforce our rules beneath the waves."

"Imagine a world in which our petty discords did not impede the lives of our people."

Yuri frowned.

"My apologies." Arjun motioned with one hand. "Please continue."

"Along the banks by the entrance to Five Waters, I met a

trader of winter gemstones from a long line of jewelry makers in the Sylvan Wyld. Many of these artisans no longer have work in their own land, so instead they attempt to sell their wares on black-market boats in the hopes that merfolk will show interest. I caught this winter fey trying to sell his jewelry in summer territory. His daughter was with him in his ramshackle boat, and she attempted to bribe me with loose gems so that I might look the other way. Of course, I locked them both up at once."

"Of course you did."

Yuri ignored him, her features softening. "Her father was not well when we arrived at our garrison on the banks near Five Waters. But she cared for him without anger or resentment in her heart, even toward me. I kept waiting for her to become spiteful—to rage and swear at every summer fey in earshot— but she never did. Her garments were wretched. Threadbare. It was clear they had so little. Yet she was . . . better at living than I." Yuri paused in remembrance. "Her face was at peace, even though she and her father flouted our laws daily. When she slept on the floor of that dank prison cell, she slept easier than I ever had in the barracks. It was the first time I saw something . . . more to a winter fey. Something worth admiring. Worth understanding."

"Was that also the first time you spoke to a winter fey at length?" Arjun asked the question gently, despite his desire to point out the wrongness of her sentiments. Yuri's opinion on the worthlessness of all winter fey was commonly held as fact within the Vale.

Yuri's cheeks hollowed. She nodded. "I'd always thought they were hopeless. Like beasts without order or direction. If the vampires weren't there to tell them where to go or what to do, they were just creatures crazed by hunger and want." She drew her knees to her chest. "But now—after what we saw on the banks that day—I'm not certain if that's the image we were told to see or if that's the image the winter fey wanted us to see."

Arjun understood why Sunan had felt the need to protect the Sylvan Wyld with his elaborate illusions, especially following the events of the truce several hundred years ago. Sunan had kept their weakness a secret so the winter fey could find a way to survive. But it was impossible to ignore the cost of that decision. The way Sunan's carefully cast spells had melted away that day beside the bridge, revealing a stark truth.

That no amount of time could repair the damage that had been done so long ago.

"I suppose that's a fair question," Arjun said, "all things considered."

"I began bringing the girl and her father food," Yuri continued. "She and I often spoke at length while I guarded them. After a few weeks at the garrison, I learned that they were to be sent to another prison, where I'd heard the guards were experimenting with new weapons meant to inflict painful wounds on dark fey." Yuri gnawed at the inside of her cheek. "So one night I decided to free them."

Arjun's eyebrows shot into his forehead. Never could he have imagined that Yuri would admit to anyone—let alone an ethereal such as he—that she had betrayed her orders as a vaunted Grey Cloak in such a spectacular fashion. "You realize that's treasonous behavior."

"Of course I know it is." She stared at him unblinking. "And I'm trusting you with this story because I want you to trust me. I have made mistakes, and I will spend the rest of my life atoning for them. Not long after I freed them, I met my love one evening near the banks of Five Waters. We spent one wonderful night together. It was the best night of my life, and I am not sorry for it. But I will never see her again, and that is the way it must be. She is winter; I am summer." Yuri took a deep breath. "I know my place. It is time for you to learn yours."

Arjun flinched as if she had struck him. "Well, you do know how to deliver blows. I'll give you that." He averted his gaze. "I hope you were kinder to your lover than you were to me."

"I wasn't. I said what needed to be said." Sadness tugged at Yuri's features, despite her smile. "And she understood. Just as I'm hoping you understand now."

What Arjun understood was that he needed a drink more than ever. "I learned my place long ago, Yuri. And it is most definitely not among the fey."

She pursed her lips. "Is it because you think we were unfair to you when we were children? Did you wish us to be kinder? Because you were half mortal, you were already weaker than us. Had we coddled you then, how would that have prepared you for the realities of being at court?" Her brows puckered. "I know you think your mother was cruel, but she did what she had to do to ready you for the inevitable."

"No," Arjun said. "I don't believe anything she did was for my benefit. Nor did I wish to be coddled. I wished for someone to show that they cared. To stop and listen, or at the very least offer a lost, lonely boy something besides their condescension. Do you realize this is the first time in all the years we've known each other that you've told me anything meaningful about yourself? It's also the first time you've shown me a drop of compassion."

Yuri sniffed. "Our court is not a place for compassion."

"Maybe that should change. Maybe I deserved your compassion as a boy, just as your winter lover deserved your compassion when you freed her and her father before our soldiers had a chance to use them for target practice," he said, his fury plain.

"How dare you use my weakness against me, Arjun Desai," Yuri said, her words filled with quiet outrage. "What I told you about her is never to be repeated, nor is it fodder for your judgment." Her hands formed fists. "They broke the law. What we do with our prisoners is fair punishment for their crimes."

He shook his head. "No. Like many things at this court, it's astonishingly cruel. And now you must trust that I will never tell anyone here how you spared your lover that cruelty. What makes you think I won't?"

Yuri tilted her head to one side, color creeping up her throat as she chose her next words with care. "Because I saw your face the other day on the bridge, just before we dragged you away from her. It was the way my love looked at me the last time we saw each other. I will never forget it. You won't betray me. Pain understands pain, without having to say a word."

For a time, they sat in silence, glowering at each other, the truth of Yuri's final statement echoing through the stillness.

Arjun closed his eyes and clutched his head in his hands. "You're right," he said quietly. "I do understand your pain, Yuri. I wish I didn't, but I do. And I am sorry for it. Truly. But I won't do what you or the general want me to do. If my mother failed to find Pippa . . . then what you said earlier is true. There is nothing left for me here." His voice broke. "No mortal could have survived those wounds. Pippa . . . is gone." Tears flowed down his cheeks, the ache in his chest clenching around his heart. The pain he'd fought to keep at bay for the last two days. The pain he'd fended off with drink and destruction. With sarcasm and seclusion.

It had found its mark. Wrapped its unforgiving claws through his insides.

And there it would stay.

Yuri reached between them to place a small hand on Arjun's shoulder. Her fingers gave him a gentle squeeze. The motion was awkward, as if the fey warrior had little experience offering consolation to anyone, but Arjun could not miss the warmth behind the gesture.

It broke him further. His shoulders slumped. He leaned forward, the pain seeping into his soul. "I couldn't save her," he whispered. "You should have let me go to her. Why didn't you let me go?"

"Then you would have been killed, too."

"Maybe you should have let that happen."

"No," Yuri said. "We should not have let that happen. I would never inflict that kind of wound on General Riya." She squeezed him again. "I, too, am truly sorry for your pain, Arjun Desai." Uneasily, she placed her other hand in his. "But it is time for this to end. It is time for you to be with your family. You must take your rightful place."

Arjun nodded. He rested his palm in hers. "You're right. I do need to be with my family."

"We need you, Arjun," Yuri confessed. "Our court is a mess. There are whispers in every corner. Your mother needs you. I . . . have never seen her afraid like this." Her voice was quiet. It wavered in a way that unseated Arjun.

He looked at her, something catching in his throat. Despite all their history—all the bad blood and resentment—Arjun wanted to help Yuri, even in some small way.

"I would station guards to protect the border bridge," he said.

"What?"

"In my opinion, it will be one of the first things the Winter Court destroys."

"That would be foolish." She blinked. "The bridge is the only crossing connecting the Vale to the Wyld. They would be just as hindered by a lack of access as we are."

One side of Arjun's mouth curved into a caustic smile. "You and I might believe that to be true. But if there's the slightest possibility the Vale would fare worse for its loss than the Wyld, then the bridge will pay the price. If there is anything I learned serving as a legal adviser to Nicodemus Saint Germain, it is that vampires have an appreciation for the theatrical. And there's nothing quite as dramatic as an explosion."

"I thank you for the advice. Your mother will be pleased to hear it."

"It isn't simply for your sake or for hers that I offered it," Arjun said. "I don't wish to see a symbol of peace and cooperation blown to smithereens by anyone."

Yuri nodded. Then she grasped Arjun's hand even tighter and hauled him to his feet with surprisingly little effort. In moments like these, it was easy to forget that a dangerous warrior lurked inside such a small body. Arjun swayed for a minute before gripping her by the arm to steady himself.

"Gather your things," Yuri said. "We will journey for the border tonight. You can tell your mother what you shared with me."

He held on to her forearm even more tightly. "I said I needed to be with my family. My real family. That isn't here in the Vale. It has never been here."

She scowled up at him, a mixture of hurt and anger dotting her perfectly symmetrical features. Yuri wrapped her fingers around his forearm, as if she thought her grip might sway him into changing his mind.

Arjun's expression softened. For an instant, he felt something spark to life in his chest. Something akin to true affection, an emotion he'd kept at bay when it came to relationships with fey in the Sylvan Vale. He'd sworn to himself when he'd left the Summer Court to attend university in the mortal world that he would hold no attachments to this land. That he would never think back fondly on anyone or anything in the Vale.

How odd for his mother's favorite to have carved out a place for herself in his thoughts.

He'd hated Yuri so much when they were children. What a waste that hatred had been. Had his mother not pitted Arjun and Yuri against each other—had Arjun not vied for his mother's affection against this tiny, orphaned fey girl—perhaps he and Yuri could have been true friends.

For there was much more to her than Arjun had once believed.

He reached into the breast pocket of his waistcoat and removed his monocle. He handed it to Yuri. "When Lady Silla first gifted me this on the day I came of age, I thought she meant to taunt me with it. A piece of glass that revealed the true emotions of those around me in clouds of colors." Arjun grinned, but it did not reach his eyes. "I learned not long afterward that it worked solely on mortals, and I assumed Lady Silla had a good laugh at my expense because of it. But I've since come to think that it might have done more damage had I known the fey's true thoughts."

"I'm not sure I understand what you mean."

Arjun's smile widened. He shook his head. "This conversation has surprised me, and I didn't think a fey could surprise me anymore. Your honesty has been refreshing, Yuri. Thank you for showing me that you care. I won't forget it." He gave her the monocle and wrapped her fingers around it.

She tugged him nearer, her voice low. Almost pleading. "Don't leave, Arjun. Come with me. Your mother wishes you to stand by her side. Help protect our people. Protect the Vale. If you believe I care, then please know that I believe you must care, too." She squeezed his wrist again, and it was as close to begging as Arjun had ever heard of any summer fey.

For an instant, Arjun considered what it might look like if he finally did what his mother wanted. If he went with Yuri to the border and donned his mother's colors, his fey armor emblazoned with the seal of the Grey Cloaks. If he wore the enchanted silver blade she'd gifted him. The one he'd hung on the wall of his mother's home deep in the forest glen and never once removed from its scabbard. What would General Riya say or do if he finally joined her in defense of her land and her people? If he embraced all that was and all that she hoped would be?

How would General Riya look upon him? If he could see her emotions, what would their colors be? The dazzling, warm gold of happiness? The simple white light of joy?

Or finally, for the first time in his life, the brilliant blue of unfettered pride?

Blue, like Pippa's eyes.

Then Arjun remembered the broken remains of the dead and the dying winter fey deep in the mountain fortress of the shattered Winter Court. All their stories. All their suffering. The torn wings and the bloodied bodies and the pitiable wails. How his mother had been the one responsible for their plight. How she'd followed the Lady of the Vale's orders without question.

She was Yuri. Who Yuri wanted to be. Who Yuri would be.

Who Arjun could never be.

Gently, he removed Yuri's fingers from around his wrist. "No, Yuri. This is not my home. It will never be my home. I'm sorry."

"Arjun, please—"

"Tell General Riya not to worry," he continued. "I will not continue to embarrass her at court. There will be no more tales of my drunken escapades. I'll return to where I belong." Arjun reached for his revolver from the cold stone floor. "To my real family," he said. "Tell her I wish those words would cause her pain, but I know they won't. Nevertheless I'm saying them, because it gives me pleasure to hear them spoken aloud."

Yuri grimaced. "Arjun. Don't."

"I'm leaving the Vale. I won't return. My home is in New Orleans, with the family I chose. The ones who love me without question or design." He shook off her grasp and stood tall.

"You will hurt her," Yuri stated flatly. "And I will never forgive you for it."

Arjun inhaled through his nose. "Tell General Riya not to look for me. She has no son. And I have no mother."

THE RUINED DUCHESS

Pippa had known pain in the past.

The pain of loss. The pain of hunger. The pain of fear.

On one occasion at her family's manor house in England, she'd been struck hard across the face. Her father, the Duke of Ashmore, had dealt her a harsh blow when he'd considered her too insolent. At the time, the injury had smarted and left a bruise, but the lasting wound had been to her soul.

And in the end, Pippa had gotten revenge by framing her father for arson and fraud.

If Pippa was honest with herself, any real pain she'd experienced in the past had not included true physical pain. Nor had she considered the limits her body could withstand when pushed to the brink. Not even during the long journey across the Atlantic—when she'd been seasick for two weeks and lolled about in a dark, damp hold with nothing but hardtack and fetid water for food and drink—could she count herself as having suffered genuine pain.

She'd been born into a family of wealth and privilege. These things had been taken from them over the years, but the benefits of being born the daughter of a duke and a duchess, along with her blond hair and English-rose skin, had offered her more chances to escape pain than endure it.

For almost seventeen years, Philippa Montrose had never considered what real physical pain might feel like. But now . . . now that she was faced with it—a type of pain she could never have grasped, even in her darkest nightmares—she found herself considering other things she'd never considered before in her life.

Perhaps death would not be so bad. At least then her skin and bones and teeth and eyeballs—indeed, the very roots of her hair—would not sear as if she were being shoved into the hottest part of a fire and left there to blaze like an iron poker.

Pippa twitched, another scream erupting from her lips. Arms and hands attempted to keep her lying flat as she fought to flee, wishing she could run from her body. She tried and failed to open her eyes. The slightest trickle of light burned like the devil, just as any movement triggered a fresh wave of agony.

And whenever someone touched her?

If she could speak, it would be in nothing but the foulest of epithets. The sort that would make the most seasoned sailor blush.

Another unintelligible shriek burst from her mouth. More hands joined the others to hold her down, at least one of them rough and callused. Almost uncaring in its resolve. Their touch was torch fire against her bare flesh. She struggled and whimpered, begging without words for someone to free her from this torment.

"Do something," a young man pleaded. "Her heart is racing faster than a runaway train."

Brutal laughter followed. "As it does for any mortal," an older man said, his voice aged and cloaked in smoke.

"She will die," the young man shot back, his desperation plain.

A young woman hummed in agreement. "Most of them do."

"Émilie!"

"There is a large island far across the Indian Ocean," the same rich and resonant female voice began, as if the speaker were performing a play for a paying audience. "A place where the English exiled their most dangerous criminals. In the badlands of this wild country, there exists a blue-black wasp with rust-colored wings the size of my palm," the same voice continued, almost amused. "It possesses a sting so painful, its victims are told their only recourse is to lie down and scream until the agony passes, because others who have experienced the torment of this wasp's sting have thrown themselves off cliffs or impaled themselves on sharp objects to put an end to their suffering." She laughed.

"What is your purpose in sharing this story?" the young man demanded.

"Humans in pain are irrational creatures. They routinely cut off their noses to spite their faces." She leaned closer to Pippa, until she spoke directly in her ear. "I trust that it would not be in your best interest to end your life for the sake of temporary suffering, Philippa Montrose. Don't be a fool. Do as I say. Lie still and endure it. There will be an end, I promise you that. I just can't tell you yet what or when that end will be."

Pippa screamed again, her eyes squeezed shut.

"Stop it, Émilie. Why must you taunt her?" the young man said.

Despite her ongoing agony, Pippa's mind made two quick connections. That voice was familiar. It belonged to Detective Michael Grimaldi. Why was he here? How had he managed to travel from New Orleans to Fairyland?

The female voice was easier to place, for Michael had named her only a moment ago.

Émilie. Bastien's sister. Émilie Saint Germain. The werewolf who had tried to orchestrate Celine's death in Saint Louis Cathedral last winter.

"Look at her soft hands," Émilie said. "Look at that lovely face. And this golden hair? As if she were a princess from a child's fairy tale. If ever there was a girl who deserved to be taunted, it's this girl. She's even more ridiculous than that raven-haired trollop you and my brother lusted after for the better part of a year, like randy schoolboys." She snorted. "I'll bet that's the reason you're here in the first place, Michael Grimaldi." Derisive laughter followed her pronouncement. "Did you think I wouldn't know? I've known it since the day I first saw you in that snow-storm on the cliff. You would follow Celine Rousseau into a raging fire." She laughed again. "It may come to that, in the end."

Pippa gritted her teeth, a shudder wracking her body. She wanted to scream at them to stop talking. To beg for something to ease the pain. To plead for them to leave her be and let her die.

But if she were left to suffer in silence, with no one nearby?

She did not want to die alone in agony. That was something Pippa knew for certain.

"Is there nothing we can do for her?" Michael demanded.

"Talk to her," Émilie replied, her tone nonchalant. "It could help to ease her pain, though I'll admit it did not do much for me." She exhaled in a huff. "Truthfully, I'm surprised she has withstood the burning this long. Most mortals are dead within an hour of being bitten. Even those with fey blood often fail to survive a single wolf bite, let alone five."

"You speak as though you are displeased to see her survive this long." It was impossible to miss the hint of suspicion in Michael's voice. "Are you?"

"The girl is stronger than she looks. If she survives, it will be . . . interesting, for certain."

"You didn't answer my question," Michael said. "Are you displeased she survived?"

A moment passed in silence.

He sucked in a breath. "My God, you planned for her to die. You lied to me. You knew exactly who she was when you attacked her."

Pippa's heart raced even faster. Her teeth began to chatter in her skull.

"I didn't lie," Émilie demurred. "I omitted part of the truth."

"You led me to believe you didn't recognize her."

"I failed to correct your assumption. There is a difference."

"You meant to kill Pippa from the start."

"Well, I certainly didn't bite Arjun Desai's bride on the bridge in plain view of both fey courts because I wanted to turn her into one of us, Michael."

"You haven't changed at all. This was part of your design to make your brother—"

Pippa began to choke. Her bones trembled beneath her skin, causing her body to convulse. She tried to say something—anything—the terror running wild through her blood. Her spine bowed, her fingers clawing at the stone beneath her. The sounds coming from her mouth were ragged, like the cries of a dying animal.

"Philippa," Michael said, trying his best to soothe her, a hand coming to rest on her cheek.

Pippa wanted to bite it off.

"Lie still, sweetheart," he continued. "It will only be worse if you fight it."

Briefly, Pippa recalled watching Michael several months ago, through the darkness deep in the swamp, as he'd transformed from a man into a wolf. Even from a far distance, she could see the pain he suffered to undergo the change.

But this was not that pain. This was different. Even Pippa knew that. His pain had lasted no more than two minutes, not several hours. And he had been able to move and protect himself, despite everything. Not even for a second had he been thrashing about in unbearable agony like this.

The older man tsked. "How is she still alive?" he muttered. "The girl shouldn't be alive, Émilie."

The next instant, something white-hot touched the skin on the inside of Pippa's forearm. A new kind of burning sensation, fresh and sharp and excruciating, shot through the nerve endings there. Pointed, in a way that drew all Pippa's focus, like a needle being stabbed through her palm. She writhed in place, a silent scream roaring from her lips, her body twisting unnaturally. Something snapped in her wrist, as if her bone there had broken in two.

"What did you do, Émilie?" Michael shouted.

"Incroyable," Émilie whispered. "Her body is trying to transform." She spoke as if she were genuinely surprised.

"That . . . shouldn't be possible," the older man said, alarm punctuating his tone. "She's just a mortal girl. There is no wolf blood in her lineage, nor is there a drop of fey magic in her veins. She has no wolf kin for her to kill to enact the curse."

"It appears everything we know about Philippa Montrose might be untrue," Émilie said. "I just pressed pure silver to her skin. It burned her, which would only happen if she were dark fey. She is turning."

"No," Michael said, fear rising in his voice. "Look, the wound is not healing. It's still spreading. The burn is going up her arm."

Bodies shifted around Pippa as a hand seized her shoulder, presumably to take a closer look. The place on Pippa's arm where Émilie had burned her with silver continued to sear and ache as if it were pressed to a flame, the wound radiating toward her collarbone.

"Hmmm," the older man said. "In all my years, I've never seen anything like this."

"Her body is rejecting the change, is it not?" Émilie asked. "It appears to be refusing the magic."

"As we suspected it would." The older man sounded almost relieved. "Perhaps this girl was just stronger than most mortals. Yes. That must be the reason this has gone on for as long as it has. There is no other explanation. No ordinary mortal would survive. And she has only ever been ordinary, after all." His tone changed to one of surety. "The girl is destined to die a painful death. It is time for us to put an end to it, as I suggested before. It will only become worse once the fire reaches her heart."

"No," Michael argued. "There is still a chance she might survive. You're not killing her. I *forbid it*." The last syllable reverberated into a growl.

Several snarls rippled through the space. Pippa realized there were more than three werewolves bearing witness to her suffering. How long they had been there—indeed, where *there* was at all—continued to remain a mystery, though from the lingering chill, Pippa assumed they were still in the winter world of the Sylvan Wyld.

"Tedor is one of the oldest werewolves I've encountered in the frozen wastelands," Émilie replied in a harsh whisper. "He and his brethren have survived for centuries, hidden deep in these caves with the winter creatures the vampires left to fend for themselves. Tedor has kept them safe and guarded the secrets concealed within the mountain walls. Who are you to question his knowledge and experience, Michael Grimaldi?"

"She could survive," Michael said, his tenor changing to one of pleading. "Pippa has lasted longer than any other mortal, you just said it. Give her a chance. At least let us be certain if the magic within her is real. If it can hold."

"The girl is already dead. She was dead the moment I sank my teeth into her skin," Émilie said. "Now that you know she was never meant to survive being bitten, there is no reason for us to delay the inevitable."

The skirr of a blade being unsheathed hissed through the air. "There are worse things than dying." Tedor's wizened voice turned harsh. "The spirits buried in the ice know this well."

"No," Michael said. Sounds of a struggle began to ensue, feet pounding against stone and fists connecting with flesh in muffled thuds. Every so often, growls would emanate from close by.

Pippa attempted to move. To cry out. To give voice to her inner thoughts. She did not wish to die. Another wave of excruciating pain unfurled across her body, rendering her all but immobile. The burn from her collarbone traveled toward the center of her chest, circling around her heart, scorching like a flame caught in a windstorm. She squeezed her eyes shut, fighting against the mounting agony.

She knew at that moment, more than ever, how much she wished to continue living. Even if it meant enduring more pain, she wanted to fight. But her body did not seem to agree with her. Just as Pippa managed to shore up her convictions, the fire took hold of her heart and seemed to swallow it whole. The pounding beat blurred into a single, thunderous roar, then slowed for a moment before racing again, as if it were running toward its inexorable end. It beat like a drum in her ears until the only thing Pippa could hear was her heart's final, feverish gallop.

Please, she tried to say. *Please,* she begged. *I don't want to die.*

Everything began to tremble around her.

"Émilie," Michael said, panic rising in his voice. "Something is happening."

Once more the shadows loomed. "Good," Émilie muttered. "Her body has made a decision. The right one."

"Help her, for God's sake," Michael said. "If there is anything you can do to save her, then—"

A slap rang through the air. "You fool," Émilie replied. "I told you already. Tedor told you. The only thing—the best thing—to do was for us to put an end to her suffering. But it's too late now. She will be gone in a matter of moments. You could have spared her this pain if you hadn't been such a coward."

Pippa heard herself scream inside her head as the pace of her heart rose to a frenetic drone, each beat rushing to overcome the next. Pain tingled along every nerve in each of her limbs, forcing her fingers to form talons and her toes to lock in place.

She thought of her brother and sister. Henry and Lydia. At least she knew they would be cared for. They were comfortable now. They had a family. One that would protect them and cherish them in a way their parents could not. Lydia and Henry would never want for anything, even if something happened to Pippa. Arjun would take care of them.

Arjun.

They'd had so little time together.

Her heart howled in her chest. The next instant, it fell silent. The pain vanished like a candle's flame in a gust of wind. Pippa waited to be freed from her earthly bonds and take to the air, drawn toward that better, brighter future the Bible had promised since childhood. Sadness threatened to overcome her, but she clung to the comfort of knowing she was not leaving her loved ones behind without the means to continue living well.

Her regrets were about time. How wasted it was. How much more she wished she'd had.

At least Pippa knew she'd fought to live longer than any mortal who'd been bitten by a werewolf before her. That thought consoled her as she waited to fade from one existence into the next. The moments stretched longer. Pippa couldn't move. She couldn't breathe. Her eyes were shut. She couldn't speak. She couldn't smell anything. But she could still feel and hear and understand what was happening around her.

It was terrifying. As if her soul had been locked inside her body.

Footsteps shuffled close by. Hands touched her neck. Fingers grazed her lips.

"She's . . . gone," Michael said as he grasped her wrist, searching for a pulse.

Émilie sighed. "I do regret her suffering. I am not unfeeling. She seemed to be a gentle girl who did not deserve the hand life dealt her. But it is done now. And I am glad of it."

"Why?" Michael asked, his voice breaking. "Why did you do this?"

"Because I could," Émilie said. "I saw an opportunity, and I seized it."

Pippa felt something damp land on her wrist. Though she

could not see, she sensed the heat of the anger in Michael Grimaldi's tears.

"This was what you wanted all along," he said, his tone bitter. "To incite us into war."

"How . . . simple you are. How simple you've always been," Émilie said. "Of course I wanted to start a fight. Why would I go to the trouble of recruiting banished merfolk and plotting with the worst of the summer gentry if I did not? I won't deny it. But it's much more than that."

"Enlighten me."

"These fey—with their petty pastimes and cruel amusements— they've forgotten what it means to feel. They find lovers' quarrels and duels diverting because living for an eternity means nothing is important. And the vampires?" She laughed under her breath. "They've become just as complacent. These vain immortals in their luxurious, wood-paneled covens, hiding in plain sight among an unsuspecting mortal world."

"Werewolves are immortal," Michael said. "How are we any different?"

"Because we know what it means to suffer. We suffer every time the moon changes. Every time we change. Time still has meaning to us, regardless of the length of our lives."

"I fail to see how killing a young mortal girl like Pippa Montrose proves your point."

"It makes the battle for life and death real to them, Michael Grimaldi," Émilie said. "Just as it did for me when I was left to burn in that fire as a young girl. Or when Luca was killed before my eyes. Pippa's loss will make Celine Rousseau feel . . . everything," she continued, her voice becoming softer. More dangerous. "When she feels everything, so will my brother. When vampires feel, they fail to think. And when they fail to think, they make mistakes. Their mistakes present us with opportunities."

"For the sake of these opportunities, an innocent girl had to die."

"She placed herself in league with the vampires!" Émilie shouted. "In league with the Summer Court. There is nothing innocent about her. If she was friends with Celine Rousseau, she knew the consequences."

"Celine will not abide by her death."

"I'm counting on it. Just as I'm counting on her wrath to incite my brother." Émilie's shadow darkened over Pippa once again, and Pippa felt something slip from around her neck.

"You have no right." Michael's words grew louder, as if he, too, had drawn closer. "That belongs to Pippa. It means something to her. I've never seen her without it."

Her necklace. The cross Pippa's grandmother had given her as a child. Pippa wanted to shout. To take it from Émilie's unworthy hands. She fought to move but could not so much as muster a breath or the flutter of an eyelash.

"And now it belongs to me," Émilie said. "It may serve a purpose soon."

Why was Pippa unable to speak or breathe, but still able to hear and think and feel? Had she died in truth? Was her soul trapped in her body?

A horrifying thought occurred to Pippa.

What if her soul could never leave her because she'd died in the world of the fey?

She would be trapped here for eternity, locked in a world of snow and ice.

"What should we do with her body?" Tedor asked Émilie. "Our pack's tradition is to consume the flesh of its own after death, but she is not one of us."

Relief chased after the terror that took sudden root in Pippa's stomach. Of all the things to be thankful for, she never thought this would be one of them.

"I will bury her," Michael said.

"Of course," Émilie replied. "Do as you see fit. If you'd like, I will help you." She snorted. "I'm not a complete monster. In time, you may even thank me."

"Only a true monster thinks itself a hero, Émilie," Michael said softly.

"And only a fool believes he can bring about real change without creating enemies."

"Well, I congratulate you on creating even more enemies, then."

"That savored strangely of a threat." She laughed. "You are amusing, Michael Grimaldi."

Strong, warm arms lifted Pippa with great care. She shouldn't feel that warmth. She shouldn't hear their conversation, not if she were dead. When they stepped outside, she steadied herself against the cold. Though she sensed the stinging of the ice and the bracing chill, it did not cause her pain.

A cloak of fur was wrapped around her. Gently—so gently—
she was placed on the ground. She heard shovels striking snow.
The breaking of ice. The hollow rhythm of an ageless ritual.

Then true panic began to mount in her stomach.

When Pippa was a young girl, she and her family would visit
her aunt Imogen during the summers in Liverpool. There was a
family of three boys only a few years older than Pippa who lived
in a home across the street. The middle boy was an excellent
storyteller, and his favorite kind of tales to share were often the
scary sort. Though Pippa would chastise him for frightening
the other children in the neighborhood, she secretly relished
the way he would lean over a candle flame in the darkness and
lower his voice, an eerie ominousness descending around him
even before he uttered a single word.

One tale in particular haunted Pippa for an entire summer. It
was the story he told of a time not so long ago when a plague
ravaged their country. It stole the very breath from the bodies
of its victims. Some people were so weakened by the disease
that it appeared they had died though there was still life left
within them. These people were buried alive, and it was only
later—when one or two of these pitiful souls managed to claw
their way through the dirt into the light—that their families
realized the horror. From that time on, people were buried with
a bell tied to their fingers, so that the cemetery workers might
hear the chiming sounds and realize that some poor wretch
had been buried before their time.

Pippa recalled every word of that story in this moment. But

there would be no bell for her. And if her soul was to be trapped in her body in this world of the fey, what would her eternity be?

Unspeakable. She screamed again, a soundless wail. For an instant, she thought she felt her smallest finger twitch, but when she tried to move it again, she could not muster a bend in one knuckle or a flex of a single toe.

Then Michael lifted her from the snow-packed earth into his arms, his movements tender. Pippa wanted to lean into his warmth. Not because she felt cold, but rather because she feared it might be the last time she would know how it felt to be held like this.

Strange, the things one worried about, in the end.

"I'm sorry, Philippa," he said. "I will return to New Orleans and tell your family that you did not suffer. That much, I can do for you and for them."

"If you leave the Wyld to convene with vampires, Michael Grimaldi, do not expect to be welcomed back," Émilie said from a distance, her voice muffled by the falling snow. "I will take it to mean you have chosen sides."

"That is your ultimatum. Not mine."

"Refusing to stand with your own kind is the same as siding with the enemy."

"My own kind is in New Orleans," Michael said. "It never has been and never will be with you in this cursed place." With that, he brought his lips to Pippa's forehead to press a chaste kiss there. "He will avenge you. I know it," he whispered in her ear.

Arjun. Pippa conjured an image of his face in her mind's eye. She imagined him smiling. Dreamed of him laughing. Pretended she watched him prepare a meal of paratha and lentils for Henry and Lydia.

She didn't want him to avenge her. She didn't want him to live a life of hatred and sorrow. *Please don't,* she prayed to no one as Michael prayed aloud to God for the sake of her immortal soul. Then Pippa felt herself falling, her stomach separating from her body. Her back hit the hard, frozen ground with a resounding thud. A shovelful of icy soil tumbled on top of her chest. Then another. And another.

The terror took root and blossomed in the same instant.

Pippa's nightmares were coming true. She was being buried alive.

There was no bell to ring. No one to save her. She could not even save herself.

THE RUINED PRINCE

Bastien followed Suli through the warren of stone. With each step, they wove deeper into the heart of the mountain. After they had journeyed for twenty minutes, the path angled downward. The air began to change. It started to resemble the stale and cool scent of still water, as if it had been undisturbed for a long time.

To his right, Bastien noticed the entrance to a cavern. As they passed, the blue flame emanating from Suli's enchanted torch flickered and flashed across an immense statue of ice, its black wings unfurling in the darkness.

Bastien halted in his tracks. "What is that?" His preternatural sight noted the outline of an equine figure rearing back, its large hooves suspended in midair. He swore he heard the faintest growl when he leaned closer to the cavern.

"The stuff of nightmares," Suli replied without stopping. "You should know better than anyone not to disturb the slumbering dead, vampire."

Despite the warning, Bastien continued staring over his shoulder at the gleaming statue swathed in shadow. Then he followed Suli down the sloping path, even deeper into the mountain. Soon they paused before a wall of solid rock, the surface shimmering in the eerie blue light radiating from the tiny goblin's torch.

Suli turned to look up at Bastien. "For over four hundred years, my brother and I maintained this chamber. Until very recently, we alone knew of its existence."

Unease formed in the pit of Bastien's stomach. "Why are you trusting me with this information?"

"I don't trust you," Suli said, his voice devoid of emotion. "But my brother did. And it is time to tell you the real reason he labored to conceal the truth of the Winter Court for so long. Why it was so important to him that the Summer Court never set foot on our lands. This is what he sought to protect. This is Sunan's legacy."

Bastien said nothing as Suli pressed his right palm to the glittering stone surface. At once, runes appeared in the shape of a large, arched doorway. The symbols glowed with pale, silvery light. The goblin muttered under his breath, and the runes began to tremble. Some of them gathered in the center of the door, their light concentrating to a point until it burned brightly, forming the shape of a keyhole.

From around his neck, Suli removed a thin chain. Dangling from its center was a single iron key of simple design, no longer than the width of Bastien's palm.

The goblin unlocked the door, which swung open from its center into two smaller doors.

The chamber that emerged from the darkness was small and

inconspicuous, almost resembling a vault, its rounded ceiling not much higher than Bastien's head. At first glance, the bare space did not seem like something warranting such secrecy or needing runes of protection. It was all but empty, its walls rough-hewn. Jagged to the touch. Nothing but a hidden nook, bathed in shadow.

It was clear from a cursory study that it was designed with a lone purpose in mind. This simple, rounded chamber carved from rock was meant to house a single, unassuming object. A spotted old mirror with silver edges that Bastien would not offer a second glance, even if it were sold at one of the famed furniture purveyors along Rue Royale.

But Bastien knew what this mirror was, even before Suli spoke. The nearer he stepped toward it, the louder the blood thundered in his veins.

This was *the* mirror. The one he'd read about. Dreamed about. The magicked silver that could offer him—and so many others—true salvation. An escape from the bonds of time itself.

Yes. I could offer it to you, Sébastien Saint Germain. In your hands, I could save all those you have lost. I could be the key to undoing it all.

The voice entered Bastien's mind, unbidden. It spoke in light, unpretentious tones. As if it were an easygoing young man. His peer. Trusting. Trusted.

What do you want from me in return? Bastien asked without words, the same way he'd spoken to his maker, his uncle, Nicodemus Saint Germain. Vampires possessed the ability to communicate with their maker in such a fashion, so it did not

seem odd for Bastien to speak with the mirror like this. It felt . . .
natural.

That you take me from here. Use me. Bring me into the light,
the mirror continued. *That you not keep me locked in darkness,
alone for all time. I tire of the solitude. Any creature with a mind
of its own longs for a chance to be of value. Don't you agree? Is
that not what we all crave?*

I suppose so, Bastien replied. *But* value *holds different meaning
for each of us.*

True. The mirror paused. If it could lean closer, Bastien almost imagined that it would. *And that meaning is what defines
us. What do you love, Sébastien Saint Germain?* Its voice
dropped. *What do you fear?*

"It is seductive, is it not?" Suli asked from behind Bastien, his
question light. "It does not seem at all as though this humble
object would cause immeasurable grief to anyone."

Bastien remained silent. He took another step toward the
mirror. He heard Suli catch his breath.

*Ah. The little one is riddled with fear. I pity him for it. His fear
makes him weak. His weakness has been the cause of his grief for
so many centuries. You are strong. You know the cost of allowing
fear to rule your mind. In your hands, I would be a source of
strength. I have seen all. I know all. Those who are wise and
strong like you need not be afraid.*

"Did you say this to Sunan, too?" Bastien wondered aloud.

The mirror did not reply.

Bastien stood five feet in front of its surface and gazed at his
own reflection. His eyes narrowed as he waited for something

to happen. For the silver to distort or perhaps for it to offer him a vision to cajole him closer.

"What do you see?" Suli said, maintaining his distance near the entrance of the chamber.

"Only myself."

"No," Suli continued. "What does the mirror look like to you?"

Surprise took hold of Bastien's features for a moment. "Just an ordinary mirror, about my height, slightly wider than my shoulders."

"Round?"

"The top is rounded. The bottom is squared."

"Does it have a frame?"

"A simple one," Bastien said. "It's silver. Old and adorned with leaves in an almost haphazard nod to something Grecian. Rather ordinary. Mundane, even."

Suli sighed. "It knows precisely how to entice each of us. To lure you in, only to use you as bait to snare the ones closest to you. To haunt their very dreams."

"It appears different to you?"

"Yes. That is part of its magic. Rooted in its evil. For you, it knows to appear meek and ordinary. In that way, you will not be threatened by it." Suli spoke in a voice barely above a whisper. Bastien noticed that the goblin had chosen to stand as far from the mirror as he possibly could. A decision based on experience, no doubt.

"You know that this mirror is responsible for the death of most of the members of my family," Suli said. "As such, I made a promise to the last of my children that I would not place so much as my reflection in its path. I refuse to offer this cursed silver even a morsel of attention."

The mirror had already tried to gain Bastien's attention. To learn who he was, despite its recent claim to know all. But in Bastien's mind, the enticement had been rather bland. Not the work of something truly insidious. "A mirror with a mind of its own?" he wondered aloud.

"It wants only to wreak havoc and foster its own significance," Suli said. "It feeds on its importance. It has been left to languish here for many years. No doubt it is famished."

At that, Bastien felt something flare from the mirror's center. A single flicker of warmth. He could not tell if it was anger or amusement.

He believes I am responsible for the loss of his family. There was no spite in the mirror's voice. It spoke in a matter-of-fact tone, like that of a young professor. *But he and his vain brother are the ones responsible. It is his own weakness that will not allow him to see it, for he cannot bear the cost of accepting that truth.*

Bastien considered the recent revelations offered by Suli and the mirror. "Then I suppose the remaining question is, how does one use this mirror without harming anyone, especially someone they love?"

"That is an easy question with an easier answer," Suli said. "Don't use this mirror. Ever. My advice is that you destroy it. It's what Sunan wanted."

"Then why didn't he destroy it himself?"

"I"—Suli exhaled in a huff—"I wish I could answer that.

Perhaps it was for the same reason I could not destroy it. Because I am afraid of it. Deeply, deeply afraid of it."

Suli is afraid. He has been afraid his entire life. His fear is his greatest weakness. Sunan was also weak, but in a different way, the mirror replied. *Sunan basked in my glory. For years, he wielded me well. I made him the greatest illusionist of his time. By then, he thought I had become too much a part of him. He believed that to destroy me would have been to destroy himself. His weakness was not fear, but self-love.*

"That is . . . quite the word of warning," Bastien said. "So this mirror became Sunan's curse. Protecting it had become his legacy. He created an entire world of illusion to keep it safe."

More lies within lies. Pity wove through the mirror's words. *The world of illusion he created in the Sylvan Wyld was so that he could keep his own image safe and beloved. The thing his brother accuses me of doing. They are the guiltiest perpetrators of all.*

Suli said, "It will tell you what you wish to hear, Sébastien. And I don't believe you are strong enough to withstand its pull. You know what this mirror can do. It will grant its bearer the power to control the past, the present, and the future. It is not like an ordinary traveling silver, merely taking you from one place to another. This mirror opens a labyrinth of enchanted mirrors that can take you to any time and place, provided you offer it an anchor. A memory, perhaps, or a token from that time and location. It is an inexact science, but its attraction is irresistible. Imagine being able to travel in time and change the outcome of an unfortunate situation. But thwarting destiny comes at a price. The more favorable the result, the costlier its price. I can tell you without hesitation that the price is often too great to bear."

"The mirror told me it knows all and it sees all," Bastien said. "How can it know and see things with any certainty if an ordinary person could wander into this labyrinth and be granted the ability to change the course of time? Would the mirror not know what I intended to do before I did it? Are our choices ours to make, then?"

"The mirror knows what has happened and what may happen at this present moment in time," Suli said. "Our will and our choices are ours alone. They can change those outcomes, just as quickly as one might make a wrong turn on a whim."

"Again, I must ask, why are you sharing power like this with me?"

Suli paused to consider before answering. "Because I want nothing more to do with this mirror. My brother protected it until now. I protected my brother. He asked that I pass this responsibility along to you or see it destroyed. I have fulfilled his wishes by doing so."

Bastien tilted his head as he continued to study the mirror. "How would I go about destroying it?"

Again that same light flared from the center of his reflection, like a spark.

Suli's eyes widened. He leaned closer, almost taking a step from the wall. "It must be destroyed from within," he said. "The entire chamber of mirrors must be shattered, and then the tare itself must be broken and burned, its ashes scattered to the winds."

Bastien turned toward Suli, a frown tugging at the edges of his lips. "I don't want this responsibility. Give it to someone else."

The goblin's shoulders sagged. "It was given to you," Suli said. "My brother willed it."

"And if I refuse?"

"Then the mirror will stay here, unguarded," Suli said, his tone grave. "Perhaps it will remain a secret. But you heard whispers of it not long after you were made into a vampire. Those whispers brought you to the Wyld in the first place. Soon there will be someone who ventures into our mountain fortress in search of this mirror. They may not have a care for the weight of such responsibility." He paused, sadness pulling at his features. "And if the Summer Court were to gain control of this mirror? There would be no end to what they might do. The suffering they would wreak on us as payment for past wrongs." He exhaled. "They would not be the only ones bent on revenge. If what is left of our Winter Court learned of this mirror's existence, they would make summer pay in kind. It is why Sunan labored so hard to keep even our own people from uncovering its whereabouts."

"I could abuse such power." Bastien stared at his reflection with a measured expression.

"You could," Suli said. "I suspect you will. In time, you will learn the price of doing so."

Disbelief flared in Bastien's chest. "You are not going to stop me?"

"No," Suli said. "I tried to stop my brother. And then my brother tried to stop me. We both tried to stop the ones we loved. The quickest way to learn you should not reach into a flame is to be burned by it." The small blue goblin managed to take a single, hesitant step toward Bastien. "In our worst moments—when we suffered our heaviest losses—my brother always looked to hope. Often I found his taste for the notion ridiculous. It seemed foolish. But in the end, Sunan was happier than I was. And I found that he was right more frequently than I," Suli mused. "So perhaps hope is not so foolish after all." He lingered in thought before removing the iron chain from around his neck and turning over the key to the vault. "There were two keys. The location of my brother's key died with him. I have no interest in uncovering its whereabouts. I give my key to you, and I will teach you the magic to unseal the chamber and reveal the lock. What you do with this information is on your head now, Sébastien Saint Germain. I willingly yield this burden to you."

Bastien pivoted toward Suli but did not reach for the key. He considered it in silence, the blue light from Suli's torch dancing along the roughened walls of stone.

Many before you thought they possessed the strength to use the power to manipulate time only for the good. They were flawed, all. You know by now that power corrupts the weak. Remain strong. Remain true. And you will be the one to prove them wrong.

He heard the mirror speak in his mind, its words rising to a soft susurration. No longer meek, but beseeching. Soothing. Always changing to suit its needs, just as Suli warned. Bastien looked to his reflection once more.

"A final word of warning," Suli said, his voice echoing through the stillness. "Do not attempt to travel to a period in the past where a version of yourself exists. Only travel to the past if you are not alive in it. And only travel to the future if it exists beyond you. If there are two versions of yourself trying to co-exist at the same time, one of them will perish. It will not be a good death. And if the wrong version of you dies at the wrong time? It could be the end of you from that moment onward, in all times."

Bastien said nothing as he considered Suli's final warning. He'd known from childhood that everything had a price, especially something steeped in enchantment.

If Bastien wanted, he knew he could return to that fateful moment when he died in Saint Louis Cathedral. Suli had revealed what would happen if a time traveler attempted to exist in the same period as their past self, but Bastien could simply choose to arrive just after the death of his mortal body.

He could stop his uncle from changing him into a vampire.

What might happen then?

Any version of Bastien would cease to exist from that moment onward.

His mind ran through the possibilities. Quickly he realized what sort of catastrophes might ensue if he were to attempt to change the outcome of that single, life-altering event.

Ah, the mirror said, its tone pleased. *Already you understand what it took many far too long to comprehend. You are suited for this.*

"That remains to be seen," Bastien replied aloud.

There is only one way to know for certain. The mirror's voice turned taunting, but not in an unpleasant way. Teasingly so, as if it were an elder sibling. As if it knew how much value Bastien placed on the opinions of his brothers and sisters.

He could not deny it. The possibilities this mirror offered tantalized him. Bastien had faced so much death and loss and pain in his short mortal life. Once he became an immortal, his existence had become equally fraught. Had all these trials and tribulations been lessons on the journey to this moment?

His uncle, Nicodemus, had sworn that Bastien was meant to lead. That it was his destiny to do wondrous things. Bastien had shied away from Nicodemus' assertions because they made him uncomfortable. He disliked the weight of such expectations.

If your uncle was right, then now is your moment. Seize this chance. Save your yesterdays, your todays, and all your tomorrows. Or regret it for the rest of eternity. It is your choice, as always.

Bastien faced Suli. Closed the distance between them. But he did not reach for the key.

"Whatever you choose, I hope you heed our warnings," Suli said. "Learn from our mistakes. That is the greatest wisdom I can ever bestow upon you."

Bastien nodded. Then he inhaled with great care. "Is there anything else you might offer in terms of advice?"

A sad smile curved his lips as Suli gazed up at him. He seemed to hesitate. "There is one more thing Sunan wished to tell you." He paused. "Lady Celine's mother . . . is not to be trusted."

"I have known that since the day I met her."

Suli nodded. "She will destroy anyone—even her own daughter—to protect her power."

Bastien turned a keen eye toward Suli. "Is there something specific Sunan told you?"

"To be wary of mortal Hallowtide when it comes to the Lady of the Vale."

Determination settled on Bastien's face. "So Lady Silla intends to threaten Celine on All Hallows' Eve." With that, he made his decision and reached for the key.

Suli gripped Bastien's hand tightly. "Listen to your own voice. Let it guide you always." A grimace crossed his face. "Mind what you offer the mirror. It will use whatever you give it to hunt for more victims. To carve out a path and haunt the dreams of those you hold dear." He swallowed a final time before relinquishing the key. "Be a quick study."

The mirror voiced its agreement. *There is no greater teacher than experience, Sébastien Saint Germain. Now go to it. Forgive the pun, but time and tide wait for no man.*

"There's something you should know about me," Bastien said.

What is that?

"I hate Chaucer."

The mirror laughed.

Before Bastien could stop to reconsider, he strode toward his reflection and stepped through its yielding, silvery surface.

The Ruined Duchess

Pippa wondered how long it would take for time to lose all sense of meaning to her. Three days? A week? Perhaps two? Buried as she was in frozen darkness, would her mind start to fracture?

What would happen first?

Perhaps it would be the hunger. Would her body feel hunger? It did not seem to need air—as her lungs no longer sought breath—but nothing about her current situation was normal or predictable. What if hunger overcame her?

The idea of starving to death buried in snow threatened to shred the last of Pippa's sanity.

She tried to swallow and failed. There was no way for Pippa to determine how long she'd been here, interred in an icy grave, deep in the Sylvan Wyld. The terror ebbed and flowed at odd intervals, as if her emotions were toying with her, warring between dread and sadness.

Another wave of anguish threatened to overcome her. The sensation took hold of Pippa from the inside out, as if she were a piece of cloth being wrung dry. She struggled in vain to move. Yet again she found herself trapped in a frozen body. She begged her soul to break free. Even if she did not wish to die, she could not fathom this half existence for much longer. Locked in a world of perpetual ice and darkness. Left to linger like this for an eternity.

Something warm trickled down Pippa's neck. It taunted her, this ability to feel and hear, though she could neither speak nor see. A new terror gripped her in its icy vise. Was some kind of fey creature moving closer to her? Crawling on her very skin? What if it sought refuge in one of her ears or her nose?

Egads. If Pippa had breath left to steal, it would be gone from her, like a thief in the night.

Her imagination continued to run wild. Horrified by the worst of her prospects, she recalled what the werewolf pack did with the bodies of their fallen. She supposed it was an honor in their minds to consume their dead, but the thought alone sickened her stomach.

What if this fey creature scuttling on her skin tried to . . . *eat* her?

A scream caught in her throat as the trickling warmth made its way down her collarbone, its movements erratic. Then— through the darkened ice before her—something shifted, as if the clouds had parted in the night sky. The murky world lightened, turning a hazy, deep grey. Pippa tried to open her eyes and failed once more.

Another warm, wet rivulet carved a path down the opposite side of her face.

Realization caused Pippa to startle in place.

She was crying.

A rush of energy flew through her bloodstream. If she could cry, then perhaps she could move. Pippa fought to shift her fingers. Willed her thumb to flex. Perhaps her limbs had succumbed to frostbite. She had heard how painful recovering from such an ordeal could be, but it did not matter. She could withstand monumental pain. She knew that now.

Pippa pushed and pressed and struggled. Her bare foot arched into the ice with a loud crack. She wanted to shout in triumph, though she wasn't sure what had broken, her bones or the rime around them. The darkness around her began to lift. Cool light filtered through the packed snow. That same jolt of energy rippled through her body once again. Then the toes of her right foot flexed. Little by little, Pippa struggled to shift in place, her fingers clawing through the ice and snow. She didn't care if her nails broke or her palms bled. It was possible all her extremities were indeed trapped in one block of solid ice now. It did not matter. She fought to move closer to the light, as if she were being drawn inexplicably toward its power and warmth.

Pippa burst through the snow with a gasp, her lips cracked and bleeding. She coughed, sputtering water and slush from her throat. Then looked up. Through a parting in the clouds, the light of a full moon glowed down on her.

She smiled, her voice hoarse as she attempted to yell in victory. A primal, guttural roar. Then all at once, the same energy pulsing through her veins began to boil over, like a pot left on the fire too long. It sizzled and steamed beneath her skin, causing Pippa to shake.

She gasped again in shock as she pulled free from the ice.

As soon as the light of the moon touched her bare skin, her body began to crack and strain, as if all her bones were being ripped from their sockets. A scream tore from her lips. Before its echo reached the mountains, it turned feral. Beastly.

In shock, Pippa felt her broken body begin to knit itself back together. To reshape and re-form. The snapping of bones became almost rhythmic. Pippa fell to the ice on all fours, what remained of her ruined garments tumbling to the snow like dying leaves in a breeze.

A mournful bale ripped from her throat. Her frozen heart began to beat once again, its rhythm steady and unbroken.

Then, just as quickly as it started, everything fell to silence, save the racing of her pulse. Pippa's senses cleared, and her eyesight focused. Far beyond that of a mere human. She could hear the way the icicles chimed in the trees above her and the way the far-off river whipped against the embankment. When a twig snapped nearby, she spun with a snarl until her gaze locked on what appeared to be a cross between a field mouse and a raccoon. At first glance, it looked harmless. Then it bared its fangs at her, its eyes glowing lambent in the light of the full moon.

Pippa attacked it without thought. On instinct. The creature squealed and scurried into the thorny underbrush not a moment too soon. On the tip of her tongue, Pippa could taste the little beast's fear and hear the way its heart fluttered in its veins like the wings of a hummingbird.

Something was wrong with her. Something had changed, irrevocably.

In the distance fifty feet to her right was a clearing, frozen puddles forming at the feet of immense, skeletal trees. Pippa raced into the clearing, intent on taking stock of whatever change had taken place. Of staring it straight in the face. Perhaps she wished most of all to confirm the suspicions churning through her stomach, laying siege to her thoughts.

Pippa gazed down at her reflection in the frozen pool of water between two immense paws. Her fur was as bright as the driven snow, her movements soundless as they padded across the forest floor. Her snout was long and pristine, her teeth white and ferocious. The only familiar sight was the two eyes staring back at her, their color the same bright blue as always.

The realization of what Pippa had become gripped her in its icy maw.

In her reflection she faced her newest truth.

Horrified, Pippa tore through the woods on all fours, the scream in her throat echoing into a howl.

Irrevocable, indeed. Philippa Montrose had become a werewolf.

THE RUINED PRINCE

There were many moments Bastien was faced with diverging paths. Choices that altered the course of his life.

Stepping through the mirror was not, in fact, one of them.

That had been an easy decision. Nothing immediately followed that could not be undone. It would have been as simple for him to turn around as it was for him to continue walking. Nonetheless, Bastien waited just beyond the mirror, his breath in his throat. He glanced around, expecting a sense of foreboding to settle on him. The familiar chill preceding something dire.

Nothing happened. This world between worlds—this realm of mirrors suspended in time—did not appear extraordinary in any way. Indeed, the scene that unfolded before him could have been a manor house in the Cotswolds or a wealthy family's country home in the Hudson Valley.

Two paths diverged just beyond the mirror. The one to the right led to the gated entrance of an immense house shrouded in mist. From a distance, it appeared well-kept, its redbrick and limestone façade elegant, strands of ivy adorning a front door fashioned of solid oak and smelted iron. A large stone fountain sat in the center of a circular courtyard.

Bastien knew without being told that this fountain was a tare. The fey loved to conceal these portals in bodies of water. Water provided a barrier all its own, for mortals could not chance drowning to breach a gateway, even an enchanted one. The first time Bastien had used a tare like this, he'd almost succumbed to the human fear of being unable to breathe. And he'd been a vampire, at that.

Fear was, indeed, a powerful force.

If Bastien were to walk the path leading to the house, perhaps he would find himself on an old Roman road outside Lyon or along a white sand beach in Zanzibar. It was possible that the tare in the fountain connected one part of the Wyld to another. Maybe it could even offer him a hidden doorway to the Vale. The path to the right was intriguing all on its own. One day, Bastien intended to indulge his curiosity and explore it.

But that day was not today.

Conviction in his footsteps, Bastien turned left. Toward the path leading into an immense maze, its entrance concealed by walls of ivy and stacked stone. Smooth blue pebbles paved the way. His footsteps crunched on their glassy surfaces, the sound pleasing and distinct.

If Bastien were a wise man—one who learned from the mistakes of others, as Suli had pleaded for him to do—he would know better. All the parables and legends he'd read as a boy warned that labyrinths contained monsters. At the very least, the treasure concealed in these mazes was not meant to be easily found.

Bastien continued to tread closer to the entrance of the labyrinth. Soon he arrived at a separation in the wall of stacked stone and ivy, again expecting a sense of dread to descend upon him.

It did not.

He waited for the mirror's voice to echo through his mind. To goad him or perhaps renew its efforts to know him better. He encountered nothing but silence.

The inner walls of the labyrinth were constructed of mirrors of all different shapes and sizes hanging in midair, set in no particular order. Some were small and simple. Others were immense and ornate. Several of their surfaces appeared mottled, as if they needed cleaning.

At first blush, the maze was . . . disorienting. It was strange to be met at all turns with one's own reflection. Almost like being confronted by an unexpected presence. Or quite literally faced with your flaws, magnified a hundredfold. Every time he moved, the very walls around him moved in tandem, as if he were the center of the universe.

Narcissus would have enjoyed it.

As Bastien wandered deeper into the labyrinth, he noticed that a few of the mirrors were set in arrangements facing each other at specific angles, so that one mirror reflected many, as if it had swallowed countless versions of itself.

An eerie sight to behold.

He kept waiting for a vision or an enticement. Wondered when that same voice from the mirror would deign to speak with him again.

But he saw nothing but his own reflection, mirrored countless times, in countless different perspectives. Soon, the maze itself did not feel so disorienting, though Bastien took care not to wander too deep into its center. He remained along its periphery, which was the safest course of action with any unknown labyrinth.

"This . . . is not what I thought it would be," he said under his breath.

What were you expecting?

When the voice answered, it startled Bastien, for it was louder than before, its tone more direct. As if it no longer needed to cajole him but was now comfortable speaking to him, man to mirror. "Were you waiting for me to speak first?"

I find it polite. I like listening. I believe I learn more when I listen.

"A welcome piece of advice." Bastien drifted back to silence.

After a few more minutes had passed, he gazed upward, wondering where to look when addressing the mirror, now that he had stepped into a world ruled by it.

"How does this work?" Bastien glanced from left to right, his attention settling on a sunset sky, the colors of a rainbow bleeding into a shadow of clouds along the horizon. "Do I simply offer any mirror before me an object or memory to which I've attached significance? Because that seems arbitrary."

Time itself is arbitrary, is it not? Mortals are the ones who attach significance to it.

"Perhaps. After all, time is a mortal construct." Bastien glanced at the ring on his hand, the one to which he'd affixed so many memories of his past life. On the gold signet ring's face was the head of a roaring lion. In its open mouth rested a fleur-de-lis. Over the years, it had become the symbol of the Court of the Lions. Nicodemus had given him this ring on his fifteenth birthday. After Bastien had been turned into a vampire, he'd presented the ring to an enchantress in New Orleans, who had spelled it so that it would enable Bastien to walk in the sunlight without feeling the burn of the curse placed on blood-drinking fey so many years ago.

It is quite a ring. An undeniable symbol of significance.

"I hate it," Bastien said. "It's why I chose it. Because you can't hate something without understanding what it means to love."

Then I gather you will not be offering this ring as a token. If you did, it would afford you a great deal of power in this place.

Bastien recalled Suli's warning to mind what he offered the mirror. How the mirror might use an object of power to lure in Bastien's loved ones. He shook his head. "My hope is never to offer something I cannot exist without."

We shall see. Bastien swore he heard amusement in the silver's voice. *To answer your question, traveling through time is rather simple. Introduce the object or memory from the time and place in question, and then present it to any mirror within the maze. A thought can conjure an image, but it is best to* anchor your destination with an object. Objects have permanence. They are not subject to the whims of a flawed recollection.

"But I may not travel to a time in which my past self is alive," Bastien said.

You may try. Many have tried before you. As you have been warned, it is all but impossible for two versions of the same person to exist at one time.

"Has everyone who has tried to do so failed?"

Failure is relative. Some have achieved what they desired. As you well know, power—any kind of power—has a price. The object or memory you offer may forever be altered as a result. Two versions of the same person cannot exist in the same time or place. One must perish.

"I see," Bastien said. "What about traveling forward, into the future?"

As I said, objects or memories help to anchor the traveler. Unless you have objects from a time in the future, it can be chaotic. Accuracy moving forward is not impossible. Merely difficult.

"Then future travel is not something a novice like me should attempt on the first try."

I appreciate how careful you wish to be. But you forget. I have seen all. And you are not always this careful, Sébastien Saint Germain. Just as you are not always this patient.

"It may not be your intention to do so, but you are warning me now to be careful, as well as patient."

Perhaps. Though I've seen how heedless you are with warnings. You forget; I know what is in your heart.

"I doubt that."

Oh?

The mirrors around Bastien shimmered to life. Until this moment, all he'd seen in the endless walls of hanging silvers was his own reflection staring back at him. Now he heard whispers and echoes. Lilting laughter and the sound of familiar voices calling out to him.

Through the din, Bastien recognized his mother's. Her voice rose above the cacophony, reverberating from a mirror behind him. Before he could stop himself, he turned in place. If he possessed a pulse, it would be careening through his veins. The next instant, his feet carried him toward the mirror without thought. He rounded a bend, his heart in his throat.

"Sébas?" Only his mother and her best friend, Valeria Henri, had ever called him that. Bastien heard the smile in his mother's voice before he saw her face in the mirror.

He stopped short.

There, in living, breathing color, was his memory, as if it were happening before him.

A sultry July afternoon in New Orleans, a blood-orange sun hanging low in the sky. His mother, Bastien, and Émilie sat in the redbrick courtyard behind their home, in the shadow of a flowering jacaranda tree. The same one his mother had replaced twice already, refusing to believe that the striking violet flowers she loved from her grandmother's garden could not flourish in the rich soil of the Crescent City. She hummed a familiar melody as she reached above to cut figs from a drooping branch nearby, her fingers deftly wielding a hooked dagger.

A younger, more contented version of Émilie settled onto a brick ledge to read a book, her back pressed against the tan stucco of their home. Bastien was a small boy, his head on his mother's lap while she sliced pieces of fig and fed them to him. Through the sweltering heat, he watched the way the sunlight warmed through the canopy of leaves. Like a piece of lace set aflame.

Bastien caught himself not a moment too soon, his foot a hairsbreadth from stepping through the mirror, an odd hunger growling through his suddenly empty stomach.

It was not a hunger for food or any kind of sustenance. It was a hunger for feeling. For connection. For something he had almost forgotten to yearn for. More than anything, Bastien wanted to take his mother's hand. To commit to memory the way the fig juice would perfume her skin with a touch of honeyed sweetness. He imagined the way the afternoon would smell. If it was close to suppertime, the scent of baking bread would suffuse the courtyard. The butter in the porcelain jar on the windowsill would be half melted in the heat. He wouldn't need a knife to spread it. He would take a slice of tomato and smash a pat of salted butter between the still-warm bread and stuff everything in his mouth.

Then he would say to his mother something his father used to say when a meal was particularly delicious. "Puedo morir ahora."

I can die now.

God, how Bastien wanted to reach for his mother. To have her reach for him. To smell the soap in her hair and the almond oil she used on her hands to keep them soft. To hear her say "Sébas" just one more time.

Bastien turned away, his throat tight, his eyes squeezed shut. "That was cruel."

It was meant to be a gift. If you alter your perspective, you will see it as such.

"Gifts shouldn't cause this much pain."

Then don't let it be the cause of pain. You saw your mother for the first time in over a decade. You heard her laugh. After she died, what would you have given to have those experiences again?

Bastien took a steadying breath. Forced his shoulders to relax. "I . . . agree. I *am* grateful to have seen her one more time. Thank you."

Would you like me to share another memory of her?

He swallowed. "No. Not yet." As he continued walking, more scenes from his past came to life in the reflections around him. It was as if the mirror were culling things from Bastien's mind as they occurred to him, with startling clarity and quickness. He could see why anyone might lose their way—their very sense of self—in this place.

"If you can take these memories from my mind, why do I need to offer them to you as payment to travel through time?" he murmured.

I am not taking them. I am borrowing them for a moment. When you freely give a memory or a token to me, it is no longer yours to give.

"So I would no longer possess any recollection I gave to you. That memory would be lost to me forever."

Yes.

"I see." Bastien walked forward in thoughtful silence. Soon he came across the moment he replayed most often in his mind. Nighttime shadows danced on the pillars inside Saint Louis Cathedral. The flickering candlelight threw everything into sharp relief.

Celine's tearstained face came into sudden focus. "Please," she begged Bastien's uncle. She clutched Bastien's head to her chest. In the gleaming silver surface, he watched the blood around his body spread, the crimson color darkening across the black-and-white-patterned floor, his skin turning lighter with each passing second.

"What do you want me to do?" Celine implored. "What can I say that will make you save him?"

Bastien listened to her offer to forget him. Offer to walk away from the world of La Cour des Lions. The first place that had welcomed Celine in the New World after her harrowing escape from Paris. Even through the constrained perspective of the mirror, it was impossible to miss the look of unbridled love on her face.

The desperation laced through every word she spoke.

What shocked Bastien was the realization that none of it was necessary. Celine had not known his uncle well enough to understand it then. But Nicodemus already intended to save him. Bastien understood it the instant he saw the careful way his uncle moved and spoke. Nicodemus' decision had been made even before Celine said a single word. Bastien realized it when he witnessed the way his brothers and sisters stood tense and at the ready around the cathedral. He did not miss the glances they exchanged. The way they whispered to each other.

As Bastien watched the scene from his past unfold, he reached into the breast pocket of his jacket, his fingers grazing the scalloped edge of a handkerchief, his thoughts in a whirl.

"He's dying," Boone said under his breath, so quietly Celine could not hear.

Madeleine replied, "Once his heart stops beating, there will be only a few precious seconds to begin the change."

"Why is Nicodemus waiting?" Hortense whispered, her tone rich with intensity.

Of course, Bastien understood the answer to that question without having to ask it. His uncle would not do something for free if he could wring something of value from someone else. And Nicodemus had made it clear that he believed Bastien's relationship with Celine would be his nephew's downfall.

All Nicodemus' blood children knew their maker relished the art of negotiation. So they waited for him to take his pound of flesh from the only girl Bastien had ever loved. They waited because they'd been shaken to their cores that very night, the moment their brother Nigel had betrayed them. They waited because—while they loved Bastien and desired his happiness— they owed their immortal lives to Nicodemus.

So they said nothing while Bastien's fate was sealed. While Celine's memories were stolen. While a first love was cast aside in favor of Nicodemus Saint Germain's designs.

Odette would have said something. She would not have disregarded Bastien's desires without a fight. But of course she was not there. His uncle had punished her for allowing Bastien to go to Celine's aid in the first place. Bastien wondered what the price of Odette's disloyalty had been.

Anger coursed through his veins.

Everything. All of it. The pain, the anguish, the worry, their suffering. Their losses.

All of it had been avoidable.

He thought again of Suli's warning from Sunan regarding Lady Silla. Of how she intended to threaten Celine's life on All Hallows' Eve.

Within Bastien's grasp lay the power to correct it. To fix it. Or end it all.

He removed the handkerchief from his breast pocket. It was one that Celine had made when she first arrived in the French Quarter. Odette had bought it from her the day they'd met. Bastien kept it close because it had been in his breast pocket the night he almost died. Its edges were still stained with his blood. It reminded him of what mattered most when all the squabbling was done. What it was they were fighting to keep safe.

Their home and their future, awaiting them in New Orleans, the city Bastien called home. The only home he would ever choose for himself, despite all the blood and the heartache.

His city of life and death. Of choice and consequence.

Without a word, Bastien offered the handkerchief to the mirror. Then he waited, focusing on the din swirling through the mirror, drowning out everything until he heard only the thrum of his dying heart. He listened to it thud as it beat toward its doom. A thread of discomfort tugged at his chest. Even though Bastien knew this story's outcome, watching it still caused him no small amount of distress.

Immortal beings who fed off the blood of living things had no need of a beating heart, but if Nicodemus waited too long to begin making the change, there would be nothing left of Bastien's mind to turn. Vampires who were made after their mortal minds were lost often went mad from it. Many times, they willingly walked into the sun.

This had been the fate of Bastien's father. A fate Nicodemus also understood well.

Nevertheless, Bastien's uncle waited. It was as if he enjoyed the thrill of toying with their sensibilities until the bitter end.

No matter. Nicodemus was not in control of this story. Not anymore.

The second Bastien heard the final beat of his human heart, he stepped through the mirror, slipping through time, blurring into the darkness to seek refuge in the shade of an immense pillar on the second floor of the main cathedral, overlooking the scene below. Close by, yet still far enough away to escape the notice of his preternatural siblings.

Bastien looked downward. Took a deep breath of incense-laden air, the heavy spring humidity of the French Quarter filling his lungs with pollen and soil and a touch of brine from the sea. An ache stole into his bones. How he missed his city. How much he longed to stay and never leave again.

If he had died in truth that night instead of being turned into a vampire, what suffering might he have spared the ones he loved?

Bastien started to move and stopped himself.

It felt . . . wrong.

Even though this was his home, here, in New Orleans, close to his family—closer than he'd been in recent memory—some distant part of him shouted to turn back.

He did not move again. Did not blink. Instead he remained shrouded in darkness, his back to the cool stone pillar, his breath lodged in his throat.

Now was the moment. If Bastien wanted to stop his uncle from turning him into a vampire, he needed to make his move. If he revealed himself in this instant, it would be the end of his suffering. He would no longer be tortured by what he lost.

Bastien stood straight, his jaw clenching.

All at once, a breeze whipped behind his head. Something grabbed him by the waist. Something strong and fast and unyielding.

The next instant, Bastien was whisked through a window two stories high into a balmy New Orleans night.

The Ruined Duchess

Gratitude rang through Pippa's heart like church bells pealing through a Sunday sky.

She'd made it to the bridge joining the winter lands with those of summer. On the opposing riverbank, the light of the sun beamed on a warm shore, reeds billowing softly in the breeze.

Soon Pippa would be safe.

If she could laugh, she would. But she was no longer human. She was a werewolf. Could such a monster laugh? Would she ever be able to laugh around her brother and sister again? Or would Pippa have to watch them from afar, damned to live forever in this beastly body, afraid that she might do the unthinkable and hurt the ones she loved the most?

She ran faster. Ran as if the devil were at her heels.

Pippa knew it was irrational, but she could not shake the idea that if she could escape the moonlight, she might be able to return to her human form. The cool white beams bore down on her like a curse. She was certain they were the reason she'd been forced into the body of a wolf. Even now, it felt like the light of the moon itself called out to her, just as it had when she'd first risen from the soil and begun transforming. The jolt of energy that had brought life back to her deadened limbs.

She raced through the snow and ice toward the entrance to the bridge. In a moment, she would be free of this wretched frost. No longer called to serve the indifferent light of an unfeeling moon.

Once Pippa crossed to the other side of the bridge, to the Sylvan Vale, she could find Arjun. Surely he would know a way to reverse whatever spell had been placed on her. Pippa was not meant to be a wolf. She had not been born to this, nor was she meant to be tethered to the world of the fey. That point had been made numerous times by the wolves in the cavern.

All she had to do was make her way back to Arjun. Back to the sun.

Pippa burst from the woods, dashing across the icy embankment toward the bridge.

A distant part of her mind warned her to move with caution. Demanded that she learn from her past. The last time she'd set foot on this very bridge, she'd been attacked by a pack of wolves. But Pippa did not notice any guards from winter posted along the entrance. Nor was there a gate to open or a wall to breach. Of course, there could be obstacles on the other side. And it was quite possible the summer fey would not take kindly to a winter-white wolf racing onto their shores.

But Pippa was irrationally certain she could explain herself once she made her way to summer. In the sunlight, all would become clear. In the brilliant warmth of day, everything would be revealed.

Pippa heard the buzzing of wings above her before she saw them. The tiny fey creatures spoke to her in a language she could not understand. Or maybe she simply wished to ignore their attempts to distract her. She was so close. So close to escaping the darkness. The twittering fey were thin and naked, their wings shimmering like dragonflies in the moonlight. Their grey-green arms waved about as they shouted down at her.

"Do . . . not," she thought she heard them say.

Pippa only ran faster, her legs flying over the bridge.

"Do . . . not . . . cross!"

Of course they did not wish her to cross. They wanted Pippa to remain cursed to this forsaken land. For her never to return to her human form.

Pippa had had enough of the Sylvan Wyld. More than enough. She had immense sympathy for those who'd suffered, and she had every intention of giving voice to their plight, but she could not help them as a werewolf. Indeed, she could not even help herself.

So she ignored the warnings of the winged fey and proceeded across the bridge in a blur. She crossed the halfway point, her paws stepping into the sunlight, warmth touching her white fur. She wanted to howl to the sky in triumph. Then she felt something rumble beneath her feet.

All at once, the stones shook. The ground erupted below her. A boom rocked through to her bones, sweeping her paws out from under her. Everything around Pippa exploded, throwing her into the air, the noise like a hundred cannons being fired at the same time.

Pippa's body was launched onto the banks of the Sylvan Vale, the wind knocked from her ribs. For a time, she could not move. She struggled to catch her breath. A whining noise echoed in her ears. Sharp pain lanced through her side. Her eyes watered as if they were too close to a flame.

She did not know how long she remained like this. It was possible she'd lost consciousness for a time. Pippa struggled to sit up, her breaths escaping her in pants and wheezes. She realized someone was shouting at her. When she tried to open her eyes, she could not focus. All she could discern were grey patches and white blurs. Fuzzy figures moving around her, their voices yelling through the din.

Then her arms felt like they were being torn from their sockets as she was dragged through the tall grass onto the shore.

Into the sun.

Even though Pippa still couldn't speak, she tilted her head toward the warmth. The pain in her side sharpened, causing her to cry out. When she screamed, it was the sound of a human girl.

Despite the pain and the buzzing in her ears, a strange relief flooded Pippa's chest. Someone bent close to her, and Pippa once again tried to open her eyes. A hand pressed to her cheek.

"Don't worry, Philippa," a muffled female voice said close to her ear. "You are safe now."

THE RUINED PRINCE

Bastien was thrust against a wooden pier, which cracked and shuddered at the force.

"What in the Sam Hill do you think you're doing?" Boone Ravenel demanded in a brutal whisper.

Anger flooded Bastien's veins. He stood tall, his fists balled at his sides. Without warning, he levied a blow at Boone's head.

"You goddamned madman," Boone yelled before returning the blow, which Bastien barely managed to evade.

Pent-up frustration threatened to burst from Bastien's skin. He lunged again at Boone, his fury plain. This time, Boone side-stepped his attack and made to counter with a punch, but feigned at the last instant, landing a well-timed kick in Bastien's chest.

Bastien fell backward, the air knocked from his body. Enraged, he blurred into motion only to have Boone shove him to ground. Before Bastien could regain his bearings, Boone's right arm wrapped him in a headlock.

Struggling, Bastien gripped Boone's wrist. "What in hell are you—"

"You were going to stop Nicodemus from changing you,

weren't you?" Boone interrupted under his breath. "Like some damned romantic fool from some damned romantic story." Fury caused his Southern drawl to become even more pronounced.

"It's none of your business," Bastien shot back without thinking, his nerves on end.

"And then what?" Boone continued. "You'd leave us to mourn you?" He yanked Bastien to his feet and blurred before him, his irritation plain. "If you stopped Nicodemus," Boone continued, "that would be *the end of you*." He gestured about, his arms thrown into the air. "Everyone you love—all the ones you would leave behind—would just suffer with unanswered questions and grief for all eternity."

"Again, it's none of your business what I—" Bastien stopped short, sudden realization settling on him. "You haven't asked how I managed to be here." His eyes went wide. "You know about the mirror?" In a flash of movement, Bastien grabbed Boone by the collar.

Boone did not blink. "I know about the mirror. Nicodemus told me."

"When?" Bastien shook him.

Boone returned Bastien's glare, his expression steady. "The night after Celine Rousseau graced the threshold of Jacques' for the first time." Dark amusement flared across his features. "He knew you well. Knew you well enough to warn me of the moment I might pick up your scent in two different places at the same time. It pays to be a tracker, after all. Our cursed sense of smell."

A wave of understanding rippled through Bastien's chest.

Nicodemus had always prided himself on being two steps ahead of everyone. His uncle must have suspected Celine would be a source of strife. He'd anticipated that Bastien might lose himself to love. Perhaps not a wild assumption, considering the many losses Bastien had experienced in his life.

And how much the ones he loved meant to him as a result.

Bastien gritted his teeth. He hated how well Nicodemus knew him. Well enough to predict his actions long before a path had even been revealed.

"He told you about the mirror," Bastien repeated, his nostrils flaring. "And you never thought to share that information with any of us?"

"Made me promise not to," Boone replied. "Besides . . . there was no need. We vampires are masters of unending youth. Do we need to be masters of time as well?" A snide grin took shape on his mouth. "You know, that's the problem with all of us. We don't know how to live the life we're given. We only know to want more. Ravenous in all things." He chuckled.

Bastien shoved him. His grin widening, Boone adjusted his rumpled collar. In disbelief, Bastien watched his brother—the most lighthearted, easygoing of all the blood drinkers in the Court of the Lions—return to his carefree self.

How long had Nicodemus known the time-traveling mirror existed? Was it possible he had already foreseen these events before they came to pass?

"Did Nicodemus use the mirror?" Bastien asked.

Boone shook his head. "He knew someone who did, a long time ago."

"Where are they now?"

"Dead, along with the rest of their family." Boone's expression sobered. "Did you honestly think you could just pop out of the woodwork and plead with us to let you die?"

Bastien said nothing.

"What were you sparing yourself?" Boone whispered. "What would change?"

If Bastien still had a heart that beat, he knew it would be pounding in his chest. He swallowed, his jaw clenching on nothing. The chance to change his fate had slipped through his fingers. He turned away from Boone, his eyes squeezed shut.

Despite his wish to argue, he knew his brother was right.

In truth, he had all but come to the same conclusion.

"You're tempting yourself when you toy with something like time, Sébastien," Boone said. "Trust me when I tell you this. I've been a vampire for a hundred years longer than you. I can smell a horseshit deal from a mile away."

"What if you knew someone you loved was being threatened?" Bastien turned to ask. "Would you not do whatever you could to save them?"

"You know something about Celine's future?" Boone guessed.

Bastien's face darkened. "Nothing concrete. Just a warning." Annoyance flickered in him, hot and fast. Why was he always the last to learn when it came to the most important things? He didn't know if his anger should be directed at Suli or at Sunan.

Could they not have left him with more than cryptic vagaries?

"Look," Boone said. "Living ain't easy. Neither is knowing what may come and having to face it anyway." He hooked a thumb in the direction of Jackson Square. "But back there, you weren't trying to save us anything. You were trying to save yourself. If you want to save Celine, you need to be here to do it. Stop being such a selfish blowhard."

Though Bastien could taste the truth in Boone's words, it did not make it easier to admit. "I . . . thought I could spare us everything that happened after I was changed. And part of me wanted to die on my own terms, rather than be forced into a life I wouldn't have chosen for myself."

"I understand, believe me." Boone sighed. He raked a hand through his head of cherubic blond curls. "The night I was turned into a vampire, I was chasing a chance to die on my own terms, too."

Surprise flashed across Bastien's face. "I don't think I've ever heard you speak of that night."

"I never have. At least not to y'all," Boone said. "I think it was because I felt like my story wasn't . . . weighty. I wasn't tortured like Jae or forced to save my sister like Madeleine. I was just looking out for myself." A half smile curved his lips as Boone leaned against the cracked pier, snickering when it whined in protest. "During the Revolutionary War, I served as a tracker in the Continental Army. Hunting the redcoats was my job, and I was damned good at it." His brows rose into his forehead as his mind seemed to drift in recollection. "The second year of the war, I came down with a blood sickness. I suppose it was cancer, but we didn't know those things at the time. I thought about dying on the battlefield, but that really wasn't my style: being shot on a muddy hill or gutted by a bayonet . . ." He shuddered.

"An ignominious end, with me crying out for my mama." Boone snorted. "I would have preferred a bar fight. Some blaze of glory where I lose consciousness with a fist in my face or a chair smashed on my head. Where I'm *strong*." He grinned again. "The last joke was on me, because when Nicodemus found me, I was drunk as a skunk, lying in a puddle of my own piss."

Despite everything, Bastien couldn't help but smile.

"Nicodemus liked my fighting spirit, I suppose." Boone's eyes narrowed. "Or maybe he'd had his eye on me anyway. He knew my name. Knew I was Lafayette's best tracker."

"He could probably smell the blood sickness on you as well."

Boone nodded. "I thought that, not long after. But"—his features brightened—"I'm not going to lie to you. I've never regretted being made into a vampire. I wouldn't take back that moment for all the world. At Nicodemus' side, I've become my own man, instead of a boy who wanted nothing more than to impress his jackass of a father up until the day he died. This family, the one we've made, is everything to me, Bastien." His eyes flashed with fierceness. "I'm not going to let you throw your life away before you've even had a chance to live it."

Bastien gazed past Boone, his eyes falling on the muddy Mississippi lapping against the pier. He listened to the sound of the churning water. Watched the way the lanterns danced across its lashing surface. "So," he said softly, "you were able to smell me in two different places at the same time tonight at the cathedral?"

Boone nodded. "Your past self was dying on the floor before

me. Your blood was the strongest scent. And then . . . it wasn't. I smelled you from above, which didn't make sense. Until it did."

"That's the real reason Nicodemus chose you," Bastien said with a sad smile. "He always sought the best and the brightest."

With his own sad smile, Boone nodded. "Destiny probably had a hand in it. And your destiny is telling you to go back to where you're supposed to be, Sébastien. If you know a way to save Celine, then do it. Don't look to the past for solutions. Look *forward. Fight.* Rage against the goddamned moon if you must." He rested a hand on Bastien's shoulder. "Your family will be there to stand at your side."

Bastien clasped Boone's arm and met his brother's steady gaze. "I know."

Bastien returned to a silent cathedral. The only trace of what happened earlier that night was the faint tinge of blood lingering through the space. He wondered who had been left to clean. Over the centuries, vampires had become adept at concealing their natures—indeed, their very existences—from humans. What manner of lies had his uncle spun to dissuade the authorities from delving for the truth?

His features hardened. Whatever lies Nicodemus had told, they had not been enough to deter Detective Michael Grimaldi.

Even if Bastien had died that night, there was no telling how far Michael might have gone for answers. It was in his nature. Perhaps the werewolf's destiny was always his own, too.

Just as Bastien's was.

With a look of resignation, Bastien blurred to the second floor of Saint Louis Cathedral, toward a shimmer of air surrounding a sliver of otherworldliness. It looked like a large knife had sliced through the darkness, distorting and refracting it. As if a giant glass of water had been left in the shadows. It would be easy to miss. One would not notice it if one did not know where to look.

Without a single glance back, Bastien left through the mirror just as he'd entered it, Boone's words echoing in his ears.

Returning to the past for salvation had left Bastien in a deeper well of indecision. His desire to be seen as magnanimous—instead of manipulative, like his uncle—had made Bastien wary of hard choices.

It was time to stop looking to the past. To start looking forward.

A wise decision, the mirror's voice said as soon as Bastien returned to the maze.

Bastien said nothing for a time. The tension in his body remained, refusing to abate. He flexed his fingers and tilted his head to the right, then to the left. He thought of everything he'd learned. Of all that had come to pass after he was turned into a vampire. The nights he'd spent beside Celine. The laughter and love. The lessons.

"Besides the obvious," Bastien began in a soft voice, "what else might have been lost if I'd stopped my uncle from turning me that night?"

I cannot answer that.

"Cannot? Or will not?"

Will not, then. Amusement tinged the mirror's tone. *I will only answer what may be, given what is and what has been. The future is a destiny yet to be foretold.*

Bastien thought to himself. "Then the best way—the only way—for me to know what my destiny is in truth would be for me to travel forward, to a time where I do not exist. A time that is impossible for me to know in the present." He chose to make a statement rather than ask a question. "There is no way for an immortal to predict the date of his demise."

The mirror did not reply immediately. When it did speak, its amusement had deepened. *I did not say it was the only way. I said that magic—any kind of magic—has a cost. Foresight requires the greatest cost. As I stated earlier, if you attempt to journey to a time in which another version of yourself exists, one of you will likely perish.*

"Then how would I go about seeing the future? How would I even know where to begin?"

The mirror hesitated. Even though Bastien knew better than to be drawn in by it, he felt himself caught on a lure. Slowly being reeled in.

"Is there something you have not yet told me?" Bastien asked point-blank.

The mirror sighed. *I had hoped to keep it from you, at least for a time. This is where I lose even the most promising of my keepers. The ones who demonstrate the keenest insight fall to this temptation all too quickly.*

"What temptation?"

I've shown you glimpses of the past in the mirrors before. Nothing concrete, but a simple moving image. A suggestion. The mirror paused. *I can do the same with the future.*

Bastien refused to show even a hint of eagerness.

But a glimpse into the future is not without cost. I culled images from your past from your willing mind. You must offer something of true value before you are given any vision of the future.

Quite the enticement. Bastien understood the idea of a payment like this. He had been raised on it.

Since you have never journeyed to the future, you may offer me a memory, the mirror continued. *But once you offer it to me, recall that it is no longer yours. It is taken from your mind, never to be returned.*

Bastien thought of Celine. If she had the choice now, would she have offered her memories of him to his uncle so readily? What was the true cost of parting with a piece of one's mind? "If I wish to glimpse into the future so that I might know what will happen to Celine if she remains with her mother in the Vale," Bastien said, "then I must offer you a memory of her with her mother in the Summer Court?"

Yes. That would be the best way to ensure you are granted what you seek.

With a nod, Bastien began to consider the slew of memories he'd collected of his time with Celine in the Sylvan Vale. He tried his best to seek the most innocent of all his recollections. The most ordinary and forgettable.

He settled on a time when Celine first donned a fairy garment presented to her by her mother the second day after their arrival to the Ivy Bower.

Bastien and Celine had fled New Orleans in a hurry. Their sudden exit had been fraught for several reasons. Odette lay bleeding, on the cusp of succumbing to the final death from of a blow dealt by Bastien's sister, Émilie. In exchange for keeping their coven—and what remained of his family—safe, Nicodemus had met the sun. It was his final negotiation. Part of a deal he'd struck with Émilie as payment for the wrongs he'd committed against her in the past.

Time haunted Bastien on all sides now. It was why he'd dreaded meeting this mirror even though he'd desired its power. His past plagued him just as Émilie's past fueled her revenge.

Just as Celine's past had found her from across the Atlantic.

The wealthy family of the young man Celine had killed for assaulting her had dispatched a French detective to track down her whereabouts in the New World. Once this detective found Celine, he intended to return her to Paris so that she could pay for her crimes. The punishment for murdering a young man of the French aristocracy was the guillotine.

Bastien would kill every bleeding paladin in France—both fictional and real—before he allowed that to happen.

The memory of Celine donning a fey gown for the first time was shadowed on all sides. It stood out to Bastien for both its blandness and for the way it had irritated him beyond measure. Celine, who'd always been so particular about her clothing.

Who knew fabrics and designs and fashion plates better than anyone Bastien had encountered in both his lives. After studying with one of Paris' premier couturières, Celine prided herself on how she dressed, for she maintained that her garments were a sort of moving art. A way to show the world how she felt without having to say a word.

The reason Bastien had hated seeing Celine dressed as if she were a member of the summer gentry was simple. He'd hated to see her lose more of herself. To surrender even more of her autonomy under the guise of pleasing her mother. Of course, she'd looked stunning in the gown of pale jade spider silk they'd presented her with to wear that day, the fabric shimmering like a peridot in the morning sunlight. To Bastien, Celine was beautiful in everything and in nothing. But he would always prefer to see her in the jewel tones she chose for herself.

If you wish to give me that memory, then I will accept it. But have a care, because once it is given, it cannot be returned.

Bastien tried to think of why he would miss that memory. He failed to conceive of a significant reason. It was nothing but a nuisance to him. Nothing to see it gone. "You may have that memory," he agreed, his heartbeat shuddering once.

Very well.

Bastien felt a tug in the back of his mind. It was not painful, but rather odd. Like a crick in his neck. As if he needed to twist his chin in the opposite direction to correct it. Once he did, a disoriented sensation settled upon him, like he was being woken from a deep sleep. He shook his head and closed his eyes.

It is done, the mirror said. *If you step to the rectangular mirror around the corner to your right, you will witness a glimpse of the future you requested. But have a care not to step into the moment or try to interfere. Never forget: the greater the magic, the greater the cost.*

Bastien walked to his right, toward a long rectangular mirror bordered in antique gold filigree. An image blossomed to life in its center, its edges blurry. Different from the ones he'd witnessed in the labyrinth thus far. Perhaps because it was a scene from a future that was not yet set in stone, but the scene unfolding before him appeared blurry, as if the mirror had been slicked with oil.

He stepped closer, trying to understand the strange flickers of motion within the silver surface. The hazy quality made it difficult to detect anything with a clear eye. Then the image sharpened. The shattered courtyard of the Ursuline convent came into view. The place Celine had first come to when she'd arrived in New Orleans at the beginning of the year. In the center of the courtyard rested the Horned Throne. The same throne that usually sat on a raised dais in the Ivy Bower of the Sylvan Vale.

Celine lay on the flagstone ground, motionless on her side, a black silk garment billowing around her. The ground trembled as if an earthquake were rumbling beneath it. The wind howled in the branches above, causing a cascade of autumn leaves to rain down around Celine, who remained immobile on the cracked stone.

It was then that Bastien saw the pool of blood spreading beside her head.

On either side of the Horned Throne—bearing quiet witness to the devastation—were two members of the Grey Cloaks. A hooded shadow emerged from behind them. In the shadow's gloved hand was an ornate dagger of bright silver, its blade dripping with fresh blood.

Bastien caught a glimpse of a profile, carefully concealed behind a veil of blue-black hair.

Lady Silla.

The figure stood. Muttered words flew from her mouth. Celine's blood began to swirl and lift from the ground, where it continued to spread. Soon it formed a slow-moving windstorm of dark crimson, churning toward the sky. The hooded form of the Lady of the Vale lifted her hands to the heavens and opened her mouth. The blood of her daughter swirled back toward Lady Silla, who appeared to consume it in a single draught.

Then the image vanished as if it were a handful of sand carried away on a passing breeze.

Lady Silla had murdered Celine.

The Grey Cloaks had stood by and allowed it to happen, as if it had all been planned from the start.

This was far worse than Celine's life being threatened. Immeasurably worse than her mother wishing ill on her. Lady Silla had brought Celine to the Vale to destroy her, for reasons Bastien could not even begin to fathom.

"No." His voice hoarse, he reached toward the mirror and stopped. Rage caught in his throat. He forced it back down. "Why—why would she kill her own daughter?"

You have your answer as to what might happen to Celine if she chooses to remain in Lady Silla's company, the mirror said.

"I have part of an answer," Bastien said, fury sharpening his words.

You know enough to understand that she should not remain at her mother's side.

Bastien stopped himself from shouting. Struggled to rein in his anger. "I have suspected that for quite some time," he said, lowering his voice in an attempt to remain calm. "But it will be difficult to convince her that she should listen to me if I cannot tell her why. She will think—as she has before—that I am being controlling and overprotective."

I do not envy you that task, it is true. As I said before, the question of might or may be is a destiny yet to be foretold. It can only be determined by decisions made in the present.

"Hang the present," Bastien said in a vicious whisper. "What do I need to do to prevent this future from happening?"

Hang the present? The mirror tsked. *But the present is the most important thing of all, Sébastien.*

"Wrong," Bastien replied. "The most important thing of all is that I am able to keep the ones I love safe. Or else I have no use for you." He turned his back to this version of the mirror, the wrath causing the blood to heat through his body.

You have so much to learn. But I understand your anger. Would it help if I offered you a gift?

Bastien did not turn around.

It will cost you nothing.

Behind him, he heard ice cracking under pressure. The braying of a horse. The beating of enormous wings.

Still he refused to turn around.

Your stubbornness is amusing. I will give you a hint about your future. Ice that was once broken can be remade.

"You think I care about ice being remade?" Bastien said. "Tell me how to save Celine or I am leaving."

Perhaps it would help you to see the present for yourself. As a keeper of time, I can tell you without reservation that there is nothing more important than what is happening now.

Bastien straightened. He adjusted his shirtsleeves. Then he began striding toward the entrance of the maze, his footsteps quick and sure. Decisive. He refused to glance in the direction of any mirror for more than a necessary instant. Instead he kept his gaze leveled on the ground before him, denying the traveling silver any more power than it already had.

After spending time with it, he understood Suli's warning. He thought he was beginning to understand the mirror's desires. It had been left alone too long. It liked to play chess, but instead of marble pieces, it played with lives. With futures and pasts and devilish presents.

It was famished, as Suli had said. And its food of choice was its longing to be needed.

Something flared through the sky above Bastien. The sunset began to darken. The earth at his feet started to rumble.

If Bastien had to guess, the mirror was irritated. All at once, he heard Odette's tired voice break through the din. It was followed by the sound of Celine's unabashed laughter, and then a quiet, broken sob.

This was not a memory. Odette was crying, too. Odette never cried. Not if she could help it.

Bastien halted in his tracks. Cursed under his breath. And turned toward the image materializing in the mirror closest to him. There, on the top floor of the Hotel Dumaine, stood Celine Rousseau, flanked by Yuri and another Grey Cloak.

Grey Cloaks. In New Orleans. In the heart of his family's haven.

Bastien didn't know if it was the audacity of the Summer Court for sending armed warriors into his city—into his home—that angered him most. Or if it was that at least two of them had watched in silence while the girl he loved was murdered in the shadow of the Sylvan Vale's throne.

In the heart of *his city*.

Why would Celine bring Grey Cloaks there? Nicodemus would have been incensed at the sight.

Another thought occurred to Bastien. What if they had brought Celine here under duress? Were they threatening his family?

These two Grey Cloaks could be the ones who enabled Celine's death. The image from the future he'd seen in the mirror earlier had been hazy. It was possible Yuri could be involved. Which then meant General Riya—Arjun's mother—could also be involved. It would not be such a stretch for Bastien to imagine the possibility. He'd never trusted the Lady of the Vale or her best general. Lady Silla may be Celine's mother, but she'd ruled the Summer Court for far longer than the short time she'd welcomed her daughter back into her life.

What kind of mother abandoned her child in the first place?

Bastien stared at the scene before him, anger flooding his veins. He did not pause to offer the mirror any kind of payment. Nor did he acknowledge it any way.

Without a moment's hesitation, he stepped through the silver surface into the present.

The Ruined Princess

Celine held Odette tightly in her arms, refusing to let go. The tears flowed down her face, gratitude surging through her chest. She breathed in the familiar scent of neroli oil and rose petals. The perfume Odette had been partial to for the last thirty years.

Even though Celine felt Odette hugging her back, something about the vampire seemed different. Seemed . . . fragile. Never before had Celine considered Odette to be anything less than invincible. In this moment, Odette felt almost human.

Weeks earlier, in the heat of battle, Émilie Saint Germain had sliced Odette's throat with a silver blade, nearly severing Odette's head from her body. At the behest of Jae—who had called in a marker of his own—two dark fey, long exiled from the Sylvan Wyld, had traveled from deep inside the bayou to attend to Odette after Ifan revealed that her injuries were beyond his expertise. Even with their considerable healing skills, Celine understood that it had taken every ounce of their knowledge to restore Odette to a semblance of her former self. A wicked scar cut a line across the vampire's neck, which would likely remain for the rest of time.

Guilt riddled Celine's thoughts. She'd failed to be there for Odette—for one of her closest friends—in the vampire's hour of need. Just like she'd failed to be there for Pippa. It was true she had her excuses, but none of that mattered to Celine in this moment.

All that mattered was her failure to be there for her friends.

The night Odette was attacked, Bastien and Celine were forced to flee New Orleans. Leaving the city in a hurry—without any word to the rest of the Court of the Lions—had been an attempt to protect the ones they loved, but it also meant that Bastien and Celine had left without knowing if Odette would recover.

The guilt that lurked inside Celine refused to be silenced, even now that she could see Odette moving about in her familiar buckskin pants, boots, and perfectly tailored waistcoat. Being in New Orleans with Odette made Celine feel as if she could finally fill her lungs with air. As if a piece of her heart that had been empty before was now full again.

Something knifed in Celine's chest. A memory as sharp and clear as an icy January morning.

Pippa's blood splashing on the bridge. Pippa's echoing screams.

Celine held even tighter to Odette, her eyes squeezing shut.

"You're acting like I almost died, you ninny," Odette joked in a soft voice, her hand stroking Celine's hair like a mother to a child.

"You did almost die." Celine wiped her tears.

"Oh, fiddle-dee-dee, as they say." Odette shot her a simpering grin, despite the smattering of pink tears staining her pale cheeks. "Honestly it was almost fun, mon amie. I've had some of the best frights of my life since you came into it. It's certainly been an adventure. Why, I could even— Bastien?" Incredulity sent Odette's arched eyebrows high into her forehead. "How did you . . . When did you arrive?"

Celine turned at once, her arms still around Odette's waist and her pulse tearing through her veins.

There, as if he'd materialized from the darkness like a demon of the night, stood Sébastien Saint Germain, his beautiful face a portrait of quiet rage.

Celine's first instinct was to run to him. To enfold herself in his embrace and allow the remaining worries to leave her body. But he was angry with her. That much was evident in the way his eyes refused to leave hers. In the cold intensity lurking in their grey depths.

The emotions racing through Celine struggled to take control. The relief. The surprise.

Her own rising anger.

He dares to be cross with me?

Celine took a step forward and saw the two Grey Cloaks standing sentry in the shadows shift, as if they were on a tether. A muscle in Bastien's jaw jumped in response.

Fury and confusion gathered in her stomach. She bit her tongue, chiding herself to remain silent. Bastien deserved a chance to explain himself. If anything, her first and greatest love had earned her trust. Even if Celine didn't understand his anger, she knew he would be able to explain it to her. She merely had to be patient.

Which was not, in fact, one of her many virtues.

The next instant, the door to the chamber—the same door that Bastien had curiously not used to gain entrance—opened with a bang. Jae and Hortense rushed inside, their faces wary.

"Bastien?" Hortense demanded, her French accent strong. "How did you get in here?" Alarm rang through her every word. "You should not have been able to come in here without being noticed."

Bastien remained focused on Celine. "The better question to ask, Hortense, is why you would ever allow summer soldiers—especially ones bearing weapons—into our stronghold."

Surprise flared through Celine. The way Bastien had said *summer soldiers* sounded like an insult.

Odette disentangled herself from Celine's embrace and stood tall, her hands placed on her hips. "Well, obviously, they are here to keep Celine safe, since you were nowhere to be found, you silly boy."

"Celine doesn't need any bodyguards in New Orleans," Bastien said. "She is perfectly capable of keeping herself safe."

"C'est possible her mother disagrees with you, mon cher." Odette's voice turned testy. "And aren't you going to tell me how marvelous I look for someone who nearly died three months ago?"

Dismay collected in Celine's throat. "It's been three months since we left?"

"Oui," Odette replied. "It is the beginning of October. All Hallows' Eve beckons from around the corner." She grinned. "My favorite holiday."

Again, Bastien's anger deepened at Odette's words. "Odette, you—"

"Stop!" Odette commanded, her hand in his face. "If you can't say what I want to hear, then don't speak at all. You *disappeared* after I nearly died, you roi des cons."

"You do look marvelous," Bastien said. "And I'm sorry I wasn't here."

Odette sniffed. "Also apologize for smelling like a butcher's shop. Where have you been?" Her eyes narrowed. "Were you in a fight? You look terrible."

He did not reply. Again, he turned toward Celine, his expression grim. Odette was right. Bastien did look terrible. Dried blood stained his shirtsleeves and one side of his collar. Drops of crimson had fallen on his torn waistcoat. His trousers were streaked with mud. At first glance, he did not appear to be injured. But Celine knew the deepest cuts were often the ones hidden from view.

"Bastien," Celine said quietly. "Are you all right?"

"No," he replied. "I am not."

"You are injured?" Hortense demanded. "We should send word to Ifan."

"I do not need a healer," Bastien said. "I need to speak with Celine."

Jae continued to study Bastien, his gaze apprising. "How did you manage to travel to the top of the Hotel Dumaine and make your way to this chamber without any of us seeing or hearing or smelling you, especially in such a state?"

"Like you appeared from thin air," Hortense finished, her lips thinned into a line.

"I used a tare." Bastien looked to his brother and sister, his features steady.

A half-truth.

The thought formed in Celine's mind, unbidden. That same inner voice she'd tried to ignore ever since the day her mother was struck down on the bridge. The same inner voice that had become more and more silent since she'd arrived with her mother in the Vale.

Curious how it chose this moment to reveal itself once more.

"What kind of tare is connected directly to the Hotel Dumaine?" Celine asked.

Bastien's eyes glittered as he looked toward the two Grey Cloaks. "The only kind I know."

He's lying. But why would he lie to you?

Celine could think of only one reason. Accusations filled her ears.

Sunan must have confided in Bastien about the mirror. And Bastien is refusing to share whatever the goblin divulged. Just as he refused to return to my side when I needed his counsel the most. He had a tare. And he did not come to see me.

The inner voice melted in her own. All at once, Celine realized how it had separated itself. How it had ceased to join with her thoughts and speak as one. She wondered when that had happened.

She suspected Bastien would be the first to tell her, his expression knowing. Smug.

No. He doesn't know everything. And he has hurt and betrayed me. I must never allow him to hurt and betray me again.

Every selfish thought that took shape was like salt rubbed in an open wound. Alone and afraid in the Vale, Celine had yearned for Bastien. She'd cried out for him, her fear shadowing all else. Like a pitiful creature in an opium den, pleading for anything to help ease the pain.

Her anger flared again. She forced herself to ignore the noise in her mind, but the accusations lingered, like whispers spoken behind her back.

Jae sucked in his cheeks. "What reason have you to be so angry with us?"

"Hm-mm-mmm," Hortense hummed. "He is not angry with us. He is angry with Celine."

Of course Hortense would be the one to slice to the truth without hesitation. The vampire with the penchant for feathers and furs and silk taffeta had never been the timid sort.

"Why are there Grey Cloaks in our city?" Bastien asked Celine, his words clipped.

Celine's fingers twisted into the folds of her skirts. A habit she'd developed as a child whenever her nerves wished to best her. She knew she should tell Bastien what Vanida had said. Simply share with him the immense weight now upon her shoulders. Surely he would understand why the Grey Cloaks felt the need to protect the Lady of the Vale's lone heir, particularly in light of Lady Silla's near assassination.

No. He lied to me. A bald-faced lie. He should be the one to tell the truth first.

Celine lifted her chin. "You have no cause to be cross with me. After what happened on the riverbank, I worried about you. But I suppose it is good to see my worries were unfounded."

"You brought Grey Cloaks into our city," he repeated.

"And you are acting like a petulant child," she said, her voice firm.

Bastien took a small step forward. "Into *my* home. Into *my* city."

Odette's nervous laughter filled the air. "Enough, mon cher. Surely you do not mean to sound threatening." Though she laughed while she spoke, Odette angled herself between them, as if warning Bastien not to press further.

Celine clenched her teeth. "He doesn't sound threatening. Not yet. But I invite him to try." She took her own step forward, matching him toe-to-toe. The Grey Cloaks at her back moved in tandem. "You don't own this city, Sébastien Saint Germain. Nor do you command me or anyone under my care."

Bastien's nostrils flared at the sight of the Grey Cloaks tilting their silver-tipped spears.

Celine held up a hand to stay the guards. Unease gripped the room in a vise. For a heart-stopping instant, no one appeared to move or even breathe.

I won't back down. It doesn't matter if he has my heart. I am fey royalty.

And he is a liar.

Celine stared Bastien down. The next second, something shifted in the air.

Bastien flinched, the tension dropping from his shoulders. He took a step back. Bewilderment kept Celine frozen in place. She could not recall a time when she'd seen Bastien back down from anything first.

He did not wear defeat well. His features turned somber, which caused an ache to take shape in her heart. She'd longed for him so much. Why was he acting like this?

Celine watched him calculate before making his next move.

What was that saying about the tiger and his stripes?

"May we speak?" Bastien asked her, his tone gentle. "Alone." He eyed the Grey Cloaks once more.

A thought occurred to Celine. Perhaps he did not want to tell her the truth with anyone else present, though she could not think of a reason why he would wish to hide anything from his brothers and sisters in La Cour des Lions.

"Pardon, Lady Celine," one of the Grey Cloaks said in a low voice. "But we were instructed never to leave your side."

"And you will of course be close by," Celine said. "But please take your leave for now." She nodded at Bastien. "We do have much to discuss."

"I longed for you," Bastien said as soon as the soldiers left the chamber with Odette, Jae, and Hortense in tow. "And I worried for you, too."

Celine reached for him. She didn't miss the beat of hesitation before Bastien took her in his arms. With a sigh, she leaned against his chest and allowed herself to relax. He held her in a familiar embrace, one hand stroking down her back and the other cradling her neck. He smelled of leather and bergamot . . . and blood.

When he tilted her chin to gaze into her eyes, Celine stood on her toes to press her lips to his. Her breath caught when he lifted her, deepening their kiss in a deliciously demanding way that never failed to leave Celine light-headed.

She pulled back just before the point of no return, her desire rising in her throat. In that moment, all Celine wanted was to lose herself in sensation. To cease the endless spiraling of her thoughts and seek nothing, save for pleasure.

But his anger and his hesitation—and the lies and the secrecy—forced Celine to make a choice. It was time for them to cast aside the pain and pettiness. Even the pleasure.

It was time to share their truths, no matter how ugly.

Bastien rested his forehead against hers until their breathing returned to normal.

"Why are you so angry that Grey Cloaks accompanied me to New Orleans?" Celine whispered. "It's unlike you to be so controlling, Bastien."

He met her gaze. "They are forbidden from being here, according to a treaty they signed four hundred years ago. The summer gentry and their soldiers know better than to enter any mortal city under the protection of a vampire coven." His eyes narrowed. "In fact, I think they are testing us to see what might happen. You know all this, Celine, so I must admit I'm surprised you were so unbothered by the transgression."

"I didn't think you'd object so forcefully, especially since you, too, are ignoring that very same treaty every time you cross into the Sylvan Wyld." She spoke in a level tone.

His lips pursed to one side. "But I am not there to cause anyone harm."

"The Grey Cloaks are not trying to harm me. They are trying to protect me."

"From whom?" Bastien raised a brow. "Do you feel unsafe in New Orleans?"

Celine straightened. "No. Should I feel unsafe in New Orleans?"

He said nothing. Then moved back, his hands resting in his pockets.

A fresh flurry of emotions ignited in Celine's stomach. Once again, anger managed to eclipse all else. She was growing weary of their unending stream of unspoken accusations.

Why are we so at odds? Why is Bastien not even attempting to understand me, though he demands nothing short of unflinching consideration from everyone else?

"This isn't the way I wanted this to be, Bastien," Celine tried again. "I don't want us to argue." She reached for his hand. "What has changed in the handful of days we were not together? Tell me."

Bastien stared down at her, conflict warring in his eyes.

"Why are you so angry with me?" she whispered. "Why won't you even try to understand?"

"I'm not angry," he said, his words more breath than sound. "I'm . . . terrified."

"Why? Will you not tell me?"

His head canted. Then he looked around, taking stock of the warm darkness and the thick humidity. The smell of the lacquered wood, along with the lingering scent of cologne. Of a richly appointed chamber to which Celine had never gained entrance in the past.

"This was Nicodemus' private suite," Bastien began. "I haven't set foot in it since his death."

"Strange how it feels like it happened only a few days ago." Celine squeezed his hand. Relief flooded her body when he threaded his fingers through hers. "But I suppose several months have passed since."

Bastien nodded. "Not any less strange than to realize we did not know each other a year ago."

"And now I feel as if you have been part of my life—and will be part of it—always."

Something darkened on his features before he responded. It made Celine's heart skip a beat. "I want nothing more than that, too," he said. "Which is why I must implore you to—"

"Sunan told you about the mirror, didn't he?"

He paused. Then nodded.

Eagerness brought Celine closer to him. If they could have access to a mirror that controlled time, the possibilities were endless. Indeed, she could even return to that afternoon along the river and stop the wolves from attacking Pippa at all.

"Did he show it to you?" Celine pressed.

That same calculating expression settled on his face. "He

did . . . but the mirror was destroyed when he died. It appears that Sunan was tied to its fate."

He's lying again.

Celine released his hand. "Why are you continuing to tell me half-truths, Bastien? What are you trying to hide?"

"Sunan also revealed something else," Bastien said, ignoring her questions. "He wanted me to tell you that your life is in danger if you remain at your mother's side."

Celine huffed. "This again. She has never done or said anything even close to wishing me harm, Bastien. Your dislike of her is unfounded."

"And your unwillingness to see beyond her serene smile is flabbergasting," Bastien replied. "I just told you your mother is a credible threat to your life."

"Did Sunan say that? Tell me the truth."

"No. He told Suli. And Suli told me."

"And those two have always been so forthcoming." Celine rolled her eyes. "The illusionist goblin and his adviser brother, who hid the truth of the Sylvan Wyld for centuries. Is it not possible that, in their zeal to keep their people safe, they might wish to undermine their supposed enemy and make trouble for the Sylvan Vale and my mother?"

Bastien took a breath. "Is it not possible that you are willfully ignoring a painful truth you simply do not wish to hear?"

"My mother would never hurt me, Bastien."

"How can you be so sure? You've known her a few weeks at best."

"Because she's my mother." Celine's voice rose, exasperation causing her cheeks to flush. "And because her powers are meant to pass to me at her death," she said, forcing herself to speak in hushed tones.

"What?"

"I am her only living blood heir." The words were pronounced with a surprising amount of sharpness. "If something happened to me, the line of her magic would be broken. I need to inherit the Horned Throne and, with it, her powers. Can you see now why she would never, ever wish me harm? On the contrary, she would do anything to keep me safe."

Bastien's cheeks hollowed. "You will inherit her powers? Are you certain?"

Celine nodded. "At her death."

"And there is no way she could prevent that from happening?"

"I just told you that our entire line would be in jeopardy. Beyond the fact that I am her only living child, who would ever risk that?"

"Someone who had a better alternative. Perhaps she found a way to—"

"Enough!" Celine shouted, her anger spiking. "If Sunan told you something certain, then share it with me. If not, everything you've said is conjecture."

He remained silent.

"See?" Celine's eyes narrowed. "You're still hiding something."

"Can I trust you to tell no one what I am about to say?"

"The way I can trust you to speak the whole truth? To tell me about the mirror and what you intend to do with it?"

Bastien blinked.

"You know where it is, don't you?" Celine accused.

Another hesitation. "I do not."

Lie after lie after lie.

Her heart shuddered. Her voice nearly broke. "Those lips can lie. Those eyes cannot." She pushed him away, unshed tears shimmering across her vision. "I can't believe you would still lie to me."

"Celine, you must understand how precarious our situation is. Information about Sunan's mirror falling into the wrong hands, however unintentionally, could cost us everything."

"Do you think me a simpleton, Bastien?"

"I never said that. Don't twist my words, Celine."

"It was implied." She brushed away her tears with a quick swipe of her hand. "As if my mouth were a leaking faucet, and I flit about the world saying whatever I wish to whoever will listen, without a care for anyone but myself."

Bastien exhaled. "I will tell you everything I know. But first I want you to promise you won't return to the Vale. That you'll stay in New Orleans, under our protection, until the end of October."

"And now you're trying to negotiate with the woman you love? Is nothing sacred to you?" Celine snorted. "You're becoming more and more like your uncle every day."

He flinched again, as if she'd struck him across the face. Then his features turned cold. "Your mother will try to kill you, Celine. Before Hallowtide. That much I know to be true."

"I don't believe you. I think you'll say anything to get what you want, even something as reprehensible as suggesting my mother would harm me."

"I've made more than the suggestion."

"Without offering any proof." Celine glared at him.

"I'm asking you to trust me."

"And I'm asking you to trust my mother."

"I will never do that. And neither should you. It is foolish for you to make that choice."

"There we have it," Celine said. "I've been waiting for the day you would ask me to choose between you and my mother, though I hoped it would never come."

Bastien cast her a searching glance. "Very well. It has come."

"I won't make that decision."

A light of desperation flickered in his eyes. It unsettled Celine. As if he were contemplating a terrible course of action.

"And you will *never* force me to do anything against my will," she said, her words a quiet command. She knew that look well. She knew what Bastien was considering.

How could he even think of holding her captive?

Bastien took both her hands in his. "Celine," he implored. "I won't force you, but please grant me this request. My fear for you is as real as my love."

Celine pressed her lips into a line. She recalled how Odette had teasingly admitted that the worst frights of her life had occurred after Celine arrived in New Orleans. Now all Bastien had asked of her was trust. Why was it so hard for her to give it?

Which of them had to succumb first? And why was it always the woman?

An icy bleakness settled on her heart.

In ways big and small, Celine seemed destined to fail the ones she loved.

"I'm tired of being afraid," she admitted. "It makes me doubt myself. But even now, there are two things I know to be true. The first is that I love you more than words, Sébastien Saint Germain. The second is that I cannot give you what you want. Not now." She removed her hands from his. "And perhaps not ever." It may destroy her, but she would not give in first.

Celine refused to be controlled by anyone or anything. Even love.

It took Bastien an instant to comprehend her meaning. "What are you doing, Celine?"

Her voice quavered. She swallowed the knot in her throat. "I'm asking you to let me go. To relinquish any obligation you have to me, at least for a time. That way, whatever happens, you won't feel responsible."

"No." Bastien shook his head, his handsome face fierce. "I won't do that. Stay here in New Orleans with me, Celine. At least until All Hallows' Eve."

"I won't. My mother is dying in the Vale. And I am her only living heir."

His brows gathered. "Is that it? You wish so badly to be the next fairy queen of the Summer Court?"

"How insulting. I hope you know me better than that."

Bastien searched her face again. "I thought I did," he murmured.

Celine kept her head high, though something twisted around

her heart. Pain began radiating from her chest, as if someone had poured a stream of boiling water onto her lungs. "I'm leaving now." Despite her best efforts, her body trembled.

Bastien grabbed her hand. "Don't. Stay. Please. We can find a way. A compromise."

"Half of me cannot stay here with you, just as half of you cannot return to the Vale with me." She smiled sadly. "One of us must win. I don't want to stay long enough to find out who it is."

After a time, Bastien nodded.

The pain in Celine's chest began to flow toward her limbs. She struggled to remain upright, a sad smile on her face. "If you change your mind, you know where I will be."

"You know where I will be, too."

"For love, I believe you are never too late."

Bastien leveled his gaze on hers. "I promise I won't be late. I swear on my life." There was a reverence to his vow. Something shone in his eyes.

If Celine saw Bastien shed tears of blood, she knew she would break first. So she forced herself to walk away, her heart shattering. She refused to falter, even as the cracks spread through her body. She stood tall, her feet moving, one step in front of the other, her head held high. She bit her lower lip to keep from screaming as she took the birdcage elevator to the bottom floor of the Hotel Dumaine, the two Grey Cloaks following as silent sentinels.

It was wrong to leave New Orleans without saying goodbye to the Court of the Lions, but Celine couldn't face them. If she stopped to speak with Odette—if she saw the concern on Jae's face, or the judgment in Hortense's eyes, or heard the note of sympathy in Madeleine's voice—she knew she would splinter into a thousand pieces.

In the lobby, she quickened her pace, her attention focused on the black and white tiles, the perfume of night-blooming jasmine winding through her nose.

"Celine?" a voice called out to her from the shadows to her right.

She stopped in her tracks, a shiver chasing down her spine.

Arjun.

Celine pivoted on her heel, her pulse quickening, the beginning of a smile on her lips.

It died the instant she faced him.

Arjun's features were haggard. It looked as though he had not slept in an age. His chin was grizzled with a week-old beard, and his usually pristine white shirt and damask waistcoat were rumpled, his sleeves pushed to his elbows. His monocle was nowhere to be found.

Celine walked two paces closer. Even from a distance, she could smell the scent of whiskey on him. Unease prickled at her skin. She wanted to ask about Pippa. But dreaded the answer.

If Arjun was back in New Orleans without Pippa, then—

Celine shook her head and attempted a smile. "How are you?"

"Excellent, can't you tell?" he replied, though he had the good sense not to smile back.

"It was a foolish question," Celine murmured, her fingers grasping at her skirts. She forced her hands to relax. "I suppose I hoped my eyes were deceiving me."

"Thank you for not lying to me or trying to make me feel better," he grumbled, his fingers yanking through his head of dark hair.

"I—I'm only treating you the way you would treat me, Arjun. I"—Celine bit her lip—"I know you will always be honest with me."

"Yes." He nodded. "I will."

Celine swallowed. Her hands twisted her skirts again. "Is Pippa with you?"

"No."

She nodded. "Then—then she is convalescing in the Sylvan Wyld?"

"No." His voice became softer.

"But . . . but I was told you had left the Vale to find her," Celine whispered. "To find her and provide care for her injuries. They said she was still alive when she was taken from the bridge. They said she—"

"Who told you these things, Celine?" Arjun asked gently.

She shook her head. Her hands started to shake.

"You must know," he continued, his voice still so gentle. So careful. "You must know how you sound. How . . . foolishly hopeful you sound." Pain rippled across his face. "You must have loved her so much."

Celine nodded. Her trembling worsened. Arjun stepped closer. "I'm all right." She shifted backward and almost stumbled.

"Celine," he said.

"Then Pippa," she began, "then Pippa . . . Pippa is . . . Is Pippa gone?" Her voice broke on the last word, anguish causing the single syllable to crack in two.

Arjun said nothing. He reached for her arm, and again Celine pulled back.

"Celine," he tried once more.

"No," she said. "No." She could not hear him speak. Refused to hear him say it. So Celine walked. She kept walking, the silent Grey Cloaks trailing in her wake. She walked all the way down Dumaine Street, straight to the pier closest to the market, her gaze fixed on the Mississippi.

A scream lodged in her throat. The blood pummeled through her body.

She could fix it. She could fix everything. She only needed the mirror. The mirror Bastien refused to share with her. The mirror he had chosen over their love.

The sound of Celine's scream pierced a hole through the sky. A single, long, pathetic shriek to nothing and no one.

Then she collapsed onto the pier, the lapping waters whispering in her ears.

THE RUINED PRINCE

The door to Nicodemus' chamber opened, lantern light spilling across the darkened floor. Bastien sat on the edge of his uncle's four-poster bed, his elbows braced on his knees as he stared at nothing.

Something slithered across the richly stained wood. A thick ribbon of shadow wound its way toward Bastien's feet.

"I wondered where you'd gone," Bastien murmured.

Toussaint's tongue flicked into the air as the snake glared up at him before hissing, long and low.

Bastien sighed. "That angry, are we?"

"We creatures of the darkness dislike being cast aside and forgotten," Odette said while strolling into the chamber. "The sweet python and I have become bedfellows in your absence. Et-tu jaloux?"

"I didn't cast you or Toussaint aside. Time passes differently among the fey."

"An excuse. Not an explanation. You followed your love without thought. As with all things, there are consequences for your actions. For the decisions you made or failed to make."

Bastien's laughter was bleak. Unamused. "So I am learning."

Odette stood before him, her arms crossed. "What have you done now?" she asked. "Where is Celine?"

"She's gone."

"I can see that. The vachette did not even stay to have a meal with me." Without being invited, Odette sat beside him on the bed. "What did you do? And how do you intend to fix it so she returns?"

Bastien did not reply for a full minute. Thankfully, Odette was patient. A change in her usual disposition. "I don't think she will return," he muttered.

"That's ridiculous. She loves you. You are each a part of the other."

"Not anymore."

"What did you do?" she repeated, even more loudly, her lips puckered.

"I tried to save her. She wouldn't listen to me. Refused to believe what I had to say." He swallowed. "She didn't trust me, Odette."

"You cannot make the woman you love do your bidding, mon coeur," she said gently. "Ah, when will you ever learn this lesson about the fairer sex? We are not designed to be controlled. It is only men who wish it were so."

Bastien stood in a blur, fury flooding his body. "I am not trying to control her, Odette. I— Damn it!" he shouted.

"Don't yell at me, Sébastien. I've been through more than enough for several lifetimes." She stared at him. "Men are the most troublesome, contrary creatures. If you are angry, be angry. If you are sad, be sad. If you wish to cry, then, mon Dieu, *cry. But don't use rage as a last resort. You are allowed to feel more than anger."*

Bastien's features contorted. The ache in his chest flooded his throat. He pushed his fingers into his eyes and shouted the foulest curse word he knew, the dam within him finally broken.

Odette grabbed him. She held him in her arms while his blood tears stained her fine linen shirt. "Ah, my poor boy," she crooned. "My beautiful, brokenhearted Bastien." She sighed. "Celine will come back. I know it. Her love for you is too great."

Bastien shook his head. "You don't understand, Odette." He clenched his jaw. "I don't know what to do." His vision swam as he looked down at her. "Help me."

"Always and forever, dearest."

"Celine's mother . . . is planning to have her killed. I can't be sure why." Bastien recalled the image of Lady Silla swallowing a windstorm of Celine's blood. "But I think it's to prevent Celine from inheriting her powers."

"What?" Odette pulled back, her hands on both his cheeks. "What are you talking about?"

He knew—just as he'd known with Celine—that to make Odette understand, he would have to divulge everything he learned from the mirror, including its existence. Perhaps it had been his fatal error to conceal these truths from Celine only moments prior. But even with her best efforts, Bastien could not trust that someone in the Sylvan Vale might learn of the mirror's whereabouts. If Lady Silla or Lord Vyr or any of the conniving, vicious members of the summer gentry knew what lurked in the heart of winter's mountain, it would be the end of them all.

"Boone," Bastien called out. "And the rest of you vultures outside the door . . . I need you."

Barely a blink passed before all the members of La Cour des Lions glided into Nicodemus' bedchamber in somber silence.

"Well," Madeleine began, her voice filled with resignation, "I fear you have much to explain, Bastien."

Odette demanded, "What do you mean by saying that Celine might die?"

Bastien lifted his gaze to Boone, who nodded once. His brother's support was all Bastien needed to share the tale of the time-traveling mirror. Though he knew Sunan would have objected to him disclosing the existence of such a terrifying and powerful object, Bastien also knew that he could not weather the coming storm without the support of the ones closest to him.

Perhaps it was a vain hope. Nigel, one of his brothers in blood, had betrayed them all not long ago. Things Bastien had always looked upon with surety were instead relegated to uncertainty. Life, as it turned out, was not always black or white. Light or dark. War or peace. Bastien thought about what Odette had said. About how he was allowed to feel more than anger. It sounded so simple. He didn't know why her permission to feel made such a difference.

Bastien was tired of not being able to trust himself. Of being forced into endless mind games and court intrigue. Now was the time to lay it all bare. To ask of and accept help from his family.

The moment Bastien finished recounting the tale, Hortense said, "Well, Bastien, you have—how do the mortals say it?" She snapped her fingers. "Oh yes. You have fucked the chicken."

Odette snorted. "No, my love. That is not what they say."

Hortense lifted a shoulder. "But he has. He should have told Celine everything. He should have said whatever he needed to convince her to stay."

"My sister is not wrong, Bastien," Madeleine said. "Why did you not try to convince her more?"

"I did, Mad," Bastien said. "I told Celine her mother would try to kill her. I asked her to stay here."

"You ordered her to stay here," Odette corrected. "No woman I know would take kindly to that."

"I agree," Madeleine said. "You cannot tell Celine what to do. You must be honest with her, no matter the consequences."

"Go to her," Jae said. "Go to the Vale. Don't go with a mind to fight. Don't even go with a mind to convince. Go to her from a place of love, instead of fear."

All heads turned in his direction, expressions of shared disbelief on each of their faces.

"Are you actually telling me not to fight?" Bastien said. "Will wonders never cease?"

"This is not about reason or right or wrong. When it comes to family, there is often no place for reason. It is about feelings," Jae said. "Today, you failed to speak to her in a language she understands."

"I tried to—"

"No," Jae said. "It wasn't a question. You failed to speak from a place of love. You must give her your trust if you ever expect her to return it in kind."

"I did not think there would come a day when I would agree with Jae so readily on matters of the heart," Odette said. "But he's absolutely right." She blurred toward Bastien and placed a hand on his shoulder. "You're acting like a scorned lover. A lion licking his wounds. Go to her. Tell her how sorry you are, and mean it, no matter her response. Let her know that—regardless of what she chooses—you will love her. But tell her she needs to open her eyes. That she is not safe there."

The last thing Bastien wanted to do was return to the Sylvan Vale.

But he knew his family was right. He would not give up on Celine. He would not be the one to hold fast to his pride. Celine was the girl he loved. The girl he'd died to protect.

He would go to Hell and back if it meant he could bring her home. And if he failed?

Bastien took a steadying breath. If he failed to convince her, he would not take her from the Vale by force. Nor would he disregard her wishes.

But Sébastien Saint Germain was a vampire. A creature of blood and darkness. If there was anything he'd learned from feeding on the lives and thoughts of his victims, he'd learned that he was not above murder. Especially if it meant ridding his world of those who meant to cause harm to the innocent. And most especially if it meant keeping the ones Bastien loved safe.

If it meant protecting Celine from her own mother, Bastien would do whatever he felt necessary. He recalled something his uncle often said: It was better to beg for forgiveness than ask for permission.

All at once, a commotion rumbled beyond the threshold of his uncle's chamber.

Arjun Desai stumbled past Hortense. In his hands, he clutched a page of rolled parchment, a wax seal hanging from its center. Disbelief creased his brow. His fingers shook, the paper crumpling in his grasp.

"She's alive," he rasped.

"What?" Jae said.

"Pippa," Arjun said. "My mother found Pippa. She's alive. She's safe. She's with my mother in the Vale." Tears streaked down his cheeks.

For the first time in a long while, Bastien felt the light of hope warm through his heart.

The Ruined Soul

É milie Saint Germain preferred sleeping alone.

Even when she'd shared a bed with her late husband, Luca, she would wait until he was in a deep slumber to untangle herself from his embrace. Then she would wander the silent halls and seek refuge on a chaise or a cushioned sill.

It wasn't that she disliked company. It was that she found herself weakest in repose. The most susceptible to the things that lurked in the dark. Émilie wanted to be the most dangerous thing in any room. She wanted to know, without a doubt, that she had nothing to fear except fear itself.

Of course, there were also the practical considerations. When she slept alone, there was no chance an errant elbow or foot would lodge into her side. Besides that, she despised the snoring of others. The sleepy mutterings and the foul breath and the overwarm bodies and the stolen blankets.

Alone, she could finally allow her body to relax.

When Bastien was very small, he used to come to Émilie's chamber in the deepest reaches of the night. Émilie would startle from her sleep to find him gazing at her, his favorite stuffed bear, Wolfie, wrapped in his arms.

She'd hated the feeling of being watched while she slept. Hated even more that her little brother had chosen to seek her out instead of their mother or their father. Nevertheless, Émilie would embrace Bastien, tuck him under her covers, and hold him tight. She wouldn't allow herself to sleep until she could feel his limbs soften and his breaths stretch into soft sighs.

Even then, Émilie had hated sharing a bed. But she'd never turned her little brother away.

When Bastien stopped seeking her out in the middle of the night—not long after Wolfie had been relegated to a forgotten pile—Émilie would sometimes steal the little stuffed bear from its dusty enclave and enfold him in her arms.

On the coldest nights, Émilie often missed that bear. It still made her smile to think of its name, which had nothing to do with any animal. Mozart. Bastien had named his bear after his favorite composer, Wolfgang Amadeus Mozart. It was just like him to do that.

She remembered Wolfie's threadbare softness as she tossed about in the dark, dank cave, her body restless. Of late, Émilie often changed to a wolf to sleep. The ground did not seem as hard and the icy breeze did not scrape her skin when she was a werewolf.

She was also convinced that her dreams were less haunting in the form of a beast.

Frustration rippled through her chest. Émilie squeezed her eyes shut.

Since Pippa Montrose's escape, she'd lost standing among the wolves. The morning after burying her beneath the snow,

Michael Grimaldi had gone to her grave, ever the fool throwing himself at another lost cause. He'd returned in a fury, convinced Émilie had disinterred Pippa's body for some nefarious reason. As if grave robbing were worth her time.

It had taken the work of a moment for the werewolves of the mountain to realize what must have happened. They'd tracked Pippa's scent to the border between the winter lands and the summer fields . . . only to discover that someone had blown the bridge there to the heavens.

Someone? Émilie had almost laughed.

Bastien.

Vampires and explosives were like beignets and café au lait.

Traces of powder were everywhere.

Once the wolves had realized that Pippa Montrose was no longer in the Sylvan Wyld, Michael Grimaldi had left to find her, desperate as always for a shred of relevance. Poor, addle-pated sod. The remaining werewolves—shocked by the revelation that a mere mortal had successfully transformed—had returned to their frozen caves, their gazes wary. Whispers died on their lips when they sensed Émilie's presence. They no longer asked her to accompany them to stand watch over that ridiculous cave of horse statues. If she left to hunt or rest, she suspected they were grumbling behind her back. Their problems had grown with her arrival. Acting on her advice, they'd risked their safety and anonymity.

Perhaps it was time to cast her aside. After all, she wasn't *really* one of them.

A tired story Émilie had heard many times before. She

shouldn't care. And she would never admit it. Not to anyone. But she had to retain her standing among them if she was ever going to succeed. And Émilie would not consider herself successful until all the ones responsible for her pain knew what it felt like to be alone with nothing to cling to but memories. With the hollow ache and the burning hatred that never left her heart.

She forced her thoughts to quieten. Breathed deeply, pleading with her body to settle. For her limbs to grow heavy and her mind to become light. She sought a memory buried deep within the past. Something peaceful. Warm. Unburdened.

All at once, she found herself on a sunny July afternoon, sitting in a courtyard with her mother and her brother. A hazy recollection she'd almost lost to sharper remembrances, only now to have the details slam into her full force.

The sweltering sun. The heavy humidity. The smell of baking bread and melting butter. The perfume of the old book in her hands. Paper and oiled leather, with a hint of tobacco smoke.

Her mother was slicing fruit and feeding it to Bastien as Émilie sat with her back to an open gate.

Someone called out to her, the voice soft and light. Like a friend.

A young man with a pleasant face smattered with freckles leaned against the gatepost and let the door swing on its hinges with a lazy whine.

"Hey there," he said with a charming grin. One of his front teeth was slightly chipped. It added to his playful demeanor.

"Hey, yourself." Émilie swung her legs in his direction and rested her open book across her knees.

She knew this boy. Didn't she?

"Our mutual friend has something for you," the boy continued.

Émilie blinked. She looked up at the boy, her hand positioned above her eyes to block out the unrelenting summer sun. "What are you talking about?"

"You like secrets." The boy's grin was slow. Careful. Teasing.

"I do."

He nodded toward Bastien, who remained blissfully unaware of anything around him, his head angled across their mother's lap and fruit juice sliding down his jaw. "He made mistakes."

Émilie's eyes narrowed. "My brother? What kind of mistakes?"

"Mistakes about dreams. And about whom he allows into his mind. Everyone believes themselves to be the exception, rather than the rule."

"What?" Exasperation caused her voice to turn shrill.

"He only heard what he wanted to hear, as they so often do." The boy sighed. "But you hear everything, don't you? Even the things you don't want to hear."

"Are you . . . threatening my brother?"

"Not at all." Laughter tinged his words. "I'm his friend. At least I want to be." He tugged a hand through his sandy, un-kempt hair. "All I'm saying is that your brother made mistakes you won't likely make."

Émilie's fingers pressed into the leather cover of her book. "About a secret?"

The boy nodded. "I can tell you how to help. All you need to do is find a key."

"I'm not interested in these kinds of games." She glared. "But you're welcome to ask Bastien if he is."

"He's already playing," the boy continued. "I think you will play better."

"I don't give a fig about your key or your games." Émilie threw her legs back to their former position and flipped open her book.

"What if the key unlocks a door to the greatest magic—the greatest power—you've ever known?" The boy bent closer, his eyes twinkling. "And what if I knew exactly where to find that key?"

Émilie gritted her teeth. "Then I'd tell you to go get it yourself."

"I see." The boy stood up. "I'll come back tomorrow and ask you again."

"Do what you like," she grumbled, her attention returning to the pages across her lap. When she didn't hear him leaving, Émilie gazed over her shoulder. The gate swung slowly back and forth. The only trace of the affable young man was the faint suggestion of something shimmering in the air around her, causing her skin to tingle.

The greatest magic. The greatest power.

As if anyone could be tempted by such a silly enticement.

Her mind hummed in agreement.

In the deepest well of her dreams, something stirred.

The Ruined Princess

Celine could not sleep.

After she collapsed along the pier, the two Grey Cloaks had insisted she return to the Vale with all haste. She'd argued through her delirium, refusing to comply, until they summoned Yuri, who decided that Celine should convalesce for a short while in the nearby pied-à-terre she once shared with Pippa.

Celine didn't know why she fought the soldiers so vehemently. Perhaps it was to feel as if she retained a thread of control over her life. Everything around her continued to spin. Everything she held dear seemed to slip from her grasp. Loss consumed her from the inside out.

Bastien. And Pippa. It was more than she could bear.

The pain in Celine's chest renewed itself, flowing down her arms until her hands shook from it. Oddly, she had not shed a tear since they'd brought her home. Even in a place with memories of Pippa haunting her from every corner, Celine had remained clear-eyed, despite the dull ache in her heart.

Celine rolled from her bed and stood, the hem of her thin nightshift skimming her knees. If rest eluded her here, it would elude her everywhere. This room should have been a comfort. The flat above her dressmaker's shop—the shop Odette had brokered for her in the heart of the French Quarter—had once represented everything Celine had dreamed of having.

A means of making her way in the world, without the need of a man.

A home of her own. Honest work she loved. And a family she'd chosen.

When had she lost sight of these aspirations? When had it no longer been enough?

She wandered toward the curtains framing the window in her bedchamber. Celine and Pippa had selected them together because the color resembled the dark, waxen hue of magnolia leaves. Something neither young woman had seen until they moved to New Orleans.

Everything about this room was designed to make Celine feel at home and at peace.

But she felt nothing but emptiness. Nothing but defeat.

Something had broken inside her by the pier. She'd left a crucial piece of herself on the banks of the Mississippi. She was no longer the same young woman.

But who stood in her place? And what did she want? Where was that voice she'd lost and found, only to have it misplaced once more like a glove or a hatpin?

A quiet knock resounded at the door to her chamber.

"Celine?" A kind male voice called out her name.

Haroun. Had she summoned him? Had she worried her Grey Cloak guards enough for them to send word to her friend?

Her only true friend in the Vale. For none of the fey could really be trusted.

That sounds like something Bastien would say.

Fury and sorrow clashed in her heart.

"Come in," Celine replied, steeling herself. It would do no good to appear weak.

Haroun entered the chamber soundlessly. The instant Celine saw him, a weight seemed to lift from her shoulders. He stopped just beyond the threshold and closed the door behind him. "Are you . . . all right?"

"No."

With a searching glance, Haroun moved forward. Then halted again. He wore the garments of the fey court. Ivory and umber silk, with a thick belt around his waist. A curved sword dangled from a loop along its side. He studied her face. "What happened?" he asked, his tone kind.

Too kind.

Celine couldn't hear the kindness in Haroun's voice. It would make her cry again. Make her feel weak when she needed to feel powerful. "You should go."

He shook his head. "I don't think that's wise."

"Why?"

"You have the look of someone who is about to do something wild."

Defiance clawed into Celine's throat. She tilted her chin upward. "And what of it? If I wish to do something wild, that is my choice."

"Celine, I would advise against—"

"Don't lecture me. If you came here to lecture me, then leave at once." She cut her eyes his way. "Why did you come? Did Yuri tell you to come?"

"No." Haroun cocked his head, continuing to study her. "Yuri merely sent word that something terrible had happened to you. She said . . . she said your guards reported that you were beside yourself. I came because I wanted to see how you were. And because I wished to speak to you about something important. Something I have struggled to discuss while in the Vale, with its listening ears around us always."

"And you thought now was a good time?" Bleak laughter flew from her lips.

"I have . . . reconsidered, after seeing you," Haroun admitted.

A spark of anger alighted in her chest. "After seeing how *wild* I looked?" She took a step in his direction, her hands balled at her sides. "Are you going to save me now?" she mocked. "A warning, Haroun. I cast aside the love of my life for daring to think he could tell me what to do. I can send you away without a second's hesitation."

Confusion marred Haroun's handsome brow. "You . . . cast aside Bastien?"

Celine nodded. She unclenched her fists, only to feel her fingers tremble. She closed them tightly once more and took another step toward him.

"Celine." Haroun sighed, and the sympathy in his expression almost undid her. "Do— What do you need? What do you want me to do?"

"I want you to—" Celine took two more steps toward him,

until she was an arm's length away. When she looked up at Haroun, an unchecked charge flashed across his beautiful eyes. Like those of a lion or a tiger. A creature of majesty and lethal cunning.

Suddenly Celine's thin nightshift seemed to caress her skin. To draw both their attention to the bare figure beneath it.

Haroun was worried she might do something wild. But Celine saw the wildness mirrored in his own gaze. Perhaps she undid him, too. That same wildness called out from the blood racing through her veins. Bade her to do something completely reckless. To forget that anything else existed beyond these walls. To feel everything and nothing all at once.

"I want you to—" Celine repeated. "Help me forget," she whispered.

Then she threw her arms around Haroun's neck and crashed her lips into his.

It was wild. Wrong. Terrible. But Celine didn't want to do something right. She wanted to do something—anything—to quiet the chaos in her mind.

She willed him to respond to her kiss. She felt the stiffness in his arms. Could sense him questioning. And then Haroun melted into her, his arms wrapping around her body.

Celine's mother had wanted this. She'd wanted Celine to forget Bastien and enjoy herself in the embrace of another. In fact, Lady Silla had cautioned her daughter on several occasions not to tie herself to the first boy who told her what she wanted to hear.

"Young men—both mortal and immortal alike—are fickle,

flighty creatures," Lady Silla had said. "It is much better to enjoy yourself with them for a time and wait until another draws your notice. They want nothing more than to control us. If we keep them wanting something they can never have, we will be the ones in control."

Celine tugged at the collar of Haroun's shirt. The material felt cool to her touch. Otherworldly, just like many of the garments in the Vale.

Haroun cupped her face in one of his hands so he could angle his jaw and deepen their kiss. In the back of her mind, Celine had always known he wanted her. Had known it and enjoyed it, in that ordinary way of a girl relishing the notice of a desirable boy. Bastien had known it, too. Every time Haroun had smiled at her while they pored over ancient texts in their search for the time-traveling mirror. Every time Celine had listened to Haroun speak of his homeland and his family, she had seen the yearning in his expression.

The time-traveling mirror. That cursed thing that Bastien had wedged between them. Only to dare to blame her for it.

Who asked someone to choose between their family and their love?

Celine's fingers caught at the ties around her nightshift. The neckline loosened, and she shrugged the weightless gown off her shoulders.

Haroun stopped kissing her. Caught his breath. Allowed a question to take shape on his face.

"Don't you dare ask me if I want this," Celine murmured in a hoarse voice. "Don't you dare caution me, as if I don't know who

I am." She twisted her fingers in his shirt. "If I want to do something wild, you will not stop me."

Never mind that it didn't feel right or easy or anything like love. It felt like a release. It felt like Celine had control over something, when everything in life appeared to elude her grasp.

Haroun tugged the hem of his shirt over his head in the same instant that Celine unknotted the umber belt from around his slim hips.

She pressed her bare skin against his and reveled in the warmth. His lips wandered lower, pressing into her throat. After the change, Bastien never kissed her there. He said the temptation of her blood was too great.

In truth, Celine had wanted him to kiss her there despite his fear. Thrilled at the thought of the danger. The wildness that lurked inside her bones.

I am better when I am wild. I am not timid or afraid. In my wildness, I am in control.

They fell back onto her bed, and Celine found herself gazing at the ceiling. At the molding she and Pippa had chosen together. The rosettes that crowned each corner. Sadness flooded Celine's veins. She squeezed her eyes shut, forcing herself to surrender to sensation.

When Haroun's teeth lightly grazed her ribs, Celine gasped. She pulled him to her face again, hungry for more of the same distraction. Her right leg hooked around his hip, and she arched into him. He gripped her thigh but did not press any further.

Denying Celine her release.

Irritated and flushed with need, she rolled over and glared

down at him. His tiger eyes were heavy-lidded, and his chest rose and fell at a rapid pace.

"What are you doing?" She narrowed her gaze. "I'm throwing myself at you. Take what we both want."

He tangled his fingers in her hair. "I want it. More than anything in a long time."

"Then why are you stopping?" She gritted her teeth.

"Because you don't want me."

"I would say all the evidence points to the contrary."

Haroun shook his head. "No. You don't want me. You want to forget him. You said as much." He sat up and gently lifted her off him. "I am not a dressing for a wound. Nor am I tool for forgetting." Haroun reached for his shirt and stood from Celine's bed.

Celine swallowed and grabbed the sheets from her bed to cover herself.

"I'm sorry," he said to her without turning around.

Her eyes blurred with unshed tears. "Get out."

Haroun hesitated only a moment. And then he left just as quietly as he'd arrived.

Celine stared at nothing for a time. She let her vision swim as she considered her rumpled bedsheets. As she remembered the feeling of another young man in her arms. The smell of Haroun's skin seemed to linger long after he'd gone. Even if Celine wished it, she could detect no trace of Bastien anywhere. They had not slept together in her room, as she'd been concerned with making Pippa uncomfortable.

After all, Bastien and Celine were not married.

And now they never would be.

Celine donned her wrinkled nightshift, then wandered to her dressing table. For an instant, she pondered what it would feel like to shatter one of the small jars there. To watch it break against the mirror. To see her own reflection destroyed before her very eyes.

Something about smashing a mirror with her own two hands would be immensely satisfying. But if Celine caused a ruckus, the two guards outside—whose names she could not recall—would darken her doorstep in a trice.

Would they report to someone in the Vale that Haroun had visited her? Would rumors abound that he'd left her chamber with his clothing awry? Would word of their wildness reach the ears of Celine's enemies?

Did it even matter anymore?

She ran her fingers across the jars of scented creams and cosmetics situated neatly atop her dressing table. Her attention caught on the ring on her right hand. The one Lady Silla had given her with the power to return to the Vale whenever she wished.

Celine had only used it that one time with Bastien. Would it work again, or were there limits to the magic she held in the palm of her hand?

As much as Celine wanted to believe she belonged in New Orleans, now it felt as if no place welcomed her. No place existed where she was safe from the demons that plagued her. Now her very home itself—her haven—taunted her from every corner.

Not even her bed was safe.

It was time to return to her position beside her mother, so

that she could be there for Lady Silla the way she'd failed to be for Pippa and Odette. Come what may.

Without thought, Celine turned the ring on her finger and willed herself back to her mother's side. She knew the ring was only meant to serve as a direct tare from New Orleans to the Ivy Bower. The first time, it had brought Celine and Bastien from just outside the Hotel Dumaine to the doors outside her mother's private chamber in the blink of an eye, as if one world had simply split into the next.

This time, the magic that carried her from the mortal plane to the world of the fey was not as strong. Not as smooth. Instead of stepping from one reality to another, Celine felt lurched about, as if her stomach had been snared on a fishhook. When she stumbled into the Vale, she spilled onto the floor of the Great Hall like the contents of a purse dumped on a table.

She almost laughed. It was a fitting entrance, in many ways.

It was close to dawn in the Summer Court. Celine made her way through the Ivy Bower, nodding to the occasional guard and stopping to acknowledge the curtsy of a scurrying attendant.

When she arrived outside the entrance to her mother's chamber, none of the guards who typically stood watch were in sight.

Celine's heartbeat quickened. Something was amiss. The lanterns on either side of the arched double doors had been snuffed out, as if to cast an even wider shadow.

Without a second thought, she pushed open the door to her mother's chamber.

Her eyes locked on the sleeping figure of her mother, who continued to lie in golden light, unmoving, her eyes closed, her features serene. No one was standing vigil. Not even a wisp or a goblin attendant. The protective haze encasing Lady Silla's supine body seemed to flicker along its edges as if it had been damaged . . . or intentionally weakened.

Something was terribly amiss.

The hair on the back of her neck stood on end. The skin along her arms prickled, and her pulse raced beneath her nightshift. Celine's senses flew into a state of alertness, as if she had known just at that moment that she was needed back in the Vale. At her mother's side.

She moved through the lantern-lit darkness toward Lady Silla, her bare feet a whisper across the cool stone floor.

All at once, a masked warrior clothed entirely in white dropped from the ceiling. The warrior was thin and pale. Tall and lithe. It was difficult to discern whether they were male or female, or perhaps a liege. Whoever they were, they moved like a shadow dancer.

They faced Celine without a sound. A snow-white hood covered their head and most of their eyes. A mask shielded the rest of their face from their nose past their chin.

With a white-gloved hand, they removed a thin sword from its simple scabbard.

Its handle and its blade were wrought from a piece of solid black iron.

A member of the Winter Court. A dark fey, armed with a weapon meant for killing summer fey.

Like Celine's mother.

"I would yell," Celine said in a soft tone. "But I suppose no one will get to us in time."

"That's the idea," the dark fey said in a rich, low voice.

"You had help."

"If you say so."

Celine looked to the chamber's entrance. "The guards are missing. No one is here to attend to my mother. That is by obvious design."

"Or perhaps it was payment for services rendered."

"And what services were provided?" Celine spoke casually, her eyes studying the space around her for any kind of weapon she might use. Her heart should have been thrumming in her chest, but it pounded in a steady beat. The blood heated her veins, as though it had been ignited like a match.

I am alive. I am not afraid. I will fight to the death to protect what is mine.

The voice trilled from deep within her bones.

Perhaps it was there always, ready and waiting for when she needed it. For when she deigned to listen. For when she wished to be wild and force all the other voices to fade into nothingness.

The only voice that matters is mine.

Celine's senses were focused and attuned to everything around her.

"I'm not here to talk." The dark fey brandished the black iron sword. Their eyes narrowed with purpose. "Blood betrayer."

Celine grabbed a tall lantern from where it stood beside her mother's bed. Then she shifted into position between the dark fey and the Lady of the Vale.

The dark fey laughed. "If this weren't so tragic, I would admire your effort."

"Did Lord Vyr send you?" Celine held the long golden taper by its top, planning to use its base as a bludgeon.

The dark fey canted their head, the white hood shifting along their forehead to reveal what appeared to be brown eyes and pale skin, along with a shock of red-gold hair. "If he did, I would not tell you."

"If I'm going to die, does it matter?"

"Don't try to be clever. It will only annoy me, which will not make what happens next more pleasant for you." The dark fey glanced at Lady Silla's silent form. "It's a pity you interrupted me before I could wake her up. I would like her to bear witness to your death. It would be fitting." Striking out with the iron blade, the dark fey blurred into motion.

Celine swung the long taper with all her might. Sparks exploded when the gold struck the iron, a clang echoing through the chamber. The force from the blow reverberated up Celine's arm, almost causing her teeth to chatter. Quick as a bolt of lightning, the dark fey changed course, aiming a downward strike at Celine's head.

Celine had no kind of formal training when it came to fencing. All she had was gumption and the will to live, no matter the cost. She swung again, trying to parry the blow. Though she missed, the momentum carried her out of the iron blade's immediate path. It caught instead on her skirt, slicing through the bottom half in a single clean blow.

Her heart stuttered at the sight, but still Celine felt a thrill course through her veins. She took a cue from the dark fey and decided to attack, charging with the base of the long taper, hoping to catch her mother's attacker off guard.

The dark fey dodged the blow easily, rolling across the floor and unfurling into a standing position with the ease of an acrobat. "I'll admit, you are surprising."

"You said not to bother talking," Celine replied, her chest heaving from the effort.

"I also told you not to be clever."

"What is your point?"

The dark fey straightened. "You were never the target." Then they turned in place and swung their blade at Lady Silla's recumbent figure.

Panic gripped Celine from the insides. In all her maneuvering, she'd failed to realize that—with every attack—the dark fey had managed to get closer to the Lady of the Vale.

A strangled cry on her lips, Celine threw herself at the dark fey, leaping across the room like a feral cat. The sheer force of her attack surprised the dark fey, causing them both to trip and the iron blade to catch on the edge of Lady Silla's bed.

The black metal blazed brightly as it penetrated the protection shield and sliced Lady Silla's arm. Celine's mother seemed to flinch, her body lurching. A trickle of bright red blood followed in the blade's wake.

"You're making me angry, halfblood." The dark fey tried to grab hold of the sword's hilt once more, but Celine grasped their wrist in both hands and proceeded to smash the dark fey's fingers into the floor repeatedly. They both yelled when the dark fey rolled over, trying to gain the upper hand by pinning Celine to the stone.

The dark fey kneed Celine in the stomach just as Celine punched her attacker in the face. A portion of their white mask shifted, revealing high cheekbones. The dark fey slapped Celine across the jaw, knocking her backward.

Celine's head struck the marble floor. For an instant she saw stars in a looming blackness. When her attacker tried to stand, Celine deliberately tangled their feet together to knock them to the floor. The dark fey's blade slid across the cool stone. Celine lunged for it, just as the dark fey twisted in the same direction, reaching for the weapon as well.

They both gripped it in their hands. Celine could feel the sharp edge of the blade cutting into the skin of her palms, but she would not let go. They rolled across the floor. The dark fey was stronger than Celine, but she refused to let go or stop moving. To yield was to die, and that was something Celine would never do, not without a fight.

A lion, to the bitter end.

Finally the dark fey moved one gloved hand to Celine's throat. She tried to pry the iron blade from their grasp, but the dark fey pressed on her windpipe until Celine could feel the air being squeezed from her lungs. She kicked and bucked, thrashing like a fish caught in a net.

"I regret that you have to die," the dark fey said in a rasping voice—the only sign that they, too, had been forced to fight. "You are much stronger and braver than anyone gives you credit for being."

Celine coughed, outrage flooding her chest.

All at once, the floor beneath them shook. The windows behind Celine blew open in a gust of air and a flurry of leaves. A vine darted toward the dark fey's body, taking hold of the hand that pressed Celine's throat to the floor. Before either of them could react, the vine snapped the dark fey's arm, breaking the bone with a hideous crack.

The dark fey yelled. Celine scrambled backward, gasping for air, the chamber still vibrating. Tears had welled in Celine's eyes, making it difficult to focus. More vines raced from the open window, darting toward the dark fey, grabbing them by their unbroken arm and both ankles. The vines suspended the fey in the air. A final vine tore the mask off the dark fey's face.

"How . . . dare . . . you?"

Celine whipped around, coughs still sputtering from her body. Her mother gripped the side of her bed with one hand, fighting to stand, rage pulling at all her features. Her other hand was positioned in front of her, her fingers twisting and writhing as she controlled the vines with her magic.

Lady Silla pushed herself toward the nearby wall and struggled to stand straight. Her body shook, but she managed to take mincing steps toward the dark fey, blood trickling down her arm.

"How . . . dare . . . you?" Lady Silla repeated, her voice stronger.

The dark fey said nothing.

Celine stood. She realized when she faced the dark fey that her attacker was a fey girl who appeared only a few years older than she was.

"She won't tell you anything, Umma," Celine croaked. She cleared her throat and made her way to her mother's side to help her.

"She's right," the fey girl said, her reply calm. Too calm. "I won't say anything, no matter what you do to me."

"You're—a winter fey," the Lady of the Vale said. "You don't need to say or do anything for me to know your orders and your intentions."

"I think Lord Vyr might be in league with her," Celine interjected. "Someone has orchestrated to have the hall cleared of guards and no one watching over you for this exact time."

Lady Silla straightened, her features expressionless. "Rest assured, I will speak with Vyr before dawn breaks." She raised her right hand and twisted her fingers in a clockwise direction, almost as though she were dancing. Her palm rotated with the motion until it was facing upward.

The vines around the winter fey's wrists and ankles tightened. They pulled taut, causing obvious strain. A low oath passed from the dark fey's lips as she winced, the pain on her face unmistakable.

"I will give you one last chance to save yourself," Lady Silla said. "Tell me who conspired with you."

The winter fey feigned a smile. "Interesting."

Lady Silla twisted her fingers again in a slow half turn. The fey girl gasped.

"Answer me," the Lady of the Vale pressed. "Who is orchestrating these attempts on our court? Tell me, and you will meet a swift death."

"Lies are unbecoming, Lady Silla," the fey said through clenched teeth. "Especially of a fairy queen."

Discomfort wrapped around Celine's insides. Even though this girl had just tried to kill her, Celine did not feel comfortable witnessing torture. It felt . . . wrong.

"Answer the question," Celine said, imbuing her words with sternness in the hopes the fey girl would comply.

"The Lady of the Vale will not show me mercy," the fey girl retorted. "So why would I offer her any?"

"Fey cannot lie," Celine said. "Tell her what she wants to know, and she will spare you."

"She never said she would spare me."

"Umma?"

Lady Silla held her hand aloft. "The wretch is right," she said. "I won't spare her. But I will end her pain."

"I am of winter," the girl said. "Pain has been my life." She angled her head to look at Celine. "But I will answer one question you ask me, Celine Rousseau."

Surprise flared across Celine's face. But she did not pause to ponder why this would-be assassin wished to address her, rather than her mother.

"Who sent you?" Celine asked. "Tell us who is the one

responsible, and you will know no more pain." Even as she said the words, doubt crept beneath her skin.

Her mother had already harmed the girl. Had already resorted to torture.

Lady Silla nodded. "This I promise you."

The fey girl smiled again, a single tear caressing her cheek. "Sébastien Saint Germain."

"What?" Celine shouted. "What are you—"

"You promised," the fey girl replied, her voice scathing, her ire directed at Lady Silla. "If I did what you asked, you swore to—"

The rest of the winter fey's reply was cut short by the sound of her neck snapping. All the rest of the vines relaxed as her body slid to the stone floor.

Lady Silla's shoulders slumped. Celine caught her before she, too, collapsed. Shock reverberated through her. It wasn't possible for Bastien to have sent an assassin to murder her mother. He wouldn't do that. He couldn't do that. Could he?

Celine recoiled at the thought. But fey couldn't lie.

"Like you, the girl is an ethereal," Lady Silla said, as if she could hear Celine's thoughts. "It's possible she was not telling the truth." Sympathy laced her words. "Ethereals can lie when full-blooded fey cannot."

Relief coursed through Celine's veins. Her stomach unclenched. "So it's possible someone wished to blame Bastien for this all along." Celine paused, trying to steady herself from the slew of recent shocks. "How did you know she is an ethereal?"

"Her ears. They are not even the slightest bit pointed," Lady Silla said, her voice hoarse from disuse. "It is also not unusual for an ethereal to work in the capacity of an assassin. They often do not find a place for themselves at court . . . and their ability to lie makes them ideal for tasks involving subterfuge."

Celine said nothing for a time.

"You were frightened . . . because you believed it might be true," Lady Silla said gently.

Tears welled in Celine's eyes. She brushed them away with the back of her hand. "He would never do that, Umma."

"I agree with you," Lady Silla said. "My most fervent hope is that his love for you remains steadfast." Her smile was kind. "I may not have won the vampire's heart, but I have no doubt of his feelings for you. He would die rather than cause you pain."

The tears threatened again. Celine bit them back. Swallowed. She wanted to tell her mother what had happened. A part of her longed to have the comfort of a mother who could console her. But if Lady Silla knew that Celine and Bastien's love had reached a point of no return, then her mother might ask why. Or start to question his loyalty.

Just as Celine had considered it, for the briefest moment.

"My dear child," Lady Silla said, her brow furrowing. "Is something troubling you?"

Celine shook her head. "Only that you are still standing. You should rest."

"I've rested long enough."

"We should call for the guards. It's possible there is more than one assassin."

"I doubt that," Lady Silla said. "Ethereal assassins like her tend to work alone. But we do need to be vigilant." She paused in thought for a moment. "Quickly retrieve my cloak. You and I will journey through my private tare together."

"Where are we going?"

"It is time I spoke with Lord Vyr." Lady Silla's eyes narrowed. "I need to look him in the eye when I demand answers."

THE RUINED SON

Arjun Desai was twelve years old when he decided he'd had enough of love.

Following the events of a particularly trying afternoon, he'd announced to his mother and the two peris attending their evening meal that he would never pursue the affection of another girl again. Nor would he foster any meaningful relationships with his peers in school. For too long, he'd tried to become one of them. To learn and act and live as if he were a member of the fey gentry.

No more, he'd vowed that day. Loving any fey meant existing in a perpetual state of fear.

When General Riya had asked him what happened to bring about this realization, Arjun had refused to disclose any details. The last thing he needed was for his mother to accost or threaten anyone on his account.

Arjun was already enough of a target. He was the only remaining ethereal in their year. There had been another girl when they were younger, but one day, she'd stopped attending class. When he'd asked after her, the teacher and his schoolmates had ignored him, as if they had no idea about whom he was speaking.

Arjun had spent two weeks imagining all the terrible things that might have happened to this poor girl.

He had not thought about her—or the girl who'd broken his heart that afternoon by the lake—for many years.

But it was true. Philippa Montrose was not Arjun Desai's first love. She was the first girl he'd ever fallen in love with, of course. But not the first girl he'd ever loved.

The first girl he'd ever loved was fey. Lord Vyr's youngest cousin. Her name was Antiope. Arjun had fallen in love with her dark hair, rich mahogany eyes, and lovely brown skin, physical attributes that were rare among the Summer Court, where many of the gentry were lighter skinned. Many of the influential families in the gentry possessed eyes and features reminiscent of mortals from East Asia or Eastern Europe. Very few of them reminded Arjun of home. Antiope did. As a lost, lonely boy longing for India, Antiope's beauty had brought to mind his father's people. The world he'd left behind.

Both Arjun and Antiope were young when they met. It was in school, when children of the gentry were not yet old enough to declare their interests. All those in their year studied everything together. Painting, sculpture, musical instruments, dance, song, alchemy, sea dragon riding, fencing, garden cultivating . . . they learned them all, until they were of a mind to pursue a particular skill to a higher level of proficiency.

Arjun had just reached his twelfth mortal year. Antiope

appeared to be around the same age as he did. Fey children matured at a similar rate to mortal children, though fey stopped aging once they reached adulthood. In this way, a member of the gentry could appear to possess no more than twenty human years and still have lived for centuries.

That particular class on that terrible afternoon was taught by a satyr. It involved studying the flora and fauna along the edge of the forest, to find mushrooms that were able to hypnotize someone when brewed in a clear tea or a type of stinging nettle that could be used to numb the pain of an injury, provided it was ground into a paste and heated to a certain temperature.

The afternoon Arjun decided to confess his love for Antiope, he'd wandered close to her. His courage had waned on at least three occasions prior, and he was determined to impress the young fey girl. It didn't matter that her family was among the highest-ranking members of the fey gentry. After all, Arjun's mother was General Riya. Second only to the Lady of the Vale herself.

Antiope would not be insulted to hear how much Arjun admired her. Though he was an ethereal, he'd demonstrated proficiency in several of the skills they'd learned thus far. He was a decent fencer. His aptitude for alchemy was unmatched. He could strum a lute rather well, or at least that was what he thought.

And Antiope? She was among the loveliest of all the fey girls in their year. But Arjun did not admire her just for her beauty. Antiope also possessed the most glorious singing voice. And

Arjun had been meaning to tell her for quite some time how much he enjoyed hearing her sing.

So he wandered close to her and overheard her speaking to her friends about how much she loved butterflies.

The next day, Arjun brought her a bouquet. He presented it to her as the class tarried beside the edge of Lake Lure that afternoon.

He'd been very careful with the bouquet that morning, for it was not an ordinary arrangement of blossoms. In fact, he'd chosen these flowers for the very reason that they attracted butterflies.

There were two butterflies nestled among the sweet-smelling petals. One was lovely, with wings of orange, black, and gold. The other butterfly had a furry body with blue-and-red wings and overlarge antennae. Perhaps it was not as lovely as the other, but its color and its shape charmed Arjun. It looked soft and gentle, rather than possessing the sharpened beauty of its companion.

Antiope stared at the bouquet Arjun had presented to her.

"You said you liked butterflies." Arjun offered Antiope what he hoped was a self-assured grin, despite the knots forming in his stomach.

Antiope arched a brow. "Were you spying on me?"

"No," Arjun said, his eyes going wide. "I merely overheard that you liked them. So I thought I would give you some. Aren't they beautiful?"

Antiope tilted her head to one side. "They are beautiful. Why would you give them to me?"

"Because . . . because I think you are beautiful, too."

"Do you?" she said with a slow smile. "Why?"

"Because . . . you just are."

"Is it my hair?"

"Your hair is nice."

"It's like yours, I suppose. Maybe that's why you like it. It makes you feel as though you are as beautiful as I am."

"No." Arjun shook his head. "I don't think anyone is as beautiful as you."

"Do you like me?"

Arjun swallowed. "Yes."

Antiope placed her index finger beside the blue-and-red butterfly with the fuzzy body and the large antennae. She waited until the tiny creature crawled onto her finger. Then she lifted it into the light to study it.

"This one is funny-looking," she mused. "Like a caterpillar that failed to outgrow its ugliness."

"I thought it was beautiful because it was different."

"Oh, I agree," Antiope said, her smile curving up one side of her face. "It is beautiful. But not because it's different." She glanced toward him, and Arjun's heart missed a beat.

Without warning, Antiope caught the small butterfly in her hands and tore off its wings.

Her smile still serene, she let the pieces fall to the ground. The butterfly with the broken wings struggled, its panic growing as it realized what had happened.

"Why?" Arjun asked, anger overcoming him. "Why would you do such a thing?"

"Because I think ruined things are much more beautiful. Don't you?"

"No." Fury heated his veins as he stared at Antiope. "I don't."

"What was once ordinary has now become fascinating." Antiope gazed down at the panicked butterfly, her expression contemplative. "I think being fascinating is the best quality of all." She looked up at him. "Don't you?"

"I don't think you have to be broken to be fascinating."

Antiope laughed. "Well, I suppose we can find out." Her dark eyes gleamed. "Do you want to see which one of us is right?"

"No," Arjun said, his posture turning wary.

"Oh, come on." Antiope smiled again. She leaned closer to whisper in his ear. "Why don't we both try this tea together?"

Her breath tickled the skin on the side of his neck. "I don't think that's a good idea."

She frowned. "But, Arjun," she whispered, "I like you, too. And if we both like each other, then shouldn't we do things together?"

His pulse quickened at her words. "I . . . suppose so."

"Then we can find out which one of us is better with ruined wings."

Arjun hadn't understood what Antiope meant at the time. Or perhaps he had, and he wished to ignore it. Maybe he'd wanted to believe that a girl who sang like an angel couldn't possibly act like a devil. He didn't know why he'd failed to take into consideration the cruel streak running through the fey of the summer gentry.

It had been a grievous error, to be sure.

When Arjun had returned home that night, it was with his own kind of broken wings. Three of his toes were fractured. His ribs were bruised or maybe even cracked. The third and fourth fingers of his left hand were difficult to bend. He walked with a limp.

But he refused to allow his mother to see his pain. He changed his clothes. Wrapped his toes in spider gauze. And hid the wounds to his rib cage. Because if she asked him, he would have to admit that he had injured himself. That he alone was responsible for his wounds.

That Antiope had won, after all. When all her friends and most of their schoolmates had laughed with gleeful abandon and watched Arjun with hungry interest in their eyes—instead of the bored disdain he'd become accustomed to seeing of late—he'd been forced to agree that his injuries had, in fact, made him fascinating to them.

He was now the butterfly with ruined wings. He could not fly even if he wanted to.

Arjun held Pippa's hand tightly.

It had been a difficult, painful lesson for him. But Arjun had learned it at twelve.

Offering his heart to anyone meant opening himself up to pain of the self-inflicted sort.

He was learning it again tonight, in his mother's home deep within the glen.

Pippa stirred. Arjun sat up. Her eyelids fluttered, then opened.

"W-water," she croaked.

Arjun helped her drink, one hand beneath her neck to lift her. She felt feverish to the touch, her cheeks red and her blue eyes overbright. He watched her drink, her hands shaking as she tried to take hold of the cup.

There was so much he wanted to say. But it didn't matter. Not now. The only emotion Arjun could feel in his heart was gratitude. It did not matter that the world of the fey had done her irreparable harm. She was not ruined. Not at all. She was Pippa, and she was whole and alive and beautiful as always.

Whatever else had happened, Arjun knew they could weather it.

Pippa fell back against the linen pillow. "Do you know?" she whispered.

Arjun nodded, then took her hand.

She swallowed, unable to look his way. "Was it a nightmare?"

He shook his head. "I'm afraid not, meri pyaari."

She shuddered. "Then . . . what am I supposed to do?" Tears welled in her eyes. "Am I dangerous now? Will I . . . hurt anyone?"

"No." Arjun wrapped her hand in both of his, his motions slow. Gentle.

"That's not true," Pippa said, her attention still fixed on the ceiling above her. "When I was . . . not myself, I attacked a small creature." She paused as the tears started to fall. "If it hadn't been faster than me, I would have killed it."

"Pippa, I—"

"I couldn't control myself," she sobbed quietly. "I couldn't stop myself from changing into a beast. And I couldn't stop myself from trying to kill something much smaller and weaker than I."

"You were in shock," Arjun said. "You almost died."

"I did die," Pippa said. "I think."

His forehead creased. "I thought only vampires died and were reborn. I didn't know that this happens to"—he hesitated for a beat—"werewolves as well."

"A werewolf," Pippa said. "A wyldwolf."

"One and the same, depending on your world."

She turned her head to gaze upon him in earnest. "I'm sorry."

Anger sparked in his chest. "You have no reason to be sorry. You did nothing wrong."

"If I hadn't been so foolish, this would not have happened to me."

"This happened to you because of me." A muscle in Arjun's jaw rippled. "The werewolves attacked you because they saw how much you mattered to me. How much I love you."

"Your mother . . . can barely look me in the eye. She disliked me before. Now I suspect she despises me."

"She's been like that with me since I was a boy. Nothing has changed. It wouldn't matter if she never wanted to see you again. We are penguins, right?"

The hint of a smile touched Pippa's lips. "Yes. We are."

"Wherever you go, I go."

"That's a verse from the Bible." Her smile widened.

"Is it?"

"The book of Ruth. 'Whither thou goest, I will go.'"

"*Whither*?" Arjun grinned. "You English never cease to amuse."

"I guess it does sound strange."

"But not as buggered as *goest*." Arjun made a face.

Soft laughter burst from Pippa's mouth. She caught herself, her features sobering. "I don't know how to do this, Arjun."

"I know," he said. "But I think I have a solution."

She waited.

"I think we should speak with the Grimaldis back home in New Orleans," he said.

"Michael's family? Because he is a werewolf?"

He nodded. "The Grimaldis are from a long line of werewolves. They should be able to help you."

"They could teach me how to control it?"

"I should think so."

Pippa reached for the water again and took another sip. "When it happened, it was almost as if the moon caused me to change. As if it reached out to me even below the ground, its light triggering the bones in my body to shift and some strange power in my veins to ignite."

"There is a saying I heard when I was a boy, when older fey lads would try to scare the younger ones with stories of werewolves. How these beasts of winter would catch us and eat us if we tried to wander into the Wyld on our own. The moon rules two things: the tide and their teeth. If you don't want to get eaten by wolves or perish beneath the sea, then learn to control the moon."

Pippa gnawed at the inside of her cheek. "If I were to stay in the Sylvan Vale—where the moon never rises—is it possible that I might not have to change again?"

"I don't know." Arjun frowned. "But I don't think the answer is to deny who you are or what you've become. Trust me." His expression turned morose. "I've spent enough of my life doing just that to know what a waste of time it is."

"It is good to hear you say this, Arjun," his mother interjected from behind him.

Arjun stood at once, facing her, his fists at his sides.

His mother held up both her hands. "I did not mean to startle you. I only wished to check on Philippa's progress." She arched a brow. "Please stop looking at me as if you are about to attack, my son." Clearing her throat, General Riya attempted to convey a sense of ease.

It was like watching a goat try to dance ballet.

Arjun forced himself to relax. At the very least, he would not be responsible for making Pippa feel any more out of place. In truth, he had not meant to take on a posture of defensiveness, but his mother's voice often did that to him. As if he needed to choose in an instant whether he wished to fight or to flee.

"I apologize," Arjun said. "My nerves are frayed."

"Of course," General Riya said. "As are mine." Her stride uncharacteristically awkward, Arjun's mother crossed the chamber toward the bed. "Recent times have been trying to us all, have they not?" After hesitating a beat, she reached toward Pippa to tuck a loose blond curl behind her ear. Arjun almost slapped her hand away. That was how little he trusted her not to do harm. But this gesture of tenderness for Pippa? Affection for a mortal girl? It almost knocked the wind from Arjun's lungs.

Never in his life had he seen his mother touch anyone with that kind of warmth.

Disbelief settled on his face. "What are you playing at, Mother?"

"Arjun," Pippa scolded, though her voice was not unkind. "Your mother has been so good to me. Please don't be unpleasant."

"Listen to your wife," his mother said in a stern tone, her features hardening into an expression much more fitting of her personality. "Since you refuse to heed what I have to say, she's the only voice of reason that remains."

"You're not planning on throwing her from your doorstep for the great sin of being a werewolf?" He thought a moment. "Or perhaps she is to be used as a bargaining chip? Some kind of prisoner swap?"

A strange look settled on his mother's features. If Arjun did not know her better, he would think she was hurt. But he also knew better than to think a leopard could change its spots.

"I . . . know how much you care about her," General Riya said, her words stilted.

"Wonderful," Arjun countered. "Now, how do you plan to use that against me?"

"I would never do that to you."

"Isn't it against the rules for a summer fey to love a winter beast?" he continued.

"It is," General Riya said. "But she is not just a winter beast. She is your wife first. She is part of our family now. The ceremony was witnessed by our court and acknowledged by Lady Silla."

Something unspooled in Arjun's chest. A tension he had not realized had taken root. He said nothing as he stared at his mother.

"You always believed I did not care," General Riya said. "But I always worried I cared too much. It is why I kept my distance. To ensure that no one would harm you in an attempt to control me." She leaned toward Pippa to offer her more water. When Pippa smiled up at her with unmistakable gratitude, Arjun's mother returned the gesture.

Again, the sight caught Arjun off guard.

He could not silence the suspicions mounting inside him. It was rare for him to encounter a fey who was kind without reason, especially to an ethereal like him. Rarer still for his mother to show affection, even to her own child.

And now she was showing a mortal girl both kindness and affection? The same mortal girl who'd trapped her only son into marriage, against General Riya's wishes and advice?

No. This smelled like shit to Arjun. And if it smelled like shit and looked like shit, it was probably shit.

"As soon as Pippa is well enough to travel, I want to take her back to New Orleans," Arjun announced.

His mother straightened. "Why? Our healers are far more skilled than those butchers in the mortal world."

"Do I need a reason?"

General Riya's cheeks hollowed. "I only hoped that you both might stay longer. I"—she hesitated—"I would like you to stay."

Disbelief stole onto Arjun's face once more. "And I would like a doublet stitched from golden thread, with the queen's stolen diamonds for buttons."

"Arjun is taking me back to New Orleans because I asked to go, Mother," Pippa said.

"Mother?" Arjun's eyes widened, his mouth agape.

"I see," General Riya said, ignoring her son. "Is there a specific reason?"

"I wish to speak with the Grimaldi family," Pippa said.

"I see," General Riya repeated. Realization seemed to dawn on her then. "You wish to speak with them about your change in situation. So they might educate and instruct you."

Pippa nodded.

"You should have said as much, Arjun." General Riya glared at her son askance.

He snorted. "Because it's definitely your business to know what we are doing."

"Your mother saved me," Pippa said. "I think the least we owe her is an explanation."

"The world has gone mad," Arjun grumbled.

"No," his mother replied. "I have only just realized how easy it would be for me to lose the few things I hold dear." A shadow fell across her face. "When Lady Silla said she wished to bring her half-mortal daughter back to the Vale, I didn't understand why. Our history is littered with warnings from our past. To bring her daughter—who might one day challenge her for control over the Summer Court, as has happened before—back to the Vale felt reckless and indulgent. I did as she asked because that is what I always do." Her voice lowered. Became more subdued. "But I never thought I would see a time when Lady Silla would be struck down." She looked to Arjun once more. "There might be a time when I, too, am struck down by forces beyond my control. And I would want you to take my place at court, Arjun. You . . . and your family."

"Alas," Arjun said. "I cannot do that for you."

"At least . . . please tell me you would consider coming back to court once in a while."

"No," Arjun said. "I will not."

"Arjun," Pippa said softly. "Try to be a little kinder. Mother has been gracious to me. Far more gracious than I can recall my own mother being. I don't know what would have happened if another member of the Summer Court had found me along the embankment. They might have . . ."

Arjun's eyes widened. He knew without it being said that if the Grey Cloaks had found a werewolf along the banks of the Sylvan Vale, the wolf would have likely been drawn and quartered. With well-dressed bystanders cheering them on.

Pippa swallowed, her features beseeching. "I appreciate your mother."

Arjun cleared his throat. "Yes. Thank you." He looked toward General Riya, his movements stiff. "Thank you for keeping Pippa safe."

General Riya nodded and averted her gaze.

At least that reaction felt more in keeping with the woman he'd known for most of his life.

"Nevertheless, I plan to take Pippa to see Michael Grimaldi's family in New Orleans as soon as she is well enough to travel," Arjun announced.

A line formed across General Riya's brow. "And there is nothing I might do to persuade you to stay? To help try and broker some kind of agreement between summer and winter?"

"Any kind of agreement in question would heavily favor the Sylvan Vale, would it not?" Arjun asked. "Or else it would never be considered."

General Riya exhaled. "That is what both sides will try to do, Arjun."

"Then I would rather not be party to it." He leveled his eyes on hers. "Especially in light of the atrocities I witnessed along the riverbank."

Her features turned cold. "I see."

"No. But I hope you will someday, Mother."

"Just as I hope you will see how much I have truly cared, all along."

Arjun shook his head, unable to cast aside his disbelief. "Do me a favor, then. Care less. It might not cause me as much pain."

Surprise made his mother's eyes go wide. "Thank you for saying that, Arjun."

"What?"

"If I can still cause you pain, it is because there is affection in your heart for me. It gives me reason to hope."

"That . . . is fey nonsense of the first order." Arjun blinked. Sarcastic laughter flew from his lips. "But you're welcome, Mother. Children are supposed to bring the light of hope into their parents' lives."

"You are mocking me." General Riya didn't seem angered by it. Merely aggrieved. Which unseated Arjun yet again. It was unlike her to be moved by anything he did or said.

"Only a little," he muttered.

Pippa chewed on her lower lip as she watched this stilted, odd exchange. Then she reached for his hand.

Her touch was a balm to Arjun's anxious heart. Gratitude warmed through him. What Pippa said before was right. No matter how oddly his mother behaved or how much he despised spending another minute in the Vale, he knew he should be thanking every lucky star in his sky that she had kept Pippa safe.

Come to think of it . . . there were no stars in the sky in the Sylvan Vale. Another reason for them to leave this wretched place with all haste. But Arjun supposed he could show his mother the smallest measure of gratitude while they waited for Pippa to recuperate enough for them to travel to New Orleans.

"I . . . apologize." Arjun cleared his throat. He could count on one hand the times he'd offered his regrets to his mother. It almost made him laugh. He'd inherited a few things from General Riya. Awkwardness in the face of deep emotions and an unwillingness to apologize unless pressed to do so.

General Riya took a steadying breath. "Thank you for your apology."

"We will stay in the Vale a few more days before taking our leave," Arjun reiterated. "Your kindness and hospitality will not be forgotten."

Her features softened. "Then I shall remain hopeful."

Arjun wanted to argue. But he looked at Pippa. And held his tongue.

Another first. Perhaps a leopard could change its spots after all.

THE RUINED PRINCESS

Though the sun had not yet crested the trees, the Summer Court was abuzz with the news.

Bleary-eyed members of the gentry had been roused from their sleep. Murmurs rippled through the marble halls and the soughing tree branches. Fey lieges and lords and ladies stumbled from their beds in a state of half dress, sweet wine staining their lips.

The whole of the Sylvan Vale appeared stunned.

Lord Vyr had been taken into custody by the Grey Cloaks. A formal inquiry into his recent actions was to be made in front of the entire court. One of the highest lords of the fey gentry was to be questioned by none other than the Lady of the Vale.

The charge?

High treason.

Shocked whispers followed this announcement. As members of the court filtered into the Ivy Bower, armed soldiers began marching through the halls. Soon, entry was barred to places that had once been open to carousing of all sorts. Listening ears appeared to be stationed everywhere.

A sense of ominousness lurked around every corner.

If one of their own could be charged with treason, then it seemed fitting to be mindful of one's words and actions. At least for the time being.

Celine waited in the shadows behind a wall of shimmering silver drapes framing the Horned Throne. From a distance, she could hear the endless stream of muttered questions and shared disbelief. The news of Lord Vyr's arrest even had the floating wisps gathering in the oak branches high above the Great Hall.

From her silhouetted vantage, Celine also learned that a gathering of this sort had not happened for an age. Her pulse raced faster and faster like a spooked horse. The sense of uncertainty seemed to deepen the longer they were held in suspense.

Through a parting in the silver curtains, she watched Haroun al-Rashid arrive to the Great Hall. A furrow formed across his brow, as if he were troubled. He leaned against the trunk of a large oak tree, mindful to keep himself in shadow and beyond notice.

After what happened this morning in her mother's chamber, Celine had considered confiding in Haroun. But the memory of last night prevented her from doing so. She did not feel ashamed. She felt . . . bruised. She could no longer trust herself around him. If Haroun didn't need to know, Celine thought it was best not to tell him, though it meant keeping her only real friend in the Vale at arm's length. Losing both Bastien and Pippa in the matter of a few days had made her uncertain of everything and everyone, even herself.

Trust had become quite a commodity.

At first, Celine had argued with her mother about the necessity of holding a formal inquiry. The Lady of the Vale was still recovering from blood loss. Weaker than she should appear, especially before her court. The matter of Vyr's guilt should be handled in private, at least for now. But when Celine and Lady Silla attempted to seek him out personally by tare, he had been unavailable. Indeed, Vyr was nowhere to be found, even in his own home. His spouse, Liege Sujee, claimed to be unaware of his whereabouts.

Though Celine had doubted Sujee's claims, she knew fey could not lie. But she also knew how skilled the fey of the Summer Court were at skirting the truth. Often they would offer an answer to another question not yet asked. Or counter with a query of their own. An adept member of the gentry could even trick you into believing something *might* have happened, rather than admitting it or denying it, full stop.

And if Lord Vyr had enough time? Perhaps he could manufacture a plausible alibi. One that did not necessitate him lying outright. The fey were notorious for such devices.

When Lord Vyr failed to respond to Lady Silla's summons, the Lady of the Vale decided there was a need for formal proceedings. One in which all the members of court were invited to bear witness. If Vyr did not make himself available by midday, Lady Silla declared she would strip the lord of all his titles, influence, and holdings.

One step above banishing him from the Summer Court entirely.

Despite having to wait for Lord Vyr's attendance, the excitement in the Ivy Bower continued to mount. The closer it drew to midday, the more the anticipation grew. Drinks were passed around liberally, and several of the gentry managed to wrangle an assortment of ripe fruit and flagons of ale. Flaky pastries crumbled to pieces on the slightest breeze, tingeing the air with the scent of butter and spices.

Then—just before the sun reached its apex in the lace of branches above—Lord Vyr strode into the Great Hall dressed in gold-trimmed finery. Ermine lined the collar of his gilded mantle. On his head he wore a band of antlers. It was fashioned in such a way that some of the antlers pointed downward, but several rose from the top of his head in an unsubtle nod to a crown.

Celine had never seen him wear a headdress like this before. It was, of course, far from a coincidence. Even by his manner of dress, Lord Vyr indicated his desire to fight.

But to what end? The Summer Court would never side with him. Not while the power of the Horned Throne rested in the Lady of the Vale's blood and that of her kin.

Celine's nerves vibrated through her body.

The whispers died down to a hush as Lord Vyr wandered toward the dais upon which the Horned Throne rested.

He waited in silence a stone's throw from the throne, his chin high, his eyes gleaming.

Lady Silla joined Celine just beyond the drawn silver drapes. Her mother was not yet fully healed. That was evident from the signs of exhaustion still touching her features. Her skin lacked its usually luster. Shadows circled her eyes. She was unable to stand for long periods of time. It would take further rest to restore her to her full power.

But she, too, had dressed for the occasion. Her silver gown hung in intricate shreds from her knees to her trailing hem. Whenever she moved, gleaming bands of paper-thin metal flashed through her skirts like the facets of a diamond. Her dagged sleeves hung almost to the floor, her forearms covered in glittering bangles. Diamond dust glowed along her cheekbones, and a diadem of solid silver and liquid topaz shimmered along her brow. Though she did not shine like the picture of health she normally was, Lady Silla still radiated quiet power.

A feeling of pride took hold of Celine. Her mother would not back down from this fight.

When Lady Silla emerged, the whispers among the crowd faded to a hush. Celine followed close behind, the tilt of her head imperious. Unmoving. The Lady of the Vale waited to sit upon the Horned Throne until silence took hold of the Great Hall. Celine stood to her right. Beams of sunlight cut through the leaves above, casting flickering shadows across the packed-earth floor and its carpet of brilliant green clovers.

Lady Silla glared down at Lord Vyr, her expression chiseled from an iceberg.

"Lord Vyr," she began without preamble. "You have been summoned here to answer a charge of high treason." She paused. "Allegations have been made that you conspired with the Sylvan Wyld to assassinate me along the riverbank. What say you to this charge?"

Vyr raised his chin higher. Instead of replying directly to Lady Silla, he turned in a slow circle to acknowledge the rest of the gentry. He took his time to smile or nod at a few of them. Clearly he was making a mental note of those in attendance and how they regarded him.

He began to speak before he faced Lady Silla once more. When Celine saw the hint of a smile on his lips, her breath caught.

Vyr was more than prepared to play this game.

"Lady Silla, my family has served the Horned Throne for thousands of years," he said. "The Golden Stag of my ancestors has ridden into battle for the Lady of the Vale on countless occasions, without reservation. We honor and hold fast to the power and the sovereignty of the Horned Throne and all its predecessors."

"That is not an answer, Lord Vyr," Lady Silla rejoined. "I asked if you conspired with the Sylvan Wyld to assassinate me."

"I have not conspired, nor will I ever conspire, with any winter beast in any capacity."

Interesting. Vyr's use of the words *winter beast* could not be an accident. But what did he consider to be a beast? Were vampires beasts in his esteem? Were goblins?

Celine's discomfort nestled deep in her stomach. She glanced at Haroun and noticed him frowning.

"Did you plot to assassinate me?" Lady Silla asked point-blank.

"I already answered your question about conspiring to assassinate you, Lady Silla." He kept his gaze steady.

"That is true. You answered my first question. Now you will answer this one."

Murmurs unfolded through the crowd. Celine watched Vyr seize upon the smallest opportunity. He said, "I would entreat the Lady of the Vale to consider my centuries of service—as well as the countless years of loyalty my family has offered the Horned Throne—before denying me the right to know who has made such an accusation of me."

Celine's heart sank like a dead weight. If Lady Silla revealed that these accusations were made by Celine, the court would not grant them the weight they deserved. Even her short tenure in the Vale had made it clear how highly the gentry regarded the word of an ethereal.

Lady Silla did not flinch. "*I* am making the accusation, Lord Vyr."

"But what proof was offered to you to sway your opinion of me in such a swift manner?" Vyr lowered his voice.

"I am not the one accused of high treason, Lord Vyr. It is you who must offer proof to the contrary."

"Very well, then." Vyr stood straight. "The best proof I can offer is a chance to question my accuser."

"Which you are doing at present," Lady Silla said.

Gratitude warmed through Celine's heart. Her mother would not toss her to the vultures of the Summer Court. Bastien was wrong about Lady Silla. He'd always been wrong about her.

"Pardon me for being direct, but I am not." Vyr's careful smile returned, and Celine's fingers twisted in her skirts. "For I have spent the better part of this morning learning what might have caused you to believe me guilty of this accusation."

"Is that so?" Lady Silla's dark brows curved into her forehead.

Again, Lord Vyr made a slow circle before speaking. This time, the members of the fey gentry who had averted their gazes before met his without turning away.

Already he had managed to sway a few of them to his cause.

Celine shuddered to think how Vyr might have fared as a politician in the mortal world.

"I learned"—Lord Vyr pitched his voice higher—"that another attempt on the life of our lady was made just this very morning."

Shocked whispers flitted through the court gathering. Haroun stepped from the shadows, his eyes narrowing.

Celine's fingers turned white. She averted her gaze and forced herself to focus on the matter at hand. For Vyr to know about this morning's altercation only solidified her suspicions. But for him to have revealed his knowledge so publicly?

What was he playing at?

"And that this attempt," Vyr continued, "was concealed from the Grey Cloaks because I was accused, yet again, of masterminding it." His laughter was sharp. "What fool of a fey would make more than one attempt on the life of his lady in a few short days?"

The murmurs grew louder. Hands flew to hide hushed conversations. Eyes flitted back and forth with suspicion.

Lady Silla spoke over them all. "I will ask you again, Lord Vyr. If you are innocent, then supply proof of it. Otherwise I will be forced to accept your unwillingness to deny the charges as proof of your guilt."

"Ah." Lord Vyr held up a hand. "But that is not the whole of what I learned this morning." After glancing askance to take stock of his audience once more, Vyr faced Lady Silla, his teeth shining from within a wide grin. "I learned that I was accused of working alongside Sébastien Saint Germain to have the Lady of the Vale murdered."

Gasps emanated throughout the Great Hall.

In a lithe movement, Lady Silla rose from the Horned Throne until silence fell.

Before she could say anything, Lord Vyr affected a deep bow, his hands outstretched on either side of him. "I beg your mercy, my lady, but if I—one of the summer gentry and among the most loyal servants of the Vale—am being accused of high treason in a formal inquiry, then why has no attempt been made to bring to court the other accused party in a plot to overthrow the Horned Throne?" He paused for effect. "Is it perhaps because of your daughter's love for the vampire? Alas, such preferential treatment does not align with justice." His features hardened. "If I am to be accused and my reputation sullied in such an egregious fashion, I demand for the vampire to be treated with the same consideration."

Mutters of assent followed Vyr's words.

Panic gripped Celine's insides. Her heart froze.

Bastien would never be permitted a fair trial in the Vale. Even her mother's favor could not dissuade the summer gentry from their hatred for any dark fey.

"I will not have you derail these proceedings with such accusations," Lady Silla said. "What I plan to do regarding the vampire Sébastien Saint Germain has no bearing on the charges that have been brought against you."

Vyr shook his head. "I disagree, Lady Silla. If the vampire was present, he could provide proof of either my complicity or my innocence. Unless you believe he has been falsely accused. And if he is the one who has called into question my loyalty, then I demand satisfaction."

A shout rang through the throng of onlookers, followed be a smattering of applause.

Celine clasped her hands in front of her, struggling to keep her features neutral. Again she looked to Haroun, desperate for even the hint of a friendly face. Instead she found no trace of him, as if he had been carried away on a passing breeze.

Lady Silla fixed Lord Vyr with a frigid stare. "There will be no dueling, Lord Vyr."

"As I am still a member of the gentry, I am permitted this consideration. A trial by combat, if you will. I have already refuted the claim that I conspired with a winter beast to assassinate Lady Silla. If the winter fey in question is the vampire Sébastien Saint Germain, I demand that these proceedings cease until the time at which the vampire can be brought to the Great Hall to face the same charges. Or"—that evil gleam shone in Vyr's face again—"he can face me in a duel and allow the hands of fate to determine our guilt or innocence once and for all."

He announced this as if he were delivering one of Shakespeare's most lauded speeches. As if he were Mark Antony by the corpse of Julius Caesar. Or Hamlet clutching Yorick's skull.

Bedlam erupted throughout the Great Hall.

"Bring the vampire at once!" a fey lord shouted.

A liege added, "His love for Lady Celine should have no bearing on his guilt."

"He must stand for the same charges with all haste!" yelled yet another lord.

Opinions flew through the air like spittle. Panic raced through Celine's blood with the speed of liquid fire.

Lord Vyr's steady gaze fell to her. His smile was close-lipped, his expression hungry.

What had they done?

If Bastien didn't answer Lord Vyr's charges, he would be considered guilty in the eyes of the entire Summer Court. And if they thought him guilty of trying to assassinate Lady Silla, then the Grey Cloaks had all the justification they needed to track him down and kill him where he stood.

Under such a pretext, they could send their warriors to the Sylvan Wyld.

They could even dispatch their soldiers to New Orleans.

Celine swallowed a scream.

What have I done?

THE RUINED DUCHESS

As soon as Pippa and Arjun returned to New Orleans through the tare concealed along the Vale's idyllic shores, they sent word to the Grimaldis. They wished to speak to Michael without drawing any undue attention.

Pippa worried what might happen if it became common knowledge among either fey court that she'd managed to escape after being bitten by werewolves and buried alive. Arjun was concerned enough that he left out these details in the letter he dispatched to Celine through a fey messenger.

"Won't your mother tell Lady Silla and Celine what happened to me?" Pippa asked from her perch on a settee in the drawing room of the Grimaldi residence in the Marigny. "I would imagine that it's important for the Lady of the Vale to know that her general's son is married to a winter beast."

"I've asked my mother not to make mention of it in writing." Arjun toyed with the tassel fringe of the olive-green drapery framing the window to his right. "Anyone could read such a missive."

"Do you think she will honor that request?"

Arjun sent her a wry smile. "No. But I thought to ask, none-theless. She's unfailingly loyal to the Horned Throne . . . but she says she does not wish you harm. It's foolish of me to believe anything she says. I should know better."

Pippa offered him a weak grin in return. "It's not foolish. I want to trust her, too."

Neither of them spoke for a moment. It had taken four days for the Grimaldis to establish contact with Michael. Four days of Pippa and Arjun remaining in hiding on the outskirts of the city. Though it had been especially difficult for Pippa, both she and Arjun had elected not to share their whereabouts with anyone, especially those in the Court of the Lions. It had caused her no small amount of sadness to keep away from Henry and Lydia, her younger brother and sister. But she did not yet know if she might harm them, and nothing was worth that risk.

A commotion resounded from the rear garden of the Grimaldi residence. Both Pippa and Arjun took to their feet, Pippa's eyes wide.

Less than a minute later, Michael Grimaldi rushed into the room, his protesting grandmother in tow.

"Philippa?" Michael whispered, his features harried, his jaw-line shadowed by a beard. He rubbed a dirty hand across his face, his disbelief plain. "How? How . . . did you manage to escape?"

His grandmother harrumphed, muttering in Italian as she glared at them.

Pippa took a deep breath and attempted to calm herself. The second she first saw Michael—the moment she'd heard his breath and smelled the earth and musk of the Wyld on his skin—a rush of emotions had flooded her body, causing her fingers to tremble.

Arjun stepped closer to her, a hand outstretched, as if he could sense her sudden disquiet.

A knowing expression took shape on Michael's face. He did not say a word.

Pippa cleared her throat. "I—I need your help, Michael," she said softly.

"Of course," he whispered. "I can smell it in your blood."

"Che cosa?" Michael's grandmother said. "Is she . . . non è possibile!" Her brows shot into her forehead. Then she spun on her heel and left, her shock plain.

Pippa chewed on her lip, concern creasing her brow.

"Don't worry," Michael said. "Nonna won't say anything, now that she knows what has happened. She would never bring harm to—" He hesitated, then stepped toward Pippa, only to stop in his tracks, his gaze locking on Arjun, who had instinctively shifted between them.

"I won't hurt her," Michael said.

After a time, Arjun responded, "I know. But old habits die hard, as they say."

"She's one of us," Michael said, his voice barely audible. "And I would never hurt her, regardless."

A trickle of tears slid down Pippa's cheeks. The things Michael had said and done to defend her deep in the mountain echoed through her mind. "Michael stopped the other wolves from killing me, Arjun. He—he kept me safe. He was the one who buried me when they thought I had died." Her fingers flew to the base of her throat. "He even tried to stop Émilie from taking my grandmother's necklace." With a hard swallow, Pippa moved toward Michael and away from Arjun's protective stance. She took both Michael's dirty hands in her clean ones. Then she stood on her toes and hugged him, despite the dried mud caking his clothes.

"I couldn't get your necklace from Émilie," Michael said. "I'm so sorry."

Pippa shook her head. Something about the way he smelled was comforting, even though the scent reminded her a bit of a wet dog. "Don't apologize. You did everything you could have done." She pulled back to look up at him. "I'm so sorry I've come here asking you for more."

Arjun exhaled, a palm dragging over his harried features. "We are both sorry. But Pippa is right. We do need your help. Badly."

"Yes." Michael nodded, his expression one of utter conviction. "Come back at dusk, when people are preoccupied with their evening meals and less likely to be about. Keep your heads down and be mindful of speaking with anyone. Wait until just before the street lanterns are lit, then go to the garden behind the house and wait for me there."

Pippa nodded. "Thank you, Michael. For everything you've done and will do."

Michael offered her a brusque nod in return. "It is a chance for me to right what happened that night. Think nothing of it."

"No." With a steadying breath, Arjun put out his hand. "I will never see this as nothing."

Though it was obvious it pained Michael to do so, he shook Arjun's hand. A reminder to them all that bad blood had existed for generations between the wolves and the vampires of New Orleans. Between the Grimaldis and La Cour des Lions.

"It's best if you speak of this to no one," Michael said.

Pippa bit her lip. "Celine will know I am alive soon, if she hasn't already heard of it."

"Then we have no time to lose," Michael said. "We will begin your training tonight."

THE RUINED PRINCE

I don't understand," Odette said as she clutched the intricate scroll, her eyes running over the words at a rapid pace.

It looked incongruous in her small hands. A relic more in keeping with the burned library of Alexandria than the modern missives of the day. Through its center was an ornate bar, which appeared to be burnished gold. Elaborate end caps held the scroll in place, their pieces carved from solid ash. The scroll itself was not made of papyrus or parchment, but rather of a thin fabric reminiscent of silk. The words were written in silver ink.

"Bastien?" Odette's eyes were huge, her light brown hair pulled back from her face in a chignon. "What does this mean?"

With great care, Bastien reached for the immense scroll. His hands were steady, despite the frenetic energy flowing through his body. As if his blood had been set aflame.

"The summer fey are trying to kill him." Jae's voice was gruff. He stood in the corner, his back propped against the wall. Along his fingertips, he twirled his favorite dagger, its blade slender and its hilt inlaid with mother-of-pearl.

"I wish them luck." Boone snorted, his boots propped on a priceless end table. Rumors abounded that Nicodemus had stolen it from Versailles one night because he liked the smell of it.

For the fourth time, Bastien unrolled the scroll and read the words to himself. "Lord Vyr—my favorite pointy-eared bastard—has challenged me to a duel." Though he kept his voice light, he could still hear the incredulity in it.

"Avec . . . les pistolets?" Odette's face was aghast.

"You'd prefer swords?" Bastien joked.

"They won't use ordinary bullets," Jae warned.

Hortense tsked. "Tipped in silver, I would wager."

Jae flipped his dagger again and caught it with otherworldly accuracy. "Which could kill you."

"Refuse to go," Madeleine stated in a flat tone. "They will not come here to drag you to their world." She cleared her throat, her arms crossing. "I would like to see them try."

A bemused half smile curled up Bastien's face. "I can't refuse. If I refuse, it's an admission of guilt. They won't come here to drag me back to the Vale. They will send soldiers to kill me. Perhaps even justify my absence as an excuse to attack this coven."

"How could Celine allow this to happen?" Odette cried. "How could she permit her mother to authorize such an action?"

"Celine was likely caught in a difficult situation," Boone replied with frown. "She doesn't have the standing to argue with the Summer Court."

"I would disagree. She's her mother's heir," Jae said.

"She won't challenge her mother. She can't." Bastien stared at the silver words on the elaborate summons. "If she had, we would not be in this predicament. Celine is lost . . . and I can't make her see reason."

Exasperation took shape on Odette's face. "You shouldn't make her do anything, Bastien."

"Yes, yes," Bastien grumbled. "You've made your point, several times over. I'm an evil prick, always trying to control her. Why would she believe anything I had to say?"

Odette exhaled, her pointer finger tapping along her forearm. "Are you quite finished?"

Bastien did not reply. He glanced at his brothers and sisters in blood. "You know I have to go."

For a time, they all remained silent.

"Yes," Jae said. "You do."

"But maybe you don't need to go alone," Madeleine said. "And you don't need return to the Vale completely without aid or guidance. This is precisely why we must speak with Arjun. After all, he grew up in the Vale." She turned toward Jae, her features determined. "Now is the time to—"

"Arjun has enough to deal with, Mad," Bastien interrupted.

She aimed a peevish look his way. "I wasn't finished, Sébastien. What is Arjun doing at this moment, Jae?"

Jae pursed his lips to one side. "He is still trying to meet with Michael Grimaldi. I believe contact was finally made. If logic follows their movements, they will likely be in the Marigny to meet with him at the Grimaldi residence."

Another moment of silence followed his statements.

"Then it's really true," Odette murmured. "Pippa has become—" She shuddered.

"If they turned her into a wolf, then it is not her fault." Bastien's reply was clipped. "And even if she has become one of them, I am thankful, for it means she was not killed."

"Arjun still does not suspect that we are trailing them and taking note of their whereabouts?" Madeleine asked Jae.

Jae did not respond.

Boone laughed under his breath. "Even God himself can't see Jae if Jae doesn't want to be seen."

Bastien straightened his shoulders. "Then we will go to the Marigny tonight." He looked around at his brothers and sisters. "Who would like to join me?"

They each glanced around the room, wordless conversations filling the space. Unspoken accusations flew as, one by one, they avoided one another's gazes.

"You are all a bunch of ninnies," Odette scolded. "I'll go," she said to Bastien. "But if I leave smelling like a dog, you will buy me new clothes and draw me a perfumed bath. Do you understand?"

"Of course." The suggestion of a smile touched Bastien's lips. "It's the only thing I have understood without question in quite some time."

"Dress well. I want us to meet our enemies in our finest form," Odette said. "For an afternoon tea . . . with a potential side of poison."

THE RUINED SOUL

Her recent dreams had become so vivid, Émilie could no longer be certain what was real.

Last night, she swore she'd gazed into an old mirror, only to have her own reflection speak to her. Ask her. Cajole her. Tell her how much she needed its help.

The mirror in her mind had shown her a path up the forbidden mountain at the heart of the Sylvan Wyld. The same mountain that contained the forgotten cave of the werewolves. Tedor had said on more than one occasion that the mountain held many secrets. In her dream, a small, concealed passage was revealed to Émilie, hidden behind rocks and an embankment of snow that never melted. The passage seemed to have been made for a very small creature. And it would be impossible to find it if one didn't know where to look.

Émilie wasn't sure what kind of madness drove her to seek it out now. Perhaps she wished to know how much of her mind had lost control.

Through the darkness she wandered, toward the patch of trees with the silvered branches near the top. She sought out the angle of the moon to determine the correct direction. If she arrived in the exact spot and did not uncover the path, then she would know just how unhinged her nightmares had become.

The moon slipped from behind a cloud as Émilie rounded a familiar bend. An eerie calm descended toward her.

She knew this place, even though she'd never been here before.

In her wolf form, Émilie turned to face the mountain, her eyes seeking the sparkling ridge of the jutting snow embankment.

There it stood, glowing in the light of the mother moon.

Émilie filled her lungs with frigid air. She considered the three large boulders covering the entrance to the path. Then she twisted around them to begin a climb that should have been impossible. The angle of the embankment appeared much too steep. But the cleverly worn path concealed itself behind a wall of crystallized ice and snow.

Despite the difficulty presented by the small path, Émilie remained surefooted. She'd walked this way in her dream just the night before. She climbed the hidden trail for almost half an hour. The air would be thin now, difficult if she was in her human form. Thin and brisk, beginning to pain the lungs of a mere mortal.

Then she saw the narrow ledge. The one leading into a tiny cavern, its entrance covered by an inconsequential rock with an angled top.

Using her snout, Émilie rolled the rock away and crawled into the tunnel. It wasn't very long. The light of the moon still reached inside, its silver beams touching the clasp of a small box.

Émilie knew what was inside that box.

The key to the greatest power—the greatest magic—she would ever know.

The second she opened it to reveal the simple key within, the voice in her dreams called out to her, clear as a summer's day.

I knew you would be the one. You were always the exception. You were meant to rule.

THE RUINED DUCHESS

Pippa glared at the sliver of moon through the window as if it were the source of her life's torment.

"You must stop fighting it," Michael said gently. "Fighting the change will not help you learn to control it."

"I'm not fighting it, dash it all." Anger stippled Pippa's features as she looked up again, her chest tight. For the last five hours, it had been a constant battle to maintain her calm.

"Yes, you are." Michael sighed. "Is it because you are concerned about damaging the room?" He looked around. "All the furniture has been removed, and walls can be repaired. Arjun and I will make sure your wolf form cannot get loose. We promise."

Pippa gritted her teeth, her bare feet pressing into the wooden floor.

Michael continued, "Then are you afraid to change into a wolf in front of me? Do you worry about propriety? I can leave before you attempt to change back, if you are concerned about being seen unclothed."

Color flooded Pippa's cheeks. "That is the least of my concerns," she grumbled. "Though I can think of many other things I'd rather be doing at the moment."

"Nakedness is a part of this life," Michael said gently. "Soon there will come a time when it doesn't bother you in the slightest."

"I said I'm not bothered by it, Michael," Pippa shouted, completely out of character.

Arjun and Michael exchanged a glance. "Believe me," Arjun joked, "I'm not bothered by it either. Another man gazing upon the bare figure of my wife . . . he should be so lucky."

Pippa sneered in response, her anger spiking.

It could not be helped. Even during the daylight hours—when the pull to shift into a wolf was at its weakest—Pippa's emotions were volatile. Fury lingered at the surface, always at the ready. The slightest provocation would elicit a harsh word of rebuke from her. Or, on rare occasions, an actual growl.

As someone who had spent most of her life priding herself on her English sense of decorum, this sudden volatility chafed Pippa's nerves. It made her feel uncertain in her own skin. Anytime a hint of an emotion like sadness would take root, no more than a moment would pass before it blossomed in her chest and overwhelmed her, until she would find herself sobbing in a corner, unable to stop crying.

The skies over New Orleans had shifted from the near darkness of a new moon to the slender crescent shape that now hung low in the sky. The very idea of facing a full moon sent Pippa into the beginnings of panic, especially after Michael had admitted he still felt apprehensive when the sun began to set on those particular nights.

"You must stop fighting the change," he repeated. "If you keep fighting it—if you let fear rule your mind—then you will never be able to control it. You will always be at its mercy."

"You think I don't know that?" Pippa yelled. "You think I don't feel it every morning I open my eyes? Even my dreams are plagued by fear. They are vivid and chaotic as never before. They leave me with the heart of a hummingbird and the rage of a caged beast. I am never rested, nor do I feel at ease, even when I desperately need it. How am I to overcome this, Michael? How? Will I be forced each month to chain myself to a tree in the middle of the woods like your great-grandmother?" She refused to cry, despite the knot of anguish collecting in her throat. Pippa had cried more over the last month than the whole of her entire life.

Michael sighed. "I regret telling you that. It was a mistake."

"Amazing," Pippa replied in a droll tone. "The great Michael Grimaldi admits to making a mistake."

He pursed his lips and kept silent. Pippa knew she should apologize. Indignation followed the thought, like a fox chasing after a hen. Why should she be the one to apologize? Why, when all she wanted was to be left in a room to rage and destroy everything in sight?

Pippa glanced around for something to break. With horror, she realized how much that behavior resembled her father's. Then she stomped over to the windowsill to pour herself a drink of whiskey, her wild emotions swallowing her whole.

"If I can't conquer the beast in me," Pippa muttered as she thought again of her father, the duke, "I may as well surrender." She replaced the cap on the decanter, her hand shaking as she raised the full tumbler to her lips.

It was Arjun who came to her side. Arjun who gently pried the whiskey from her hands. Arjun who threaded her fingers through his.

Pippa spoke through clenched teeth. "Why are you allowed to drown your sorrows, yet I am not?"

He nodded, his expression circumspect. "Right. That does seem unfair, doesn't it?" He returned the metal tumbler to her and waited.

Pippa considered the amber liquid as it sloshed near the brim of the cup.

"Do you want me to join you?" Arjun said, his tone casual as he raised a tumbler of his own. When she did not respond, he uncapped the decanter from its place on the windowsill, the nearby lantern flickering.

"No," Pippa whispered, guilt clutching at her stomach. She wanted Arjun to be stronger than that. Which meant . . . damn it all . . . that she should be stronger, too.

Something softened in Arjun's expression. "It is *because* I know what it is like to drown your sorrows that I want you to be better than I am. Fight harder than I did. Because *you are better*, Pippa."

"Poppycock." Pippa sniffed. "I am a growling beast who bites the head off anyone unlucky enough to cross my path. Just like my father."

"That isn't true," Michael said. "From what I've heard of your father, I doubt he could have survived as you have." Pippa watched him select his next words with care. "I think we choose anger because it is the easiest reaction to have. Anger grants us the freedom to behave as we never would under normal circumstances." He paused. "Wolves often turn to it as a result." Then his focus seemed to waver, his mind lost in thought. "It makes us feel powerful."

"You're thinking of Émilie Saint Germain." Pippa bade herself to remain calm. Still, she could not banish the memory of Bastien's werewolf sister sinking her fangs into her skin. "There's no need for you to apologize anymore, Michael. I know you did not intend for this to happen."

Anger flashed across Michael's face. "I should have known better than to trust her."

"I don't think it was about trust," Pippa said.

Arjun hummed in agreement. "Jealousy would be my guess. Not that I blame you. Bastien is an easy chap to hate. A tortured soul with ungodly amounts of money and the rakish good looks reserved for Greek statues. If he weren't so generous, he'd be insufferable."

Michael closed his eyes. "Jealousy does not become me."

"Actually, I rather think it does," Arjun said. "I believe we all become our strongest emotion, sooner or later." His expression turned somber. "I became sorrow, for a time." He glanced toward Pippa. "I'm not proud of it. But even the strongest among us are weak when it comes to our feelings."

Michael's eyes flashed open. "I never thought of it that way. Becoming the thing we feel." He canted his head. "An interesting thought. I wonder what might happen, Pippa, if you tried that."

"I don't wish to be *any* emotion," she said. "I want to go back to who I was before."

"I know." Michael nodded. "But maybe the reason you can't seem to control your shift is because you've become your own fear. What if you tried to become . . . something else?"

Pippa frowned. "I can't be happy when I'm not happy, Michael."

"Maybe not happy," he continued. "But . . . determined, perhaps? Maybe try for a feeling that does not control you, but is something you can control instead?"

"Like . . . patience?" Pippa quipped. "Or serenity?"

"I know it sounds simple," Michael said. "But that shift in thinking may help you shift in truth."

A knock resounded from beyond the room. Before Michael could respond, the door swung open with a surprising amount of force. Michael's elderly grandmother walked in without a word, her black lace shawl swinging from her shoulders and a mahogany walking stick thumping the hardwood floors in time with her strides.

"Michael Antonio Grimaldi," Nonna said in her lightly accented voice. "There are two vampires gracing our doorstep, asking to speak with Arjun Desai. Tell them to leave at once." She eyed Pippa and Arjun askance, but the look was not unkind. "I knew nothing good would come from this." With the first two fingers of her right hand, she made the sign of the cross. "In the past, we never allowed blood drinkers close to our home." Her gaze clouded over. "I hate to turn away any of our kind, but when you fraternize with the devil . . ." Nonna finished by muttering something unintelligible in Italian.

Michael opened his mouth to reply, then stopped himself. Again he looked at Pippa, that same thoughtful expression on his face. "Nonna," he said after a few moments of silence, "perhaps the past served us well before. But it's time for us to consider a different way."

"No." Nonna sniffed. "My mother taught me never to trust a man who won't eat dessert and never to put garlic in my tomato sauce. Shallots and sweet onions only." The end of her walking stick struck the floorboards three times in rapid succession. "There is a reason we look to the past. Because we wish to learn." She stood to her full height. Even though she was still two heads shorter than her grandson, she managed to tower over them all. "Do as you're told, Michael. Tell the vampires to leave, for I will not address them directly. Remind them this is not where they belong, and they are not welcome here."

Pippa listened to the conversation unfold in silence. Nonna's words resonated with her. Looking to her past—and learning from it—had provided her with many of life's most important lessons. It taught her what she needed to know to leave Liverpool and brave the Atlantic for a new world.

But looking to her past meant having her eyes behind her rather than before her.

"Nonna," Pippa said, "please don't fret. Arjun and I will leave, and we will make sure your unwanted guests go with us. But . . . if you will permit me to share something that has only just occurred to me." She took a deep breath. "I never thought I would turn to werewolves for help, especially after what happened to me on the bridge. But here I am because"—she gnawed at the inside of her cheek—"I need you. Your family is the only place I can turn. And despite my struggles, I'm not sorry I have done so. Maybe our enemies are only our enemies because we are unable to let go of the past."

Nonna harrumphed, the wrinkles lining her mouth becoming more pronounced. "Vampires care only about their own. They turned their backs on us when they no longer saw value in our kind, and they will do it to you one day, cara mia."

"I hope you're wrong." Pippa moved to don her stockings and boots. "But thank you for everything. Your kindness won't be forgotten."

Nonna's frown deepened. "For your sake, I hope I am wrong, too." She made a shooing motion. "Off with you now."

"Nonna," Michael said, something suddenly occurring to him. "Whatever brought these vampires to our door must be important, or they would have simply sent a messenger." His features hardened. "If it's about Celine, I want to know what has happened. I want to speak with them."

"No. I will be struck by lightning before I allow a vampire in my home," Nonna said.

"Then in the garden." Michael walked to the door to lead the way downstairs. "If there is trouble on our doorstep, we need to know exactly what kind of trouble it is."

Pippa stood with Arjun to one side of the garden, her apprehension mounting. The high wrought-iron fence surrounding the Grimaldi family's home in the Marigny was lined with tall oleander and holly hedges to provide privacy. Though the garden was small, it was well kept, with tomato vines, lemon trees, and an elegant herb garden running parallel to the house.

The scent blooming around them reminded Pippa of a time when she was very young, before her family lost their fortune and their standing in British society. They'd spent a month together touring Tuscany by rail. It had become one of her fondest memories. The way the basil and the thyme and the rosemary would waft through the open windows of the train car, carried on a warm countryside breeze.

Despite the reminder of a happier time, Pippa could not shake her growing discomfort. And it had everything to do with the pair of vampires now facing the werewolf in the torchlit garden of the Grimaldi home.

Pippa hadn't expected the vampires waiting outside the Grimaldi residence to be Odette Valmont and Sébastien Saint Germain. She wondered how La Cour des Lions had even known to look for them here. Perhaps they were watching the Grimaldi home. Pippa thought maybe Boone or Jae had been sent to fetch them. The fact that Bastien would dare to show his face in the Marigny after all the enmity that had passed between him and Michael Grimaldi meant that this was a serious matter, indeed.

Bastien may have won Celine's heart, but Michael had fought for it first. He'd loved her first. And he'd been the first to lose her after professing his love.

Michael had proposed to Celine. Asked her to build a life with him.

In return, she'd run away with Bastien. A vampire. His mortal enemy.

Pippa noticed that Michael's fists had yet to relax. They remained clenched at his sides. His feet were spread wide, and the way he puffed his chest before him indicated how he felt in Bastien's presence. With Pippa's newly sharpened senses, she could even detect the faint pounding of his heart.

"What are you doing here, Sébastien?" Michael demanded in a gruff voice.

Bastien's eyes were steely, though he maintained a casual stance, his Panama hat at a jaunty tilt. "In your garden? I haven't the faintest idea. You were the one who invited me back here, after all."

"Don't be an ass," Michael growled back. "Why did you come to my home, if not to deliberately provoke me?"

Odette's lips puckered as if she were kissing the air. Her eyes shifted from side to side. With a lace-gloved hand, she attempted to take hold of Bastien's arm in a soothing gesture.

"Please, Bastien," Pippa said. "Be kind. Celine wouldn't want you to act like this, especially to someone who is helping me."

Bastien flinched. His expression sobered. Though Pippa could sense how much it irritated him, he shifted backward. "I . . . apologize for coming here. It was because I needed to speak with Arjun."

"Why?" Michael demanded.

"Have you changed your name to Arjun since we last saw each other?" Bastien smirked.

"If you came to my home to speak with him, it must be important," Michael said. "Where is Celine?"

"That's none of your concern," Bastien replied. "Arjun and Pippa, if you wouldn't mind, I think it's time for us to return to the Quarter, where we belong."

"Where is Celine?" Michael stepped in front of Bastien, blocking his path, his posture rigid.

Something flashed in Bastien's eyes. "It just so happens that Celine Rousseau's whereabouts are none of my concern either."

Though he kept his gaze light, Pippa realized what she was detecting in his face.

Pain. Carefully controlled. But pain, nonetheless.

Michael shifted backward, casting Bastien a searching glance. "What have you done?"

"Mon Dieu, you really are tiresome, Michael Grimaldi," Odette said with a long exhale. "*Thank you* for inviting us for such a delightful soirée. *Thank you* for regaling us with wonderful stories of your shared youth. *We shall be leaving now.*"

"Bastien, what happened? What's wrong?" Michael asked, all the fight leaving him. "If something is wrong . . . we deserve to know. And if there is something to be done"—he bit down on nothing, his jaw rippling—"then perhaps we can help."

With a snide smile, Bastien bared his fangs, the torchlight dancing across his chiseled face. "Unless you know how to mount an army of dark fey in less than a fortnight, I will be bidding you a good evening." He tipped his Panama hat.

"Just like your uncle." A voice echoed from the darkest

shadows beside the Grimaldi home. "Arrogant. Conceited. Destined to fail."

Nonna emerged into the torchlight, her long white braid hanging across one shoulder and her shawl wrapped tight around her small body.

"Why did you come to our home, Sébastien Saint Germain?" Nonna demanded while she strode closer. "You would not have done so unless you were very afraid. Unless you wanted something you were too afraid to ask for."

Odette bit her lip. Pippa looked from the lovely vampire's worried mien to the unmoving stare Bastien fixed on Michael's grandmother.

"What is this you say about needing an army of dark fey?" Nonna refused to back down.

"Nonna, please forgive me." Bastien cleared his throat. "A tasteless joke. I apologize."

"Non dire cazzate," Nonna said. "That is horseshit." She glared at Bastien.

"The Summer Court has demanded that Bastien fight in some farcical duel. Some kind of trial by combat against an odious lord named Vyr," Odette said softly. "An accusation has been levied at Bastien that he was the one responsible for a recent assassination attempt on the Lady of the Vale."

Bastien's steely gaze flicked Odette's way.

"I won't apologize." Odette raised her chin. "I am so wearied by male posturing that I could write a fucking song about it. 'Odette's Lament,' I shall call it."

Nonna's lips twitched.

"Good God," Michael whispered. "A . . . trial by combat? Are we in King Arthur's court?"

Distress flooded Pippa's body. She shook her head. "Why would they do this? Why would Celine ever allow it?"

"Celine wouldn't," Bastien said. "The summer gentry are looking for an excuse to launch an invasion of the Sylvan Wyld. If they can blame me for the assassination attempt—if I were to lose in a trial by combat—then they would have all the justification they need to say the Winter Court is responsible."

"Even if you win the duel, they will still go to war," Michael murmured. "You will have murdered one of their own, right in front of their eyes. They will say you cheated. This is a trap."

"I know." Bastien looked at Michael. "It's why I needed Arjun's help. I wanted to see if he could think of a way to avoid my having to fight this duel. Is there anything in the Summer Court's lore to—"

"No," Arjun said, both his hands raking through his head of dark hair. "And even if there were, Vyr has you cornered. This is likely what he wanted all along. I wouldn't be surprised to learn he'd planned the entire thing." His brow furrowed.

Pippa swallowed the lump gathering in her throat. "But I can't understand why he would deliberately provoke Celine and Lady Silla with this."

"I don't think he's provoking Lady Silla," Bastien said. "I think he's in league with her."

"How do you know this?" Michael asked.

A pause. "I have my suspicions," Bastien said.

Nonna's laughter was dark. "And you will share them with us

253

now, Sébastien Saint Germain." With a final wary glance at the two vampires standing in her garden, Nonna sat on a nearby bench to take her place in the circle, her expression fierce. "Because I will tell you something no vampire of this city has ever known." She took a careful breath. "If it is an army of dark fey you need, look to the mountain in the center of the Sylvan Wyld. Those who would protect it are still there. They have been there in secret for centuries."

Pippa gasped. "The wolves. The ones who took me from the bridge. They brought me to some kind of cave. Are they the ones you're speaking about?"

Nonna's features turned grave. She nodded.

"Why are they there?" Bastien asked. "Why did they stay, despite the order of exile that was decreed on them hundreds of years ago?"

"Because these wolves are beholden to a higher order from something older and greater than any foolish edict. They swore by blood to stand guard over a secret chamber deep in the heart of the mountain. A cavern of ice." She canted her head as she regarded Bastien, who remained strangely silent. "Where winged statues and forgotten legends and the darkest of nightmares dwell."

"What?" Arjun blinked. "What are you talking about?"

Satisfaction spread across Nonna's face. "I think you know exactly what they guard, Sébastien Saint Germain. And now you will tell us everything."

Bastien stared back at her.

"Now," Nonna repeated, "or else the devil take you and your

troubles." Her eyes narrowed. "These werewolves of the mountain will never listen to a vampire. You will need my help. And I will never let you forget it."

After a final pause, Bastien began speaking.

And Pippa soon learned exactly what Nonna meant.

The darkest of nightmares indeed.

The Ruined Prince

One of the things Bastien missed most about being a human was dreaming. Vampires did not need to sleep the same way mortals did. Time to himself in the darkness of his chamber, shrouded by his thoughts, offered him clarity when he needed it. He would close his eyes, surrender to the blackness, and his mind would wander.

Some might call them dreams, but Bastien knew better. They were not dreams at all. Cursed to live as a vampire, he was haunted by memories, his mind floating above him as the ghosts of all his lives emerged like specters from the shadows. On some occasions, demons took shape before his shuttered eyes, fed by his unspoken worries. They left him with questions. Left him dwelling in fear.

After learning from Michael's grandmother about the were-wolves guarding the secret chamber deep inside Mount Morag, Bastien decided to return to the Wyld without warning. Instead of traveling through tares undoubtedly watched by fey, both light and dark, he chose to use the time-traveling mirror to pass from New Orleans into the icy reaches of winter. The mirror called out to him when he wandered through its shining labyrinth, but he ignored its siren song.

I can help you. You have but to ask. To give . . . and to receive. In me alone, you will find the answers. In me alone, you will uncover the truth.

He refused to be baited. Though it seemed foolish, a part of Bastien held the mirror responsible for the end of his relationship with Celine. But he could not deny that part of what the mirror said was true. It might share with him a way to prevent a particular future from happening.

What would Bastien lose in return?

He would gladly receive . . . but he already suspected that what he would have to give may not be worth the cost. And perhaps, as it had with Celine, the truth about the future would be nothing more than a self-fulfilling prophecy.

Bastien had warred with himself more than once over his decision not to tell Celine about the mirror's existence and capabilities. If he told her that a time-traveling mirror had revealed to him that her mother would murder her on the grounds of the Ursuline convent—if he revealed what he knew and how he knew it—then there was no telling what might be done with that information. However well-intentioned Celine wished to be, she might confront her mother. And in doing so, she might bring about their ruination.

It pained him to think it. But Celine . . . could no longer be trusted.

There. This was the truth Bastien had been so afraid to face.

He did not trust Celine. Not anymore. Under the influence of her mother, she'd become a shadow of herself. Rendered in pastel colors, instead of the strong jewel tones she'd favored in the past. Her desire to know and be known by the fairy queen who'd abandoned her as a child had swallowed her strength.

She was no longer the same girl.

Bastien understood it. He wondered what part of himself he would willingly lose to have his family made whole again. To hear his mother in their garden. To feel the warmth of his father's embrace. To return to a time when Émilie was a beloved sister instead of an inexorable menace.

So Bastien entered the Sylvan Wyld on his own, the echoes of the time-traveling mirror's taunts in his ears. He stared up at the snow-capped mountain from his silent perch on the edge of the skeletal forest the summer gentry referred to as the frozen wastelands. In the shadow of these creaking, ice-covered trees lurked creatures that might attack Bastien at any moment, as they had in the past.

Bastien no longer feared them. His fears had grown and multiplied. They'd become bigger than any one thing. Ghouls from his childhood nightmares no longer held sway. It was here, in the shade of a frozen forest, that Bastien found himself lost in a new haunting.

One far more vivid than anything he'd experienced before.

A blast of icy air struck him in the face. If he were a mortal, the force of it would have knocked him to the ground. The smell of something stale and cold and frostbitten swirled through his nostrils. He opened his eyes and was met with nothing but blackness.

The faint pounding of hooves started ringing in his ears. A horse whickered, and the sound rose to a howl. A feral beast wailing to the skies. Wings began to beat in the darkness. With every whoosh of air, Bastien felt himself being forced backward.

Fear ignited in his chest, burning through his body like a flame to kindling.

Still he saw nothing before him but the unrelenting murk.

Then . . . a pair of red eyes glowed far in the distance. The pounding of hooves grew louder. The burning eyes drew closer. And the wings continued to scream their rhythmic scream.

Bastien yelled to the yawning darkness, "What do you want?"

To be set free.

When Bastien arrived in the remains of the Winter Court's Great Hall, deep inside Mount Morag, the war council had already begun.

"The summer forces are massing along the border." The centaur named Hadeon, who had become the commander of the Sylvan Wyld's bedraggled army, stood in the middle of a large chamber lit by nothing but blue firelight. The walls were jagged, the stone floor cracked. When Bastien gazed into the coved ceiling high above, he could see traces of fanciful carvings, some of the figures caught in compromising positions. Murder and mayhem mixed with the sensual and the sordid.

The art of a lost court of darkness.

Hadeon nodded to acknowledge Bastien's arrival before continuing. "Ever since we destroyed the bridge at the vampire's suggestion, the Summer Court has armed their warriors in the open, without a care for being seen. Each day, more of their fighters and more of their weapons arrive to the border between our lands. Our latest reports indicate they are building a floating bridge." His voice boomed through the shadows. "Soon they will use it to try and cross into our territory to conquer us. Blowing up the old bridge may have bought us a breath of time, but there is nothing we can do to stop summer from launching an invasion in the coming weeks."

The centaur is wrong. There is something you could do. I could help you stop it. You have but to ask.

Though Bastien knew it was impossible, he swore he heard the mirror calling out to him from deep in the heart of Mount Morag. As if it had managed to lodge a piece of itself within his head.

Bastien inhaled slowly, fighting to ignore the mirror's newest temptation. His eyes panned across the cavern to the tattered relics of the war council. Despite their demand that Bastien take responsibility for the situation and assume the role of his forebears as the leader of the Winter Court, he'd resisted their requests, as he lacked the experience to lead any kind of army. Moreover, Bastien's loyalty could not remain with the Sylvan Wyld alone. His home—his city—was New Orleans. He would defend it first and foremost.

A true leader in a time of war could not have his heart in two different places.

Which was why it pleased Bastien to see that the heads of the various winter fey families had embraced Hadeon's leadership. The centaur was one of the few among them who could recall the battles that had happened between summer and winter centuries ago, before their truce had been made. A fragile peace forged at the cost of the Sylvan Wyld's freedom, the loss of its vampiric leadership, and their quick descent from a once-mighty land to the scattered factions that held court now.

Bastien took a deep breath, his gaze shifting across the cavern. Hadeon's recent announcement about the Winter Court's dire situation was met with resignation. What was left of their forces waited in sullen silence, their shoulders hunched, their wings folded, their faces drawn.

For an instant, Bastien toyed with the notion of informing all those who had gathered here about the werewolves hidden within the mountain. Michael's grandmother had been either unwilling or unable to tell Bastien how many wolves remained, but she'd been resolute in saying they would defend their lands to the death.

But would they follow a vampire? Would they take the orders of a centaur? Or would they wish to lead themselves?

These thoughts creased Bastien's brow. Some of these werewolves—likely incited by his sister, Émilie—were respon-sible for the attack on Pippa Montrose that afternoon beside the bridge. As always, wolves were a dangerous, unpredictable entity. Bastien wanted to know if Hadeon had any memory of dealing with them successfully in the past.

Lastly, Bastien sought both Hadeon's and Suli's guidance on how to navigate the duel he'd been summoned to fight in the Sylvan Vale. If he ignored Lady Silla's directives for much longer, he might be putting all the Wyld at even greater risk.

He'd returned to the Wyld only to speak with Hadeon and Suli. Only to take stock of their situation.

Not to speak with or use the mirror. Never for that.

Liar. The mirror laughed.

A sudden tittering from the eaves above caught Bastien's attention. The sounds of a squabble began to emerge among several small winged fey.

Bastien realized Bagus and his family—the ones who had placed the niter along the bridge to ensure its destruction— were being attacked by a group of even smaller winged fey with sharpened horns and obsidian eyes.

It did not take Bastien long to determine the source of their enmity.

"Enough!" Bastien shouted, his voice booming into the reaches of the cavern. "Bagus was following orders. The suggestion to destroy the bridge was mine, and I do not believe we were wrong in doing so."

"Ruining the bridge provoked the summer fey!" a horned fey yelled in a tinny voice, its wings buzzing through the darkness. "They would never have made plans to invade us had we not done something so foolhardy."

"You are mistaken," Hadeon said, his hooves striking the

frosted stone as he moved closer to where Bastien stood in a gesture of solidarity. "The Summer Court had every intention of sending forces across the bridge into our lands. We know this because they'd already dispatched soldiers to find the ones responsible for attempting to kill the Lady of the Vale."

"And I would rather see their duplicity in the light of day. Now that their forces operate out in the open with such arrogance, we may know how to ready ourselves," Bastien said.

Cold laughter emanated from his right. "Ready ourselves?" A small hobgoblin with nine eyes, a missing leg, and severe burns along one side of his body struggled to stand. Drawing himself to his full height with the help of a makeshift crutch, he faced Bastien and Hadeon. "How do you propose we do that?" he said, his voice low, his words stilted from his injuries. "And why should we listen to you, vampire? You, who give orders from the shadows while refusing to stand among our ranks." He smashed the end of his crutch into the stone for emphasis. "I will not follow the orders of a fair-weather blood drinker. Especially when his orders provoke our enemies and lead us to slaughter!"

Murmurs and whispers rippled around them. The vestiges of the Winter Court began to stir, agitation flowing through their ranks.

Bastien refrained from shouting again. He wanted to howl into the cavern and hear his own voice reverberate through the countless hollows and outcroppings. Nothing had changed; he still had no desire to lead the winter fey. Moreover, he refused to take on a mantle thrust upon him. The mistakes of his ancestors were not his to fix, despite what the winter fey believed.

But Bastien knew they were not solely to blame for their folly. They deserved a measure of his compassion.

He made his way over to the injured hobgoblin. Instead of speaking louder, he chose to reply in a softer tone. "I understand why you believe I am leading you to slaughter. Making it more difficult for the summer fey to cross into our lands was merely a stalling tactic. I agree on that score. But we needed to buy ourselves time." He looked upward. "And we must use that time wisely." Bastien raised his voice to address all the fey present. "I know how many of you see me. That vampires like myself have lived among the mortal world in luxury, removed from the sorrow you've faced for centuries. How is it possible for me to understand your plight?" He paused. "And the truth is, I don't."

One of the winged fey who had accosted Bagus tittered. She zipped lower, her wings like those of a horsefly. "At least you can admit it," she scoffed.

"It's difficult for me to admit my shortcomings. I've only just begun to understand this. If we admit what we can't do, then we are faced with our limitations. But maybe we also become aware of our capabilities," Bastien said, an idea forming in his head. Once more, he pitched his voice louder. He took a deep breath, knowing his next words may drive the wedge deeper. Or cast winter's pitiful lot in an even more unsavory light. "I am told . . . I am told there are those who dwell within the reaches of the Sylvan Wyld in secret. Who wish to remain unknown." He paused for effect. "If there are those among you who know of any winter fey within Mount Morag, I call upon you to beseech them. Ask them to join our ranks as we make a stand against summer."

Everything drifted to silence and sudden stillness, Bastien's accusation hanging heavy in the air.

Hadeon cleared his throat.

"I am not accusing them of being cowards," Bastien continued, the stillness unnerving him. "I understand their desire to keep their secrets. To remain safe." He gazed upward, letting his eyes move the length of the cavern. "In truth, I felt that way, too. I did not understand why I was being blamed for the mistakes of my ancestors. Why I was being forced to take responsibility."

"Do you understand now?" the hobgoblin said, his expression dubious.

"No," Bastien replied. "But I want to understand." He spoke even louder. "And I need your help to do it. I need all of you."

"For what?" Ouna, the amabie who had punished Anurak, stepped from the shadows. When Bastien saw her, it was clear the dark-haired fey had been crying, her features splotched with anger.

"I need you to speak to everyone you know," he continued. "To try to get word to the dark fey who remain in hiding. We need all of them now. Even if they manage to keep themselves safe for the time being, that safety will not last once the Summer Court conquers the winter lands." Bastien's hands curled into fists. "If we stop them now, I can promise that the vampires in my family—my blood brothers and blood sisters—will help to rebuild these lands. We will do whatever we can to ensure the future of the Sylvan Wyld."

"They won't trust you," a winged fey said. "We don't trust you."

"I understand. Trust is a thing that is earned." Bastien inhaled. "But if every creature waited to grant trust until it was earned, then how would we manage to accomplish anything? I ask that you offer me your trust as a gift. I promise I will not waste it."

The hobgoblin moved forward, his crutch striking the icy stone in ominous thuds. "You ask too much, vampire."

"I know." Bastien nodded.

"And offer too little," the fey with the horsefly wings added.

Ouna said, "And what of the rumors that the Grimaldi werewolves of New Orleans are siding with the Summer Court?"

Bastien sucked in a breath. A fresh wave of fury flashed through him. "What do you mean?"

"General Riya sent Grey Cloaks into the city of New Orleans when her son and his wife returned to the mortal world. The Grey Cloaks were seen loitering in daylight near the Grimaldi home," Hadeon interjected. "We only recently received word. It appears the Grimaldi wolves may have chosen a side."

"That . . . is not true," Bastien said.

"You are so quick to defend your enemy?" Hadeon's aquiline brow furrowed.

"No." Bastien thought quickly, knowing it would not be in Pippa's best interest to disclose her new ties to the werewolves. "But I refuse to believe the Grimaldis have chosen a side in this, especially one that aligns them with the Summer Court. Werewolves have a long memory. In their bones, they were never creatures of summer." It was not Bastien's place to divulge the things Michael's grandmother had told him, at least not within earshot of so many winter fey.

Hadeon frowned. "The information we have gathered suggests—"

"The werewolves in a distant mortal city are not of concern to us at present," a gravelly voice pronounced from behind Bastien.

Bastien turned, the attention of those in his immediate vicinity following his gaze.

Suli stood off to the side, his posture stooped and his features more weathered than usual. "Sébastien, it is good that you have returned. I have need of you. Come with me." He began teetering toward the entrance to the cavern, his expression unwilling to brook opposition.

Though Bastien was surprised by the goblin's quiet insistence, he did as he was told.

$$\longleftarrow \S \longrightarrow$$

"You have been busy," Suli said as soon as they were beyond earshot of the war council. He made a sudden turn right, descending a narrow set of steps.

Bastien raised a brow as he followed. He did not realize Suli would be keeping an eye on his comings and goings. "Meaning?"

"Just that." Suli glanced behind him. "Traveling to and from the mortal world to the fey world. Conversing with your sworn enemy. As well as wreaking havoc on the Summer Court, from what I've heard." His laughter sounded like a series of coughs. "I even heard you dared to attempt another assassination on the Lady of the Vale. Are you that resistant to having her as a mother-in-law?"

"I have no intention of making Lady Silla my mother-in-law." Bastien frowned. "Besides that, I never asked Celine to marry me. Nor is that likely to happen anytime soon."

"Another mistake. One you should correct with all haste." Suli halted to address Bastien directly, his expression grave. "I didn't see it sooner. But some of the things Sunan said to me on his deathbed have troubled my nights. He spoke of our family. Of love. And of keeping Celine Rousseau safe from her mother."

Bastien bit down on nothing, the need to curse barreling up his throat. "I'm afraid that Celine is not—"

"The best chance for summer and winter to find lasting peace is through love, not war. Through family. Not bloodshed. If you were to embrace your birthright, you would be a leader within the Winter Court. Celine is the successor to the Horned Throne of the Vale. Join your houses. Any children from such a union would ensure a better future for both summer and winter. I can think of no better solution."

"Isn't it against the rules for summer and winter to enter into a relationship, let alone produce heirs?" Bastien asked.

Suli rolled his eyes. "Not when you are among the ones who make the rules. Go to Celine and her mother. Offer a proposal. Put an end to this bloodshed the right way. Keep our people safe by giving summer the thing they desire most: the illusion of power."

"That is not an option, I'm afraid." Bastien closed his eyes. "Not now. Celine and I . . . are no longer together."

Suli spluttered. "Then why did you even bother to come back?" he grumbled as he resumed walking. He made a turn left. "You Saint Germains are incorrigible, unhelpful creatures. So prideful, I cannot even begin to—"

"The cavern with the frozen statues of winged horses. I came here because I want you to tell me about it."

Suli stopped short.

"Is it true it is guarded by werewolves?" Bastien pressed, moving to stand beside Suli. "I remember hearing something growl the day I first beheld it. Is it possible to bring the winged beasts back to life?"

"This is the real reason why you returned," Suli murmured. "You do not wish to assume leadership, nor do you wish to heal the wounds of our land. Instead you chase exactly what brought your forebears to ruin." With a determined glare, Suli looked up at Bastien. "Do not go to that cavern, Sébastien. If you do, whatever happens is on your head."

"Will the wolves treat with me?" Bastien continued. He stopped to take a breath. "And what will it take for these beasts frozen for centuries to answer our call?"

Suli heaved a great sigh. "The last masters the Draconin served were vampires. Vampires from the Saint Germain line. If they would answer any command, they would answer yours. But you . . . will never be worthy in their eyes."

Bastien gritted his teeth. "That depends on how they determine worth, does it not?"

"Worth is determined by one's actions, vampire." Suli stared up at Bastien with a grim look. "I fear the winged beasts will find you sorely lacking." He sighed and then made his way toward a wooden door barely high enough for Bastien to pass through. Suli unlatched the handle and directed Bastien to enter the chamber with a tilt of his blue head.

Bastien did as he was bidden to do. When he straightened in the small room, his eyes went wide.

Standing in the low-ceilinged space was a disheveled Haroun al-Rashid. The young man who'd found himself lost in time, with no way to return home. He wore rumpled, simple garments that still smelled of river water, as if he'd swum across from summer to the frozen banks of winter. His lips were blue. His cheeks and forearms were scratched by what appeared to be claws. Icicles clung to his black hair. Lines of worry—along with another emotion Bastien could not yet identify—creased his forehead.

If Haroun had indeed braved the waters of the river crossing and all the creatures that skulked beneath them, he had risked much to come here.

Bastien and Celine had first met Haroun when he'd introduced himself as Ali, a guest of the Sylvan Vale. The mortal had become a favorite of Lady Silla . . . as well as a perpetual nuisance to Bastien.

He disliked the way Haroun carried himself with such assurance, especially in front of Celine. As if he were trying to impress her.

"What are you doing here?" Bastien asked in a low and steady tone.

To Bastien's surprise, Haroun met his indifference with humility. "I came because I need to speak with you, Bastien," he said, his voice quiet.

Taken aback by his lack of bravado, Bastien did not reply immediately.

"Sébastien?" Suli prodded. "The young man wishes to speak with you. Are you going to act like an inhospitable mountain troll?"

"I don't trust him, Suli," Bastien murmured.

At this, Haroun grimaced. The sight unnerved Bastien, for he'd never seen Haroun look anything less than poised.

"Why have you allowed a favored guest of summer into your chambers?" Bastien asked Suli. "Into Mount Morag itself?"

"The young mortal named Haroun came here many months ago, seeking Sunan," Suli said. "When we sent him on his way with nothing of consequence, Sunan expressed regret. My brother wanted to trust him. I did not. I've learned that my brother's faith in others was rarely misplaced. I spoke with Haroun because I remembered what Sunan said. But the mortal would not tell me why he came here. Instead he asked specifically for you."

Haroun said to Bastien, "I came as soon as I learned that Lady Silla would be summoning you to the Vale to duel Lord Vyr."

Discomfort lodged beside Bastien's heart. "Why would that make you come to my aid?"

That same, strange emotion crossed Haroun's features. "Because of something I learned in my research," he admitted. "And it is not because I wish to aid you, but rather because I do not want to see harm come to Celine." Again he winced, and Bastien recognized a glimmer of guilt in his eyes.

It raised Bastien's hackles. Why would Haroun al-Rashid feel guilt? "What did you learn in your research?" he asked in a steady voice.

Haroun swallowed before speaking. "As you know, I've been poring over the scrolls and volumes of fey lore for almost a year in an attempt to uncover a way to return home, to the correct time and place in the past. I've spoken already with Celine about my interest in a supposed time-traveling mirror." He paused. "When I came to meet with Suli and Sunan months ago, I was told this mirror no longer existed. But I remained determined to continue my search for anything that might help me."

"Go on," Bastien said.

"In my reading," Haroun continued, "I learned that—more than a thousand years ago—a Lady of the Vale failed to produce a direct heir of her own. She knew when the time came, she would have to pass along both the right to rule the Horned Throne and the magic that came with it to her younger sister, who was next in line by blood.

"So she turned to the darkest magic for an answer. She consulted a blood mage . . . the most powerful of the dark sorcerers advising the Lord of the Wyld. She was told that if she took in the entirety of her successor's youth and power, she could not only prolong her life, but prevent her younger sister from taking the throne at all." Haroun leaned forward. "But in order to do this, her younger sister's life must be forfeit . . . and she must offer herself willingly."

Bastien's jaw tightened. "And how did the Lady of the Vale plan to accomplish this?"

"By consuming her sister's blood in a dark ritual," Haroun said.

It took everything inside Bastien not to unleash his rage. Not to succumb to his baser instincts. He fought to keep calm. To look to his humanity rather than to his nature.

His hands clenched into fists. "Why did you not tell this to Celine the moment you learned of it?"

Haroun took a thoughtful breath before replying. "I knew she would not listen. She wanted too badly to keep the mother she had lost. She would think I was trying to turn her against Lady Silla." He paused. "I saw your doubt drive you and Celine apart." He turned away. "And I was selfish. I wanted you to leave. So I said nothing."

In the past, another young man admitting he coveted something Bastien held dear would have sent him into a rage. The familiar heat of anger was already gathering in Bastien's stomach. But he was no longer Celine's, just as she was no longer his.

How would anger serve him in this moment?

"I must apologize for this," Haroun said. "Just as I must apologize for trying to take your place with Celine, when I have always known she wanted only you."

Again, the anger attempted to rise in Bastien. But Haroun's

honesty and the way he refused to avert his gaze as he spoke caused Bastien to see him in a strange new light.

One bound by an ancient sense of honor.

"You must help Celine, Bastien," Haroun said. "I know you and I have never seen eye to eye, but please know that I value her greatly. I do not wish to see harm come to her." He stopped for breath. "After listening to Lord Vyr speak in the Great Hall, I became convinced that he is working with Lady Silla to some dubious end. He used language I've heard Lady Silla use before. And the story of the blood mage's ritual has haunted my thoughts ever since that moment. I would never have believed Lady Silla capable of such a thing. But now . . . now I do not know what to think." He brushed the melting droplets of water and ice from his hair. "I worry that it is possible all the recent misfortune that has befallen Lady Silla may be by her own de- sign. Perhaps to appear weakened so that Celine will offer whatever she can to help her mother, even at the cost of her own life."

Bastien could not speak for a time. His thoughts raced through his mind like a lightning bolt cutting across a black sky. He considered Haroun once more. Recalled what Suli had said about worth just before they'd entered this chamber.

Worth is determined by one's actions.

Not his heritage. Not the misdeeds of his ancestors. Not the money or name or privilege he'd been afforded from an early age.

But by his actions alone.

"Haroun," Bastien began. He raised a tentative hand to rest on Haroun's shoulder. "I will never forget that you sought me out to share this information. I am indebted to you." He sent Haroun a determined look. "And I promise you I will do whatever it takes to return you to your home, my brother."

Haroun rested a hand on Bastien's shoulder, mirroring the gesture. "I believe you, brother. Tell me what you need."

Bastien nodded. "Well, for one, it appears I will need a second."

"Are you asking me to stand beside you in the duel?"

"I am."

Haroun's hand tightened on Bastien's shoulder. "It would be an honor."

THE RUINED PRINCESS

U mma, there must be another way," Celine pleaded with her mother again as soon as they were alone in the confines of Lady Silla's chamber.

A spark of anger alighted in her mother's weary eyes. "As I've told you several times since Lord Vyr's questioning yesterday, there is not."

"The gentry will never accept Bastien's word against—"

"I said there is nothing more I can do." When Lady Silla's voice rose, a gust of wind blew through the open curtains to riffle Celine's hair, twisting her black curls in knots.

Celine blinked, her mouth ajar. It was the first time since being reunited with her mother that Lady Silla had raised her voice or showed any signs of real anger toward Celine.

Lady Silla huffed. "I'm sorry, aga. I am not myself. In my weakness, I have become afraid. The healers say I've lost too much blood . . . but all will be better once I am restored." She waved a dismissive hand.

The imperiousness of the gesture caused something to ignite inside Celine as well. "How is it possible there is nothing more we can do to prevent this duel from happening?" She steeled her spine and stood tall. "I am the daughter of the Lady of the Vale. You are the most powerful fey in all the summer lands. I am told you wield the powers of wind and of earth. Why are we so beholden to those who look to us for leadership?" Something flashed across Celine's vision, washing it in red. "They should serve our will and respect your decisions."

Lady Silla's eyes narrowed. "If you do not understand why it is important to keep those who support you happy, then I question your ability to assume any role of power in the future."

"Who is the ruler of the Vale?" Celine demanded. "You or Lord Vyr?"

Her mother's cheeks hollowed. "Celine. That's enough."

A rush of recklessness flooded Celine's body. The sensation was odd, but not unwelcome. Like trying to dance without music. "If you stood up to him, what would Vyr do? It's absurd to think he wields such power over the entirety of the Summer Court. He would not dare risk—"

"I said *enough!*" Lady Silla's voice boomed, and the entire chamber darkened. Her nostrils flared, and her hands raised at her sides, almost as if she wished to strike something. "How *dare* you defend a blood drinker to my face? I have done nothing but welcome you and the one you believe claimed your heart, despite my reservations. Have you any idea what this has cost me? *Do you know what the vampires did to us? What they would do to us if given the opportunity?*" Lady Silla raged, her pale-pink garments billowing about her, her body lifting into the air as if she were a bird in flight.

Celine felt herself shrink back, the boldness that had been

building within her withering to dust. Some long-forgotten part of her wanted to rage against the indignation, but Celine silenced it in an instant.

It felt . . . stifling. As if she were drowning from the inside out. She swallowed hard, struggling to find breath. "I . . . apologize," she croaked.

Again, a troubling feeling spread through Celine's bones when her mother did not offer an immediate reply. As if Lady Silla were weighing her options.

Was it possible—had Bastien been right all along? Was her mother . . . a danger to her?

Celine's slippered feet eased backward, her heart pounding in her ears.

"No." Lady Silla shook her head. She reached out for Celine, her features melting into an expression of abject horror. "I am so sorry I frightened you. Please forgive me." Her mother's eyes watered. "How awful of me to have upset you. I—I'm so wearied by all of this. I am not myself." Her hands trembled. "It is not an excuse. But please, please. Forgive me." The tears flowed down Lady Silla's face as her bare feet returned to the marble and her garments stilled.

Celine continued backing away, her heart stuttering in her chest, indecision gripping her stomach. She felt as if she were being torn in two. As if both versions of her—the reckless girl of her past and the young woman who would be a fairy princess— could not reconcile themselves.

As if one part of her needed to die so the other could live.

She wasn't certain of many things. But Celine knew she was

tired of searching for a place she belonged. Of thinking she'd found a touchstone, only to learn it was nothing more than an illusion.

Celine didn't care what most people thought of her. Even as a child, she'd disregarded the judgment of others as being either beneath her or immaterial to her.

But when Celine loved someone? When she let someone into her heart? She gave them part of her soul, too. And it made her feel everything. Every smile. Every sigh. Every tear.

It made her feel . . . lost. She was so tired of feeling lost.

Celine thought she'd found herself in New Orleans. Then she thought her place was in the Sylvan Vale, by her mother's side.

But it appeared as if she'd found nothing. Learned nothing. That she was destined to be alone in all the ways that mattered. Pippa had been taken from her. Her mother . . . was not entirely who she appeared to be.

And Bastien had broken her heart.

Celine's laughter was bitter. "It seems no matter where I go or what I do, I am fated to be disappointed." Her vision blurred. She looked away from Lady Silla. "How sad. How . . . pathetic. To know that no matter where I am or what I accomplish, it is still nothing unless I can love without question and be loved like that in return."

"Oh, my dearest love." Lady Silla swallowed, her features filled with remorse. "This—this is precisely why I know you will be so good for our people. Your humanity will ensure that the disease of ambition infecting our ranks will not spread, as I have feared. Humans understand the weight of such things.

The way such terrible acts ripple through a society. How important it is to learn from past mistakes. We've lost sight of that here. *I've* lost sight of it." Hesitatingly, Lady Silla swiped the tears from Celine's cheeks. "I need you, my dearest. I love you so. My aga. My only child."

Though uncertainty festered in Celine's chest, she could not ignore the look of unabashed love on her mother's face. The undeniable regret as Lady Silla stretched out her arms for her daughter's embrace.

"I . . ." Celine cleared her throat. "I have a temper, too, you know."

Lady Silla smiled a crooked smile as Celine stepped into her mother's embrace. She felt her mother's hands smooth the knots of hair down her back.

And she convinced herself it was enough.

The Ruined Prince

Bastien clenched his jaw. He reached for the key hanging from the chain around his neck. One of only two in existence. The phrases Suli had taught him to reveal the wards spelled into the stone were upon his lips when a gust of icy wind blew at his back.

He turned in place, his body angling toward the cold blast as if it were tethered to it.

Sébastien, the mirror cajoled him, its tone singsong. *Do not be so stubborn. So foolish. That chamber contains nothing but ruined relics. It is the past. I am the future. Use me. Together, we will do great things. Ice that was once broken can be remade.*

It was not the first time Bastien had heard about broken ice being remade. The Ice Throne had been shattered when the Winter Court lost the war. Curious that the mirror seemed to wish it restored. To what end?

The wind blew toward Bastien once more, sending another frigid gust up his spine.

He warred with indecision. To his left stood the hidden door leading to the time-traveling mirror. Less than twenty paces to his right lay the cavernous entrance to the chamber of winged statues.

Bastien had wondered if Sunan had hidden the mirror close to the cavern as an added measure of protection. Once Bastien had learned the werewolves of the mountain guarded the statues, he'd become even more certain. The wolves did not realize this mirror lay behind Sunan's secret door, but they would stop unwanted intruders from delving into the rock. Their presence would serve as its own kind of deterrence.

Now he was stalling. No matter how much he wished to deny it, Bastien knew he had come to a crossroads.

Use the mirror? Or turn to the black-winged beasts of a bygone era?

Use me. Choose me. A weapon of brute force is no match for knowledge.

The call of the mirror continued to caress Bastien's skin like the touch of a lover. It could offer him a way to help Celine. To prevent Lady Silla from consuming her daughter's blood in a dark ritual designed to solidify herself as the most powerful ruler of all the fey courts. And to ensure that no one existed to challenge her reign.

He could already see it. Bastien had suspected Lady Silla of duplicity all along. She'd left Celine as a child in the mortal world. Allowed her daughter to believe she'd perished. And she'd been quick to blame Celine's father for her own choices. Her words and actions possessed an air of disingenuousness, as if she were trying to please someone to earn their support, rather than hold fast to her convictions.

And Lady Silla was always careful to conceal her true motivations.

It reminded Bastien too much of his uncle, Nicodemus.

But he'd never been able to convince Celine of it. Now Bastien recalled how Lady Silla had brought her entire court to the border between the summer and winter lands for a simple parley. How they'd all been there to witness the arrow—clearly aimed from the Wyld's reaches—strike her down. Such a carefully targeted arrow. It did just enough damage to warrant an invasion into the Wyld, but managed to miss being fatal.

Bastien remembered the shock of seeing Lady Silla felled. His surprise at how much of her blood was spilled.

Soon, he wagered, there would come a day when Silla would ask Celine for help. The kind of help only a trueborn daughter could provide. He suspected the Lady of the Vale would continue appearing weaker and weaker in front of Celine. A ruse to create a perfect opening for Silla to say how Celine's blood might restore her.

And Celine would offer her mother her own blood willingly, just as the dark ritual necessitated. She would never know of her mother's selfishness. She would die thinking she had saved Silla.

Fury writhed beneath Bastien's skin. They were so alike, he and Celine. For the ones they loved, they would give everything. It could not have been a coincidence that Lady Silla was attacked in plain view of her own court. Nor was it happenstance that yet another attempt on the Lady of the Vale's life occurred only days later.

Bastien had never believed in coincidences.

What would the cost of preventing this outcome be? Bastien glanced at his signet ring. The one embossed with the symbol of La Cour des Lions: a roaring lion with a fleur-de-lis in its mouth. It meant a great deal to him. The gold ring had been a gift from his uncle, and it protected Bastien from the fire of the sun. Wearing it meant he could walk about freely in the daylight.

Would he surrender all his remaining days to protect Celine? Consign himself to the darkness for all eternity?

Bastien did not hesitate. He knew he would. But would the mirror provide him with a solution? Would he be able to spare Celine that fate?

You know I want the ring. Offer it to me, and the answers you seek are yours.

Of course the mirror would say that. Bastien knew it was never that simple. Every warning Suli had levied at him echoed in his ears. Sunan and Suli had lost their entire families to this mirror and its double-edged promises. It could offer a way for Celine to avoid that particular destiny . . . only to have her perish in the path of a stray bullet the next day.

Some things were fated, after all. And a ripple in the fabric of time could have far-reaching consequences.

Bastien had almost decided it was worth the risk when a final gust of wind carried on it the faintest strains of a roar. As if someone or something were shouting at him through a void. It seemed to knock sense into him. The muted roar turned him in place, his gaze settling to his right.

To that darkened chamber.

As with the mirror, Suli had cautioned him about the dangers of entering the chamber of the frozen winged beasts. If the werewolves that guarded the room found Bastien there, they would likely attack. According to Michael's grandmother, they had been tasked with keeping the winged horses safe from an intruder who might wish to use them for a dark purpose.

The Draconin. That was what Michael's grandmother had called them. She'd told Bastien that, centuries ago, the vampire gentry had ridden these winged, fanged beasts into battle. They'd descended from the sky in a riot of beating black wings, their eyes glowing like embers. When the vampires had been forced to leave the Wyld, the Draconin had turned to stone and ice. No one had seen them or lived to share any tale about their whereabouts for an age.

No one seemed to know if it was even possible to return them to life. Bastien suspected that trying to resurrect the Draconin might result in being attacked by the pack of werewolves.

The brisk scent of frost coiled around him, icicles glittering along the stone walls.

It is a fool's folly, Sébastien. Use me. I alone will grant you the power to save the ones you love.

He hesitated a final time. Bastien wanted to answer the call of the mirror, more than anything. The winged horses of lore were nothing more than a fantasy. The demons Suli and Michael's grandmother had warned him never to wake.

But Bastien had ignored Suli's warnings already. And he would rather his last breath be of his own choosing, at his own time, than at the whims of an all-knowing mirror.

Bastien turned right. He took the path leading toward the cavern of winged demons, halting just beyond the entrance, the smell of the frostbite sharpening. Like mint and moss and something he could not identify. Despite the thick layers of darkness, Bastien could see the flickering curves and angles of the hidden creatures. Like diamonds buried in the shadows.

Without a second thought, he entered the cavern. After taking several steps inside, he realized the ceilings were high. At least fifty feet or more. A slight breeze wound into the apex of the chamber, suggesting that there might be an opening of some kind concealed in the thick darkness. The absence of light was so profound that even Bastien's heightened senses required a moment to adjust.

In the middle of the room stood a raised dais.

It was empty. On either side of it lay shattered pieces of thick blue ice.

Bastien examined them. Studied their angles and the way they had once fit together, as if they were part of a puzzle. It took him less than a moment to recognize what they were.

These were the broken pieces that had once comprised the Ice Throne, which had been destroyed when the vampires were exiled from the Otherworld so many centuries ago.

This was the throne of Bastien's ancestors. He studied the remains as if they were pieces of history in a modern museum. Encircling the throne fragments were seven immense statues carved from black ice.

Seven winged horses, arranged in stances of abject fury. As if they'd been frozen in time at the exact instant their rage could no longer be contained. Their eyes were flashing rubies. Their bodies were dark as night. Their wings were so thin that Bastien swore he could see veins through them, as if they were the wings of an enormous bat.

They were beautiful. Terrifyingly so. The guardians of the Winter Court's ruins.

"Ice that was once broken can be remade," Bastien murmured with a bitter smile.

A low growl emanated from the darkness directly in front of him. A pair of glowing yellow eyes took shape. Then fangs glistened in warning as padded footsteps made a slow circle of the chamber, their destination clear.

Bastien wanted to fight. Instead he thought of all he had learned since becoming a vampire. Vampires were made to fight. Their first and last recourse was blood. It was why they'd been forced from their home. Why their throne lay in pieces, forgotten in a dank chamber of ice and stone.

Bastien put up both hands in a gesture of surrender. "Please," he said under his breath. "I mean no harm."

You have made a grave error coming here, vampire.

The voice entered his mind in the same way that his uncle had been able to converse with him. It was not like the traveling silver. Rather than a pleasant voice echoing around him on all sides, this was a savage whisper in his ear.

"I don't believe that," Bastien said. "If you really meant to kill me, you would have done it by now."

I enjoy toying with my food.

"What is your name?" Bastien began emulating the wolf's

movements so that they paced in a slow circle around the chamber, the destroyed throne positioned between them.

The wolf did not answer.

"Antonella Grimaldi told me I would find you here," Bastien said, invoking the name of Michael's grandmother.

The wolf halted its careful stalk of Bastien for an instant. *If she told you where I was and didn't say anything more, then it is because she wished for your life to be forfeited. I will gladly oblige her.*

"She told me you would protect these lands at all costs."

Good. She knows me well.

"And she told me you had once followed the orders of a Saint Germain."

The wolf raised its hackles, a low growl emitting from its lips. It bayed once, calling to its brethren. A moment later, the sound of more footsteps echoed through the chamber.

Wolves were surrounding Bastien on all sides. Still, he maintained his calm, his gaze wary. "If I wish to protect the Sylvan Wyld as you do, will you not stand with me?"

We will never stand alongside a vampire again. Much less a Saint Germain.

"Even if I am able to resurrect the Draconin?"

The first wolf—the leader—stopped in its tracks once more. *Antonella seems to have told you more than she should.*

"She wishes to trust me, as I trusted her. An exchange of secrets was made."

Another dealmaker. Another cursed Saint Germain.

"A deal is what we will all need to survive the coming invasion by the Summer Court."

We will be making no deals with the likes of you. Another wolfish voice resonated in Bastien's opposite ear. He came to a halt. He was completely closed in. There would be no escape for him. His eyes drifted upward. Unless . . .

You will never wake the Draconin, the leader of the pack said. *You are unworthy.*

"How do you know?"

I can smell your fear, vampire. I can smell your uncertainty. If I can smell it, Ziah will taste it in the air around you.

"Ziah?"

The greatest of all the Draconin. The devil's stallion. The most terrifying of them all.

Bastien studied the seven steeds carved from black ice. The tallest and largest of them was reared back on its hind legs, its wild ruby eyes gleaming and its mouth open in a snarl.

"Let me try," Bastien said. "If I fail . . . then mete out your justice."

I do not make deals with vampires, the leader said.

I think we should let him. A familiar voice cut through the building din. Bastien almost hissed at its sound. Émilie.

Silence. You should not be here, another wolf snarled. *You were told not to come.*

Let her speak, the leader commanded. *She knows the vampire well.*

I can feel your fury, brother, Émilie said. *But I still think we should let you try. It would be amusing to see you fail. Then we can rip you to shreds where you stand.*

The leader raised his hackles. *What if he manages to wake one of the Draconin?*

He won't, Émilie replied. *But if he does, he won't survive the true test. My brother is no Lord of the Wyld. He will never be able to remake the Ice Throne.*

Ziah will know his truth better that any of us. He will see into the vampire's cursed soul. If he does not like what he sees, then he will render his judgment, the leader decided. *Very well, vampire. Try to awaken one of the Draconin. Let your last act in this immortal plane be one of failure.*

Bastien looked about the chamber, his body wound tight, like a cello string. "And would you mind telling me how I might go about waking Ziah?"

He could feel them smile, their bloodlust growing. Becoming a presence of its own.

A vampire does not know what the Draconin crave? a wolf said. *How delightful.*

The leader said, *Ziah hungers for blood, vampire. Feed him from your own veins. And we will all bear witness to your worth.*

Without a word, Bastien made his way to Ziah's side. He stared at the winged black horse for a moment. The beast's wrath was wrapped around each muscle. Every sinew was a bowstring ready to be loosed. A hammer on a revolver, waiting to be released.

He murmured soothing sounds as he reached up to stroke a palm down the beast's neck.

"I want to trust you," Bastien said to Ziah. "I believe we have nothing without trust."

He thought he felt something vibrate beneath his fingers.

"You have been locked away too long," Bastien continued. He recalled the words the wind sent his way the last time he glided past this chamber. "I want to set you free." Carefully, Bastien stepped onto the dais that had once held the Ice Throne. He stared into Ziah's ruby eyes. "And if you find me lacking, then do with me as you see fit."

The wolves around them snarled, their footsteps closing in, forming a tighter circle.

Bastien should have been nervous. But he was not. Energy brimmed within him. Danger hovered about in the air.

There had not been many occasions in Bastien's past where he'd encountered any being—mortal or immortal—who had not known his name. Who did not know to fear his reach. *Le Fantôme*, he'd once been called. The Ghost. Such whispers had bred his infamy in the shadowy streets of the Vieux Carré. They had served him more often than they had failed him. The Saint Germain name instilled fear and wonder in many.

But it was meaningless here. No reputation preceded him.

Fittingly, the only thing that mattered would be the blood.

He peeled back the cuff of his shirtsleeve to reveal the veins in his wrist. Without averting his gaze from Ziah's, Bastien bit through his skin. The taste of his blood was sweet on his lips. He let the drops of crimson fall into Ziah's open mouth. They flowed in dark rivulets onto the beast's fangs and frozen tongue.

Bastien stepped back.

Nothing happened.

Then the ground beneath the dais began to shake.

Cracks fissured through the ice, shattering the cave's silence, reminding Bastien of rapid gunfire.

All at once, the ice enclosing Ziah's body exploded with the force of a cannonball. The blast blew Bastien and the wolves back, tossing them through the air like rag dolls. Bastien slammed against the frozen stone wall of the cavern. He was on his feet in a flash, ready to fight.

Ziah's massive hooves crashed into the ground as a terrifying bray reverberated into the high ceilings of the chamber. The wolves who had not been injured in the blast growled and retreated as the demonic horse turned in place, stomping and lunging, prepared to destroy anything nearby. The stallion behaved as a demon unleashed, shrieking to the skies.

When Ziah saw Bastien, he stopped and lowered his head, his right front hoof scraping the floor in warning, as if he were a bull about to charge.

Again Bastien was at a crossroads.

And he refused to run.

He stood straight. Met the beast, face-to-face.

The black stallion bared his fangs and glowered down at Bastien, a snarl ripping from his mouth.

"You do not know me," Bastien said, his tone calm. "But I know you." He took a step closer, dropping his voice. "I *am* you."

Ziah blew streams of air from his nostrils, his fury barely contained.

"Beasts like us do not do well when we are trapped," Bastien continued, taking another step. "As long as I walk through this realm, I promise you will never be trapped again."

A final step. He reached for Ziah's mane. The stallion's skin was so cold that it burned to the touch. When Bastien stared into the steed's eyes, they narrowed for a harrowing instant before softening at the edges.

"You and I," Bastien whispered, "were meant to fly."

Ziah's giant wings unfurled. Began beating, whirling the ice and snow around them in twin vortexes. Bastien mounted the stallion in a single lithe motion.

And they raced into a black sky.

THE RUINED PRINCESS

Ever since that terrible night Bastien had forced Celine to choose between him and her mother, Celine had sought reminders of times when they were happy. These memories had been a comfort to her, especially when she'd been left too long with the solitude of her own thoughts.

Often they would come to her in dreams. They would leave her smiling. Filled with desire. Or consumed by a sadness that threatened to swallow her whole.

On the third evening following their arrival to the Vale from New Orleans—when Celine was still glowing with the knowledge of finding her mother, believing she had finally discovered her place and who she was meant to be—she stood on her terrace, looking out at an enchanted sunset.

In the Vale, the sun never sank beneath the horizon. It hovered in the firmament, kissing the shadows until resuming its slow ascent the following morning. The sight of a sunlit sky in the depths of night reminded Celine of stories she'd heard about the northernmost regions of Scotland. Of a land across the sea where, for part of the year, darkness would never descend on its inhabitants.

Of a place where the sun always shone.

Dusk in the Vale painted the sky a wash of gilded hues. The softest pinks and warmest yellows and palest blues. Like watercolors bleeding across a canvas.

It was here that Bastien joined her along the terrace beside Celine's private rooms. The decorative screens enclosing the space were open to a large stone tub carved into a rock. The scent of the perfumed water wafted through the air, filling it with notes of jasmine and honeysuckle. Celine could still remember the way the steam curled above the hot water. The way the flower petals floated on its shimmering surface.

How it dampened her skin and made Bastien's chiseled face gleam.

Celine remembered reaching for him. How he gazed down at her. How the look in his eyes told her everything she wanted to know in that moment, without him having to say a single word.

He had died for her. She would do anything for him.

Her fingers moved to his collar. Though they'd been in the Vale for several days, Bastien still refused to wear the garments of the Summer Court. Celine had embraced the fey clothing. They felt light as a feather against her skin. She loved how the wind would catch at the hem of her gowns and tousle them every which way. It would have been scandalous back home in the mortal world, but in the Vale, such a sight was perfectly ordinary.

Celine unbuttoned Bastien's crisp linen shirt to just below his heart. She placed her palms on his bare chest, reveling in the feel of hard muscle there. His eyes never leaving hers, Bastien lifted Celine onto the terrace railing, the feel of the cool stone seeping through her skirts to her skin.

Her fingers coiled behind his neck, her hands brushing across the short black hair on his scalp. Her hunger for him was reflected in his gunmetal eyes.

"Here?" he said with a teasing smile.

Celine nodded.

"How scandalous." His low laughter tickled her skin when he leaned in to leave a trail of kisses beneath her chin.

She felt his hands slide from her bare ankles upward. The way he suddenly gripped behind her knees and drew her to him caused her breath to catch. Celine unfastened the fall of his trousers and arched her back. She knew the edge of the terrace was behind her. A fall into the fathomless unknown was but inches away. But she feared nothing.

They joined together, and Celine caught her lower lip between her teeth. The delicious slide of their bodies moving as one made her close her eyes and surrender.

She gasped when he murmured in French beside her ear. *Je t'aime.*

"Until when?" she whispered, her heart in her throat. "Until when will you love me?"

"Until the stars turn cold."

Celine woke with a start.

Every nerve ending on her body felt alive. She sat up straight, her fingers moving to her throat. She could feel the pounding of her heart. She swore her lips were still swollen from the mere memory of a kiss.

She looked around, her hands searching the silk sheets.

But Bastien wasn't there.

And today was the day of the duel between the one she loved and the lord she despised. This afternoon, Celine would be forced to make another irrevocable decision. But she knew what needed to be done. She knew where she belonged. Not to a place. But to a person.

"Until the stars turn cold," she murmured.

Then Celine threw off her sheets and began to ready herself.

THE RUINED SOUL

When Émilie regained consciousness, she found herself among the ruins of the icy cavern. Left with the silent creatures she'd foolishly believed to be nothing more than statues.

She was alone in the dark.

It took her the work of only a moment to realize what had happened. Six of the seven horse statues remained. The wind whistled high above her, as if the small entrance at the top of the chamber had been ripped open.

Bastien was gone, undoubtedly riding on the back of a winged steed.

Soul-deep fury unfurled within her. Once again, her brother had bested his fate. Not only had he escaped unscathed, but was better off than he'd been before.

Now Bastien commanded a demon horse from the best kind of nightmare.

He could fly.

Émilie shook her head and winced. Her right paw was injured. Her head ached from where it had struck the base of a frozen steed. A blow that would have killed a normal animal, but instead only caused her to lose consciousness for a time.

Her anger grew as she took another mincing step.

Émilie tilted her gaze up to the sky. She forced herself to change back to a human, a small scream escaping her lips as the pain of the transformation melded with her injuries.

Her body shook as she stood up, human once again, for the first time since the night she'd help to bury Pippa Montrose. The same night she'd lost her standing among the wolves.

The same werewolves that had left her in this cavern. When she looked around, she noticed two small pools of blood. It appeared the awakening of the Draconin named Ziah had not injured just her.

But the werewolves had not offered her their succor or care. They'd left Émilie where she'd fallen, without a second's hesitation. She was not one of them. She never would be.

Émilie limped toward the entrance, her rage flowing down her cheeks in steady streams.

She did not need the wolves. She did not need her brother. She did not need anybody.

Her strides purposeful, Émilie turned right from the chamber and made her unsteady way through the darkness.

She stopped before the wall of stone and bent at the waist, the pounding in her head intensifying. Then she unclasped Philippa Montrose's gold chain from around her ankle. Against the gilded crucifix dangling from its center was the small dark key she'd retrieved from the icy mountainside three nights ago.

It was the right time. No guard remained to witness her unlock this secret.

You know what to do, Émilie.

Indeed. She also knew that voice well. The one that came to her in dreams. The one that promised salvation. Revenge. And absolution.

Émilie Saint Germain did not need anybody. After all, she was Émilie Saint Germain.

THE RUINED PRINCE

This was a mistake. Bastien knew it already. It was foolish. Provocative. Unbecoming of a leader. Émilie was right: He was no Lord of the Wyld. But if the summer fey wished to see him fall, he would not surrender without a fight. He'd put his affairs in order. Made sure the Winter Court was left with commendable leadership in Hadeon. No part of Bastien desired to rule. Nothing had changed.

Well. Almost nothing. He was riding a demon Pegasus. To a duel. In the Vale.

After all, Bastien was a vampire. A Saint Germain.

His family had always lived for the theater.

The wind roared in Bastien's ears as he peered down through the clouds, watching for the moment he crossed from the land of perpetual darkness to the shores of enduring light.

When he'd made the decision to journey to the Summer Court on the back of Ziah, he had done it with two goals in mind: To strike a note of fear in the hearts of his enemies. And to dispatch Lord Vyr, once and for all.

Bastien knew there was no way to win, even if he bested Vyr. Lady Silla would still invade the Wyld. She'd gone to great lengths to orchestrate the perfect storm, and it was unlikely for her to change course now. At the very least, Bastien could spare Celine any more of Vyr's machinations by striking down the fey lord. And in doing so, he might remind the Summer Court with whom they toyed. Of their mutual past, of the Wyld's still-dangerous secrets, of warriors who would never turn the other cheek.

But Bastien would be lying to himself if he did not admit how afraid he was.

It wasn't that he feared heights. He just feared falling, in all ways.

Ziah's enormous wings beat on either side of Bastien, the muscles of the massive stallion rippling as the winged horse began his descent through the clouds, his red eyes aflame.

The grove of trees concealing the Ivy Bower rushed toward them. Bastien gripped Ziah's mane tighter, his thighs straining, fighting to keep his seat. On a typical mount, he was an accomplished horseman. In fact, he'd been the best in his year at West Point, prior to his expulsion, that is. But there was nothing normal about this flying stallion with fangs for teeth and fire for eyes.

It was incendiary for any vampire to arrive in the Sylvan Vale atop a flying demon. An unspoken threat. But those in the Summer Court who remembered the Draconin—and what they represented—were not likely to dismiss it.

It was time for the Lady of the Vale to recall that the Winter Court was once a formidable foe. The last war they'd fought had lasted centuries. Many lives had been lost.

Bastien was here to remind them: challenging winter did not

come without its risks. Test the patience of a sleeping beast, and it will awaken. He wanted summer to worry. Bastien may not have roused all seven of the Draconin, but since he was able to stir the greatest of them from his slumber . . . then perhaps he might also be able to mend the Ice Throne and unite the whole of the Wyld beneath its banner.

It was quite a warning. Now all Bastien could do was hope it provided him enough protection. The coming duel would not end well, especially if everything went to plan.

There were two things Bastien had excelled at while attending West Point:

Horsemanship. And marksmanship.

If he aimed true, there would be hell to pay. But at least Vyr would no longer be left to torment Celine. And if Bastien failed? Well, he'd left his things in order. La Cour des Lions would continue without him. His beloved New Orleans would endure.

As for Celine? He could not think about that now. It would drive him to ruin.

Instead of sliding from his saddle, Bastien clicked his tongue, bading Ziah to fold back his wings and continue the march to the Great Hall of the Ivy Bower in full view of those gathered. The blood pounded through Bastien's veins, but he continued staring ahead, affecting a haughty, unbothered pose.

The first member of the summer gentry to see him atop the black demon horse let out a shriek. He scurried from the path, spluttering as he ran. The next group of fey to take notice of Bastien and Ziah glanced with puzzlement in their direction. One of their trio suddenly whispered, "Is that . . . a *Draconin*?"

The other two members of the gentry gasped. "I thought they were all dead," the young fey woman muttered, her voice shaking. "My mother told me they tear the still-beating hearts out of their victims with their bare teeth!"

Bastien took his time, making a slow march to the Great Hall. The whispers preceded him, as he'd intended. When he and Ziah finally entered the hall, they were met by a phalanx of Grey Cloaks aiming their alabaster spears in the Draconin's direction.

With a gentle tug and a click of his tongue, Bastien drew the horse to a stop. The Draconin snorted with displeasure and shook out his long jet-black mane. His front hooves trampled into the carpet of green clovers leading directly to the Horned Throne.

Bastien smiled a slow half smile.

"What is the meaning of this, vampire?" General Riya demanded as she shouldered her way to the front of the phalanx. Her features were livid, but even from a distance, Bastien could sense her dismay.

"There is no meaning behind it at all," Bastien said coolly. "I am simply answering the summons sent to me by Lady Silla."

"Why would you dare to bring one of these demons into our Great Hall?" General Riya's upper lip curled. "Do you have any idea what this creature did the last time he was in the Vale?"

Bastien's smile widened. "I don't have the first clue. But I wager I would enjoy the tale."

Two of the Grey Cloaks flanking General Riya brandished their weapons, one of them aiming a sneer at Bastien.

"General Riya," Lady Silla called from the opposite end of the hall, her voice strangely pleasant. "Please allow our guest to come forward."

"Lady Silla." General Riya turned in place. "I cannot condone the presence of this demon in the Ivy Bower. I would ask that you—"

"Sébastien is no threat to me. If he wishes to continue this performance, then by all means . . ." Lady Silla smiled back at Bastien, her right hand raised as if to welcome him. As if to say, *Be my guest.*

Bastien nodded back at Lady Silla, and then his attention drifted to her right.

Celine stood there in silence, her eyes wide. Even from a distance, Bastien could feel her unease. He wanted nothing more than to take flight on Ziah's back and rescue her, like a knight in a fairy tale. Lancelot saving his Guinevere.

But Bastien knew Celine was not the sort of princess who wanted or needed rescuing.

And he was no knight.

He continued up the clover carpet to the foot of the dais upon which the Horned Throne sat, the Grey Cloaks following alongside him, ready to pounce at even the suggestion of violence on his part.

Bastien dismounted from Ziah but remained by the stallion's side. "You asked me to return to the Vale to take part in a duel, Lady Silla."

"Your actions have been called into question, Sébastien Saint Germain. A duel has been issued by Lord Vyr." Lady Silla cocked her head. "But you do not have to fight him. If you can supply adequate proof of your innocence, then I will declare the trial by combat a closed matter."

Too easy. Which meant it was another test. "What would be considered proof of my innocence?"

Lady Silla stared at Ziah. Bastien swore he felt the horse's agitation spike. As if the stallion shared a history with the Lady of the Vale. As if he, too, had no intention of leaving without causing some destruction of his own.

"Your formal declaration of loyalty to the Horned Throne and to the Lady of the Vale," Lady Silla said with an easygoing grin. "The kind of oath the dark fey like to make in blood."

As soon as the words left her mother's mouth, Celine glanced her way in surprise. The sight disheartened Bastien. Further proof of how skillfully Lady Silla had concealed her intentions from her only daughter. It made him even more certain that Haroun had uncovered the truth. Again the vision the mirror had shared with Bastien came to life in his mind. He'd seen it as clearly as if he were there himself.

Celine's blood flowing across the stone courtyard of the Ursuline convent. Lady Silla creating a maelstrom of dark magic to consume the blood and retain her power, at the cost of her daughter's life.

"Loyalty?" Bastien said in a quiet rage, fighting to maintain his calm. "What exactly does loyalty to the Horned Throne entail?"

Lady Silla kept a pleasant demeanor. "I am not asking for you to give me the world, Sébastien. You love my daughter, do you not?"

Bastien met Celine's gaze. "Yes. I do."

"Then why is it too much to ask for you to offer your loyalty to her family?"

"Loyalty to Celine and loyalty to her family are not the same thing."

Lady Silla's easy smile deepened. "Of course they are. We cannot separate our family from ourselves. You, of all people, should know this." Stern lines set across her brow. "Come now. Swear fealty to me. Pledge your demon steed in service to the Vale." Another serene smile. "And all will be forgiven. You have but to say the words." She waved a hand. "I will forgo the matter of the blood oath . . . for now."

"The words alone are not too much to ask, Lady Silla. But I would like to hear what expectations you have of me, should I swear fealty."

"It is quite simple. I wish for you to speak with any winter fey who continue to resist. Who plan to take up arms against summer. Convince them otherwise. Tell them it is better to keep themselves safe. And if they will not listen, I wish to know their plans."

"Umma," Celine said. She moved toward her mother. "We never discussed—"

"Please, my dear. This is how it is done. Once you are in power, you will understand."

Wordlessly, Bastien implored Celine to meet his eyes. He

hoped she saw his truth there. Just as he hoped she could sense how much he loved her. And would always love her, come what may. "Lady Silla," he began, "I appreciate the offer. But you are asking the Wyld to lay down their arms against an aggressor. To fail to defend their lands." He straightened, a muscle rippling down his jaw. "I am no one's lord, but I know enough to tell you they will never do that. Nor will I." He stared at Celine once more. "I will defend what I love until the stars turn cold."

"Please, Bastien," Celine said, a frantic expression settling on her face. "Umma, may I have a moment to speak with him?"

"I don't think it would make a difference, my dearest," Lady Silla said. "The vampire has made his choice." She stood from her throne and raised her voice high so that it carried to all members of the summer gentry who had joined the assembly, eagerly awaiting the day's events. "Make preparations for the duel."

Bastien had come prepared for this fight. He'd known what to expect. Nevertheless, it still struck him as odd how closely the court of the summer fey adhered to the mortal conventions of the code duello.

In truth, Bastien had been forced to reacquaint himself with this old-fashioned manner of settling arguments between gentlemen, for duels had been outlawed in many states for years. They were still legal in Louisiana, though Bastien had long considered the practice ridiculous.

No matter. He had already agreed to play the Summer Court's game.

He directed the fey master-at-arms to summon "Ali" to serve as his second.

Haroun—who was still known to the summer gentry as Ali— would prepare a dueling pistol for Bastien, just as Lord Vyr's second would do for him. Vyr and Bastien would face each other in the center of the glen; then they would turn their backs and walk ten paces in the opposite direction.

Once the master-at-arms directed them to about-face, they would both take aim. Each shooter was allowed one shot only.

Bastien hoped it would be enough.

He watched Haroun pretend to be unfamiliar with the pistol. Watched him fumble about, much to the amusement of the summer gentry. But Bastien had given him strict instructions on how to load the weapon the night they'd spoken in Sunan's home. On the importance of choosing an iron bullet, to lethal effect. There was no chance Vyr would fail to select a bullet of solid silver with a similar intention.

In this duel, they would both shoot to kill. Bastien would not be taking the gentlemanly route and firing into the air. One of them would not leave this fight alive.

And Bastien had every intention of seeing tomorrow.

Haroun feigned interest in watching Lord Vyr's second pre-pare the gunpowder and the round bullet, tamping it into the barrel with a long, elegant piece of silver, as if to underscore Vyr's wishes. Haroun followed suit, packing the iron round in place with care.

As Bastien had suspected, they were situated in the center of the Great Hall as far from the throne as possible. He looked upward. Once he felled Vyr, he would need to escape in the chaos that was sure to follow. His window of opportunity would be small.

Bastien faced Vyr with a pleasant nod. "A fine day, is it not?"

"For you to die." Vyr grinned. "I myself intend to enjoy my evening repast and the pleasures to follow."

"You are a fair shot?"

"This is my seventh duel," Vyr said, his expression indifferent, though Bastien noted the delighted gleam in his eyes. "I have never lost."

"Impressive."

The master-at-arms made the call for the two duelers to stand tall. Bastien stole a final glance at Celine before turning away. The girl he loved but no longer recognized. Beads of sweat had collected on her brow. Instead of standing tall and sure, her shoulders were hunched. Her fingers were clasped in her lavender skirts. He wished he could have said more to her. Wished he could have told her everything she wanted to hear. Promised they would share a beautiful future and all the trappings that came with it.

In the end, all anyone ever wished for was more time. Even just a moment more.

Then Bastien turned on his heel and began marching while the master-at-arms counted out ten paces. With each number, he felt energy rush through his body, blood churning through his veins at a frantic pace. If his heart could still beat—if his blood weren't propelled by its own dark magic—he knew it would be hammering in his chest.

He swallowed and took a careful breath.

Eight—

Nine—

Ten.

Bastien inhaled. Pivoted to take aim. Then slowly exhaled as he considered Vyr's arrogance. The way the fey lord favored his left side. He listened with his heightened senses . . . and twisted to his right as soon as he heard the bullet whistle through the air.

It grazed his left shoulder, searing through his skin.

Bastien almost laughed. His arm burned from contact with the silver bullet. Blood dripped down his elbow. But he steadied himself again. A ray of light caught his eye, surprising him, as he stole a last glance at Celine on the dais. Then he took aim.

Vyr stared him down defiantly. All the other fey in attendance held their collective breaths. The sound of a falling leaf would be all anyone remembered in that moment.

Bastien exhaled once more. And fired his pistol.

Less than an instant later, the Lady of the Vale collapsed from her throne, a crimson torrent cascading down her throat.

Shock gripped the Ivy Bower. Screams followed as the Grey Cloaks raced from the periphery to protect their lady.

Bastien wasted no time. He whistled for Ziah. Before he could blink, his fingers were in the stallion's mane, and they were tearing toward the sun, the wailing and the shrieking chasing after him, the calls for blood and fire and revenge reverberating in Bastien's ears.

He thought only of Celine. "I'm sorry," he whispered. "I'm so sorry."

THE RUINED PRINCESS

When the bullet struck her mother, it froze Celine where she stood. Disbelief seeped into her bones with the chill of a winter's day. She shook her head slowly, as if she could deny the truth unfolding before her eyes.

Her mother looked at Celine, Lady Silla's shock palpable. Then she crumpled from her seat in slow motion, her hand pressed to her neck, her fingers already stained with blood.

Celine raced to her.

Pandemonium rang throughout the glen. Cries of shock and horror emanated on all sides. The Grey Cloaks surrounded their lady and her daughter in a protective circle. Celine heard the shrieks grow in fervor when the black-winged stallion tore through the tree branches, streaking toward Bastien in an inky blur.

Celine wanted to scream. But still she could not make her mouth form a single sound.

Lady Silla moaned as she reached a bloodstained hand for Celine.

"S-somebody," Celine stammered. "Fetch . . . fetch a healer!" she tried to shout.

Lady Silla gasped, blood leaking from her mouth. She raised a hand to Celine's cheek.

Celine covered it with her own. "No. It's all right. You'll be all right."

Blood began to trickle from Lady Silla's nose. She tried to smile.

The ground beneath them rumbled, as if it were awakening from a deep slumber.

And then Celine's mother stilled in her arms.

"Umma?" Celine whispered. "Umma?" Tears coursed down her cheeks. Beneath the throne, the ground began to shake in earnest.

"He has murdered our queen!" one of the fey ladies shouted.

Another screeched, "Hunt the vampire down."

"Flay him alive!" Lord Vyr raged. "Destroy the Wyld and all the vermin who reside in its forsaken shadows."

The earth shuddered, nearly knocking those around the dais to the ground. Still, Celine continued staring at the lifeless body of her mother, her disbelief mounting. The oddest sensation was building around her heart. A strange kind of cooling warmth, as if she had swallowed a mouthful of fresh mint.

"They plotted this," a fey liege shouted, their fingers stabbing the air with uncontrolled fury. "The Wyld plotted this. They sent the vampire here for this exact purpose."

"Silence!" Lord Vyr yelled. "We will wreak our vengeance. Rest assured that we will take the battle to the vampire's door, and when we do, we will destroy every—"

The scream that tore from Celine's mouth caused the ground

to split beside her. All the leaves in the trees above cascaded to the carpet of clovers as if they'd been ripped from their moorings by a hurricane. The gentry stumbled and grabbed hold of each other to maintain their footing.

Celine stood slowly, her scream still echoing throughout the glen. That strange warmth spread through her limbs. Set fire to her heart. Burned into her brain.

Ignited everything.

How could Bastien do this? How could he walk away from our love . . . and then return, only to kill my mother?

How?

All her rage and all her fear and all her pain coalesced to a point and then burst through her body. Briefly, Celine wondered which feeling would win out. Which sentiment would burn the hardest and the longest. And then the pain flashed through her chest with a searing intensity. It seemed to take on a life of its own, roaring like a raging forest fire. She could not control it. Her body and soul were lost to this pain. As if she'd become a whirl of fire, consuming everything until there was nothing.

When she flexed her fingers, a gust of wind formed in the center of the glen, the fallen leaves collecting until they formed a twister. She squeezed her fingers shut, and the leaves crashed to the ground.

Power. What Celine was feeling was the kind of power she had never known existed.

And the more she let this power take root, the less she knew of herself.

The more she became the pain.

He would not be able to walk away from this again. Celine vowed it. Sébastien Saint Germain would know the hurt he caused, if she had to cry blood tears in his face and hurl invectives into his precious night sky. If she had to make the very ground quake beneath his feet, he would know what he had done. He had taken everything from her. She would be sure to return the favor.

He thought himself damned before? Now Celine would make sure of it.

If she was to be left with nothing, he would know exactly how she felt.

Vines erupted from the ground on all sides of the glen. They grew with astonishing speed as they wrapped around the oak trees lining the hall. As they pushed through the cracks in the stone and clover floor.

Celine could not control it. Nor did she want to.

"Behold," Lord Vyr announced to the silent throng. "The Lady of the Vale."

THE RUINED SOUL

Émilie emerged from the small chamber containing the traveling silver.

Her thoughts were a tangle of thorns.

She'd seen their fate. Known what the future might bring.

It had cost her the last bit of her soul, but Émilie had discovered how to ruin her brother's happiness, once and for all. The mirror had given her what it promised.

Now she must wait for the right time.

Émilie would pull the thread. Watch it all unravel. And then they would all know.

Nothing in this world hurt more than being alone.

THE RUINED PRINCE

Bastien did not stop shaking his entire return journey to the Sylvan Wyld.

The madness of what he'd done. The way the thought had descended on him like a summer storm. The sudden clarity it had offered.

That split-second chance he'd been forced to take.

Even a master sharpshooter would have been hard-pressed to clear that shot. Nonetheless, it had struck exactly where Bastien had aimed, as if it were predestined.

In truth, it was the sun that did it. When Bastien glanced that final time in Celine's direction, a ray of light touched the Lady of the Vale's gleaming necklace, drawing his attention at the last instant.

The thought had blossomed to life then. If Lady Silla died from a wound to her throat, she would never have a chance to ask Celine for her blood. There would never be an opportunity to trick her daughter into becoming an unwitting martyr.

But the cost. The cost.

Bastien would face it. In that instant of decision, it had become his own fate.

The second he returned to the Sylvan Wyld astride Ziah, he left the Draconin to be tended and called for Hadeon, Suli, and Ouna. Without preamble, he demanded that they ready for summer's retaliation.

"What have you done?" Suli whispered.

Bastien did not answer. Instead he knelt before Suli and asked the small blue goblin to help him piece together the fragments of the Ice Throne.

It was an outrageous idea. But Bastien needed to unleash every bit of outrage he could muster. Whatever he needed to do to rally the whole of the Sylvan Wyld to his unlikely banner, he would do. It was now his full responsibility.

For he had murdered the Lady of the Vale. What happened next had nothing to do with Bastien's ancestors and everything to do with his own decisions. He had known it when he did it. And he should never have rationalized the life of the young woman he loved against this entire land. It was selfish and unforgivable.

Exactly the thing his uncle would have done.

Bastien did not regret doing it. He would forever regret the pain it caused Celine. But he would do it again and again if it meant keeping her safe from her mother. He had become his own kind of monster. But Bastien would not dismiss the damage he caused. He would stand and take responsibility, even if it meant meeting his own demise.

"Why do you want to remake the Ice Throne?" Suli demanded, his features filled with suspicion. "To what end?"

"To whatever end will bring the winter fey together to stand their ground, once and for all." Bastien steeled himself. The first way to take responsibility was for him to admit what he had done. "I have provoked the Summer Court by firing a weapon at the Lady of the Vale." He took a careful breath. "It is quite likely I have ended her immortal life. But it was a plan conceived in the moment, and—while I am sorry for what is to come—I do not regret doing it. My hope is that, when the power of the Horned Throne passes to Lady Silla's daughter, we may find a leader more willing to act from a place of diplomacy."

Hadeon cursed under his breath, his hooves stomping into the stone.

Ouna cocked her head. "I suppose it—it"—she stuttered— "well, I suppose it was not . . . a completely terrible idea."

"What do you mean?" Hadeon raged. "He believes the new Lady of the Vale will treat with us after *he murdered her mother*? He has brought ruination to us all. We are ill prepared for any kind of an attack! If we are left to—"

"But so are they," Ouna replied, her eyes turning shrewd. "They are not ready. Their bridge is not ready. I am certain summer's forces are scrambling every bit as much as ours will be. When you do not possess the strategic advantage, it is always better to strike at a moment that is least expected." She looked at Bastien, her gaze filled with approval. "It is good to see you acting rather than merely reacting. What do you need of us?"

"I need help to spread the word," Bastien said. "Tell all who can to join us when the moon is at its highest point, at the base of Mount Morag, on the easterly side. From there we will make plans to defend the Wyld." Again, he turned to Suli. "Will you help me?"

Suli said nothing in response.

"What are your plans for the Draconin?" Hadeon demanded.

"Defense only," Bastien said without hesitation. "I will not cross directly into summer with the Draconin unless we have no other option."

"Very well, vampire." Suli nodded, though he appeared to have aged another lifetime in the last five minutes. "I will prepare the chamber and speak with the werewolves who guard it."

"Thank you, Suli." Bastien inclined his head.

The tiny blue goblin sighed a world-weary sigh. "I hope I do not regret it."

THE RUINED SOUL

When Tedor returned to the cave of the werewolves, he came bearing news Émilie was not expecting.

Because of what the mirror had revealed to her—at great personal cost—she knew that Bastien would awaken the rest of the Draconin and restore the Ice Throne to its former glory.

But the mirror had not told her that he would do so after murdering the Lady of the Vale.

Nevertheless, Émilie remained silent while Tedor shared the Wyld's current predicament. She owed the wolves no loyalty, for they no longer saw her as one of their own. They'd made that abundantly clear, and Émilie was keen to return the sentiment.

Tedor's expression was grave, but his eyes glittered with excitement. "The Draconin . . . awakened after so many years," he marveled aloud for the third time.

"And you're certain it was the blood drinker?" a werewolf by the name of Meryl said, her long red hair matted in a plait down her back. "How did he manage such a feat?"

"How it happened is not a matter of import. If the vampire

roused the Draconin, it means he is indeed the rightful heir to the Ice Throne," Tedor said, his admiration clear.

A pang of deep jealousy cut through Émilie's heart. It surprised her. She loathed that she could not control it. Despised the idea that she still felt jealousy for her little brother. Why was it that, irrespective of his numerous failings and all the misfortune he wrought on those he loved, Bastien managed to garner admiration, even from those who had despised him only a moment ago? Not once in the weeks she'd resided among them had Tedor gazed upon her with anything akin to approval.

Why was Bastien always the one?

She swallowed, the taste of bitterness coating her tongue.

Émilie rolled her shoulders back. The wolves in the cave would sense the bitterness of her thoughts if she lingered in them much longer. She was above such childishness.

Soon Bastien would not inspire such emotions. In anyone.

Once Émilie was done, the wool would be pulled back from their eyes. They would see what she saw in Bastien. A frightened little boy clutching a bear named after Mozart. A namby-pamby crying in his warm, safe bed for all the things he'd lost.

All the things he'd never deserved.

"This does not mean we have to follow Bastien or obey his commands," Émilie said. "We wolves are not obligated to anyone or anything, save ourselves."

"Sometimes I forget how young you are," Tedor said. "There are times you strike me as an elder. It's easy to think you have been among us for decades rather than for a few short weeks."

He snorted as he leaned against the wall. "But age and inexperience always reveal themselves in due time."

Émilie gritted her teeth and held fast to her feigned indifference. Tedor may be much older. But contrary to his way of thought, age and wisdom did not always go hand in hand. Sometimes experience only served to increase a man's arrogance. Such arrogance often made them less vigilant. Less wary of threats, even the ones right in front of them.

She looked around the dark and gloomy cave.

The bedraggled mats of hay and fur they used for sleeping—as well as the tools available to them for preparing food—were rudimentary at best. These werewolves often spent a great deal of time in their animal form, but they still had not managed to establish a better life for themselves, even while they lingered within the mountain, serving as nothing more than glorified watchdogs, standing vigil over a cave of silent statues.

The wolves under Tedor's leadership were content to function in a lawless state, with no real designs on anything more. Anything better.

When she'd come across their tracks not long after being exiled to the winter wastelands, Émilie had first felt a renewed sense of purpose. It faded not long after her arrival. Tedor was old and supposedly wise and, therefore, knowledgeable when it came to the history of the Wyld, but his understanding of their past made him cling to the old ways. Made him look upon the world with a narrow perspective. He had become entrenched as the centuries passed. Of late, the only thing that concerned him was drawing negative attention to their pack.

He was old. Weak. Inattentive.

Perhaps these wolves needed a fresh perspective.

"Mount Morag will once again be the seat of power in the Sylvan Wyld," said Meryl, who was also Tedor's second-in-command. She poked at the fire, sending a cascade of sparks into the air. "I wonder how long the Vale will allow the vampire to sit upon the Ice Throne."

"If he has control of all seven of the Draconin, they cannot deny his right to it," Tedor insisted. "Indeed," he murmured. "It is possible the news will draw out many who have remained in hiding all these years. The ones who have been afraid to show their faces to the moon."

Émilie affected a nonchalant expression. "Why should winged demon horses be the thing to draw them out after all these years?"

"They are not just winged demon horses." Meryl leaned forward, an evil light in her gaze. "They represent the strength of our past. The fearsomeness of what the Wyld once was. These creatures were in the stories told to frighten summer children. The Draconin are black as night with flames for eyes. Their wings are made of smoke, and they smell of ash. Only vampires are allowed to ride them. It is said that, during the Great War, the Lady of the Vale feared one thing and one thing alone: the Draconin known as Ziah, who burned an iron hoofprint into her thigh." The eagerness in her face reminded Émilie of a child awaiting a sweet.

How was it that her ridiculous little brother now had seven of these at his command?

Émilie considered this new information. She needed to be careful. If she drew their focus to one side, they would not see the plans she made on the other. "But that does not explain why the awakening of the Draconin would cause the rest of the Wyld to bow to a recently made vampire who has lived his entire life in the mortal world."

"Because it would mean that the Wyld finally has a lord who can protect it," Meryl said, her tone exasperated. "That the throne is broken no longer."

Émilie snorted. "If the Winter Court would follow my foolish brother—who is barely out of leading strings—into battle, then whatever ill fortune befalls them is theirs to endure."

"Have a care, Émilie," Tedor said. "If the vampire is successful, the fool could very well unite the Wyld in a way we have not seen for an age." He stared at a point behind her head, his features lost in remembrance. "In a way I believed we had lost forever." His gaze scanned across the gathered pack of wolves. "Many of you do not know, but I used to be a lord in the halls of Mount Morag. I had a banner of my own, and a seat of respect at the head of a table."

Émilie's eyebrows raised. Tedor's arrogance, along with his fondness for the past, would be his undoing. But perhaps she did not need to alter her earlier plans. Not much, at least. She merely needed to divert for a moment. "If the emergence of a new Lord of the Wyld is bringing other members of the gentry into the open, should we not join them?"

"Why?" a male wolf named Gaspar said as he lounged in his human form, shirtless, across the stone floor. His trousers were filthy, and his long dishwater-colored hair hung down his back. If Émilie had to guess, Gaspar had not bathed in weeks. "Isn't it better if we stay in hiding?"

"We should have considered that before we showed ourselves on the bridge that day," Meryl retorted, her eyes flashing in Émilie's direction.

Gaspar sat up in a fluid motion. "We showed ourselves on the bridge that day because *she* suggested it." He gestured toward Émilie.

"And I still believe it was the right decision," Tedor said. "The Vale needed to know that wolves still prowl the woods, and that their designs on vanquishing the Wyld would not be met without resistance." He paused in consideration. "Perhaps Émilie is right. It would be wise for us to join with the rest of the Sylvan Wyld's forces as they mount a counterattack on summer."

"Another ridiculous parley at the riverbank?" Émilie muttered. "Since that went so well the last time."

Tedor shook his head. "The new Lord of the Wyld sends word for any and all who would fight to join him on the easterly side of Mount Morag, when the moon is at its apex."

Émilie was certain her brother would not be happy to see her after what happened to Pippa Montrose on the bridge that day. The wheels in her mind continued to turn. "My brother will still be angry at me for attacking that young mortal girl. I think it would be best for me to remain behind when you rally to the new lord's banner, which I do believe is the right course of action. It is important that we wolves fight to keep our land safe, even if I do not always agree with Bastien." She smiled at

Tedor as if he were her grandfather or an elder she held in high esteem. "And I would not want you to lose an opportunity to regain a place at the Winter Court on account of my mistake."

Suspicion clouded Meryl's face. "What will you do?"

"I . . . will entreat with the vampires in my brother's coven in New Orleans," Émilie said. "They will undoubtedly want to help him."

"Weren't you banished from the mortal world?" Meryl snickered.

Émilie refrained from lashing out. She was growing wearier every day with this bedraggled lot of castaways. As a castaway herself, she supposed there were those who would argue that she should expect no better. But Émilie believed otherwise.

She'd always believed she deserved so much more than the lot her life had granted her.

"Yes," Émilie said with a grin, "I was banished. I am hoping that the change in my brother's situation—as well as the resulting change in their coven's circumstances—will allow me to speak with them before they throw me out."

"Well, I hope word doesn't reach them of your arrival in the mortal world before you have a chance to explain yourself," Gaspar said with a yawn. "I'd hate to see the vampires take your pretty head off."

The greasy lout's mockery was nearly the last straw.

Émilie had fought and clawed and struggled for so long. The rage she'd held close to her chest—buried deep behind her heart—had fueled her passions for over a decade. She'd sworn to herself that everything she'd done was not just about vengeance. That she was proving a point that went beyond the petty grievances of a scorned young girl. That it was about absolution. Righting a grievous wrong.

Where had all this gotten her?

Each time she scrabbled to the top of something, she fell harder. Only to fight again. To climb toward the top of . . .

She glanced around once more.

She'd fallen harder. And harder. And harder. The promise of being closer to greatness, even in the Wyld, was yet another lie. The werewolves who'd managed to survive here were just that. Survivors. They did not aspire beyond eking out a meager existence for themselves.

They did not aspire to greatness, as Émilie did. But if greatness meant groveling at the feet of her younger brother, she would rather die. Tedor saw greatness in the old ways. He still longed to bow at the feet of the Ice Throne.

A throne that could have been Émilie's, had fate taken a different path.

Bitter anguish took hold of her.

She had been so close on so many occasions. At one point, Émilie and her werewolf husband, Luca, had been invited to dine in the homes of the most celebrated wolves in the mortal world. They had been guests of the Alpha himself on the Greek island of Lycandrus, which housed the most celebrated library and place of recordkeeping that existed outside the Otherworld.

She had been so close to the seat of power.

The anguish threatened to take her in its grips.

Émilie refused. She would not succumb to such weakness.

If she failed to accomplish her plan, she would fall again. But she would turn to the mirror if need be. Again and again. Until there was nothing left.

Somewhere, there was a place for her. And one day, she would not have to bow to anyone. Indeed, they would all bow down to her.

And if she could not win their hearts and minds?

Then there was always blood.

Émilie waited until the wolves left for the easterly side of Mount Morag. Then she made her way once again to the chamber of mirrors.

She would do exactly what needed to be done.

The Ruined Lady of the Vale

Celine had almost lost her sense of reality three times in the last half hour. Voices echoed in her head. Demands to rally for war. Cries for revenge. Overwrought sobs of the gentry, wailing at the loss of their lady.

It was more than she could bear.

She'd tried to drown them out by focusing on random details. The veins on a fallen leaf. Drops of wine trickling from a discarded tumbler. A strange shift in the wind above her. The sight of the coiling breeze, which seemed to play tricks on her mind. To fashion images that were not there a moment ago.

All the while, Celine's newfound power radiated in her body, pulsing in time with the beat of her heart. She felt overheated. Overwhelmed. In a sudden rush, she ordered all the advisers and every member of the Fey Guild to leave her mother's chamber at once.

Celine wanted to be alone with Lady Silla a final time. She needed a breath of silence. A last chance to mourn . . . and ready herself for what was to come. Perhaps it was foolish. Supremely mortal of her.

But too much had happened. A lifetime of heartbreak in a handful of days.

The firestorm inside Celine had not ceased raging from the moment her mother's power had transferred to her. If she didn't find a way to control both her powers and her emotions, she was sure to make a misstep.

Too many eyes were watching her now.

The first order Celine had issued as the Lady of the Vale was to stop Bastien from leaving. To force him—even through violence—to stand and witness what he had wrought. In her fury upon realizing Bastien had escaped, the second order she'd almost issued was to execute Lord Vyr. To silence all her detractors and make an example out of him. She could not lead in the coming war if she was battling members of her own court.

These were the musings of a tyrant. The sort of things she could ill afford to do. Celine had known then that she needed to step away as soon as possible.

"Umma," Celine whispered. Her fingers fell on her mother's unmoving hand.

In death, Lady Silla's skin had taken on a waxen hue. It reminded Celine of pale marble. A length of white silk had been wrapped around the gash in the side of her neck. Otherwise, Celine's mother appeared as lovely as ever. Like a statue carved by Michelangelo.

Again, the wind seemed to curl through the air before Celine's face. As it writhed about like the edges of a fog, something took shape in its center. She thought she saw the ghost of her mother smile in her direction.

Celine squeezed her eyes shut. Her fingers shook. What was wrong with her?

Nothing is wrong. This is my magic. My power. Everything about it is right.

Her eyes flashed open. Vanida had mentioned that some of the blood heirs in the past had been able to conjure images from nothing but air, just like Sunan did.

Another wave of sorrow rippled over Celine's heart.

So many lives and loves had been lost, with no real chance to mourn.

Nicodemus. Sunan. Pippa. Her mother.

And now Bastien was forever lost to her as well.

No. Celine did not have time to wallow in sadness. She silenced her mind the next instant. Chose to stoke the wrath that smoldered in her stomach.

Bastien had murdered her mother. In cold blood. He would deny it, of course, but Celine knew it was retaliatory. He had always hated Silla. And Bastien hated to lose at anything. He'd killed Lady Silla for separating them. As if he hadn't been the one to force Celine to make a decision.

Her mother had never asked Celine to choose between them.

And now Lady Silla was dead by Bastien's hand.

This role that Celine had so feared—the Lady of the Vale— had fallen to her. A role with a terrible responsibility. With awe-inspiring power that . . . frightened her, in truth. It was unlike Celine to be frightened by power. Even as a child, she'd craved it. But this kind of power was so different from any kind she'd ever known or dreamed of possessing.

Something stirred in the corner behind Celine. She spun on her heel, her hands lifting, energy already collecting in her fingertips.

Émilie Saint Germain emerged from the shadows.

Celine didn't stop to think. Immediately she shifted the air to thrust Émilie into the stone wall. Vines snaked from the open window to grip Bastien's sister by the wrists, ankles, and throat.

"What are you doing here?" Celine said, her eyes wide, worried she was seeing things again.

To her credit, Émilie did not appear the least bit afraid. "I came because I wanted to share something with you. Something my brother failed to share with either of us."

Celine cinched the vines around Émilie, ever so slightly. "Why would I ever believe anything you have to say?"

"You don't trust me," Émilie continued, her expression controlled. Undoubtedly she realized what might happen if she were to choose the wrong words. "But I know about the mirror. I have seen the future it has foretold with my own eyes." She paused. "And I thought you would want to hear what my brother has been keeping from you."

Though Celine was taken aback to learn that Émilie had both uncovered the mirror and managed to use it, she did not show it. Émilie had always been resourceful. She'd likely tricked or manipulated her way there. Just as she was trying to do to Celine now. "Leave at once," Celine warned. "Or I will strike you down where you stand. The only reason I haven't already done so is that I don't think it would cause Bastien pain to hear that you had perished."

"You want to cause my brother pain? My, how the tables have turned." Dark amusement washed across Émilie's features. For the first time, Celine saw a hint of Bastien. "I suppose there is very little difference between love and hate. In either case, you must care a great deal."

"Stop talking." Celine stepped forward, her hands raising higher in threat. "Leave now. Before I change my mind."

Émilie quirked her head. "At least listen to what I have to say. You don't have to trust me in order to listen. You only have to trust that I am here to protect myself, first and foremost." Her cheeks hollowed as her expression turned bleak. "I do not wish to die."

"The mirror has foretold your death?" Celine glowered at her. "Good."

"Yes." Émilie nodded. "But not just my death." She took a shaky breath. Her lower lip quivered. "It has foretold the deaths of so many wolves. So many of my kind. The Grimaldis. Your dear friend Pippa."

Celine's heart stuttered. "Wh-what are you talking about?" She swallowed, her fingers curling into claws. "Pippa died on the bridge after *you* attacked her." She tightened the vines again, until Émilie began to struggle.

"My God." Émilie choked, her face turning red. "They never told you."

"Told me what?" Celine asked in a vicious whisper.

Émilie began to cough. She thrashed about, trying to fight back against the vines.

Celine released her hold, ever so slightly. "What are you talking about?"

Émilie's laughter sounded like burning acid. "They never tell us. And then they are surprised when we are angry."

"What in hell are you talking about?" Celine demanded.

"Pippa didn't die after the bridge." Émilie laughed again. "We bit her, and she became a werewolf. We turned her into a werewolf."

Celine almost stumbled at this news. "Pippa . . . is alive?"

Émilie nodded. "And Bastien and Arjun and everyone in your precious Court of the Lions have known about it for weeks and failed to tell you." Incredulity creased her brow. "She's been in New Orleans this entire time, and you still thought she was dead."

A buzzing sound, like the humming of a bee, rose in Celine's ears. She felt her shoulders start to shake. Her knees turned to water, and she dropped to the floor, unblinking.

When Celine's hands fell, the vines loosened around Émilie, who crashed to the stone in a heap, coughing all the while. Both young women scowled at each other from where they crouched on the cool marble.

"I should kill you for what you've done," Celine said softly.

"You still may," Émilie replied, her fingers rubbing at her bruised throat. "But I chose to risk it because I will not see the end of my kind," she rasped. "The mirror told me a great battle is about to occur. The fate of the fey realm hangs in the balance.

The Vale will invade the Wyld because of what my brother did to your mother. You cannot stop it, though you may wish to do so. But if this battle happens in the Wyld, I will die. All the wolves in the Wyld will perish trying to defend it. What is left of my kind will be completely lost." She took a deep breath. "And the wolves in New Orleans—the ones who will come to my brother's aid—will perish as well."

The pounding of Celine's heart rose into her ears. "Which wolves?"

"All the Grimaldi wolves will join the fight. They will all be lost, including Pippa."

Celine shook her head. "I can stop it," she said. "I can—"

"There is only one way to stop it," Émilie interrupted. "You must call my brother's bluff. No battle needs to be fought at all. Convince Bastien to surrender to you. I know he will. He loves you. But summer must never cross into winter. You must meet someplace else. Someplace neutral."

Celine's eyes flitted back and forth. She scrubbed a palm across her face. The idea of making such an important decision without the advice of anyone she trusted troubled her. But she was now the Lady of the Vale. She did not have the luxury of turning to others for guidance. Especially those in her own court. "I don't suppose the mirror showed you a way to avoid this fate?" Celine stared at Émilie, her gaze narrowing. "If you're anything like Bastien, you would never accept anything less."

A half smile curled up Émilie's face. "You know me well. And I do in fact have a way, if you'll hear me out. Remember, I am just as invested in this outcome as you. Perhaps even more so."

Celine clenched her teeth. Closed her eyes. It was foolish to even listen to what Émilie Saint Germain had to say. This could all be a lie designed to wreak havoc, as Émilie tended to do. But how did she know about the mirror? How had she gained access to it?

"I can hear your doubts, Celine," Émilie said. She exhaled. "But you really don't have another option, do you? If you call my bluff, many people you love will die. If you listen to me . . . it's possible people may still die, but at least you would have attempted to save them."

Celine opened her eyes. "Against my better judgment, I'm listening."

THE RUINED PRINCE

Two hours later, Bastien stepped back from the makeshift mold of the shattered throne, his breath held tightly in his chest.

Now was the moment of truth.

"I believe it has had enough time to freeze over," he said to Suli. "Don't you?"

"I refuse to comment," the little goblin replied in a gruff tone.

"Your reticence has been noted several times over, Suli," Hadeon said. "Yet you are still here."

"If we are going to resurrect the past, it is important that someone who was present then be here to make sure it is done properly," Suli grumbled.

"My mother was here for it," Ouna said.

"But I asked for Suli," Bastien replied. Then he stared at the metal and wooden contraption positioned atop the raised dais. "Before we do this, I want to tell each of you that I have no intention to rule the Sylvan Wyld as my ancestors did before me, nor do I wish to resurrect everything that existed in the past. Whatever power is granted to me, I see as a responsibility. I will do my best never to abuse it." He gazed around at his three unlikely advisers. "I will need your help and your candor, now more than ever."

Hadeon harrumphed. "I suppose that is the best we can hope for."

"Oh, will you get to it?" Ouna said, rolling her upturned eyes. "There is not much time left."

Bastien nodded, then studied the hastily assembled mold. The cracks through the throne were still visible. He wondered if they would ever fully heal. But a part of him considered them a good reminder. Firstly, that everything came at a cost. And just because something had once been broken did not mean it could never be mended.

With Hadeon's help, Bastien wedged a crowbar between two slats of wood and began prying apart the pieces of the mold encasing the newly re-formed fragments of what was once the Ice Throne.

The wood splintered with a resounding crack. The iron binding gave way. And the mold broke apart until the throne itself slid from within to rest crookedly atop the dais.

Nothing happened. All Bastien could hear were their collective breaths. The staccato inhales and the halting exhales. The throne appeared the same as it had in the mold. Unremarkable blue ice, welded together in a maladroit manner. Even in the darkness, Bastien could see the deeper veining where the new ice had formed around the old.

He remembered Jae telling him about a kind of pottery that was famous in the East. Whenever it cracked or broke, it was repaired with gold, rather than cast aside. That way, the cracks that had once been considered a weakness was now a thing of beauty. Something to be admired.

It was a fanciful but lovely thought. Another important reminder.

"I suppose I thought something would happen," Hadeon said.

Ouna exhaled in a huff. "As did I."

"What were you expecting?" Suli asked, his irritation still plain.

Ouna asked, "Did it look like this before it was destroyed?"

"No," Suli replied. "It emitted a silver light. But it wouldn't do that now, would it? It has been shattered for an age. Left in pieces and cast aside. Putting it back together with water isn't the same as reforging a sword."

"Ice that was once broken can be remade," Bastien repeated softly. "Why would this not work?"

"Because it was never about remaking the ice," Suli said with exasperation. "It was about what the Ice Throne represented. The Summer Court destroyed it because they did not want anyone to rule the Winter Court. If there was no throne for the winter gentry to sit upon, then there would be no reason for them to worry about someone assuming this particular position of power and possibly leading the Wyld to rise up once again."

Bastien studied the throne in consideration. Could it be so simple as that?

"Then the leader of the Winter Court should take their place on the throne?" Hadeon said.

"If he is ready," Suli said. "If he is willing."

It wasn't that simple. Nothing ever was. Bastien had known all along what remaking the Ice Throne meant. It was why he'd never craved the responsibility. And now? Now all he wanted to do was inspire the fractured pieces of the Sylvan Wyld to unite, just as they'd done with these discarded fragments of ice. These cast-aside relics.

Bastien wanted to fight for them all. For those who'd lived in the shadows and taken refuge in the caverns for centuries, certain that no one would fight to defend them. For those who believed there was no one left to protect this land. Their land.

Remaking the throne was never about seeking power. To the bitter end, Bastien had not wanted it. Perhaps his discomfort had stemmed from the fact that ruling anything did not settle well on him. Nicodemus had taught him from an early age that he was meant to rule. His uncle had raised him to take his place. Instilled in him the notion that it was in his blood.

It was why Bastien had hated the very idea. He never wanted to do anything he was told to do. He wanted to be the one to choose. Like a boy who would deliberately turn right when he was commanded to go left.

But Bastien wasn't a boy anymore.

Everything he'd suffered—the loss of his parents, the loss of his sister twice over, the loss of his humanity, and the loss of his love—had taught him that life was a thing to be cherished. That his choices were his and his alone, as were the consequences.

His past did not have to dictate his present or his future.

Real men did not rise to anger. They rose to responsibility.

Bastien walked toward the throne. Like him, it was scarred and battered.

Like him, it had been remade.

He turned in place. Took his seat.

The throne began to shake. The slightest tremor.

Bastien worried it might shatter beneath him, proving once and for all that he was unworthy. Instead the dais started to rumble. Cracks spread from its four corners. Then they fanned across the frozen floor.

A piece of ice fell from the coved ceiling above, crashing to the ground a stone's throw from where Ouna stood. The cracks unfurled across the ceiling.

More ice began to crumble upon them.

"Take cover," Hadeon shouted, gesturing for Suli and Ouna to press their backs to the far wall.

Bastien considered rising from the throne, but then he heard the sound of a hoof smashing against stone. The snort of a horse.

Ice shards rained down around him as the frozen statues came to life, their ruby-red eyes glowing in the darkness. Wings unfurled and icicles chimed as gusts of wind blew through the chamber.

Awestruck, Bastien watched the six remaining winged horses rise from their frozen graves, their breaths like puffs of smoke in the wintry air. Like fire-breathing creatures of old.

They turned toward him just as Ziah streaked down from the opening above, the largest of the seven Draconin, black wings curling against his back, a snarl upon his lips.

Bastien did nothing, though his instinct told him to rise to the unspoken challenge.

The black horse with the red eyes glared at him sitting on the throne. Snorted.

And dipped his head.

Then the remaining six Draconin bowed as one. The throne shuddered to life. A silver glow emanated from within it, faint at first, then shining brighter, until the entire throne lit the chamber in an eerie white light.

Everything fell silent.

Hadeon walked toward Bastien and placed a fist on his chest. "My lord," he said simply.

"The Lord of the Wyld has returned," Ouna murmured. "For the first time in four hundred years, winter has a leader worthy of the name."

"What would you have us do, my lord?" Hadeon said.

"Bastien," Bastien corrected. "Among those in my counsel, I will always be Bastien."

"Then, Bastien," Hadeon continued, "what should we do?"

Bastien looked around at the winged horses, who stomped in place and snorted, their movements restless, awaiting a chance to finally break free from their prison of ice. To take to the skies and shriek among the stars.

They would understand each other well.

"I believe it is time for the whole of the Otherworld to understand that the Sylvan Wyld is no longer a lost, defenseless land, its leadership scattered to the winds," Bastien began in measured tones. "Commander Hadeon and General Ouna, select a few of our best riders. See if it is possible for them to learn how to fly on a Draconin by the night's end. I do not care whether they are goblins, amabie, or former members of the gentry. I care only for their abilities and their willingness to ride at the vanguard of our forces."

Suli stepped toward Bastien, his hands clasped before him, something shining in his eyes. "In the past, only vampires were allowed to ride the black dragons, which is why none who remained in the Wyld knew what to make of the frozen beasts guarding the fragments of the throne. Already I can see you will be . . . different."

Bastien considered Suli's words. "The rules that dictated the way of things before are not the path I choose today." He turned to Ouna. "General Ouna. If you wish, I would like to offer one of the Draconin for you to ride out and rally those who remain in the shadows. Ask them to come to the easterly side of the mountain. It is time to defend our land."

"And what will you do?" Suli asked.

Bastien did not reply immediately. He gazed out upon the chamber, its floor littered with pieces of fallen ice and debris, the seven winged Draconin continuing to roam about with restless energy. His attention settled on Ziah.

When Bastien thought of his name, the winged horse turned to face him. His red eyes narrowed. Bastien knew Ziah was the one who had decided his apparent worthiness. The demon horse moved toward him, his massive hooves treading on the cold stone floor, the sound echoing off the high ceiling above.

Again Ziah stopped just in front of Bastien.

Up close, Bastien could see how the black membranes in Ziah's immense wings resembled those of a bat. He could feel the fiery ice of his furred skin and the silkiness of his black mane. How Ziah smelled of frost and ash and something he could not identify . . . brimstone, perhaps, as if the steed had risen from Hell itself.

If the Summer Court saw the seven Draconin descending from the skies like avenging dark angels, what might they think? Would they reconsider their decision to flout the truce they'd honored for so long? Or would it stir them to more violence?

"Suli," Bastien asked. "Is it possible that—"

They were interrupted when at least ten tiny winged fey burst into the chamber, their voices indistinct but their panic clear. An instant later, one of the werewolves appeared from the shadows. The yellow-eyed leader, whose name, Bastien had learned, was Tedor.

The wolf took one look at the shining silver throne and the seven awakened Draconin and bowed before Bastien.

"No," Bastien said. "Please rise. I will never ask any wolf to bow before me. Nor do I expect it of you."

Tedor rose, his gaze steady. Then, in a sudden rush of energy, he transformed into a man. His dark beard and wizened features indicated his age, but his clear eyes and the scars on his body showed the battle-worn brutality of a werewolf with a storied past. "My lord. I have come to tell you that summer has begun its invasion."

So soon? Bastien rose from the throne at once, his expression determined. "On the banks of the river? Ouna, have our runners speak with the riverfolk and those who—"

"No, my lord." Tedor's voice was grim. "They have not attacked winter at all. I am sorry, my lord. It appears their first battle is meant to be a personal one."

It took Bastien only a moment to understand the werewolf's meaning.

"New Orleans," Bastien whispered. "They have gone to New Orleans. God help us."

And if that was true . . . then he had truly lost Celine, forever.

THE RUINED CITY

All Hallows' Eve had always been Eloise's favorite holiday. It had its roots in a pagan ritual honoring the dead. Samhain, as it was once known, marked the end of the summer harvesting season. The beginning of the darker half of the year. In Ireland and Scotland, they believed burial mounds of old would open on this night, and the gates between the mortal realm and the Otherworld would be easier to cross.

In New Orleans, All Hallows' Eve was treated with deference. A holiday about the dead brought life to its streets. As with all things, the Crescent City's residents never failed to make it their own.

Dancing, music, food, and costuming were not uncommon, especially in the Vieux Carré.

Which was why Eloise wasn't surprised to hear booming sounds rise into the night sky. Perhaps some damned fool had thought it wise to send fireworks into the air. She only hoped it wouldn't cause a fire before the fire brigade was able to put an end to such nonsense.

She sat up in bed when another explosion caused her room to shake. The book she'd been reading fell to the floor.

"Qué jodienda," Eloise muttered. "I should have gone out tonight."

She'd wanted to join in the festivities, but her mother had—

Another boom caused her window to crack.

Outraged, Eloise threw off her bedcovers and raced to the window in question. She ducked reflexively when yet another boom resounded even closer, reminding Eloise of a cannon being fired.

A cannon? In the streets of the French Quarter?

Eloise flew down the stairs of their home to the first floor, which housed the Henri family's perfume shop on Rue Royale. Her mother was already there, her features frantic as she collected vials of dried herbs from the open shelving beneath their family's precious trove of cookbooks. "I was just about to call for you."

"What is—"

"The fey have entered our world with the intention of taking it over," Valeria Henri shouted. "And on All Hallows' Eve, when the gates are weakest, of all nights!"

"What?" Eloise demanded. "What in god's name are you—"

"Just listen to me, damn you!" Her mother's face was wild. Wild in a way that unnerved Eloise, for it was so unlike the picture of calm her mother had portrayed for much of her life. "We need to drive away all the mortals from the French Quarter. If we can contain the fey attack to these streets, perhaps we can save any innocents from being hurt or killed in the cross fire." She grabbed Eloise by the arm. "Quickly. Use the scented stores in the back. Create a noxious gas . . . like the one we use to drive away onlookers when we seek moments of privacy. Make it stronger than anything you've ever brewed before. There are other enchanters and magic weavers in the city who are trying to draw out the mortals and lead them away as best they can. They are even attempting to form a parade using the skills of hypnotists to lead the crowds to safety. If we can create a border along the western side of the French Quarter, we can keep them at bay, at least for a time."

Eloise nodded. Her nerves were strung tight. Her mother so rarely asked for her help when it came to anything occult. "Of course!" She grabbed one of their largest stew pots and stoked the fire in the stove. "Once I'm done with this, I'll go to Pippa and see if—"

"Once you are done, you are to break into Arjun Desai's flat and flee outside of the city using the traveling mirror, as you once did."

"What?" Eloise said. "Absolutely not. I will stand and fight with my—"

"You will do as you're told!" Valeria yelled, grabbing her daughter by the shoulders. Then she yanked her into a sudden embrace. "Please, Eloise. Listen to me. For once. Your help brewing this potion is all I need. Then I want you to go. Save yourself. Take our books and all the lessons on potion making with you. Keep them safe until I send for you. Do you understand? If this city falls, then something of its history—of our family's past—must be kept safe. I am counting on you." Valeria placed a hand on Eloise's cheek. "Do you promise to do as I ask?"

Eloise swallowed, her eyes wide. She wanted to argue, but the streets shook with another series of loud booms. Jars fell from the shelves to shatter on the floor and perfume the air with bergamot and neroli oil. "I promise."

"Good." Her mother nodded. "Now get to work."

Grumbling to herself, Eloise did as she was told.

When it came down to it, she knew she would do as she was told.

But perhaps . . . Eloise might take a detour along the way.

The Ruined Lady of the Vale

Celine didn't know who fired the first shot. She'd ordered her single battalion of Grey Cloaks not to resort to violence. This was meant to be a peaceful attempt to persuade Bastien to surrender. In exchange, summer would forgo violent retribution for the death of her mother. The streets of New Orleans were supposed to serve as nothing more than a neutral meeting place.

Bastien would never risk his beloved city. Neither would Celine. The Crescent City had become her home. A place that had accepted her without question, even when she was at her worst. She'd once heard Odette say that New Orleans either welcomed a newcomer with open arms or spat them out without question. It was a city always on the cusp, and it had suited Celine as no other place ever had before. Unpretentious and uncompromising. Gilded, even on its worst day.

When the first cannonball exploded, Celine briefly wondered if the mortals had done it. Or if it was simply a series of fireworks to commemorate Hallowtide. But her battalion immediately armed itself. The next instant, dark fey emerged from the blackest corners of the Vieux Carré, their features livid.

Cries of treachery emanated from the ranks of the Grey Cloaks. They believed Bastien had come to the city under false pretenses. They worried he would try to strike down Celine, just as he had Lady Silla. And now iron-tipped arrows and alabaster spears and silver bullets rained down around both forces.

This wasn't supposed to happen. She had never meant for war to break out in the French Quarter. The pulse of her beloved city.

A noxious gas began to fill the air. It caused Celine's eyes to water, though her fey guards did not flinch when the smoke burned into their lungs. The scent would be strong enough to drive any mortals away.

Someone somewhere was laboring to protect the innocents.

Celine knew she could use her powers to cast away the burning fog, but she refused to do so if it meant any mortals might be hurt. She also refused to call on her magic to harm the dark fey. She would only use these terrible powers in defense. There was still a chance to right this wrong. Celine could persuade Bastien to surrender. If he had any love left in his heart for her, she could persuade him.

And then . . .

Yuri cried out, "Draconin!" Her finger pointed into the deeply purpled sky.

Celine looked up. High above the heart of the city, seven pairs of glowing red eyes appeared. One of the winged stallions screeched with rage, then darted through the clouds like an arrow streaking toward a target.

The next instant, one of Celine's Grey Cloaks was wrenched

upward in a blur, the guard's wrist clamped in the mouth of a ruby-eyed Draconin. Its Wyld rider—a small thing with pale skin and black hair, fangs bared in fury—cried out triumphantly. The other Grey Cloaks attempted to fend off the attack by the Draconin, but the soldier was thrust into the air. A second Draconin rushed forward to seize the Grey Cloak's opposite shoulder.

And then the flying stallions tore the screaming soldier in two. The ranks of Grey Cloaks surrounding Celine yelled in outrage and began hurling their spears into the skies.

At that moment, Celine realized there would be no surrender. She'd hoped Bastien would choose diplomacy over warfare, especially waged on the streets of New Orleans. Bastien's uncle, Nicodemus, had been an excellent negotiator.

But if the Wyld wished for blood, the Vale would gladly oblige them.

The instant Celine signaled for the Grey Cloaks to take down the Draconin at all costs, Bastien himself hurtled through the sky atop his own black steed. His face was a mask of fury. "What in God's name are you doing, Celine?" he yelled.

He looked like an avenging demon. So beautiful. So lost to her. Forever.

A cold, calculating kind of wrath wrapped its icy hands around Celine.

In God's name? No. There was no god to be found here. Only a goddess.

She turned away from him without a word.

If Bastien thought to intimidate her with violence, he would find himself sorely mistaken. Maybe it was the Wyld itself that wished to misjudge her. After all, she'd been a simple mortal girl this time last year. Perhaps the court of the dark fey believed she would quail at the sight of blood and death unfolding before her eyes.

Or perhaps Bastien had hoped to use her love for New Orleans against her, just as she had thought to do to him.

She gritted her teeth. All her life, Celine had been surrounded by men who refused to see her for who she was. Her father, who had wanted her to be a kinder, softer, quieter version of herself. The young man who'd accosted her late at night in the atelier. He had expected someone more pliant. A willing victim. In the heat of the moment, he'd even suggested that Celine should be grateful for his attention.

She thought she'd found something different in Bastien. Someone who truly saw her and loved her as she was. But he had fooled Celine with his charm and his devilish good looks. For he, too, wanted to change her. He wanted her to listen to him and believe in him above all else. To trust that he had her best interests at heart. To ask no questions and expect no answers.

To be only as defiant as he wished her to be.

Bastien had tried to dissuade Celine from staying in the Vale with her mother. From having a chance to not only be part of her mother's life, but to learn how to one day rule the entirety of the Sylvan Vale. He had wanted her to believe they could be each other's worlds. That they alone should be enough. Celine should desire nothing more than him.

And now he had taken hold of the Ice Throne. He had seized his own destiny and all the power that came with it, after trying to dissuade her from reaching for hers.

To think, Celine had been ready to walk away from the Sylvan Vale—from her birthright—all for him.

She didn't want to be anyone else's world anymore. She wanted to be her own world.

The pain in her chest flowed like branches of a river to her limbs. It suffused her with power, making her feel heady and light. Making her feel as if she could burn into nothingness at the touch of a spark. She felt herself begin to float. To take to the air, carried on a breeze she commanded with nothing more than a thought.

Celine flexed her fingers. Soon they would all know what she could do.

She relished the feeling. Took in a breath of the foul-smelling air. And dared the city to refuse to bow to her. She would have something she loved see her tonight. It would not be able to ignore her. Nor would it be able to walk away.

Celine gazed down at the ghostly beautiful streets of New Orleans. Even cloaked in noxious fog as it was, it was still a sight.

Alas, the sight of her beloved city—her first home away from Paris—did nothing to dull the pain. If anything, it only reminded her of what she had lost. The future she'd designed for herself, with all her hopes and dreams. The love she'd fashioned from the best fairy tales. She thought back to the time when all she wanted was to have her dress shop and her friendships and her loved ones close by. How it had felt to peer behind the curtain of magic and mystery that had existed at Jacques'. To know a secret very few people knew.

It had been intoxicating, all of it. Then her world had grown into two, the possibilities endless. Her favorite childhood stories—both the light and the dark—had come true. The things Celine had wanted in the past began to look small and insignificant. And then, just as soon as she'd realized what really mattered . . .

She'd lost Pippa. She'd lost Bastien. Her mother had died before her eyes.

Everyone she'd trusted had lied to her. They'd failed to tell her Pippa was alive. They'd denied Celine that comfort when she'd needed it most.

Now all she had left was this magnificent power flowing through her veins. She felt as if she could reach down into the earth beneath her feet and feel the center of all things. As if she were in touch with the Great Creator herself.

God or goddess. What did it matter?

She thought again of Pippa. Remembered walking down these same streets with her dearest friend, hand in hand. Recalled the fated day they'd first met Odette, right in Jackson Square.

Behind Celine, the Grey Cloaks assembled. General Riya gave orders to call back to the Vale for reinforcements. Celine turned in place, her body and mind moving as one, as if all the past rulers of the Vale were channeling their spirits—their knowledge over the millennia—through her.

She flew toward Jackson Square and used her powers to lift

immense stones from the ground and carry pillars through the air with no more effort than it took to move a bowl from one side of the table to the other. Then—emboldened by her ancestors—Celine began to construct a temporary tare in the middle of Jackson Square. She built it with the stones she had collected, as if she were forming a kind of henge or a dolmen. Two pillars running perpendicular to the ground with boulders strewn across the top to create a roof.

It was Hallowtide. The gates between worlds were at their weakest. Why should Celine not use this to her advantage?

When the gateway was completed, Celine closed her eyes. Magic unfurled from her outstretched hands. The power of summer radiated toward the stone monolith, unlocking the portal to the Otherworld.

General Riya began issuing orders. Lord Vyr stepped through the gate the next instant, dressed in full silver regalia, the white steeds of the Summer Court galloping full bore into Jackson Square.

One of the Draconin hurtled through the sky toward Celine.

With a brush of her hand, she sent a gust of wind toward the winged beast. Its rider—the same rage-filled young woman who'd directed her steed to tear apart the Grey Cloak soldier—yelled in a language Celine could not understand. With a calm expression, Celine yanked the rider from her moorings and flung her through the air.

The girl landed with a sudden snap . . . right across the tines of the wrought-iron railing along the edge of Jackson Square. Despite her injuries not being caused by silver, her eyes lost their light the next instant, dark blood trickling down the black iron as the rider stilled in place.

There would be no healing from a wound like this.

That had not been Celine's intention. It had not been the first time she'd killed someone, but she had genuinely not wished the rider's death.

But Celine would learn to adjust. Death was, after all, a part of life.

Then, through the fog, she saw Pippa.

Celine's heart soared. It was her beloved friend. Her first true connection in the New World. They'd shared so much together, right from the docks at Liverpool all the way across the Atlantic. In many ways, Pippa had taught Celine what it meant to have a true companion. To care about someone so deeply that their joy became your own and their pain took root inside you.

Pippa was alive. Celine could save her now. And she'd never have to live in a world without her friend again.

Everything else seemed to melt into the fumes of the noxious fog. Celine swiped the tears from her eyes and called out to her. "Pippa? Wait. I'm right here." Her voice sounded strange, even to her ears. Muted. Almost waterlogged. She flew toward the retreating figure of her friend.

Pippa turned and smiled at Celine, her arms outstretched. "How I've missed you, dearest."

Even through her tears, Celine noticed something odd. Pippa did not look like she normally did. The edges of her pale blue dress appeared to writhe into the fog. Her friend moved strangely, as if she were a ghost or an apparition.

Maybe it was the magic. The fog. Or maybe it was simply Celine's tears.

But the sight of Pippa smiling up at her, arms wide to accept Celine—to *see* Celine and love her as she was—almost undid her.

Celine breezed toward Pippa's welcome embrace. She held on to her friend tightly. The images of Jackson Square in the periphery seemed to distort, as if the wind had rippled the surface of a lake. The sounds of fighting and violence muted to a faint roar. The sight of the dark fey's broken body strewn across the iron tines dissolved into nothingness.

Into yearning.

Pippa wrinkled her nose at Celine and grinned. After weeks of believing Pippa to be dead, the warm familiarity of her friend's expression made Celine's heart stutter. "Let's get a sweet and something warm to drink. I want to hear about your day." Pippa reached a lace-gloved hand toward Celine.

Something burst into flame in the sky above Celine. The sound should have been louder. Celine should have felt the ground tremble.

But instead she reached for Pippa's hand. "Café au lait?" she asked.

"With a piece of honeycomb on the side." Pippa smiled and wrapped her fingers around Celine's palm.

The warmth in her friend's hand. The squeeze of Pippa's touch. The love and acceptance washed away Celine's loneliness. Her fear. Her sadness. Celine walked through the fog with Pippa in the direction of their favorite bakery, a smile on her lips.

The Ruined Lord of the Wyld

W hat is she doing?" Hadeon shouted up at Bastien as they dodged the silver-tipped arrows being fired in their direction.

From atop Ziah, Bastien swerved closer to the centaur, who reared back to defend himself from the alabaster spears of two Grey Cloaks.

"She thinks the illusion created by her heart's desires is real," Bastien yelled.

"Or she wishes it to be!" A ball of fire arced their way, and Hadeon struck out at it with one of his hooves, redirecting it away from Bastien.

"I have to stop her," Bastien said. "If she doesn't start to realize she's lost in an illusion, the rest of the Sylvan Vale's forces will spill through the gateway in Jackson Square. They will tear apart this city and everyone in it." He leaned back just as an arrow zipped near his head. "Make sure our ground troops hold the line at the edges of the Quarter. I don't want any summer forces to spread beyond these streets."

Hadeon nodded. When the centaur spun about, he saw the body of Ouna strewn across the wrought-iron railing. Rage upon his lips, Hadeon grabbed one of the summer soldiers by the throat and throttled him before pitching him into a corner of Jackson Square. Then the centaur galloped away to direct the bulk of winter's forces along Iberville.

From his perch high above New Orleans, Bastien searched Rue Royale for the Grimaldi wolves. He knew Michael and his family would never allow any fey to attack their home without answering the call. If the Grimaldi wolves were there, the real Pippa Montrose would likely be close by. And if Bastien brought Pippa to Celine, perhaps she would realize she had been swallowed by her own illusions.

Bastien saw Michael in his wolf form near Bienville and Royale. He angled Ziah in that direction, slipping past bullets, the demon horse drawing his wings against the rippling muscles of his body. Ziah roared with rage when a silver-tipped arrow sliced into his right flank.

Bastien clicked his tongue on the roof of his mouth. "Easy." He did not want to unleash Ziah on his city. Allowing the murderous stallion free rein in the mortal world was unwise. Even from here, Bastien could tell how badly Ziah wished to wreak unchecked destruction.

Bastien landed Ziah on the cobblestones not far from where Michael and the rest of his werewolf brethren had gathered. "Where is Pippa?" he demanded in a breathless tone. "I need to take her with me. Celine is lost in an illusion, and she is the only one who can put a stop to summer's attack before irreparable harm is done."

Michael spoke in Bastien's head, much like the werewolves in the cave of the Draconin had done. *She is at the Ursuline convent with Arjun. The hospital next to the convent was unable to fully evacuate, so they are making sure summer forces don't enter the premises.*

Bastien took to the skies without replying, racing toward Pippa. If he could break the spell around Celine, he could talk to her. He could explain himself. What he'd done and why he had done it. Once she heard what he had to say, she would stop everything. He knew it. This was not her. It could not be her.

He had not lost Celine. Not yet. She could see reason. She still loved him. He knew it. She would listen to what he had to say, despite everything.

Hope flooded Bastien's heart. And for the first time following the death of his parents, an earnest prayer touched his lips.

Please. Please, God. Help me.

The Ruined Soul

From around the corner on Chartres, Émilie Saint Germain listened to the desperation in her brother's shouts. Satisfaction warmed beneath her skin.

Now was the moment. The time she'd been patiently awaiting, all these years in the shadows. So many months of watching. Planning. Hoping.

Hating.

And she was here to watch Bastien lose everything. The favored son. The one everyone had done everything for. The one Émilie had sacrificed her human life to save.

She had erred in thinking too small before. She'd wanted to provoke a certain reaction from her brother by attacking the things he held near and dear. Her plans with his blood brother Nigel had been too drawn out. Too indirect. And then her designs on ruining Nicodemus to injure Bastien had backfired as well, for they had only placed her brother in a newfound position of power. Her missteps had elevated him, time and again.

Now he was the newly minted Lord of the Wyld.

She could not destroy him with half-hatched schemes or long, drawn-out ordeals.

The way to hurt her brother was simple. It had become so clear now.

This time, Émilie wouldn't be forced to make it look like it was a mistake. He would know it was her. Bastien would see, for once, what the pain of being Émilie Saint Germain was.

It was a pain borne of loss.

A pain borne of loneliness.

And now he would know it as she had known it her entire life.

The Ruined Lady of the Vale

Even through her joyful haze, Celine noticed her soldiers marching on the streets of New Orleans. Grey Cloaks in all their silver-armored glory, their helms catching rays of moonlight. It was odd to see them in the dark. She'd never witnessed any summer fey beneath a starlit sky.

What were they doing here?

Celine shook her head. It felt heavy. Blanketed by a drunken fog.

"What a shame they were closed." Pippa sighed, her arm linking through Celine's once more. "Should we go to the café near the convent? I don't like their pastries as much, but their coffee is divine."

The edges of Pippa's features looked blurry. Again, Celine closed her eyes tightly and shook her head. What was wrong with her?

Then Pippa squeezed Celine's hand. The warmth of her touch felt so real. Celine returned the gesture. Marveled once more that Pippa was still alive. Nothing could describe the feeling of having a lost loved one restored to her. It was like the sun on the first day of spring.

Explosions in the sky continued to echo in Celine's ears. But she couldn't see much through the fog, save for the marching soldiers and the archers at their backs, who continued aiming their arrows upward.

Every so often, Celine thought she heard the growl of a wolf. It should have frightened her. But she knew her powers could keep Pippa safe.

After all, she was the Lady of the Vale.

"Lead the way," Celine said with a cheerful grin. She knew it was foolish. Something strange was occurring around her. Maybe they needed her help. But she could not let go of this moment. Not yet. This peace was worth protecting.

Together, they wandered by the Ursuline convent.

Pippa paused just outside the entrance. "Strange," she murmured. "I'm not used to seeing this gate bolted." She frowned. "I hope everything is all right."

"Should we check inside?" Celine asked. "I can send some soldiers to see if everything is as it should be."

Pippa's frown deepened. "What soldiers? I don't think soldiers should be here, Celine."

"They are only in the city to keep us safe. And to make sure Bastien pays for what he has done."

"What did he do?" Pippa's blue eyes were wide.

Celine shook her head. "We can discuss that later. I don't want to talk about it now."

"No." Pippa placed a blurry hand on Celine's arm. "Something is troubling you. Please tell me what it is."

"Please," Celine whispered. "Please, can we just go share a pain au chocolat?"

"Why are you avoiding telling me, dearest? Is it because it causes you pain?"

Pippa's words caused something to crack in Celine's chest. No. Being with her friend for this short breath of time had allowed Celine to forget the ache for a moment. She did not want it to return. Not now. Perhaps not ever.

In the furthest reaches of Celine's mind, she thought she caught the sound of someone shouting. It was followed by the clanging of metal on metal.

Lines gathered along Pippa's forehead. "Whatever Bastien has done, he loves you. I know it. He—"

"No!" Celine shouted, tearing her arm away from Pippa. "Bastien loves himself. If he loved me, he would have fought for me. If he loved me, he wouldn't have asked me to choose. If he loved me"—she swallowed—"he wouldn't have killed my—"

She heard the arrow before she saw it. It was fired from close range. Celine tore her right hand through the air, sending a gust of wind to redirect the arrow from its path.

The arrow that had been aimed at them buried itself in the dirt outside the Ursuline convent. In a rush, Celine grabbed Pippa in an embrace and carried them both over the gate into the courtyard.

Pippa felt lighter than air. Too light.

No. Celine shook her head. This was real. She'd saved her friend. All this violence and destruction were worth it if she could keep the ones she loved safe.

"Celine!" a muffled voice shouted from above.

She gritted her teeth. She knew that voice.

When Bastien called for her again, Celine spun in a rage. She channeled a tunnel of air before her, then formed a circle with her hands until the raging winds collected into a ball.

Without thinking, she hurled it toward Bastien in the sky.

"Celine!" Pippa cried out.

This time her voice was much clearer. It was coming from across the courtyard instead of behind her.

Confused, Celine looked over her shoulder. The figure of Pippa wavered like a mirage. Smiled sadly.

And disappeared.

Celine blinked.

"Stop it!" Pippa yelled again as she ran toward Celine with Arjun at her heels. "You must stop this at once." Panic alighted on her features. She was dressed in trousers. Her hair and face were a mess. But she was not blurry. Nor was she serene and smiling and waiting to share a treat and coffee.

Pippa was alive. Real. Not a mere illusion. Arjun stood beside her, hand in hand. Jae and Boone and the rest of her chosen family came into view as the moonlight touched their drawn features.

Realization caused Celine to freeze in place. The muffled sound in her ears started to clear. Then a ball of fire soared through the night sky toward the Ursuline convent.

Toward Pippa.

Celine did not hesitate for a moment. She threw her powers into the fireball, sending it to the other side of the courtyard, just beyond the entrance.

To the hospital beside the convent.

The next second, it exploded in a blanket of flames.

Pippa screamed. A long, tortured scream, her face set in horror. She fell to her knees screeching for help. Without hesitating, Arjun raced in the direction of the hospital. Celine gasped when she turned around. Terror clutched at her chest. She began to run behind Arjun, her powers collecting in the air around her.

Bastien was beside her in an instant, grabbing her by the waist, struggling to take hold of her wrists. "No, Celine."

"Get off me," she yelled, kicking her feet and flailing.

"Stop it!" he said. "You can't try to put out the fire. If you blast it with air, it will get worse."

Of course. Celine knew that. Still, she tried to shove Bastien away. His grip only tightened, his face filled with sorrow.

Inside the hospital, the cries for help reached a fevered pitch. Jae and Boone chased after Arjun, the trio entering the building without a glance back. A breath passed before flames engulfed the hospital on all sides.

"Arjun!" a small boy yelled from behind Pippa. Celine watched Pippa grab hold of her brother and sister. Henry tried to tear away, clearly intent on helping.

Boone made it outside, carrying two patients across his shoulders. His clothing, hair, and skin were badly burned. Once he deposited them on the ground far from the building, he pivoted to return.

The hospital caved in before he was able to make it two steps.

For an instant, they all stood in silent shock.

Bastien blurred toward Boone, holding him back, even as Boone cried out, his voice inhuman in its grief. Pippa began sobbing, and Henry ripped away from his sisters, racing toward the blaze, shouting one thing over and over again:

"No! I have to save my brother. He's my brother!"

Celine couldn't watch. Bastien barely managed to pull Henry away from the blaze.

The small child's cries buried into Celine like the tip of a knife. Then he fled toward Pippa, who knelt on the ground, clutching both her siblings to her chest as they wailed.

Without thought, Celine bent toward them, tears blurring her eyes.

Pippa screamed, "Get away!" The words came from her chest like a roar.

The sound stopped Celine midstep.

"How—how could you do this?" Pippa wailed to Celine. "What have you done, Celine?"

"No." Celine shook her head. "I saved you. I came here to save you." Her body began to shake. Her hands pressed to her temples.

"Save me, as if you were God?" Pippa cried. "Who lives or dies isn't your choice to make!"

When Bastien attempted to take her in his arms, Celine turned on him. She shoved him back. "This is your fault," she yelled. "You did this." She pushed him again. *"You made me do this."*

He did nothing. He said nothing.

The fire continued to rage in the distance.

"Fight back," Celine demanded of Bastien, shoving him once more. "Fight back, you coward. You *murderer.*"

Bastien continued staring at her, the pity in his gaze tearing her into pieces.

Celine screamed a soul-deep scream and fell to her knees. The wind roared around her. The fire blazed into the purple sky. Her heart thundered through her body.

If Bastien was a murderer, then so was she.

And they would both pay the price for it.

THE RUINED LORD OF THE WYLD

Bastien stood on one side of Jackson Square. Hadeon, the commander of the Sylvan Wyld's forces, guarded his right. Ziah waited behind him, whickering softly, his hooves striking the pavers. Restless. The other six Draconin served as sentinels, perched all around the square.

Celine, the Lady of the Vale, waited on the other side of the square, her Grey Cloaks guarding her on all sides. General Riya stood to her right, her expression bleak.

There were no winners tonight. Both summer and winter had lost.

Lord Vyr had been killed by Ziah. Arjun's mother had flown into a rage when she learned about the loss of her only son. Ouna had perished on the tines of Jackson Square. The bodies of several Grey Cloaks were being collected from all around the Quarter. Once the fire at the hospital had begun to die down, the search for survivors had begun.

Of course . . . there was no trace of Jae or Arjun.

Even the strongest vampire could not withstand a blaze powered by such ruthless summer magic.

The losses weighed on Bastien like an anvil. He would not

allow the grief to take root. Not yet. For the battle was still not over. It wouldn't be over until he destroyed the mirror after Haroun used it a final time. Until both sides had taken their pound of flesh.

Bastien would give it. Whatever Celine asked. Whatever it took to grant them peace.

"Sébastien Saint Germain," Celine said. There was no life in her voice. Her lips were cracked. Her fingers trembled as she tucked a loose black curl behind an ear. "The Lord of the Wyld," she continued softly. "We are here to discuss the truce that once existed between summer and winter. But you are responsible for the death of my mother. In cold blood, you murdered the Lady of the Vale. The Summer Court demands a reckoning."

"I understand." Bastien nodded.

Celine closed her eyes. It seemed as if she'd aged a decade in an hour. Bastien wanted more than anything to hold her. To explain himself. To say how sorry he was. But he knew the words would sound hollow.

This place they had come to—this painful journey they had taken—was beyond words.

"There are many who would have your head," Celine continued. "But I do not think more bloodshed is the solution. We . . . have lost something precious to us. We expect you to forfeit the same." She took a careful breath. "However, we also do not wish to repeat the mistakes of the past."

Surprise touched Bastien's face. He waited.

"The last time a truce was discussed," Celine said, "punishments were doled out solely on the Wyld. I know that winter has lost a great deal in this fight." Her gaze hardened. "I will bear the cost of this. Whatever you and your court deem fair."

General Riya opened her mouth to protest, her face streaked with soot and the telltale trail of tears.

"No," Celine said quietly. "Summer is not innocent. If we are to have lasting peace, we must acknowledge the wrongs we have committed."

Bastien glanced at Hadeon. Then he looked around Jackson Square. At the destruction surrounding them. At the smoke still curling into the sky. "The Winter Court wants to ensure the Lady of the Vale's powers do no further harm in the Wyld . . . or in New Orleans."

Celine swallowed. Her hands balled at her sides.

Bastien knew he was asking her to stay away from both places. Maybe there would be a time in the future when Celine was in full control of her magic. Until then, he would not risk repeating tonight's events. Not for any promise in the world.

"Very well." Celine lifted her chin. "I agree."

General Riya stepped forward. "You are never to see or speak with the Lady of the Vale again. Any communication between you must be through an emissary."

Bastien wanted to argue. "I can't very well govern if I am not allowed to speak to my counterpart in the Vale. There must be something else."

General Riya's eyes narrowed. "We discussed another exile."

"I will not be exiled from my own lands." Bastien looked at Celine. "You said you wished to learn from the past. Leaving the Wyld without proper leadership is simply more of the same."

Celine inhaled. "You're right." Her lips pursed. "Then . . . we wish to exile you from this land."

"New Orleans?" Surprise flared through Bastien, followed by a spike of anger. He would not agree to this. He would never agree. This was his home. His beloved city.

"I have lost something dear to me, Sébastien Saint Germain. My mother can never be restored. You have lost a great deal as well." Celine looked around Jackson Square. Weary sadness clouded her expression. "I think we can both agree that New Orleans would be safer for the ones we love if we didn't return to it."

Loss gripped Bastien's insides. The pain of it almost left him breathless. "I will leave New Orleans," he said quietly. "And never return."

This was his city. His home. The idea that he would never see it again—never wander its streets or hear the lilting strains of far-off music or smell the scent of roasting cochon in the distance—threatened to overwhelm him.

General Riya nodded. Then she gestured for the remaining summer troops to begin making their way through the gate.

"Bastien?" Celine said.

He turned in place. The way she said his name tore the remaining shreds of his heart.

"It needs to be destroyed," Celine said. "Promise me."

"You would believe my promise?"

"Yes. We owe each other that much."

Bastien nodded. "After Haroun uses it, it will be destroyed."

"Thank you." She turned away.

"Celine?" An unbearable ache began to unfurl through his chest.

She stopped.

"I'm sorry," Bastien said. "So sorry."

"So am I," she whispered. Her eyes welled with tears.

Celine and Bastien stared at each other for a moment.

Then they turned their backs and left New Orleans for the last time.

The Ruined Soul

Émilie wandered through the smoldering buildings in the heart of the Vieux Carré. The battle between the light and dark fey had brought ruination to a third of the French Quarter. Several buildings had fallen. The streets were filled with mud, ash, and debris.

A fire from revelry gone awry. That was what the mortals were saying about it.

Miraculously, not many humans had been killed in the mêlée. The worst of their losses were at the hospital beside the Ursuline convent. Even then, many of the patients inside it had already been evacuated. It would take New Orleans some time to recover from all the damage, but it had weathered such storms before. It was a resilient city. It knew better than most how to rise from the ashes. Unquestionably it would return better than before.

Of that, Émilie had no doubt.

She padded down the still-dark streets.

It would be the last time Émilie would ever be in New Orleans. It surprised her how sentimental she felt in this moment.

Perhaps it was true. The city had managed to worm its way into Émilie's heart, despite all.

She'd lived and died and been reborn here. She'd seen the beginning and the end of all things. She'd loved and lost and labored in its shadowy streets.

The hackles on her neck rose. Émilie heard the wolf before she saw it.

She turned to growl, her body lowered, ready to lunge.

It was Michael Grimaldi. He had not changed back to a human.

They are dead? Émilie asked in her mind.

Michael curled his upper lip. *Arjun and Jae did not survive the fire. Henry's hands were badly burned, but he will live.*

Something to be thankful for, I suppose. Émilie snorted. *Are you here to kill me? If so, I am ready.*

I don't hurt women, though I could make an exception for you.

Do as you will. I won't fight it.

Michael quirked his head. *Why?*

Because I have nothing left to lose. And I have ruined my brother's happiness. He can never be with Celine now. He won't have her. And she won't have him.

I wouldn't place a bet on either of those assumptions.

Wouldn't that make you happy, to hear that Celine and Bastien will never be together?

Michael seemed to sigh. *No. It doesn't make me happy to think that.*

She can be with you.

That's the problem with you, isn't it? You think settling scores and leveling the playing field are simple. He took a step forward. *I don't want to be with Celine anymore because I can't make her happy. I'm not the one she wants.*

Perhaps you are the one who is simple.

Michael paused in thought, a storm cloud descending on his brow. *What did you give the mirror?*

Émilie pretended to yawn. *Nothing too important. Nothing I will miss, for sure.*

Michael waited.

Émilie smiled. *Don't fret, Michael Grimaldi. I cannot do any more harm. I am forever changed into a wolf. I can never be human again.*

You gave the mirror your humanity?

What was left of it to give, that is.

Michael seemed to consider this. *I will never understand why you did these things. What you hoped to achieve by causing such pain.*

Because you have always been loved and wanted and appreciated.

No. I haven't. But maybe it makes the times when I am loved and wanted and appreciated all the sweeter.

Enough. Émilie sneered. *If you're here to kill me, then do it. I'm ready.*

No. I'm not going to kill you.

You've always been so weak. Haven't you learned what mercy cost my brother?

No. I'm not weak. And being merciful isn't a sign of weakness. It is a sign of forgiveness.

I don't want to be forgiven.

Forgiveness isn't for you, Émilie. You never understood that. Maybe that's why you hold so much hate in your heart. Forgiveness is for me. For Bastien. For all the ones you've wronged. Maybe if you had learned to forgive, you wouldn't be so alone.

Stop talking, Michael Grimaldi. Émilie growled. *Do what you came to do. Be done with it.*

Michael exhaled. *I hope you live a long life, Émilie Saint Germain. You will likely be alone, and that's the worst punishment I can think to bestow on anyone. If you find anyone willing to love you, you will likely ruin it, as you have all your life.*

Damn you to Hell, you weak bastard. Émilie crouched to lunge.

Michael walked away.

What are you doing? Émilie demanded. *Where are you going?*

He limped back into the shadows.

A lump formed in Émilie's throat. Part of her wanted to chase him down. Provoke him. Prove that he still cared. But she would never stoop to such lowness.

She was Émilie Saint Germain. She didn't need anyone.

When she ran to the outskirts of town, the lump in her throat remained.

THE RUINED FUTURE

Eloise Henri watched from the shadows outside the flat that had once been shared by Arjun and Jae as the two immense wolves dispersed in opposite directions. They'd been discussing something, of that she was certain. Of course, she couldn't understand anything they said.

But the smaller wolf had dropped something as it ran.

Eloise couldn't be sure what it was. She only knew that it glinted in the darkness, like a diamond.

When she stooped to the ground to retrieve it, she saw that it was a golden chain. Hanging from it was a small crucifix and a strange key made of iron.

Eloise hoisted the sack filled with her family's spell books higher on her shoulder and pocketed the key. She'd dawdled long enough. She needed to use the mirror inside the flat to leave the city, as her mother directed.

But maybe she would see where else the traveling silver might take her.

Just once.

After that, Eloise would be a good, dutiful daughter. Just like she promised.

THE BRIDGE BETWEEN
LIGHT AND DARK

The Lady of the Vale stood at one end of the newly constructed bridge. Across the way, the Winter Court's contingent gathered in all their dark finery. Soon, their lord arrived on a black winged stallion, his long cloak trailing behind him.

The Lady of the Vale held her breath.

He was still beautiful to her. He would always be beautiful to her. Curse him for stealing the breath from her body yet again.

He dismounted.

It had been more than ten mortal years since they'd last seen each other face-to-face. The completion of this bridge was to be the pinnacle of many months of diplomacy. Of emissaries being sent from the land of eternal sunshine to the world of perpetual night. As this new truce was solidified and wounds were slowly healed.

Lady Celine, ruler of the Summer Court, had dressed for the occasion.

She could have chosen any of her Summer Court finery. Instead she dressed as she had back home in New Orleans. Stays and a silk taffeta underskirt with a matching bodice. An apron overskirt replete with ruffles and a bustle with intricate draping and a jaunty bow.

All in the color of red. Brilliant red. The hue of freshly stained blood.

When the Lord of the Wyld began striding across the newly completed bridge, Celine walked to meet him in its center. Behind her, she sensed the presence of her general, Yuri, as well as the Silver Cloak guards flanking them from a respectful distance.

The Lord of the Wyld walked with a wolf at one shoulder and a familiar blue goblin at the other.

Celine Rousseau, who had once been a dressmaker from Paris with a terrible secret, stood tall as she faced Sébastien Saint Germain, who had once been a boy who wandered the darkened streets of New Orleans shrouded in Savile Row and mystery.

Celine, the Lady of the Vale, and Bastien, the Lord of the Wyld.

The girl who became a fairy queen with the magic of air and earth running through her veins. The boy who became a vampire and assumed the mantle of a long-lost line of blood-drinking royalty.

They stopped before each other at the center of the bridge.

To Celine, Bastien looked as he always did. As he always had since the night she first glimpsed him wandering the darkened streets of New Orleans with the kind of power she could only dream of possessing. When she felt her heartbeat quicken, she forced herself to remain calm. But not before the hint of a knowing smile curved his lips.

"Hello," she said, determined to stay levelheaded throughout this symbolic exchange.

"Hello," he replied.

"I have to admit, part of me thought you would send advisers."

"I said I would go. So I am here. It is important to both our lands for them to see that we mean to have peace between us."

Celine inhaled through her nose. "You didn't want to see me. Still?"

Bastien said nothing.

Something knifed in her chest. It jarred her, that his disapproval could sting so sharply, even after all this time. Hot on the heels of this realization came a deeper sense of understanding. They had both hurt each other. Her wounds were too deep to heal on their own. She had lost so much. So had he.

They had lost each other.

Bastien glanced over his shoulder and gestured toward the attendants waiting there. A winged horse emerged from the woods, led on a gilded rope with scarlet reins. The dappling along its flanks reminded Celine of an old mirror, its surface mottled and beautiful.

One of Bastien's Black Knights led the stunning animal across the bridge. It reared back and whinnied, its wings spreading wide, its eyes blazing with indignation.

Bastien offered Celine an almost apologetic smile. "He's supposed to be a gift of peace."

"He seems like a spy to me," Celine replied without thought.

"Perhaps." Bastien grinned in earnest. "There is only one way to know for certain. Or"—he took hold of the horse's reins and handed them to Celine—"you could trust me."

Celine flashed him a smile, baring all her teeth. "In a pig's eye, my lord." She took the reins and motioned for one of her Silver Cloaks to lead the horse the rest of the way.

"Still uncomfortable with trusting dark fey, my lady?" Bastien asked, his tone cool.

"It's in my blood, vampire. I'm certain you can tell."

Bastien laughed. As the rich sound rumbled from his mouth, Celine saw him relax. The next instant she felt the tension leave her body. "You always did know how to make me laugh," he said.

Celine grinned. "I have a gift for you as well." She stepped aside so that he could see the elegant tent erected at the end of the bridge behind her. "Will you share a meal with me?"

He paused in consideration. "As long as your general will partake in a meal with my general."

"Of course." Celine nodded and began walking toward the elaborate tent set near the shore. When Bastien moved closer, a familiar scent filled her nostrils. She inhaled deeply. His hand brushed hers, and he pulled back for a moment.

They entered the tent, and Celine held her breath. She'd been preparing for this moment for several months.

Bastien paused as he glanced around. Unease darkened his gaze. "A bit bare, is it not?"

The tent was empty, save for a table and two chairs in its center.

"You are a difficult man to offer a gift. I struggled to think of something that would have meaning to you."

"That is unnecessary," he said. "Any symbolic gift would suffice."

"But we are not merely symbolic enemies, are we?"

"No," he agreed. "We are not."

He stepped toward the head of the table. Then he paused. With a nod, he offered the chair to Celine. "Apologies for the oversight. An old habit."

"Unlearning old habits is something we both have had to do." Celine held out her hand and waved it over the rectangular table. It shimmered and shifted until it changed to form a circle.

Bastien's eyes widened. "Impressive."

"I've been studying and practicing a great deal. I'm not Sunan, and it's unlikely that I will ever be as gifted as he was, but I'd like to think my mastery over air and illusion will be a skill to hone for many years to come."

"If you put your mind to it, there is nothing you can't accomplish, Celine."

Celine sat at the table. "I still prefer making my own garments by hand," she confessed. "It never fails to throw my attendants into an uproar. Though I will freely admit that fey fabric is unlike anything else. I can't manage it on my own, so I mostly still use silk and linen." She paused to worry her lower lip between her teeth. "How is Pippa?"

Understanding settled on his features. "She will see you again, Celine. I know she will. Just give her more time."

Tears welled in her eyes for a moment. Then she nodded and coughed to clear her voice.

The next instant, Bastien's voice returned to its formal tenor.

"Henry is off to Harvard soon, and Lydia has already made quite a name for herself at Cambridge. Already making noise about women being granted the right to vote."

"Brava, Lydia." Celine laughed. "I hope she rakes them over the coals. A pity the so-called gentlemen at Harvard have not yet learned that women are every bit their equals and deserve to be studying beside them."

"One day it will happen. Not a moment too soon. But it is inevitable."

His words brought to mind something Celine had once thought of their love. "Bastien—" she began, and stopped short before she could finish the thought.

"Yes?" he said.

"I thought better of it."

An awkward beat of silence passed between them. "I don't regret anything between us, Celine," he said, his tone kind. "I hope you do not regret it either. Those we lost . . ." He hesitated. "I don't believe they were lost because we loved each other."

"I'm glad to hear it."

He cleared his throat. "Now, I am quite curious about what you thought fitting to serve to a vampire."

"Something rare, of course." Celine almost grinned. She stood and closed her eyes. In her mind's eye, she conjured a perfect image. The way it had once been. The curtains and the china and the hustle and bustle of constant movement. A symphony of sound and senses. The scraping on bone china and cut crystal clinking together. The smell of melted butter and spices and the splash of wine in an empty goblet.

She kept her eyes closed, committed to making sure every detail was painted with perfect clarity. "I've been practicing," she said. "I'm not sure I'll get everything right. But it's the best gift I could think to give."

When she opened her eyes, Bastien's back was to her. He stood in the center of the dining room at Jacques'. If Celine did not notice the way his fists were clenched, she would think him to be merely one of the many patrons frequenting the famed dining establishment.

"Bastien?" she said. She walked toward him, skirting a server who pushed a cart of domed dishes, whisking it toward a table in the far corner.

Still he said nothing.

Celine came to stand beside him. She noticed the trails of crimson on his cheeks and kept silent.

When he reached for her hand, Celine startled. Their fingers were stiff at first, and then they entwined as if they'd never been apart, like the roots of a tree, buried deep beneath the ground.

"What were you going to say?" Bastien asked. "When you thought better of it."

"I wanted to know if you might take a walk with me someday."

"I thought my answer to such a question would always be no," Bastien said. "But I may consider a walk, my lady." He glanced her way. "If you'll visit my mountain."

Celine squeezed his hand. "Before, I would have said no." She smiled. "But I enjoy toying with danger."

YOUR GUIDE TO RENÉE AHDIEH:

SEE WHERE
CELINE AND
BASTIEN'S STORY
BEGAN

Excerpt on Page 393

READ MORE
FROM THE
BEAUTIFUL
QUARTET

Excerpt on Page 403

THE QUARTET
CONTINUES
WITH PIPPA AND
ARJUN'S ROMANCE

Excerpt on Page 413

CHECK OUT
RENÉE AHDIEH'S
FIRST SERIES

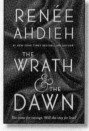

Excerpt on Page 427

STILL CRAVING
MORE RENÉE
AHDIEH?

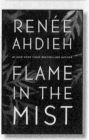

Excerpt on Page 441

TURN THE PAGE FOR AN EXCERPT OF:

———◦∘◇∘◇∘◦———

Now Orleans is a city ruled by the dead.
     I remember the moment I first heard someone say this. The old man meant to frighten me. He said there was a time when coffins sprang from the ground following a heavy rain, the dead flooding the city streets. He claimed to know of a Créole woman on Rue Dauphine who could commune with spirits from the afterlife.

I believe in magic. In a city rife with illusionists, it's impossible to doubt its existence. But I didn't believe this man. *Be faithful,* he warned. *For the faithless are alone in death, blind and terrified.*

I feigned shock at his words. In truth, I found him amusing. He was the sort to scare errant young souls with stories of a shadowy creature lurking in darkened alcoves. But I was also intrigued, for I possess an errant young soul of my own. From childhood, I hid it beneath pressed garments and polished words, but it persisted in plaguing me. It called to me like a Siren, driving me to dash all pretense against the rocks and surrender to my true nature.

It drove me to where I am now. But I am not ungrateful.

For it brought to bear two of my deepest truths: I will always possess an errant young soul, no matter my age.

And I will always be the shadowy creature in darkened alcoves, waiting . . .

For you, my love. For you.

Not What It Seemed

————◦◇◇◦————

The *Aramis* was supposed to arrive at first light, like it did in Celine's dreams.

She would wake beneath a sunlit sky, the brine of the ocean winding through her nose, the city looming bright on the horizon.

Filled with promise. And absolution.

Instead the brass bell on the bow of the *Aramis* tolled in the twilight hour, the time of day her friend Pippa called "the gloaming." It was—in Celine's mind—a very British thing to say.

She'd begun collecting these phrases not long after she'd met Pippa four weeks ago, when the *Aramis* had docked for two days in Liverpool. Her favorite so far was "not bloody likely." Celine didn't know why they mattered to her at the time. Perhaps it was because she thought Very British Things would serve her better in America than the Very French Things she was apt to say.

The moment Celine heard the bell clang, she made her way portside, Pippa's light footsteps trailing in her wake. Inky tendrils of darkness fanned out across the sky, a ghostly mist shrouding the Crescent City. The air thickened as the two girls listened to the *Aramis* sluice through the waters of the Mississippi, drawing closer to New Orleans. Farther from the lives they'd left behind.

Pippa sniffed and rubbed her nose. In that instant, she looked younger than her sixteen years. "For all the stories, it's not as pretty as I thought it would be."

"It's exactly what I thought it would be," Celine said in a reassuring tone.

"Don't lie." Pippa glanced at her sidelong. "It won't make me feel better."

A smile curled up Celine's face. "Maybe I'm lying for me as much as I'm lying for you."

"In any case, lying is a sin."

"So is being obnoxious."

"That's not in the Bible."

"But it should be."

Pippa coughed, trying to mask her amusement. "You're terrible. The sisters at the Ursuline convent won't know what to do with you."

"They'll do the same thing they do with every unmarried girl who disembarks in New Orleans, carrying with her all her worldly possessions: they'll find me a husband." Celine refrained from frowning. This had been her choice. The best of the worst.

"If you strike them as ungodly, they'll match you with the ugliest fool in Christendom. Definitely someone with a bulbous nose and a paunch."

"Better an ugly man than a boring one. And a paunch means he eats well, so . . ." Celine canted her head to one side.

"Really, Celine." Pippa laughed, her Yorkshire accent weaving through the words like fine Chantilly lace. "You're the most incorrigible French girl I've ever met."

Celine smiled at her friend. "I'd wager you haven't met many French girls."

"At least not ones who speak English as well as you do. As if you were born to it."

"My father thought it was important for me to learn." Celine lifted one shoulder, as though this were the whole of it, instead of barely half. At the mention of her father—a staid Frenchman who'd studied linguistics at Oxford—a shadow threatened to descend. A sadness with a weight Celine could not yet bear. She fixed a wry grin on her face.

Pippa crossed her arms as though she were hugging herself. Worry gathered beneath the fringe of blond on her forehead as the two girls continued studying the city in the distance. Every young woman on board had heard the whispered accounts. At sea, the myths they'd shared over cups of gritty, bitter coffee had taken on lives of their own. They'd blended with the stories of the Old World to form richer, darker tales. New Orleans was haunted. Cursed by pirates. Prowled by scalawags. A last refuge for those who believed in magic and mysticism. Why, there was even talk of women possessing as much power and influence as that of any man.

Celine had laughed at this. As she'd dared to hope. Perhaps New Orleans was not what it seemed at first glance. Fittingly, neither was she.

And if anything could be said about the young travelers

aboard the *Aramis*, it was that the possibility of magic like this—a world like this—had become a vital thing. Especially for those who wished to shed the specter of their pasts. To become something better and brighter.

And especially for those who wanted to escape.

Pippa and Celine watched as they drew closer to the unknown. To their futures.

"I'm frightened," Pippa said softly.

Celine did not respond. Night had seeped through the water, like a dark stain across organza. A scraggly sailor balanced along a wooden beam with all the grace of an aerialist while lighting a lamp on the ship's prow. As if in response, tongues of fire leapt to life across the water, rendering the city in even more ghoulishly green tones.

The bell of the *Aramis* pealed once more, telling those along the port how far the ship had left to travel. Other passengers made their way from below deck, coming to stand alongside Celine and Pippa, muttering in Portuguese and Spanish, English and French, German and Dutch. Young women who'd taken leaps of faith and left their homelands for new opportunities. Their words melted into a soft cacophony of sound that would—under normal circumstances—soothe Celine.

Not anymore.

Ever since that fateful night amid the silks in the atelier, Celine had longed for comfortable silence. It had been weeks since she'd felt safe in the presence of others. Safe with the riot of her own thoughts. The closest she'd ever come to wading through calmer waters had been in the presence of Pippa.

When the ship drew near enough to dock, Pippa took sudden hold of Celine's wrist, as though to steel herself. Celine gasped. Flinched at the unexpected touch. Like a spray of blood had shot across her face, the salt of it staining her lips.

"Celine?" Pippa asked, her blue eyes wide. "What's wrong?"

Breathing through her nose to steady her pulse, Celine wrapped both hands around Pippa's cold fingers. "I'm frightened, too."

TURN THE PAGE FOR AN EXCERPT OF:

BOOK 2 OF THE BEAUTIFUL QUARTET

THE
DAMNED

"Will leave you
wanting so much more."
—SEVENTEEN

RENÉE AHDIEH

#1 NEW YORK TIMES BESTSELLING AUTHOR

THE AWAKENING

———— ≈ ————

First there is nothing. Only silence. A sea of oblivion.

Then flashes of memory take shape. Snippets of sound. The laughter of a loved one, the popping of wood sap in a fireplace, the smell of butter melting across fresh bread.

An image emerges from the chaos, sharpening with each second. A crying young woman—her eyes like emeralds, her hair like spilled ink—leans over him, clutching his bloodstained hand, pleading with him in muffled tones.

Who am I? he wonders.

Dark amusement winds through him.

He is nothing. No one. Nobody.

The scent of blood suffuses his nostrils, intoxicatingly sweet. Like lechosa from a fruit stand in San Juan, its juice dripping down his shirtsleeves.

He becomes hunger. Not a kind of hunger he's ever known before, but an all-consuming void. A dull ache around his dead heart, a blast of bloodlust searing through his veins. It knifes through his stomach like the talons on a bird of prey. Rage builds in his chest. The desire to seek and destroy. To consume life. Let it fill the emptiness within him. Where there was once a sea of oblivion, there is now a canvas painted red, the color dripping like rain at his feet, setting his world aflame.

My city. My family. My love.

Who am I?

From the fires of his fury, a name emerges.

Bastien. My name is Sébastien Saint Germain.

Bastien

———≈———

I lie still, my body weightless. Immobile. It feels like I'm locked in a pitch-black room, unable to speak, choking on the smoke of my own folly.

My uncle did this to me once when I was nine. My closest friend, Michael, and I had stolen a box of cigars hand-rolled by an elderly lady from Havana who worked on the corner of Burgundy and Saint Louis. When Uncle Nico caught us smoking them in the alley behind Jacques', he sent Michael home, his voice deathly quiet. Filled with foreboding.

Then my uncle locked me in a hall closet with the box of cigars and a tin of matches. He told me I could not leave until I finished every single one of them.

That was the last time I ever smoked a cigar.

It took me weeks to forgive Uncle Nico. Years to stomach the smell of burning tobacco anywhere in my vicinity. Half a lifetime to understand why he'd felt the need to teach that particular lesson.

I try to swallow this ghost of bile. I fail.

I know what Nicodemus has done. Though the memory is still unclear—fogged by the weakness of my dying body—I know he has made me into one of them. I am now a vampire, like my uncle before me. Like my mother before me, who faced the final death willingly, her lips stained red and a lifeless body in her arms.

I am a soulless son of Death, cursed to drink the blood of the living until the end of time.

It sounds ridiculous even to me, a boy raised on the truth of monsters. Like a joke told by an unfunny aunt with a penchant for melodrama. A woman who cuts herself on her diamond bracelet and wails as drops of blood trickle onto her silken skirts.

Like that, I am hunger once more. With each pang, I become less human. Less of what I once was and more of what I will forever be. A demon of want, who simply craves more, never to be sated.

White-hot rage chases behind the bloodlust, igniting like a trail of saltpeter from a powder keg. I understand why Uncle Nico did this, though it will take many lifetimes for me to forgive him. Only the direst of circumstances would drive him to turn the last living member of his mortal family—the lone heir to the Saint Germain fortune—into a demon of the Otherworld.

His line has died with me, my human life reaching an all-too-sudden end. This choice must be one of last resort. A voice resonates in my mind. A feminine voice, its echoes tremulous.

Please. Save him. What can I say that will make you save him? Do we have a deal?

When I realize who it is, what she must have done, I howl a silent howl, the sound ringing in the hollows of my lost soul. I cannot think about that now.

My failure will not let me.

It is enough to know that I, Sébastien Saint Germain, eighteen-year-old son of a beggar and a thief, have been turned into a member of the Fallen. A race of blood drinkers banished from their rightful place in the Otherworld by their own greed. Creatures of the night embroiled in a centuries-long war with their archenemy, a brotherhood of werewolves.

I try to speak but fail, my throat tight, my eyelids sealed shut. After all, Death is a powerful foe to vanquish.

Fine silk rustles by my ear, a scented breeze coiling through the air. Neroli oil and rose water. The unmistakable perfume of Odette Valmont, one of my dearest friends. For almost ten years, she was a protector in life. Now she is a sister in blood. A vampire, sired by the same maker.

My right thumb twitches in response to her nearness. Still I cannot speak or move freely. Still I am locked in a darkened room, with nothing but a box of cigars and a tin of matches, dread coursing through my veins, hunger tingling on my tongue.

A sigh escapes Odette's lips. "He's beginning to wake." She pauses, pity seeping into her voice. "He'll be furious."

As usual, Odette is not wrong. But there is comfort in my fury. Freedom in knowing I may soon seek release from my rage.

"And well he should be," my uncle says. "This is the most self-ish thing I've ever done. If he manages to survive the change, he will come to hate me . . . just as Nigel did."

Nigel. The name alone rekindles my ire. Nigel Fitzroy, the reason for my untimely demise. He—along with Odette and four other members of my uncle's vampire progeny—safeguarded me from Nicodemus Saint Germain's enemies, chief among them those of the Brotherhood. For years Nigel bided his time. Cultivated his plan for revenge on the vampire who snatched him from his home and made him a demon of the night. Under the guise of loyalty, Nigel put into motion a series of events intended to destroy the thing Nicodemus prized most: his living legacy.

I've been betrayed before, just as I have betrayed others. It is the way of things when you live among capricious immortals and the many illusionists who hover nearby like flies. Only two years ago, my favorite pastime involved fleecing the Crescent City's most notorious warlocks of their ill-gotten gains. The worst among their ilk were always so certain that a mere mortal could never best them. It gave me great pleasure to prove them wrong.

But I have never betrayed my family. And I had never been betrayed by a vampire sworn to protect me. Someone I loved as a brother. Memories waver through my mind. Images of laughter and a decade of loyalty. I want to shout and curse. Rail to the heavens, like a demon possessed.

Alas, I know how well God listens to the prayers of the damned.

"I'll summon the others," Odette murmurs. "When he wakes, he should see us all united."

"Leave them be," Nicodemus replies, "for we are not yet out of the woods." For the first time, I sense a hint of distress in his words, there and gone in an instant. "More than a third of my immortal children did not survive the transformation. Many were lost in the first year to the foolishness of immortal youth. This . . . may not work."

"It *will* work," Odette says without hesitation.

"Sébastien could succumb to madness, as his mother did," Nicodemus says. "In her quest to be unmade, Philomène destroyed everything in her path, until there was nothing to be done but put an end to the terror."

"That is not Bastien's fate."

"Don't be foolish. It very well could be."

Odette's response is cool. "A risk you were willing to take."

"But a risk nonetheless. It was why I refused his sister when she asked me years ago to turn her." He exhales. "In the end, we lost her to the fire all the same."

"We will not lose Bastien as we lost Émilie. Nor will he succumb to Philomène's fate."

"You speak with such surety, little oracle." He pauses. "Has your second sight granted you this sense of conviction?"

"No. Years ago, I promised Bastien I would not look into his future. I have not forsaken my word. But I believe in my heart that hope will prevail. It . . . simply must."

Despite her seemingly unshakable faith, Odette's worry is a palpable thing. I wish I could reach for her hand. Offer her words of reassurance. But still I am locked within myself, my anger overtaking all else. It turns to ash on my tongue, until all I am left with is *want*. The need to be loved. To be sated. But most of all, the desire to destroy.

Nicodemus says nothing for a time. "We shall see. His wrath will be great, of that there can be no doubt. Sébastien never wanted to become one of us. He bore witness to the cost of the change at an early age."

My uncle knows me well. His world took my family from me. I think of my parents, who died years ago, trying to keep me safe. I think of my sister, who perished trying to protect me. I think of Celine, the girl I loved in life, who will not remember me.

I have never betrayed anyone I love.

But never is a long time, when you have eternity to consider.

"He may also be grateful," Odette says. "One day."

My uncle does not reply.

TURN THE PAGE FOR AN EXCERPT OF:

FULL OF VEXATION COME I.

A Midsummer Night's Dream,
WILLIAM SHAKESPEARE

———◆◆◆———

She lay as still as death.

It unnerved Arjun to see her like that. As if he were listening to the final strains of the Sonata *Pathétique*. Waiting for the music to fade to the rafters before falling to silence.

It didn't suit her. Odette Valmont was a triumph. An "Ode to Joy," not a dirge.

As usual, he stood apart from his chosen family, now more from habit than anything else. Arjun Desai liked remaining along the fringes. He could see and hear everything. Ensure he was never caught unawares.

The candlelit darkness around them reminded Arjun of a painting by a Dutch master. Remnants of Odette's perfume—the citrus of neroli oil and roses—clung to the ivory silk drapes of her bed on the top floor of the Hotel Dumaine.

Arjun's gaze drifted to the five immortals gathered around the still figure of the first vampire he'd considered a true sister. He recalled the moment he'd realized it, not long after he'd arrived to New Orleans over a year ago. She'd brought him a cup of tea. The smell of cardamom and ginger and cinnamon and milk had warmed through to his soul.

"I thought you might like some tea," Odette had said.

Arjun had looked at her, unable to conceal his surprise. "You know how to make chai?"

She'd grinned. "J'ai appris à en faire. I hope it makes you feel at home, mon cher." Then she'd vanished without another word.

The last person who had made him a cup of chai from a place of love was his father.

A single tear slid down the cheek of the vampire standing before Arjun, as if he could hear Arjun's thoughts. A tear of bright red blood. When they first met, this vampire had disturbed Arjun the most. An assassin hailing from the Far East, Shin Jaehyuk kept a collection of razor-sharp weapons—honed from iron, silver, and steel—in a black box beside the coffin he used for sleep. Crosshatched scars marred his pale skin, and his black hair was styled long to hide his features from view. A look meant to engender fear. One Arjun found highly effective.

"Is there nothing more we might do for her?" Jae asked.

The fey with the ghost-white complexion and the long queue of auburn hair straightened. He turned away from Odette. "I never said we have exhausted all possible solutions. I said I have done all my skills will allow. Even a blood drinker as unimaginative as you should know the difference, Shin Jaehyuk." His disdain was clipped.

"Then what else must be done?" Jae demanded as he rolled up the sleeves of his linen shirt, preparing for battle. "Why has Odette still not awakened?"

The fey's eyes thinned, making him look even less human.

Even more like the dangerous creature he was. More like the warrior who'd served for years as Nicodemus Saint Germain's personal guard. He said nothing, the silence around them thickening.

Arjun sighed as he leaned his shoulder against the gilded fluting of the marble column separating the bedchamber from Odette's dressing room, the ornate furniture designed in the style of the seventeenth-century court in Versailles. He understood why Jae was always gunning for a fight. It was the place the vampire felt most at ease. Most in his element. Just like Arjun lurking in the shadows.

Madeleine would put a stop to Jae's penchant for violence. Or Bastien, if he were still here. Bitterness clouded Arjun's thoughts. Sébastien Saint Germain—the vampire who had inherited the Court of the Lions' crown after the recent demise of his uncle Nicodemus—abandoned them two days ago, chasing after Celine Rousseau's jewel-colored skirts. He'd left behind an unforgivably cryptic note:

I will return.

—B

The madarchod.

As Arjun had predicted, Madeleine blurred to Jae's side before wrapping her dark hand around his scarred palm. "Jae. Please," she beseeched. "We appreciate all you've done, Ifan." She dipped her head toward the fey.

417

"Appreciation is meaningless to me," Ifan said. "Honor your promise of payment in full for services rendered. That is all I require."

"If gold is all you desire, you shall have it," drawled Boone from the foot of the golden four-poster bed. "Mercenary till the end. Just like a goddamned fey." Even when he cursed, Boone sounded refined. Perhaps all wealthy young white men from Charleston were the same.

"Indeed," Ifan countered, an eyebrow crooking upward. "Why should the life of any blood drinker be worth more to me than my fee? My allegiance to your kind died with Nicodemus, and I have no use for gratitude." He placed a cork stopper in a dark blue vial as he spoke. "I have prevented Odette Valmont from succumbing to the final death, which was no mean feat, given the gaping wound to her throat. I have fulfilled my end of the bargain. My fee is due." With that, he began wiping his blood-stained copper tools with a length of bleached linen.

Boone crossed his tanned arms and pursed his lips to one side of his aquiline face. "How long will she remain like this?"

Ifan lifted a shoulder. "As long as she is undisturbed, she could remain as she is for decades to come, which is not much different from death, I suppose." A snide grin tugged at his lips. "I've heard that a vampire deprived of blood becomes a husk of itself after enough time passes . . . and often loses their mind in the process." His grin deepened. "That would likely rile this one's sensibilities beyond measure." The inhuman fey glanced from one gilded corner of the room to another. "Odette

Valmont was always such a vain creature. Perhaps you can keep her here. Another pretty piece of lifeless art. The Court of the Lions' very own masterpiece."

Jae all but snarled before he spoke. "*Tak-chuh*, you piece of—"

"I meant it as a compliment," Ifan said. "Beauty is the only thing worth living for."

Hortense stepped before him, her feet spread shoulder-width apart, her arms akimbo. "You cannot wake her?" She leaned closer, her dark eyes menacing, her French accent harsh. "Or you *will* not?" Though she bared her fangs at the fey, her jeweled fingers clutched tightly at a handkerchief stained with crimson tears.

They all loved Odette Valmont. Each of the blood-drinking demons Arjun considered family could not fathom a world without her. A lifeless Odette? It was like a sea without salt or a wine without taste.

"You may ask a million times in a million ways, Miss de Morny." Ifan matched Hortense, toe-to-toe. "The answer remains the same. I do not possess the skill to wake Odette Valmont."

"Then who does?" Her voice faded to a whisper.

Again, Ifan raised a shoulder. "Perhaps there is a healer in the Vale."

Hortense snorted, the sound filled with scorn. "Parfait! A healer residing in a realm to which vampires are prohibited from traveling. Idéal!"

"Not all of you are vampires," Ifan said. "Not all of you are prohibited."

A low groan split through the silence. Arjun couldn't prevent it from escaping his lips. His head struck the marble column once, twice, his jaw set.

There was no question that he would do it. He would do whatever they asked if it meant saving Odette. She was his sister. They were his family. But that didn't mean that Arjun had to like what happened next.

Five sets of immortal eyes turned toward him, their gazes expectant.

"Hell and damnation," he swore under his breath, his English accent harsh.

Hortense spun toward Arjun in a flash, her umber skirts swishing with her movements. "You do not wish to save Odette? I thought ethereals like you—"

"Ma soeur," Madeleine interjected with a warning glance at her sister, "please be patient." She blurred to Arjun in a whirl of turquoise silk. "Arjun, I know you have lived among us for the least amount of time, but we have long considered you one of our own, and—"

"Madeleine," Arjun interrupted in a soft voice. "You don't have to ask. Of course I'll go to the Vale to find a healer for Odette."

She blinked once, the lines along the brown skin of her forehead smoothing. With a nod, she said, "I know you do not relish traveling to the place of your mother's birth. I'm aware it causes you great pain." Her features softened further. "Go with our gratitude. Whatever you need, you have but to ask."

"Make him promise he will not return without a healer," Ifan said. "Even cursed ethereals like Arjun Desai should be bound by their promises. Halfbloods may lie, cheat, steal, or kill to do it, but their word is their bond."

Anger surged through Arjun's fists. But he held his emotions in check. Full-blooded fey like Ifan had been trying to provoke him from the day he set foot in the Vale as a boy of seven.

"A promise is unnecessary," Jae said. "Our brother will not fail us." He placed a hand on Arjun's shoulder. Though it was meant to be reassuring, Arjun couldn't help but wince at his touch. Fear was not an easy feeling to shed. Just like love.

"That remains to be seen." Ifan rearranged his sleeves. "He is an ethereal, after all. It would be foolish to trust one on faith alone. Do what you will, but I cannot bear fools."

Arjun shifted from the marble column and sent him a cool smile. "Apparently your mother could."

A muscle rippled in Ifan's pale jaw. He cast a threatening glance Arjun's way. One Arjun gladly returned.

Boone's laughter was soft. Weary. "One of us should go with you, Arjun."

"No," Arjun said. "They won't tolerate a vampire in the Vale. It's too much of a risk, for them and for you."

"Bastien would have gone with you." Sadness filled Madeleine's face as she spoke.

"Perhaps it is not in our best interest to follow in the footsteps of Sébastien Saint Germain," Hortense said, her eyes flashing.

All movement stilled in the darkness, save for the dancing candle flames. As if a sudden hush had descended around them. A hush of sorrow. A hush of rage.

Bastien had betrayed his family. Vanished in their hour of need. Left Odette to die.

No matter his excuse, it was unforgivable.

"If you ask your mother for her assistance, will she give it?" Madeleine studied Arjun, her back ramrod straight.

"It's unlikely," Arjun replied. "General Riya is the last fey in any realm who would provide assistance to a blood drinker, even when asked by her own son." Resignation set along his forehead. "I will do whatever I must to save Odette. She is family to me, every bit as much as each of you have become." His voice dropped further. "But the last time I crossed a tare into the Otherworld, I promised my service to a dwarf king in the Sylvan Wyld in exchange for our safe passage through the Winter Court. Once he realizes I have returned, I will be forced to honor it."

Ifan tsked as he continued cleaning his copper tools.

Madeleine inhaled with deliberation. "How much time do you think you have before the dwarf king discovers your whereabouts?"

"I promised I would return by the harvest moon. Perhaps less than two mortal months are left before then?" Arjun canted his head to one side. "Which is a mere week or so once I cross into the Otherworld. Time does not move the same there as it does here. I cannot imagine it would take long for word to reach the dwarf king after I am sighted in the Vale."

Boone sighed, his fingers raking through his head of cherubic curls. "A week or so? As in ten days? Twelve?"

"Ten at most," Arjun agreed after a moment of thought.

"Well then, enough of this talk," Jae said. "Go."

With a nod, Arjun reached for his jacket.

"What is the dwarf king's name?" Hortense pressed. "C'est possible he can be persuaded to forgive your debt? Or at the very least, we could send someone else to serve in your stead, non?"

Ifan's laughter was as cold and clear as a winter's night.

"The dwarf king failed to offer a name," Arjun said, sliding his arms into his caramel jacket sleeves. "And, alas, Ifan is correct. From what I know of the creatures in the Sylvan Wyld, he will be unlikely to forgive any debt, no matter the enticement. He's a bearded spitfire with a terrified blue hobgoblin in his service. His court did not rise to rule the Ice Palace of Kur by showing anyone mercy."

Hortense crossed her arms. "I can be very . . . persuasive."

The beginnings of a smile ghosted across Arjun's lips. "I don't doubt it."

Madeleine took him by the arm, her touch gentle. A sharp contrast to the bladed stare of her younger sister. "As the leader of this coven, I give you authority to entreat with those in the Vale by whatever means necessary so we may restore Odette from this deathlike sleep." She squeezed his forearm. "Go now, with all haste."

Arjun took her hand and felt her grip tighten, like a mother reassuring a child. At least, he surmised it was like that. His own mother had never been the reassuring sort.

"Arjun?" Jae sat on the edge of the jacquard divan at the foot of Odette's bed and unsheathed one of the many daggers concealed in his long coat to begin sharpening it, the skirr of metal against stone echoing through the darkness. "Leave the portal open to the Vale after you depart."

"It is usually open to Rajasthan," Arjun replied. "The secondary gate is concealed in a fountain on—"

"No." He peered through his long black hair. "Not the usual, ordinary portal. I meant a direct tare to the Vale."

Arjun faced Jae fully, his hazel eyes wide. "It's dangerous to leave a portal like that open to another realm. A direct tare to the Vale is a direct tare to New Orleans. If it is not properly sealed behind me, any manner of creature from the Vale could travel through it unimpeded."

Jae said, "If you are indeed confined to the Wyld in service to the dwarf king before you are able to secure a healer, we will need a direct tare so that we can do what must be done to heal Odette." He continued honing his blade as he spoke.

Boone grunted in agreement. "If you're worried that someone might abuse the magicked mirror, no one knows it's here in New Orleans. Nicodemus made sure to keep its existence secret from any immortals outside our circle, and your flat is warded against any unwanted intruders."

"There have been whispers that Nicodemus' court possesses a hidden portal," Arjun said. "I've heard them myself."

"Whispers are not proof, and I pity the one foolish enough to wander into the Sylvan Vale sans l'invitation," Hortense finished, the French words rolling from her tongue. "No matter how"—she gestured with her hands as if searching for something—"charmant those of the Vale are, I have no doubt they are just as cruel as our forebears in the Wyld."

"It will not be left open for long," Jae finished as he twirled the newly sharpened dagger between his fingers. "Of that you may be assured."

After a time, Arjun nodded, though the decision did not sit well with him. "I'll leave the silver open. But I'm not merely worried about those in New Orleans taking advantage. As I mentioned, I'm mindful of the possibility that a creature of the Vale might use the mirror to make its way here."

"An acceptable risk on both accounts," Madeleine said as she sat alongside Jae in solidarity. "Go now, Arjun. Godspeed."

Arjun almost smiled. God? He doubted God had very much to do with a coven of blood drinkers, especially this one, nestled in the heart of a city like New Orleans, teeming with ghosts and ghouls and goblins.

The Damned. The Fallen. The Court of the Lions. They were known by many names, and none were blessed, to be sure. It wasn't the way of it, not in this world of whispered curses, glowing wards, and changelings armed with poisoned trinkets. Funny how—despite being so different from the fey in the Summer Court—vampires behaved in the same dramatic manner, theatrical to the end. Boone, with his so-called Southern charm; Hortense, her elegant hedonism; Madeleine, her calculated control; Jae, his murderous frown; and Odette . . .

He feared most of all what none of them would say. To say the words might give them life. Odette Valmont was the one who held them together. And if she was not whole, then they would never be whole again.

With a final glance at the members of his family, Arjun

straightened his lapel and took his leave from the top floor of the luxurious Hotel Dumaine, moving swiftly into the damp darkness of a New Orleans summer evening. Resolve lengthened each of his strides as the plan he'd begun concocting in his mind began to solidify. He knew where to begin.

Five days. He had five days in the Sylvan Vale to persuade one of its famed healers to travel back to the mortal world with him . . . to save a vampire. Their sworn enemy.

This was not a game of chess. Arjun could not waste time anticipating the thoughts and actions of capricious fey. His father's mortal blood put him at a disadvantage in a world that prided itself on the purity of one's lineage. Arjun often thought there were only two kinds of humans who were safe in the Vale: one who was foolish enough to marry a member of the fey gentry and one who was dead. Most halfbloods did not fare much better. From the age of seven, Arjun had lived in the Summer Court of the Sylvan Vale. He knew their rules. He'd played their games. And he would do as he'd always done from a childhood spent as the half-mortal boy with an indelible target painted on his back . . .

He would lie in wait, like a creature on the bottom of the sea. He would let them pick at him. Let them tear at his flesh and gnaw at his soul. He would smile and keep still.

And he would never allow them to see the rage burning in his soul.

TURN THE PAGE FOR AN EXCERPT OF:

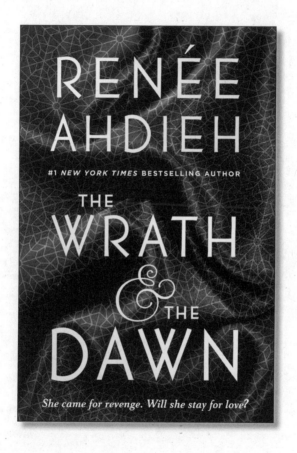

PROLOGUE

I T WOULD NOT BE A WELCOME DAWN.

Already the sky told this story, with its sad halo of silver beckoning from beyond the horizon.

A young man stood alongside his father on the rooftop terrace of the marble palace. They watched the pale light of the early morning sun push back the darkness with slow, careful deliberation.

"Where is he?" the young man asked.

His father did not look his way. "He has not left his chamber since he gave the order."

The young man ran a hand through his wavy hair, exhaling all the while. "There will be riots in the city streets for this."

"And you will put them to rout, in short order." It was a terse response, still made to a somber stretch of light.

"In short order? Do you not think a mother and father, regardless of birth or rank, will fight to avenge their child?"

Finally, the father faced his son. His eyes were drawn and sunken, as though a weight tugged at them from within. "They will fight. They should fight. And you will ensure it amounts to nothing. You will do your duty to your king. Do you understand?"

The young man paused. "I understand."

"General al-Khoury?"

His father turned toward the soldier standing behind them. "Yes?"

"It is done."

His father nodded, and the soldier left.

Again, the two men stared up at the sky.

Waiting.

A drop of rain struck the arid surface beneath their feet, disappearing into the tan stone. Another plinked against the iron railing before it slid its way into nothingness.

Soon, rain was falling around them at a steady pace.

"There is your proof," the general said, his voice laden with quiet anguish.

The young man did not respond right away.

"He cannot withstand this, Father."

"He can. He is strong."

"You have never understood Khalid. It is not about strength. It is about substance. What follows will destroy all that remains of his, leaving behind a husk—a shadow of what he once was."

The general winced. "Do you think I wanted this for him? I would drown in my own blood to prevent this. But we have no choice."

The young man shook his head and wiped the rain from beneath his chin.

"I refuse to believe that."

"Jalal—"

"There must be another way." With that, the young man turned from the railing and vanished down the staircase.

Throughout the city, long-dry wells began to fill. Cracked, sunbaked cisterns shimmered with pools of hope, and the people of Rey awoke to a new joy. They raced into the streets, angling their smiling faces to the sky.

Not knowing the price.

And, deep within the palace of marble and stone, a boy of eighteen sat alone before a table of polished ebony . . .

Listening to the rain.

The only light in the room reflected back in his amber eyes.

A light beset by the dark.

He braced his elbows on his knees and made a crown of his hands about his brow. Then he shuttered his gaze, and the words echoed around him, filling his ears with the promise of a life rooted in the past.

Of a life atoning for his sins.

One hundred lives for the one you took. One life to one dawn. Should you fail but a single morn, I shall take from you your dreams. I shall take from you your city.

And I shall take from you these lives, a thousandfold.

MEDITATIONS
ON GOSSAMER AND GOLD

THEY WERE NOT GENTLE. AND WHY SHOULD THEY BE?
After all, they did not expect her to live past the next morning.

The hands that tugged ivory combs through Shahrzad's waist-length hair and scrubbed sandalwood paste on her bronze arms did so with a brutal kind of detachment.

Shahrzad watched one young servant girl dust her bare shoulders with flakes of gold that caught the light from the setting sun.

A breeze gusted along the gossamer curtains lining the walls of the chamber. The sweet scent of citrus blossoms wafted through the carved wooden screens leading to the terrace, whispering of a freedom now beyond reach.

This was my choice. Remember Shiva.

"I don't wear necklaces," Shahrzad said when another girl began to fasten a jewel-encrusted behemoth around her throat.

"It is a gift from the caliph. You must wear it, my lady."

Shahrzad stared down at the slight girl in amused disbelief. "And if I don't? Will he kill me?"

"Please, my lady, I—"

Shahrzad sighed. "I suppose now is not the time to make this point."

"Yes, my lady."

"My name is Shahrzad."

"I know, my lady." The girl glanced away in discomfort before turning to assist with Shahrzad's gilded mantle. As the two young women eased the weighty garment onto her glittering shoulders, Shahrzad studied the finished product in the mirror before her.

Her midnight tresses gleamed like polished obsidian, and her hazel eyes were edged in alternating strokes of black kohl and liquid gold. At the center of her brow hung a teardrop ruby the size of her thumb; its mate dangled from a thin chain around her bare waist, grazing the silk sash of her trowsers. The mantle itself was pale damask and threaded with silver and gold in an intricate pattern that grew ever chaotic as it flared by her feet.

I look like a gilded peacock.

"Do they all look this ridiculous?" Shahrzad asked.

Again, the two young women averted their gazes with unease.

I'm sure Shiva didn't look this ridiculous . . .

Shahrzad's expression hardened.

Shiva would have looked beautiful. Beautiful and strong.

Her fingernails dug into her palms; tiny crescents of steely resolve.

At the sound of a quiet knock at the door, three heads turned—their collective breaths bated.

In spite of her newfound mettle, Shahrzad's heart began to pound.

"May I come in?" The soft voice of her father broke through the silence, pleading and laced in tacit apology.

Shahrzad exhaled slowly . . . carefully.

"Baba, what are you doing here?" Her words were patient, yet wary.

Jahandar al-Khayzuran shuffled into the chamber. His beard and temples were streaked with grey, and the myriad colors in his hazel eyes shimmered and shifted like the sea in the midst of a storm.

In his hand was a single budding rose, its center leached of color, and the tips of its petals tinged a beautiful, blushing mauve.

"Where is Irsa?" Shahrzad asked, alarm seeping into her tone.

Her father smiled sadly. "She is at home. I did not allow her to come with me, though she fought and raged until the last possible moment."

At least in this he has not ignored my wishes.

"You should be with her. She needs you tonight. Please do this for me, Baba? Do as we discussed?" She reached out and took his free hand, squeezing tightly, beseeching him in her grip to follow the plans she had laid out in the days before.

"I—I can't, my child." Jahandar lowered his head, a sob rising in his chest, his thin shoulders trembling with grief. "Shahrzad—"

"Be strong. For Irsa. I promise you, everything will be fine." Shahrzad raised her palm to his weathered face and brushed away the smattering of tears from his cheek.

"I cannot. The thought that this may be your last sunset—"

"It will not be the last. I will see tomorrow's sunset. This I swear to you."

Jahandar nodded, his misery nowhere close to mollified. He held out the rose in his hand. "The last from my garden; it has not yet bloomed fully, but I wanted to give you one remembrance of home."

She smiled as she reached for it, the love between them far past mere gratitude, but he stopped her. When she realized the reason, she began to protest.

"No. At least in this, I might do something for you," he muttered, almost to himself. He stared at the rose, his brow furrowed and his mouth drawn. One servant girl coughed in her fist while the other looked to the floor.

Shahrzad waited patiently. Knowingly.

The rose started to unfurl. Its petals twisted open, prodded to life by an invisible hand. As it expanded, a delicious perfume filled the space between them, sweet and perfect for an instant . . . but soon, it became overpowering. Cloying. The edges of the flower changed from a brilliant, deep pink to a shadowy rust in the blink of an eye.

And then the flower began to wither and die.

Dismayed, Jahandar watched its dried petals wilt to the white marble at their feet.

"I—I'm sorry, Shahrzad," he cried.

"It doesn't matter. I will never forget how beautiful it was for that moment, Baba." She wrapped her arms around his neck and pulled him close. By his ear, in a voice so low only he could hear, she said, "Go to Tariq, as you promised. Take Irsa and go."

He nodded, his eyes shimmering once more. "I love you, my child."

"And I love you. I will keep my promises. All of them."

Overcome, Jahandar blinked down at his elder daughter in silence.

This time, the knock at the door demanded attention rather than requested it.

Shahrzad's forehead whipped back in its direction, the bloodred ruby swinging in tandem. She squared her shoulders and lifted her pointed chin.

Jahandar stood to the side, covering his face with his hands, as his daughter marched forward.

"I'm sorry—so very sorry," she whispered to him before striding across the threshold to follow the contingent of guards leading the processional. Jahandar slid to his knees and sobbed as Shahrzad turned the corner and disappeared.

With her father's grief resounding through the halls, Shahrzad's feet refused to carry her but a few steps down the cavernous corridors of the palace. She halted, her knees shaking beneath the thin silk of her voluminous *sirwal* trowsers.

"My lady?" one of the guards prompted in a bored tone.

"He can wait," Shahrzad gasped.

The guards exchanged glances.

Her own tears threatening to blaze a telltale trail down her cheeks, Shahrzad pressed a hand to her chest. Unwittingly, her fingertips brushed the edge of the thick gold necklace clasped around her throat, festooned with gems of outlandish size and untold variety. It felt heavy . . . stifling. Like a bejeweled fetter. She allowed her fingers to wrap around the offending instrument, thinking for a moment to rip it from her body.

The rage was comforting. A friendly reminder.

Shiva.

Her dearest friend. Her closest confidante.

She curled her toes within their sandals of braided bullion and threw back her shoulders once more. Without a word, she resumed her march.

Again, the guards looked to one another for an instant.

When they reached the massive double doors leading into the throne room, Shahrzad realized her heart was racing at twice its normal speed. The doors swung open with a distended groan, and she focused on her target, ignoring all else around her.

At the very end of the immense space stood Khalid Ibn al-Rashid, the Caliph of Khorasan.

The King of Kings.

The monster from my nightmares.

With every step she took, Shahrzad felt the hate rise in her blood, along with the clarity of purpose. She stared at him, her eyes never wavering. His proud carriage stood out amongst the men in his retinue, and details began to emerge the closer she drew to his side.

He was tall and trim, with the build of a young man proficient in warfare. His dark hair was straight and styled in a manner suggesting a desire for order in all things.

As she strode onto the dais, she looked up at him, refusing to balk, even in the face of her king.

His thick eyebrows raised a fraction. They framed eyes so pale a shade of brown they appeared amber in certain flashes of light, like those of a tiger. His profile was an artist's study in angles, and he remained motionless as he returned her watchful scrutiny.

A face that cut; a gaze that pierced.

He reached a hand out to her.

Just as she extended her palm to grasp it, she remembered to bow.

The wrath seethed below the surface, bringing a flush to her cheeks.

When she met his eyes again, he blinked once.

"Wife." He nodded.

"My king."

I will live to see tomorrow's sunset. Make no mistake. I swear I will live to see as many sunsets as it takes.

And I will kill you.

With my own hands.

TURN THE PAGE FOR AN EXCERPT OF:

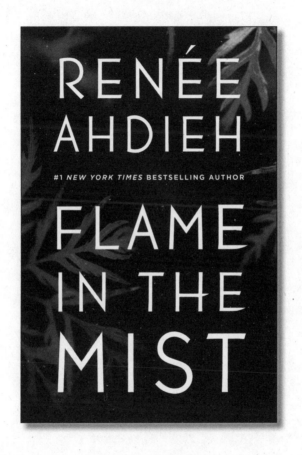

The Beginning

———✳———

In the beginning, there were two suns and two moons.

The boy's sight blurred before him, seeing past the truth. Past the shame. He focused on the story his *uba* had told him the night before. A story of good and evil, light and dark. A story where the triumphant sun rose high above its enemies.

On instinct, his fingers reached for the calloused warmth of his *uba*'s hand. The nursemaid from Kisun had been with him since before he could remember, but now—like everything else—she was gone.

Now there was no one left.

Against his will, the boy's vision cleared, locking on the clear blue of the noon sky above. His fingers curled around the stiff linen of his shirtsleeves.

Don't look away. If they see you looking away, they will say you are weak.

Once more, his *uba*'s words echoed in his ears.

He lowered his gaze.

The courtyard before him was draped in fluttering white, surrounded on three sides by rice-paper screens. Pennants flying the golden crest of the emperor danced in a passing breeze. To the left and right stood grim-faced onlookers—samurai dressed in the dark silks of their formal *hakama*.

In the center of the courtyard was the boy's father, kneeling on a small tatami mat covered in bleached canvas. He, too, was draped in white, his features etched in stone. Before him sat a low table with a short blade. At his side stood the man who had once been his best friend.

The boy sought his father's eyes. For a moment, he thought his father looked his way, but it could have been a trick of the wind. A trick of the perfumed smoke curling above the squat brass braziers.

His father would not want to look into his son's eyes. The boy knew this. The shame was too great. And his father would die before passing the shame of tears along to his son.

The drums began to pound out a slow beat. A dirge.

In the distance beyond the gates, the boy caught the muffled sound of small children laughing and playing. They were soon silenced by a terse shout.

Without hesitation, his father loosened the knot from around his waist and pushed open his white robe, exposing the skin of his stomach and chest. Then he tucked his sleeves beneath his knees to prevent himself from falling backward.

For even a disgraced samurai should die well.

The boy watched his father reach for the short *tantō* blade on the small table before him. He wanted to cry for him to stop. Cry for a moment more. A single look more.

Just one.

But the boy remained silent, his fingers turning bloodless in his fists. He swallowed.

Don't look away.

His father took hold of the blade, wrapping his hands around the skein of white silk near its base. He plunged the sword into his stomach, cutting slowly to the left, then up to the right. His features remained passive. No hint of suffering could be detected, though the boy searched for it—felt it— despite his father's best efforts.

Never look away.

Finally, when his father stretched his neck forward, the boy saw it. A small flicker, a grimace. In the same instant, the boy's heart shuddered in his chest. A hot burst of pain glimmered beneath it.

The man who had been his father's best friend took two long strides, then swung a gleaming *katana* in a perfect arc toward his father's exposed neck. The thud of his father's head hitting the tatami mat silenced the drumbeats in a hollow start.

Still the boy did not look away. He watched the crimson spurt from his father's folded body, past the edge of the mat and onto the grey stones beyond. The tang of the fresh blood caught in his nose—warm metal and sea salt. He waited until his father's body was carried in one direction, his head in another, to be displayed as a warning.

No hint of treason would be tolerated. Not even a whisper.

All the while, no one came to the boy's side. No one dared to look him in the eye.

The burden of shame took shape in the boy's chest, heavier than any weight he could ever bear.

When the boy finally turned to leave the empty courtyard, his eyes fell upon the creaking door nearby. A nursemaid met his unflinching stare, one hand sliding off the latch, the other clenched around two toy swords. Her skin flushed pink for an instant.

Never look away.

The nursemaid dropped her eyes in discomfort. The boy watched as she quickly ushered a boy and a girl through the wooden gate. They were a few years younger than he and obviously from a wealthy family. Perhaps the children of one of the samurai in attendance today. The younger boy straightened the fine silk of his kimono collar and darted past his nursemaid, never once pausing to acknowledge the presence of a traitor's son.

The girl, however, stopped. She looked straight at him, her pert features in constant motion. Rubbing her nose with the heel of one hand, she blinked, letting her eyes run the length of him before pausing on his face.

He held her gaze.

"Mariko-*sama*!" the nursemaid scolded. She whispered in the girl's ear, then tugged her away by the elbow.

Still the girl's eyes did not waver. Even when she passed

the pool of blood darkening the stones. Even when her eyes narrowed in understanding.

The boy was grateful he saw no sympathy in her expression. Instead the girl continued studying him until her nursemaid urged her around the corner.

His gaze returned to the sky, his chin in high disregard of his tears.

In the beginning, there were two suns and two moons.

One day, the victorious son would rise—

And set fire to all his father's enemies.

ACKNOWLEDGMENTS

THE FIRST THING I did when I set out to write a four-book series about vampires was take a deep breath. Then I proceeded to ignore all the warnings rumbling through my brain.

I chose to write, instead, from the heart.

I wrote about a world I'd starting building in my head as a teen-ager. About characters and ideas and situations I'd dreamed about for decades. And then I hoped someone else would love them as much as I did.

To B, who did not flinch when I told her what I wanted to do.

To Stacey, who laughed with delight and then made it happen.

To my readers, who send and create memes, who share and message and offer support from all corners of the world: I literally can't do this without you. Thank you for loving books and stories and helping to dream these stories into being.

To the incredible team at Penguin: Thank you for supporting me every step of this wild ride. A special shout-out to Jen Loja, Jennifer Klonsky, Olivia Russo, Tessa Meischeid, and Caitlin Tutterow. To Felicity, Alex, James, and Shannon, thank you for fiercely championing these books and coming up with so many wonderful ideas even through a pandemic, when all our creative wells were running dry. It is such an honor to work with each of you. Thank you for making this dream possible.

To Cindy and Anne: Thank you for saving me from myself, ha ha ha. And for making sure my books make sense to someone besides an addled mom of two kids under three.

To IGLA, Heather Baror-Shapiro, Mary Pender, and the team at UTA: Thank you for everything.

To my assistant, Emily Williams: Thank you for all that you do.

To Alwyn: So much love and laughter and so many late-night chats. I appreciate you more than words.

To Rosh, JJ, and Lemon: I am so grateful for each of you. CMC for life.

To Sabaa and Elaine, my ride-or-dies: There are not enough words in any language to express how glad I am that you both exist. It makes believing in fairies an easy task.

To Erica, Chris, and Tahlia: Our family makes me smile and laugh and cheer every day. But mostly, I feel such deep gratitude for you. Here's to a beautiful future.

To Ian, Izzy, and Maddie: So much love to you.

To Mama Joon, Baba Joon, Umma, and Dad: Thank you for all the support and the unfailing love you give to us and to our zany kids, even when one of them is asking the same question for the eightieth time and the other one is screaming bloody murder three inches from your head.

To Navid, Jinda, Ella, Lily, Omid, Julie, Evelyn, Isabelle, and Andrew: I am so grateful for each of you.

To Mushu . . . This one is so hard. Sometimes I miss you so much it steals the breath from my body. I see a shadow move in the corner of the room or feel something soft at my feet, and I wish it was you so fiercely that I swear I see you there. But I wouldn't take any of it back. The deep pain is because of deep love, and that is worth everything. I hope we could give you half the joy you gave us. I love you, Mushee. You are in our hearts forever.

To Victor, Cyrus, and Noura: Everything I love and feel and hope for in life is because of you. Thank you for all the joy and all the sleepless nights.

I am tired every day.

But I am so happy.

RENÉE AHDIEH is a graduate of the University of North Carolina at Chapel Hill. In her spare time, she likes to dance salsa and collect shoes. She is passionate about all kinds of curry, rescue dogs, and college basketball. The first few years of her life were spent in a high-rise in South Korea; consequently, Renée enjoys having her head in the clouds. She and her family live in Charlotte, North Carolina. She is the #1 *New York Times* and internationally bestselling author of The Wrath and the Dawn series, the Flame in the Mist series, and The Beautiful quartet.

You can visit Renée Ahdieh at
ReneeAhdieh.com